AFRICA39

OTHER HAY FESTIVAL PROJECTS

Beirut39: New Writing from the Arab World

AFRICA 39

NEW WRITING FROM AFRICA SOUTH OF THE SAHARA

Edited by Ellah Wakatama Allfrey
With an Introduction by Wole Soyinka

BLOOMSBURY

LONDON · NEW DELHI · NEW YORK · SYDNEY

With the support also of PEN UK Commonwealth Writers,
Royal African Society and British Council

Bloomsbury Publishing Plc
50 Bedford Square
London
WC1B 3DP

www.bloomsbury.com

Bloomsbury is a trademark of Bloomsbury Publishing Plc

Bloomsbury Publishing, London, New Delhi, New York and Sydney

A CIP catalogue record for this book is available from the British Library

ISBN 978 1 4088 5466 2

10 9 8 7 6 5 4 3 2 1

Typeset by Hewer Text UK Ltd, Edinburgh
Printed and bound in Great Britain by CPI Group (UK) Ltd, Croydon CR0 4YY

Acknowledgements

The publishers would like to thank: the judges, Elechi Amadi, Osonye Tess Onwueme and Margaret Busby; the thirty-nine authors; the translators; the editor, Ellah Wakatama Allfrey; Binyavanga Wainaini for research on the longlist; and all those, including Cristina Fuentes, Jásminka Romanos, Peter Florence, Anna Simpson, Imogen Corke and Becky Alexander, who have contributed to making an ambitious vision a concrete reality. They also gratefully acknowledge the following original publishers of the pieces listed below (pieces not listed have been taken from as yet unpublished works):

'The Shivering' extracted from the story collection *The Thing Around Your* Neck by Chimamanda Ngozi Adichie. Copyright © 2009 Chimamanda Ngozi Adichie. For the UK and Commonwealth: reprinted by permission of HarperCollins Publishers Ltd. For Canada: reprinted by permission of Alfred A. Knopf Canada, a division of Random House of Canada Limited, a Penguin Random House Company. For the USA: reprinted by permission of The Wylie Agency. All rights reserved.

'The Banana Eater' by Monica Arac de Nyeko was first published in AGNI online, 2010 (https://www.bu.edu/agni/fiction/africa/arac-de-nyeko.html).

Extract from *All Our Names* by Dinaw Mengestu. Copyright © 2014 Dinaw Mengestu, reproduced by permission of Hodder and Stoughton Ltd.

Extract from *The Wayfarer's Daughter* by Chibundu Onuzo (forthcoming Faber and Faber Ltd, 2016), Copyright © Chibundu Onuzo, 2014, used by permission of Faber and Faber Ltd.

Contents

Introduction

The Word Shall Fly Free!

I

This year, the world will mark the twenty-fifth anniversary of the fall of the Berlin Wall. The city of Port Harcourt, designated World Book Capital 2014, can justly consider her literary constituency especially privileged to be playing host to the world on the anniversary of a convulsion that profoundly impacted the world of letters and creativity. Not just Port Harcourt of course, but decolonised Africa. For the generation captured in this anthology, the connection may not be obvious. The 'wind of change' had already blown over the continent and nearly all African nations had long gained their independence from colonial rule. That wind, however, did not take long to change direction and character. Inevitably it brought with it the detritus – including shrapnel – of ideological warfare from other lands. 'Inevitably', since the struggle for independence itself was never completely devoid of a search for ideological anchors. Wherever convenient for the corralling of citizen solidarity and commitment, unity of purpose and obedience to political direction, leadership itself adopted ideological labels, either pitting itself against, or co-opting its writers and intelligentsia into strategies for, social transformation.

For a handful of that leadership, conviction in the social doctrines for radical change was genuine. For the majority, however, it was a sham, a weapon for silencing dissidence and regimenting society. Material development, productive strategies and social organisation were never considered sufficient in themselves as validation of the radical choice. The mind itself was the ultimate target, its conformity and intellectual submission to the prevailing ideology. This made the creative writer a primary objective in the struggle for power. In the Soviet Union and its captive bloc – the birthplace of what, till today, was considered the most radical manifesto of all time – the writer's creative choices became subject to clinical inspection under the testamentary microscope: theme, language, stylistics, social relationships, class consciousness or the absence thereof, revolutionary rhetoric and so on and on – under which the material of literature itself virtually disappeared, leaving only a question of conformity to, or deviation from, a Party ideology. The African intelligentsia was not slow to catch on, and the battles that raged in academia and among the general literati soon degenerated to a level of ferocity that virtually inhibited new talent altogether. Like the proverbial millipede that stopped to count its feet, they could no longer walk!

For writers and aspiring writers everywhere, Berlin was not simply a wall of concrete with watchtowers and armed guards, bristling with electronic gadgets, mined sectors and slavering guard dogs, but a structure of mind control and creative interdictions. Put at its most basic, under that ideology, the world of literature was neatly bifurcated. There was literature that advanced the revolutionary cause, whose destination was a classless Utopia, and there was – The Rest. During the extreme phases of that division, from the epicentre to the peripheries of its catchment zones, including the African continent, the rest was fit not merely for the garbage dump, it was deemed a crime against social perfectibility, if not against humanity itself.

A quarter of a century after the battle for the mind was resolved in Berlin in favour of freedom of intellect and imagination, a new (yet ancient) enemy of that eternal quest resurfaces on African soil. The vestments of today's commissariats of 'correctness' may have changed, but the credentials remain the same – a doctrinaire mentality that cannot tolerate the freedom of the mind, its exploration of a universe that continues to astonish, to take us on unique voyages of discovery both physical and metaphysical, and even into the hidden, censored and denied histories of ourselves. Was that not what Nelson Mandela had in mind when he rhapsodised: 'In the presence of Chinua Achebe'

– referring to the writer's famous work – 'the prison walls fell down'?
Yes, indeed, that is one of the attainments of literature. And not just
the walls of Robben Island but of ignorance. Prejudice. Separatism.
Mind constrictions. Robben Island could be located in Pyongyang, in
Ahidjo's Cameroon. In Pol Pot's necropolis. Where are they all?
Where will they be found at the dawn of tomorrow? Literature survives
them all.

2

One of my favourite browsing grounds remains, unrepentantly, the
garbage dump, or, to put it more elegantly – the flea market, especially
of books. Those rows and jumbled stalls and trestles of browned,
dog-eared second-hand books, pages frayed with age, evocative of
contemplative, even escapist hours in the company of unknown faces,
redolent of distant places and exotic adventures both of mind and body
– such musty, unruly way stops have the edge, for me, even over the
fragrance of newly-minted volumes on tidy rows of antiseptic shelves,
with careful labelling under subject matter, author, geography etc. You
never know what you will find in the flea market! They are spaces of
fleeting to deep self-immersions in the unknown, and a purchase does
not break your budget. Tantalising extensions of the mind in unsched-
uled directions, they engender curiosity, and a wistful regret that life
does not offer more leisure for infinitely extending such ephemeral
moments, those meagre interruptions of routine hustling for material
survival or even structured study.

Making a literary discovery becomes a bonus that is casually
savoured for days afterwards, hanging in the background of other
activities until it dissipates on its own or prods the mind (or hand!)
into sometimes unrelated undertakings. Where it takes on a life of its
own, or simply inducts the mind into new regions of awareness, is,
however, the most rewarding. Blessed be those who can swear that
they never touch a book unless it promises class conflict and pays
homage to dialectical materialism – the rest of us infidels look forward
to being surprised by an exquisite literary vignette from a hitherto

unknown hand, a work that has emerged through reinterpretative intelligence over humdrum existence, the transformation of the familiar through a new order of reality, the creation of an autonomous realm of social relations and extraction of congruence from incongruence etc. etc. The writer is a magician. Here now are three quite recent literary adventures, each exposing this secret fraternity within the world of books.

Take one of my nominations for this very *Africa39* project. It came from one such encounter in a 'garbage' pile. I have no idea, even at the stage of writing this, if the product of that encounter will make the longlist, the short, or eventually earn a place in this anthology – or indeed if others have entered the same choice. All I know is that the modest volume of short stories had me making enquiries and keeping a lookout for further works from that pen. I encountered it in a sort of Fringe Mart, in this very city, outside the confines of a previous book festival in Port Harcourt organised by the Rainbow Book Club. It was a work of acute social observation and creative empathy – the author was clearly no beginner. His collection did not spout any ideological sermons, being committed only to exposing the social fakeries and artificial values of contemporary society, delineating the delicate, and often moving, course of adolescence in a mined environment. It did not take more than the flash of one line and I knew that I held a miniature gem in my hands. I was not deceived.

The second took place in a mall in Dakar, but the subject was located in Cameroon under the late President Ahmadou Ahidjo, the action set in a concentration camp for dissidents. Political repression was common knowledge, but a full-scale concentration camp? There is propaganda and there is reality. And there is of course reality that suffers from failure of communication – in short, fails the test of literary conviction. This personal narrative, very simply written, no stylistic pyrotechnics, carried the stamp of authentic experience – victim or simply witness. I purchased a copy. Despite having had close Cameroonian colleagues since the early sixties, and having heard their outcry at the time of those events, it was only with this work that I became individually inducted into the day-to-day existence of dissident victims in such

camps, and in vivid detail. There is a difference between clinical report-
age on the one hand, and, on the other, admission as a vicarious witness
to the functioning of the mechanisms of repression – including even its
bureaucracy – that is the triumph of literature.

This Cameroonian dissident had spent nearly a decade in a detention camp instituted by my next-door dictator, Ahmadou Ahidjo, a
camp whose existence had of course been stoutly denied by the
government. Overcoming personal suffering and privation, this
author provides an intimate lesson on the loss of liberty and its
bureaucratic banalities. The book did not presume to analyse the
colonial and neo-capitalist social structures, the *rentier* and *comprador*
economics of neo-colonial surrogate leaders etc. etc. that had made
his ten-year odyssey inevitable in the first place. No, he had merely
taken time off to situate the reader in the physical atmosphere of his
detention camps, including the contrasting strategies of survival as he
was transferred to farm labour from the sterile walls of an actual
prison. In short, a work fit for only garbage for its deficiency in
progressive socio-economic analysis. Still, it rests snugly today on my
shelf side by side with other shamelessly undialectical narratives of
human resilience and survival of the spirit, and the writer's overwhelming compulsion to simply – testify!

In a class of its own for irredeemable apostasy would be my third
exemplar of these Chance Encounters of a Different Kind – a semi-
fictional narrative that drew deeply on the mythology of a part of the
Nigerian landscape. This time, the terrain of discovery could not have
been more contrasted – a fleeting escape into my own world that took
place on the freezing streets of Geneva. Walking between the trestles
of the usual potpourri of books from everywhere, my eye caught the
single word that was its title – a Nigerian place-name. The result was
predictable. I stopped, opened the volume and sighed with disappointment. The book was in French and my French – to put it kindly – is
somewhat limited. It was doubly aggravating, since that very place-
name was none other than – Onitsha!

This Eastern Nigerian city has earned literary fame as being, if not
exactly the pioneer of the flea-market publication – mostly pamphlet
format – that came to be known as Onitsha Market literature, then at

least of being a promoter of an industry of such rudimentary writing, expressing not only the social aspirations of the authors' society, the confusions of cultural transition and mixed values, but also the robust political awakening reflected through the lives and travails of pan-African heroes: Patrice Lumumba, Jomo Kenyatta, Marcus Garvey and other iconic figures. A treasure trove, perhaps more for the social anthropologist than the mainstream literary critic, its products would appeal more to an unsophisticated proletariat/peasant readership than to those who are featured in this anthology.

I was about to abandon the volume when my rudimentary French netted a sentence that arrested my motion. I struggled through that paragraph, then the entire page, then recollected as my fingers began to freeze that I had a fat *Harrap's* French dictionary at home in Abeokuta. So of course, I bought *Onitsha,* brought it back to its approximate environment, but continued to postpone the gratification of my curiosity for several months. The author was again one I had never encountered.

That same year, the designation of the Nobel Prize for Literature was announced. I dashed to my bookshelf and, yes, there it was – Le Clézio! Pure serendipity. I had nothing to do with Le Clézio's nomination, and in any case, Nobel's literary Academy does not work that way. That way, however, is simply the way, the excitement of Literature, sometimes dominated by the random spirit of *Esu,* lord of the crossroads, other times by the methodical application of *Orunmila,* the presiding deity of the divination board, *Ifa.* A blasphemous suggestion undoubtedly to the 'radical order' since, in addition to the fact that Le Clézio's novel explores the mythology of his host environment at childhood, and in a spirit of discovery, I have now attributed – albeit playfully – my encounter with his work to the intervention of obscurantist enemies of a materialist understanding of market forces and the law of supply and demand etc. etc.

Le Clézio and I eventually interacted in the flesh in South Korea, at a literary encounter, where I watched his bemused expression as the pros and cons of literary ideologies were traded. It was sufficiently sobering to share on that occasion the stark face of the world's largest and most thorough surviving Personality Cult that holds millions captive, as our colleagues from North Korea narrated their experiences and their strategies for creative fulfilment and physical survival. They had borne and finally escaped the operations of the totalitarian state that had no space for the creative estate, except, undoubtedly to dub its products garbage manifestations of deviant thinking. North Korea, where even a moronic leader, once spawned into a dynasty, can be elevated to the status of Supreme Guide and Infallible Idiot, stands virtually alone today as the structured edifice of human regimentation at its grimmest. The foundations of a 'modern' nation are the millions and millions of her crushed humanity – largely her intellectuals, writers, teachers and others who labour in the 'vineyard of the Word'. What 'consciousness' shall we attribute to such deadly manifestations, I often wonder, we who so readily resort to phrase-mongering as quicklime over the fallen victims of the rhetorical order?

I try to imagine an attempted dialogue between the architects of the Berlin Wall and the current standard bearers of theocratic closures. What a vengeful irony these no-prisoner-taken 'revolutionary' brigades of the spiritual realm have wreaked, and continue to wreak, on writers and critics alike, not forgetting practitioners in the sister arts – music, theatre, cinema etc. A theocratic actuality, a virulent strain of Islam, now swears to wipe out in entirety, and with murderous abandon, all other structures of consciousness. At the head of the receiving end of this onslaught stands – as usual – the written word, and all its associated institutions. It is against this very background, a raging homicidal actuality launched by the gatekeepers of One Consciousness that critics – more accurately, censors – attempt to reimpose ideological diktats on African writers, diktats that lie today under the rubble of the Berlin wall. It is against this background that the last-ditch ideologues continue to demand of writers that it is insufficient to denounce atrocities, to allegorise the unspeakable, to ridicule the perverse and puncture afflatus, and even to imagine the infinite – no, they must first explain the cause of localised and global dilemma through ideological prisms and tidy formulations of social development, as *is*, as *used to be* and as *should be*!

★   ★   ★

Africa39 is dedicated to an age group that occupies a significant phase, arguably considered a defining plateau before a fully confident ascent towards the peak of imaginative powers. Its fortuitous timing in this instance, with a universal celebration of the release of creative plurality, augurs well for the future, yet it is fraught with danger from an implacable enemy – a religious fundamentalist onslaught on human freedom. Emerging from the shadow of the Berlin Wall was no easy task for many African writers of that age who, in contesting colonialism and then confronting internal social malformations through their writing, seeking new forms and playing variations on the old, literally fought with one arm tied behind their back, or willingly underwent a version of critical lobotomy from the scalpel of doctrine at the most productive phase of their career. Some eventually recovered; others never! Much talent was suppressed, bullied and harried during that period of doctrinal obsession. It was a crime against literature, art and creativity. Restraint on that faculty we recognise as human imagination leads inevitably to raging crimes against humanity itself – a sequence that is amply, repetitively demonstrated throughout the history of the world: first a crime against creativity, next, crimes against humanity. It is a hard lesson learnt – it is not possible to be against creativity and hope to end up on the side of humanity. That attestation is tragically enshrined in the nation's latest contribution to world vocabulary – Boko Haram – and its transborder, power-driven conspiracies against the creative mandate.

The primary function of literature is to capture and expand reality. It is futile therefore to attempt to circumscribe African creative territory, least of all by conformism to any literary ideology that then aspires to be the tail that wags the dog. Literature derives from, reflects and reflects upon – Life. It projects its enhanced vision of Life's potential, its possibilities, narrates its triumphs and failures. Its offerings include empowerment of the oppressed and the subjugation of power. It will not attempt to do all of this at once – that will only clot up the very passages of its own proceeding. There is infinitude to the nature of Literature, but attempts to curtail or dictate to its protean propositions often strike me as a simultaneous exercise in attempted parricide and infanticide in one stroke. There is only one universal literary ideology that answers human cruelties, the excesses of power, bigotries, social inequalities and alienation: Literature. On behalf of a pursuit that lures generation after generation to partake of its sumptuous banquet of creative splendours – Welcome, *Africa39*!

Wole Soyinka
Lagos, May 2014

Editor's Note

When we reject the single story, when we realise that there is never a single story about any place, we regain a kind of paradise.
                                              – Chimamanda Ngozi Adichie

The writers featured in this anthology were chosen following intensive research by Binyavanga Wainaina, writer and founder of one of the continent's most inspiring literary journals, *Kwani?*. Following a public call out for recommendations and the work of judges Elechi Amadi, Margaret Busby and Osonye Onwueme – who had the difficult task of selecting just thirty-nine writers out of this pool of outstanding talent – *Africa39* is a celebration of writers whose work promises to inspire readers for decades to come.

In the months it has taken to bring the collection together, I have found myself immersed in texts by and conversations with some writers whose works I already knew well; others I had heard of but not yet read; and a few who were entirely new discoveries. As a reader, my horizon is broadened especially by the inclusion of works in translation from Equatorial Guinea and Cape Verde. It is my fervent hope that the stories chosen to appear here will give readers that same gift – the satisfaction of new work by familiar, beloved voices, the joy of discovering the new.

Although thirty-nine writers, representing sixteen countries from south of the Sahara, can only provide a snapshot of the potential offerings from a vast continent of storytellers, this anthology is a good place to start. There are love stories here; explorations in language that seek to bridge the gap between poetry and prose; political works of psychedelic daring; a look at the far future that comments on social repression today; re-imaginings of historical events; explorations in crime writing. There is no danger of 'a single story' here. Indeed, one would be hard pressed to find collective concerns, unifying themes or even to coin a definition that adequately describes the range, stylistic inclinations and subjects herein. At their best, the writers of *Africa39* show themselves a generation whose imaginations are unbound – time, space and circumstance are adapted, adopted and shaped in stories that are as different from each other as their creators are unique.

Ellah Wakatama Allfrey
London, May 2014

The Shivering

Chimamanda Ngozi Adichie

On the day a plane crashed in Nigeria, the same day the Nigerian first lady died, somebody knocked loudly on Ukamaka's door in Princeton. The knock surprised her because nobody ever came to her door unannounced; and it made her jumpy because since first-thing that morning she had been on the Internet reading Nigerian news, refreshing pages too often. She had minimised early pictures from the crash site. Each time she looked at them, she brightened her laptop screen, peering at what the news articles called 'wreckage', a blackened hulk with whitish bits scattered all about it like torn paper, an indifferent lump of char that had once been a plane filled with people.

One of those people might have been her ex-boyfriend Udenna.

The knock sounded again, louder. She looked through the peep-hole: a pudgy, dark-skinned man who looked vaguely familiar though she could not remember where she had seen him before. She opened the door. He half-smiled and spoke without meeting her eye. 'I am Nigerian. I live on the third floor. I came so that we can pray about what is happening in our country.'

She was surprised that he knew she, too, was Nigerian, that he knew which apartment was hers, that he had come to knock on her door; she still could not place where she had seen him.

'Can I come in?' he asked.

She let him in. She let into her apartment a stranger wearing a slack Princeton sweatshirt who had come to pray about what was happening in Nigeria, and when he reached out to take her hands in his, she hesitated slightly before extending hers.

★ ★ ★

He prayed in that particularly Nigerian Pentecostal way that made her uneasy: he covered things with the blood of Jesus, he bound up demons and cast them in the sea, he battled evil spirits. She wanted to interrupt and tell him how unnecessary it was, this bloodying and binding, this turning faith into a pugilistic exercise; to tell him that life was a struggle with ourselves more than with a spear-wielding Satan; that belief was a choice for our conscience always to be sharpened.

He prayed and prayed, pumping her hands whenever he said 'Father Lord!' or 'in Jesus' name!' Then she felt herself start to shiver, an involuntary quivering of her whole body. Was it God? Once, years ago when she was a teenager who meticulously said the rosary every morning, words she did not understand had burst out of her mouth as she knelt by the scratchy wooden frame of her bed. It had lasted mere seconds, that outpouring of incomprehensible words in the middle of a Hail Mary, but she had truly, at the end of the rosary, felt terrified and sure that the white-cool feeling that enveloped her was God.

Now, the shivering stopped as quickly as it had started and the Nigerian man ended the prayer. 'In the mighty and everlasting name of Jesus!'

'Amen!' she said.

She slipped her hands from his, mumbled 'Excuse me,' and hurried into the bathroom. When she came out, he was still standing by the door in the kitchen.

'My name is Chinedu,' he said.

'I'm Ukamaka,' she said.

'This plane crash is terrible,' he said. 'Very terrible.'

'Yes.' She did not tell him that Udenna might have been in the crash. She wished he would leave, now that they had prayed, but he moved across into the living room and sat down on the couch and began to talk about how he had heard of the plane crash as if she had asked him to stay. He told her he did not realise initially that there were two separate incidents – the first lady had died in Spain shortly after a tummy-tuck surgery in preparation for her sixtieth birthday party, while the plane had crashed in Lagos minutes after it left for Abuja.

'I know somebody who was on the flight,' she said. 'Who might have been on the flight.'

'Jehovah God!'

'My boyfriend Udenna. My ex-boyfriend, actually. He was doing an MBA at Wharton and went to Nigeria last week for his cousin's wedding.' It was after she spoke that she realised she had used the past tense.

'You have not heard anything for sure?' Chinedu asked.

'No. He doesn't have a cell phone in Nigeria and I can't get through to his sister's phone. Maybe she was with him. The wedding is supposed to be tomorrow in Abuja.'

'God is faithful. God is faithful!' Chinedu raised his voice. 'God is faithful. Do you hear me?'

A little alarmed, Ukamaka said, 'Yes.'

The phone rang. Ukamaka stared at it, the black cordless phone she had placed next to her laptop, afraid to pick it up.

Chinedu got up and made to reach for it and she said 'No!' and took it and walked to the window. 'Hello? Hello?' She wanted whomever it was to tell her right away, not to start with any pre-ambles. It was her mother.

'*Nne,* Udenna is fine. Chikaodili just called me to say they missed the flight. He is fine. They were supposed to be on that flight but they missed it, thank God.'

Ukamaka put the phone down on the window ledge and began to weep. First, Chinedu gripped her shoulders, then he took her in his arms. She quieted herself long enough to tell him Udenna was fine and then went back into his embrace, surprised by the familiar comfort of it, certain that he instinctively understood her crying from the relief of what had not happened and from the melancholy of what could have happened and from the anger of what remained unresolved since Udenna told her, in an ice-cream shop on Nassau Street, that the rela-tionship was over.

'I knew my God would deliver! I have been praying in my heart for God to keep him safe,' Chinedu said, rubbing her back.

Later, after she had asked Chinedu to stay for lunch and as she heated up some stew in the microwave, she asked him, 'If you say God is responsible for keeping Udenna safe, then it means God is responsible for the people who died, because God could have kept them safe, too. Does it mean God prefers some people to others?'

'God's ways are not our ways.' Chinedu took off his sneakers and placed them by the bookshelf.

'It doesn't make sense.'

'God always makes sense but not always a human kind of sense,' Chinedu said, looking at the photos on her bookshelf. It was the kind of question she asked Father Patrick, although Father Patrick would agree that God did not always make sense, with that shrug of his, as he did the first time she met him, on that late summer day Udenna told her it was over. She and Udenna had been inside Thomas Sweet, drinking strawberry and banana smoothies, their Sunday ritual after grocery shopping, and Udenna had slurped his noisily before he told her that their relationship had been over for a long time, that they were together only out of habit, and she looked at him and waited for a laugh, although it was not his style to joke like that. 'Staid' was the word he had used. There was nobody else, but the relationship had become staid. Staid, and yet she had been arranging her life around his for three years. Staid, and yet she had begun to bother her uncle, a senator, about finding her a job in Abuja after she graduated because Udenna wanted to move back when he finished graduate school and start building up what he called 'political capital' for his run for Anambra State governor. Staid, and yet she cooked her stews with hot peppers now, the way he liked. She left Thomas Sweet and began to walk aimlessly all the way up Nassau Street and then back down again until she passed the grey stone church and she wandered in and told the man wearing a white collar and just about to climb into his Subaru that life did not make sense. He told her his name was Father Patrick and that life did not make sense but we all had to have faith nonetheless. Have faith. 'Have faith' was like saying be tall and shapely. She wanted to be tall and shapely but of course she was not; she was short and her behind was flat and that stubborn soft bit of her lower belly bulged, even when she wore her Spanx Body Shaper, with its tightly restraining fabric. When she said this, Father Patrick laughed.

'"Have faith" is not really like saying be tall and shapely. It's more like saying be OK with the bulge and with having to wear Spanx,' he said. And she had laughed, too, surprised that this plump white man with silver hair knew what Spanx was.

Ukamaka dished out some stew beside the already-warmed rice on Chinedu's plate. Chinedu held up the fork she had placed on his plate. 'Please give me a spoon.'

She handed him one. Udenna would have been amused by Chinedu, would have said how very bush it was to eat rice with a spoon the way Chinedu did, gripping it with all his fingers – Udenna with his ability to glance at people and know, from their posture and their shoes, what kind of childhood they had had.

'That's Udenna, right?' Chinedu gestured towards the photo in the wicker frame, Udenna's arm draped around her shoulders, both their faces open and smiling.

'Yes, that is the great Udenna.' Ukamaka made a face and settled down at the tiny dining table with her plate. 'I keep forgetting to remove that picture.' It was a lie. She had glanced at it often in the past month, sometimes reluctantly, always frightened of the finality of taking it down. She sensed that Chinedu knew it was a lie.

'We met at my sister's graduation party three years ago in New Haven. A friend of hers brought him. He was working on Wall Street and I was already in grad school here but we knew many of the same people from around Philadelphia. He went to U Penn for undergrad and I went to Bryn Mawr. It's funny that we had so much in common but somehow we had never met until then.'

'He looks tall,' Chinedu said, still standing by the bookcase, his plate balanced in his hand.

'He's six feet four.' She heard the pride in her own voice. 'That's not his best picture. He looks a lot like Thomas Sankara. I had a crush on that man when I was a teenager. You know, the president of Burkina Faso, the popular president, the one they killed—'

'Of course I know Thomas Sankara.' Chinedu looked closely at the photograph for a moment, as though to search for traces of Sankara's famed handsomeness. Then he said, 'I saw both of you once outside in the parking lot and I knew you were from Nigeria. I wanted to come and introduce myself but I was in a rush to catch the shuttle.'

She restrained herself from asking what exactly Chinedu remembered: Had he seen Udenna's hand placed on her lower back? Had he seen Udenna saying something suggestive to her, their faces close together?

'Is the stew too peppery?' she asked, noticing how slowly Chinedu was eating.

'It's fine. I'm used to eating pepper. I grew up in Lagos.'

'I never liked hot food until I met Udenna. I'm not even sure I like it now.'

'But you still cook it.'

She did not like his saying that and she did not like that his face was closed, his expression unreadable, as he glanced at her and then back at his plate. She said, 'Well, I guess I'm used to it now.'

She pressed a key on her laptop, refreshed a Web page. *All Killed in Nigeria Plane Crash.* The government had confirmed that all one hundred and seventeen people aboard the airplane were dead.

'No survivors,' she said.

'Father, take control,' Chinedu said, exhaling loudly. He came and sat beside her to read from her laptop, their bodies close, the smell of her peppery stew on his breath. There were more photographs from the crash site. Ukamaka stared at one of shirtless men carrying a piece of metal that looked like the twisted frame of a bed; she could not imagine what part of the plane it could possibly have been.

In the following days, days now cool enough for her knee-length leather boots, days in which she took the shuttle to campus, researched her dissertation at the library, met with her advisor, taught her undergraduate composition class, she would return to her apartment in the late evening and wait for Chinedu to visit so she could offer him rice or pizza or spaghetti. So she could talk about Udenna. She liked that Chinedu said little, looking as if he was not only listening to her but also thinking about what she was saying. Once she thought idly of starting an affair with him, of indulging in the classic rebound, but there was a refreshingly asexual quality to him, something about him that made her feel that she did not have to pat powder under her eyes to hide her dark circles.

Her apartment building was full of other foreigners. She and Udenna used to joke that it was the uncertainty of the foreigners' new surroundings that had congealed into the indifference they showed to one another. They did not say hello in the hallways or elevators, nor did they meet one another's eyes during the five-minute ride on the campus shuttle, these intellectual stars from Kenya and China and Russia, these graduate students and fellows who would go on to lead and heal and reinvent the world. And so it surprised her that as she and Chinedu walked to the parking lot, he would wave to somebody, say hi to another.

'Do you know them from your programme?' she asked.

He had once said something about chemistry, and she assumed he was doing a doctorate. It had to be why she never saw him on campus; the science labs were so far off and so alien.

'No. I met them when I came.'

'How long have you lived here?'

'Not long. Since spring. I knew I had to make the effort to make friends in this building. How else will I get to the grocery store and to church? Thank God you have a car,' he said.

On Sundays, she drove Chinedu to his Pentecostal church in Lawrenceville before going to the Catholic church on Nassau Street, and when she picked him up after service, they went grocery shopping at McCaffrey's. She noticed how few groceries he bought and how carefully he scoured the sale flyers that Udenna had always ignored.

'I'm starving. Should we get a sandwich somewhere?'

'I'm fasting,' he said quietly.

'Oh.' As a teenager, she, too, had fasted, drinking only water from morning until evening for a whole week, asking God to help her get the best result in the Senior Secondary School exam. She got the third-best result.

'No wonder you didn't eat any rice yesterday,' she said. 'Will you sit with me while I eat then?'

'Sure.'

'Is this a special prayer you are doing? Or is it too personal for me to ask?'

'It is too personal for you to ask,' Chinedu said with a mocking solemnity.

She took down the car windows as she backed out of the parking lot, stopping to let two jacketless women walk past, their jeans tight, their blonde hair blown sideways by the wind. It was a strangely warm day for late autumn.

'Fall sometimes reminds me of harmattan,' Chinedu said.

'I know,' Ukamaka said. 'I love harmattan. I think it's because of Christmas. I love the dryness and dust of Christmas. Udenna and I went back together for Christmas last year and he spent New Year's Day with my family in Nimo and my uncle kept questioning him: "Young man, when will you bring your family to come and knock on our door?"' Ukamaka mimicked a gruff voice and Chinedu laughed.

'Have you gone home to visit since you left?' Ukamaka asked, and as soon as she did, she wished she had not. Of course he would not have been able to afford a ticket home to visit.

'No.' His tone was flat.

'Will you move back when you finish here? I can imagine the loads of money you'll make at one of those oil companies in the Niger Delta, with your chemistry doctorate.' She knew she was speaking too fast, babbling, really, trying to make up for the discomfort.

'I don't know.' Chinedu barely smiled. She drove slowly to the sandwich place, over-nodding to the music from the radio to show that she was enjoying it as much as he seemed to be.

'I'll just pick up the sandwich,' she said, and he said he would wait in the car. The garlic flavours from the foil-wrapped chicken sandwich filled the car when she got back in.

'Your phone rang,' Chinedu said.

She picked up her cell phone, lodged by the shift, and looked at it. Rachel, a friend from her department, perhaps calling to find out if she wanted to go to the talk on morality and the novel at East Pyne the next day.

'I can't believe Udenna hasn't called me,' she said, and started the car. He had sent an email to thank her for her concern while he was in Nigeria. He had removed her from his Instant Messenger buddy list so that she could no longer know when he was online. And he had not called.

'Maybe it's best for him not to call,' Chinedu said. 'So you can move on.'

She waited until they were back at their apartment building and Chinedu had taken his bags up to his apartment and come back down before she said, 'You know, it really isn't as simple as you think it is. You don't know what it is to love an asshole.'

'I do.'

She looked at him, wearing the same clothes he had worn the afternoon he first knocked on her door: a pair of jeans and an old sweatshirt with a saggy neckline, Princeton printed on the front in orange.

'You've never said anything about it,' she said.

'You've never asked.'

She placed her sandwich on a plate and sat down at the dining table. 'I didn't know there was anything to ask. I thought you would just tell me.'

Chinedu said nothing.

'So tell me. Tell me about this love. Was it here or back home?'

'Back home. I was with him for almost two years.'

The moment was quiet. She picked up a napkin and realised that she had known intuitively, perhaps from the very beginning, but she said, because she thought he expected her to show surprise, 'Oh, you're gay.'

'Somebody once told me that I am the straightest gay person she knew, and I hated myself for liking that.' He was smiling; he looked relieved.

'So tell me about this love.'

The man's name was Abidemi. Something about the way Chinedu said his name, Abidemi, made her think of gently pressing on a sore muscle, the kind of self-inflicted ache that is satisfying.

He spoke slowly, revising details that she thought made no difference – was it on a Wednesday or Thursday that Abidemi had taken him to a private gay club where they shook hands with a former head of state? – and she thought that this was a story he had not told often in its entirety, perhaps had never told.

Abidemi was a banker, a Big Man's son who had gone to university in England, the kind of guy who wore leather belts with elaborate designer logos as buckles. He had been wearing one of those when he came into the Lagos office of the mobile phone company where Chinedu worked in customer service. He had been almost rude, asking if there wasn't somebody senior he could talk to, but Chinedu did not miss the look they exchanged, the heady thrill he had not felt since his first relationship with a sports prefect in secondary school. Abidemi gave him his card and said, curtly, 'Call me.' It was the way Abidemi would run the relationship for the next two years, wanting to know where Chinedu went and what he did, buying him a car without consulting him, so that he was left in the awkward position of explaining to his family and friends how he had suddenly bought a Honda, asking him to come on trips to Calabar and Kaduna with only a day's notice, sending vicious text messages when Chinedu missed his calls. Still, Chinedu had liked the possessiveness, the vitality of a relationship that consumed them both. Until Abidemi said he was getting married. Her name was Kemi and his parents and hers had known one another a long time. The inevitability of marriage had always been understood between them, unspoken but understood, and perhaps nothing would have changed if Chinedu had not met Kemi, at Abidemi's parents' wedding anniversary party. He had not wanted to go – he stayed away from Abidemi's family events – but Abidemi had insisted, saying he would survive the long evening only if Chinedu was there. Abidemi spoke in a voice lined with what seemed troublingly like laughter when he introduced Chinedu to Kemi as 'my very good friend'.

'Chinedu drinks much more than I do,' Abidemi had said to Kemi, with her long weave-on and strapless yellow dress. She sat next to Abidemi, reaching out from time to time to brush something off his shirt, to refill his glass, to place a hand on his knee, and all the while her whole body was braced and attuned to his, as though ready to spring up and do whatever it took to please him. 'You said I will grow a beer belly, abi?' Abidemi said, his hand on her thigh: 'This man will grow one before me, I'm telling you.'

Chinedu had smiled tightly, a tension headache starting, his rage at Abidemi exploding. As Chinedu told Ukamaka this, how the anger of that evening had 'scattered his head', she noticed how tense he had become.

'You wished you hadn't met his wife,' Ukamaka said.

'No. I wished he had been conflicted.'

'He must have been.'

'He wasn't. I watched him that day, the way he was with both of us there, drinking stout and making jokes about me to her and about her to me, and I knew he would go to bed and sleep well at night. If we continued, he would come to me and then go home to her and sleep well every night. I wanted him not to sleep well sometimes.'

'And you ended it?'

'He was angry. He did not understand why I would not do what he wanted.'

'How can a person claim to love you and yet want you to do things that suit only them? Udenna was like that.'

Chinedu squeezed the pillow on his lap. 'Ukamaka, not everything is about Udenna.'

'I'm just saying that Abidemi sounds a little bit like Udenna. I guess I just don't understand that kind of love.'

'Maybe it wasn't love,' Chinedu said, standing up abruptly from the couch. 'Udenna did this to you and Udenna did that to you, but why did you let him? Why did you let him? Have you ever considered that it wasn't love?'

It was so savagely cold, his tone, that for a moment Ukamaka felt frightened, then she felt angry and told him to get out.

She had begun, before that day, to notice strange things about Chinedu. He never asked her up to his apartment, and once, after he told her which apartment was his, she looked at the mailbox and was surprised that it did not have his last name on it; the building superintendent was very strict about all the names of renters being on the mailbox. He did not ever seem to go to campus; the only time she asked him why, he had said something deliberately vague, which told her he did not want to talk about it.

She would never speak to him again, she told herself; he was a crude and rude person from the bush. But Sunday came and she had become used to driving him to his church in Lawrenceville before going to hers on Nassau Street. She hoped he would knock on her door and yet knew that he would not. She felt a sudden fear that he would ask somebody else on his floor to drop him off at church, and because she felt her fear becoming a panic, she went up and knocked on his door. It took him a while to open. He looked drawn and tired; his face was unwashed and ashy.

'I'm sorry,' she said. 'Do you want me to drop you off at church?'

'No.' He gestured for her to come in. The apartment was sparsely furnished with a couch, a table, and a TV; books were piled one on top of the other along the walls.

'Look, Ukamaka, I have to tell you what's happening. Sit down.'

She sat down. A cartoon show was on TV, a Bible open face down on the table, a cup of what looked like coffee next to it.

'I am out of status. My visa expired three years ago. This apartment belongs to a friend. He is in Peru for a semester and he said I should come and stay while I try to sort myself out.'

'You're not here at Princeton?'

'I never said I was.' He turned away and closed the Bible. 'I'm going to get a deportation notice from Immigration anytime soon. Nobody at home knows my real situation. I haven't been able to send them much since I lost my construction job. My boss was paying me under the table but he said he did not want trouble now that they are talking about raiding workplaces.'

'Have you tried finding a lawyer?' she asked.

'I don't have a case.' He was biting his lower lip, and she had not seen him look so unattractive before, with his flaking facial skin and his shadowed eyes.

'You look terrible. You haven't eaten much since I last saw you,' she said, thinking of all the weeks that she had spent talking about Udenna while Chinedu worried about being deported.

'I'm fasting.'

'Are you sure you don't want me to drop you off at church?'

'It's too late anyway.'

'Come with me to my church then.'

'You know I don't like the Catholic Church, all that unnecessary kneeling and standing and worshiping idols.'

'Just this once.'

Finally he got up and washed his face and changed. They walked to the car in silence. She had never thought to tell him about her shivering as he prayed on that first day, but because she longed now for a significant gesture that would show him that he was not alone; that she understood what it must be like to feel so uncertain of a future, to lack control about what would happen to him tomorrow – because she did not, in fact, know what else to say – she told him about the shivering.

'It was strange,' she said. 'Maybe it was just my suppressed anxiety about Udenna.'

'It was a sign from God,' Chinedu said firmly.

'What was the point of my shivering as a sign from God?'

'You have to stop thinking that God is a person. God is God.'

'Your faith, it's almost like fighting.' She looked at him. 'What's the point of God being a puzzle?'

'Because it is the nature of God. If you understand the basic idea of God's nature being different from human nature, then it will make sense,' Chinedu said, and opened the door to climb out of the car. What a luxury to have a faith like his, Ukamaka thought, so uncritical, so forceful, so impatient. And yet there was something about it that was exceedingly fragile; it was as if Chinedu could conceive of faith only in extremes, as if an acknowledgment of a middle ground would mean the risk of losing everything.

'I see what you mean,' she said, although she did not see at all.

Outside the grey stone church, Father Patrick was greeting people, his hair a gleaming silver in the late morning light.

'I'm bringing a new person into the dungeon of Catholicism, Father P,' Ukamaka said.

'There's always room in the dungeon,' Father Patrick said, warmly shaking Chinedu's hand.

The church was dim, full of echoes and mysteries and the faint scent of candles. They sat side by side in the middle row, next to a woman holding a baby.

'Did you like him?' Ukamaka whispered.

'The priest? He seemed OK.'

'I mean *like* like.'

'Oh, Jehovah God! Of course not.'

She had made him smile. 'You are not going to be deported, Chinedu. We will find a way. We will.' She squeezed his hand and knew he was amused by her stressing of the 'we'.

He leaned close. 'You know, I had a crush on Thomas Sankara, too.'

'No!'

'I didn't even know that there was a country called Burkina Faso in West Africa until my teacher in secondary school talked about him and brought in a picture. I will never forget how crazy in love I fell with a newspaper photograph.'

At first they stifled their laughter and then they let it out, joyously leaning against each other, while next to them, the woman holding the baby watched.

The choir had begun to sing. It was one of those Sundays when the priest blessed the congregation with holy water at the beginning of Mass, and Father Patrick was walking up and down, flicking water on the people with something that looked like a big saltshaker. Ukamaka watched him and thought how much more subdued Catholic Masses were in America; how in Nigeria it would have been a vibrant green branch from a mango tree that the priest would dip in a bucket of holy water held by a hurrying, sweating Mass-server; how he would have stridden up and down, splashing and swirling, holy water raining down; how the people would have been drenched; and how, smiling and making the sign of the cross, they would have felt blessed.

The Banana Eater

Monica Arac de Nyeko

Naalu and her family lived a block from us, at number G.16 in the housing estates. Many things about our houses were similar. Their size: a kitchen and store, a sitting room and a bedroom. The paint: cream and magenta against a brown tiled roof. Only our back yards were different. Theirs was almost bare – grassless and without any bougainvillea, thorn brush, or red euphorbia fencing to keep trespassers or vagabonds away. Ours was lush with paspalum grass. We had flowers, too. In the rain season, dahlias and hibiscus bloomed; so did roses and sophronitella, cosmos and bleeding heart vines. Everyone who passed by our house said the garden gave a fine display of colour and fragrance.

Ma's gardening knowledge had been transplanted from her school years at Our Lady of Good Counsel, the Catholic girls' school. Home economics was compulsory then. Ma never did like the cooking and baking bits. But she did like gardening. A house, she often said, starts at the back yard. See the state of the back yard and you'll know if you want to enter.

Gardening might have seemed viable in Catholic boarding school, but in the real world things were different. In the estates, only potato fields and cassava survived to maturity. They were unspectacular. The silly boys were not interested in them; nor were the children who liked to roam about the houses breaking windows or anything that looked fragile. Plant fences and flowers, on the other hand, were different. They were boastful. They attracted everyone. And often-times people did stop to examine the garden arrangement or to pick flowers to stick in their hair. These people were generally not trouble-some. Ma tolerated them. The lot she found unbearable, though, were the market vendors.

Every day as soon as customers turned scarce, the vendors left the market. They crossed Estate Close, the road that separated the market from the estates, and came to sit in our back yard. They were choosy, those vendors. They avoided all the other back yards on the block. They came straight for ours, and laid down their tired and sweaty bottoms. Our back yard was a place to forget about the market and its unsold sacks of potatoes and bananas, a place to gossip, a place to laugh out loud at anyone, including our distin-guished house guests.

One particular guest among all others ignited fits of laughter among the vendors. Perhaps there was something about his temperament that provoked them. Perhaps it was his German bowl haircut. Or maybe it was the fact that he often talked to himself. The man's name was Patrick Aculu, a strange little man from our church. He was thin and unassuming, watchful and quiet. Because his demeanour seemed over-tolerant, I was convinced he had suffered heavily at the hands of bullies in his school days.

The first day Patrick Aculu came to visit us it was at Ma's insis-tence. The market vendors, when they saw him, laughed with tears in their eyes. They clapped. They did not stop for a long time. I opened the door for him as soon as he made it past the vendors. I showed him into our sitting room. I even called him Uncle Aculu in the hope of pacifying him. But Uncle Aculu did not look up, did not show any interest in Ma's gold cushion covers, the new curtains, or the vase with fresh roses.

On Uncle Aculu's second visit – the next day – the vendors still laughed, but the insult was not as severe as before. Uncle Aculu sat in the sitting room. When I went to the kitchen to make him some tea, Ma followed. I thought she wanted to help, but she just wanted to talk. Ma said I should not call Patrick Aculu 'Uncle Aculu' any more. It was better to call him Brother Patrick, she said, because he was our brother in Christ. I did not tell her that the Sunday school children would not have agreed. They called him Red Devil. They thought his eyes were the colour of red devil peppers and that he talked like he was chewing fire, exactly like the devil on Uganda Television.

Red Devil became a daily guest. Every evening after his job skinning fish for export in the industrial area, he headed not to his home but to ours. Red Devil wore a brown polyester suit. He lined the suit's pocket with two sets of pens in four colours: black, blue, green and pink. I found the pens alarming and constantly worried that Red Devil's brain was not wired properly. It did not help that at dinner time he used too much Blue Band on his bread and blew at the tea. They were things Ma said that only people with no manners did.

Now that he was a regular guest, Ma started to plan him into our evenings. When she bought maize flour, she added an extra quarter kilo just for Red Devil. When she cooked meat, she added three ladles of soup. When we ate dinner, she invited his thoughts and opinions. Ma encouraged him to speak like he was part of the family. After a few weeks, Red Devil's confidence had grown bigger than the man himself.

Late one evening at the dinner table, Red Devil offered his unsolicited thoughts about the market vendors. I noticed he was careful about the way he approached the subject.

'Your back yard is beautiful,' Red Devil said. 'But those vendors are too much. Have you seen how they pluck the roses? The way they leave your beautiful garden defiled, I cannot believe it sincerely.'

Ma did not speak immediately. When she did, she said, 'Good point. Very good point, Brother Patrick.'

Chei, I thought, such nonsense!

'You are right, Brother Patrick,' Ma said.

Though she was quick to agree, she was careful about implementing his advice.

About half a week later, Ma confronted the vendors. She left her office at the printing press early, walked home as usual, and before entering the house, stopped by the back yard. She surprised the vendors. They sat up respectfully in the grass and listened to Ma as if they were schoolchildren. But being as ill mannered as they were, the vendors lost interest as soon as they realised that her stopover was not friendly. Accustomed to talking as loud as they liked without rebuke, they did not take to being scolded. I watched with amusement from the sitting room window, curious to see what the outcome might be. That evening, when Red Devil came, Ma told him it had gone very well.

'You really have good ideas,' Ma said. 'You should have been a lawyer.'

'Ah, Sister, I can still be a lawyer. With God, nothing is impossible.'

Chei, I thought. Such nonsense.

That evening there were fewer silences between Ma and Red Devil at the dinner table. The two of them talked adult things, reckless, as if I was too stupid to understand. They talked about God and his plans for the future. It was God who had widowed both of them, they said. It was God who knew what tomorrow looked like.

'You know, Sister, the book of Song of Solomon might be about God's relationship with the church, but it has also taught me many things. Very many,' Red Devil said. Ma laughed. She laughed so much she almost choked on her saliva.

'Amito, maybe it is time for you to sleep now.'

In my bed that night, I thought I ought to pray for Ma. It was true what they said about some diseases being contagious. Red Devil had infected Ma with his. Now the wires in Ma's head were not working properly either.

The next day, I waited at the window for Ma's return from work. I saw her making her way through the market joyful and excited, holding a pineapple in her hand. When she reached our back yard, she looked stunned. There were at least twenty vendors, some of them sleeping on the grass, others on the stairs. The paspalum grass was scattered with flower petals, as if someone was trying to decorate the yard. Papers and polythene bags from the market were everywhere.

Instead of threatening the vendors with eviction, Ma went directly into the house and stayed in the bedroom for a while. When she finally came out, she had changed into a black dress. She was wearing boots and carrying a spade. In the back yard, Ma found the vendors laughing and talking, happy, as if all was well. She tried to speak to them. They did not pay her any attention – not until she started to yell at them, her small arms shaking and her wig unstable on her scalp.

'Leave. I want all of you to leave my compound now,' Ma said.

'Your compound?' one vendor said. The rest joined in, and they did not allow Ma to speak again. If she wanted to live like the rich, she was on the wrong estate. She should hire a truck, load her household items on it, and head for Kampala's hills, where the houses were large and double-storied and there were dogs and long fences to keep people away.

'I am not going anywhere. I am not. This is my house,' Ma said, repeating herself until she started pointing to the ground, claiming her back yard for her own, refusing to be defeated in this fight.

'Your house? You think this is your house?'

The vendors were undeterred in their efforts to make Ma shut up. They told her that no one came into the estates with any piece of land on their heads. They called my mother a whore. They said she was a husbandless slut, a fanatic Christian, a sex-starved bitch who should migrate back to the north of the country where people were unciv-ilised and lacked manners.

I hoped Red Devil would walk up. If he did, and if he tried to come to Ma's defence, the vendors would beat him until all his teeth fell out. Maybe if he stayed in Mulago Hospital long enough, Ma would forget him. But he was lucky, that Red Devil. He only heard about these exchanges from Ma. And being the Red Devil he was, he just said, 'Um, um, if I was you, I would really make sure those men leave for good. This is your house, they need to know that.'

On the third day of the confrontations, Ma decided to return late from the office, when day would be giving way to night. The day vendors would have left, and in their place would be the night vendors, who were not troublesome. The night vendors kept away from people's back yards. They spread themselves around the market and along Estate Close with their tables full of bread and milk for sale, tomatoes heaped on sisal sacks, kerosene lamps, and large saucepans of cow-leg soup cooking, offal, pancakes, roast meat, and fried cassava, and filled the roadside with the aroma of life. Men, labourers from the industrial area, the market, and the factories around the estates, stationed themselves on benches waiting to be served. Ma always said those men fed their families on eggplant while they fattened themselves on road-side chicken and beef.

I waited for Ma at the window. I was anxious for her, hoping the vendors would be gone by the time she returned. But they weren't. When Ma arrived home, there were as many as the day before.

'You. You thought we would leave just because you came late? You thought we would leave?' The vendors started even before Ma crossed Estate Close. She avoided looking at them and hurried towards the house. They were not ready to let her pass. Everyone in the market stopped to see what was going on. Ma stopped too. She turned.

The vendors resumed the shouting, but one voice among them commanded more attention. It was the man with keloid scars all over his chin. He said no woman should talk to them like that, most especially Ma. She was unworthy. He said nothing good ever came out of her. He said even Ma's womb carried the ugliest of children, children who came out with heads the size of water basins and nostrils that could fit a man's fist. I didn't move from the window for a long time.

Later that evening, I told myself I shouldn't be affected by the stupid things those uneducated vendors said. The vendors came and went, and the market didn't even notice. But me, I was destined for greater things. I was going to end up in Makerere University, Kampala's hills, and maybe even outside countries, the ones Naalu my friend always spoke of. Naalu said that in London, which was one of the cities we could easily end up in, people were rich. They left cars by the roadside if they didn't like them. Every morning the city council worked over-time clearing the street of unwanted merchandise.

I woke up early the next morning, hoping the previous evening would be forgotten. But bitterness and doubt stayed with me like an illness. Throughout the day at school, I found myself holding a fist to my nose to gauge its size. In class, even when the teacher said funny things about Didi Comedy on Uganda Television, I did not smile. I thought it was my fault I did not have many friends. I was not pretty – and good looks, it seemed, were a prerequisite for everything, even for being at the top of the class.

On my way home that evening, I waited for Naalu at the end of Estate Close. She went to another school, and we always met by the cemetery before walking together. That evening, when Naalu joined

me, I asked her if she thought I was ugly. Yes, she said and then, real-
ising I was serious, she asked what was wrong with me.

'OK, OK,' I said, and I told Naalu the vendors must be evicted from
our back yard. I told her I was fed up.

'Eh, this is serious,' Naalu said. But she offered to help, as long as we
did whatever we were planning to do when her father was not home.

The next afternoon, I sat in the cemetery waiting for Naalu. After
an hour, I started to worry. But just when I was getting restless, Naalu
burst through the cemetery, running. She reached me and did not
stop. I ran after her, slowing only when Naalu herself slowed down
half a kilometre later, by the city council hospital.

'Is someone chasing you?' I asked.

'No,' she said, 'but it is better to run just in case.' And then, 'The
bastards must pay. It is war. It is war!'

The sun was still hot and evening seemed far away. Naalu and I
reached Mama Benja's house one block from ours to the left. From
the safety of her fence, Naalu and I threw stones. There were about
nine men under the umbrella tree that day, in the middle of our
compound. The tree was small, but in the afternoon its shade turned
generous and could accommodate several of them stretched out in
the grass beneath. It took at least three stone throws before the
vendors noticed that someone was trying to command their attention. They stood up one at a time. One of the men, the one with the
keloid scars, made as if to come towards us, squinting to peer through
the thick layer of fence.

Naalu and I ran. At the corner of Mama Benja's block, I fell and
scraped my knees bloody. Naalu raced on. She stopped at the large
jambula tree. I rose from my fall and darted through Mama Farouk's
fence. When I reached Naalu at the jambula tree, the man with the
keloid scars appeared at the corner of Mama Benja's house. Off we
raced again. We never looked back until we stopped at the road that
turned into the police barracks. But Naalu was worried that her father
would be home, and so we made our way back through the estate
houses towards the dead water point.

At one time this water point had been the main source for our
neighbourhood. Age and lack of use had rusted the taps, which looked

fit for scrap only. Naalu's father, who was also the chairman of our residential area – the man charged with settling petty quarrels and taking small bribes for writing letters of introduction and stamping passport applications – had raised funds to renovate the water point and replace the taps. Activity returned. People thought it was good they didn't have to trek half a kilometre to fetch water in Lugogo, but by six in the morning, jerry cans were lined up as people fought over whose turn it was. Then the jerry cans, even if they were carefully labelled, started to disappear. The next time the taps broke, water flowed all the way to the market. It spewed everywhere and children ran around naked, happy for the artificial rain. After that episode, no one bothered with the water point again.

After our first try at evicting the vendors, the evening of the next day came. We were inside our house. In the kitchen, I fetched a bucket full of water that I had used to clean the fresh fish from the night before. The water was going stale now, the scent of rotting tilapia fermenting and turning the house into a fish brewery.

Ma was still at work. She would not be home soon. But I was still worried that if we did not hurry, she would return to find the house still smelling of fish. So I repeated to Naalu that we really needed to be quick.

The men were still in our back yard, basking and anticipating another exciting confrontation with Ma while Naalu helped me carry the bucket of water from the kitchen to the sitting room.

'I think you can carry it from here,' she said when we reached the back door. I looked at her and frowned, I knew she would not go outside with me even if I threatened witchcraft.

I descended the stairs by myself, carrying the bucket of water slowly down. On the grass, I pulled the bucket towards the umbrella tree. I wasn't sure if the men were paying attention, but I knew they had seen me.

I pulled my bucket farther. As soon as I sensed I was too anxious to go on, I lifted. It was heavy but not as heavy as I had expected it to be. I directed the bucket towards the umbrella tree, then I poured and ran. On the stairs I said to myself, 'Hallelujah, hallelujah. Praise be to God!'

In the house, under the bed in the bedroom where I stayed the whole evening, all I thought was 'Hallelujah, hallelujah. Praise be to God!'

Ma came home to a riot – men with stones and bricks. She also came home to find Naalu's father standing on our stairs, trying to make sure everyone understood he'd come as chairman to settle the matter.

Years later, Ma would say that when she came back from work and saw him standing on the stairs trying to calm everyone, she didn't know whether to be pleased or annoyed. It was well known among our neighbours that Ma and Naalu's father did not like each other. Naalu's father thought northerners were to blame for every single thing that had ever gone wrong in the country – the *coups d'état*, the bad roads, the hospitals without medicine, the high price of sugar, his addiction to nicotine, and the fact that the country was landlocked. As for Ma, her reasons for disliking the man were simple. He was Catholic, like the unforgiving nuns of her school days; he supported the Democratic Party; and he was a Muganda, like most of the vendors who messed her back yard. According to Ma, all three things were incurable ailments. Catholics worshipped idols. DP was a dead political party led by a goat of an old man who did nothing but make dead deals. And Ma thought the Baganda were thieving traitors who'd been selling the country to the highest bidder right from the time of the British. Ma said it often that Baganda treasured money over loyalty. They would steal your hand if you turned away. The Baganda were banana eaters. They consumed *matooke* for a staple. Ma said *matooke* was a useless food, one per cent air and ninety-nine per cent water. She thought the Baganda were a weak people, fearful of confrontation and conflict, who chose the easy way instead of the upstream path of honesty, clarity and directness. My friendship with Naalu Ma had tolerated for the most part because of the day she found Naalu and me in our sitting room sharing a plate of dried fish and millet. Ma asked Naalu if she liked it.

'Yes,' Naalu said.

'Good,' Ma said. 'Tell that to your father when you see him. Tell him you eat millet these days, not bananas!'

In our back yard, Naalu's father forgot about his ongoing war with

Ma. He focused on the vendors and spoke with eloquence and serious-ness. He told all the gathered people that the market and the estates were two different entities. It was irrelevant that they were both owned by Kampala city council. If the men wanted to use such flimsy argu-ments, he said, we should as well go and camp at the state house and tell the president it was our right as citizens. If the vendors did not stop coming to Ma's back yard, or any other back yard in the estates for that matter, he would take this issue up with the market management.

That evening a new law came into force, written on plywood with charcoal and hurriedly constructed by a carpenter. It was erected right next to Ma's newly planted red euphorbia fence. Anyone caught crossing over to the estates would be fined twenty thousand shillings. When I saw the sign from the safety of our window, I thought it would be pulled down. But that signpost survived hail and dogs, vendors and trucks for years.

Red Devil came home just when Naalu's father was trying to settle the matter. With the confidence he'd built over the weeks of coming to our home, he tried to intervene on her behalf. Someone took the pens from his brown suit pocket and pocked his skull with them. They ordered Red Devil to shut up because he had no right to speak. A man who knew him well took the opportunity to embarrass him. He said that Red Devil was not a Christian. He did not care about God – only about the Christian women he infected with gonorrhoea while recit-ing verses from the Song of Solomon.

I did not see Red Devil after that, but neither did I see Naalu. Over the next days, I searched for any sign of her in their front yard. When she did eventually surface, it was only because her father had sent her to the market to buy cooking oil for the house. Naalu hurried there, running as if there was fire on her hem. When she saw me following, she broke into a sprint and left the market without buying the cooking oil. She did not look back either. Maybe she was afraid she would turn into a pillar of salt like Lot's wife. Naalu raced up the hill as if it was a flat football field. And that was the last time I saw her. Ma was not speaking to Naalu's father again, and Naalu's brother, Nviiri, was not talking to me, so I could not ask him. Only the silly estate boys seemed available to offer some answers. It took several tries before they told me what they knew. They said that Naalu's father, fearing that I would turn her into a good-for-nothing millet-eating uncivilised northerner, had enrolled her in a Catholic boarding school to join the Order of St Bruno, the crazy nuns who committed to a vow of silence and solitude for the rest of their lives.

Chei, I thought. Such nonsense.

But it was not nonsense, of course, because Naalu did not return.

from a novel in progress

Rotimi Babatunde

The Tiger of the Mangroves

Perhaps the sorry-looking, rat-infested boat that came in weekly from Fernando Po was to blame for the end of the affair. When the new steamships arrived hungry for the palm oil needed by the smoking factories of Europe, Chief Koko seized the moment to establish – with arms bought from his white merchant friends – a monopoly that stretched along the length of the palm coast.

It was a relationship that benefitted both parties. The merchants got their oil, the Chief's coffers swelled by the year, and the romance between the African middleman and Europe's merchants seemed set to last for ever. But on the last leg of the trip from Europe, the boat from Fernando Po brought, along with passengers and the mail, newspapers already a month old. After those dailies brought the white merchants the good news that the resolutions of Berlin had granted the British dominion over Chief Koko's kingdom, the merchants converted to the gospel of free trade and began grumbling about the fortune Chief Koko was raking into his palace vaults. The Crown will soon fly the Union Jack over the hinterland, Europe's merchants reassured one another, but the months lengthened into years and yet the Crown dawdled over taking possession of the territory. As the years went by, the resentment of the merchants towards Chief Koko mounted.

Almost a decade would pass after the deliberations in Berlin before the decrepit boat from Fernando Po finally brought over the boyish-faced fellow who couldn't sleep in his cabin because of the crawling vermin but instead spent most of his time on the deck with the sailors. No one paid much attention to the nondescript man who stood on the boat's prow and continued applying brushstrokes to a canvas, even after the vessel had dropped anchor and his fellow passengers were making their way down the gangplank. Only later would people come to know that the painter was no one less than Henry Hamilton, the territory's pioneer consul, who was recording his first view of the creeks Europe considered the Crown's because of a few signatures scribbled years earlier in Berlin.

Chief Koko was conducting his weekly council when he received the report that Henry Hamilton was the person mandated to oversee the affairs of his nation on behalf of Her Majesty. The Chief laughed. No wonder people from Hamilton's native land always pray that God should save the Queen, he said. Surely, the poor woman must have an appetite for sticking her nose into troubles bigger than she could handle. Why else would her subjects be forever begging God to save her from one distress or another?

He laughed again. No other person in his royal chamber was relaxed enough to laugh along with him.

Chief Koko and Consul Hamilton met under a brightly coloured parasol on a beach a long way down the coastline from the stretch where the European merchants had their warehouses. Henry Hamilton was surprised by how young Chief Koko was. The consul had been expecting a wizened warrior, like the battle-hardened sheiks he had encountered a decade earlier during his youthful travels along the fringes of the Sahara studying Maghreb art and architecture. This anticipation had been reinforced by the fat dossier containing chronicles of the Chief's military and political exploits which Hamilton had been given during his briefing at Whitehall, but the beguiling face of the man scrutinising the consul with intense but tender eyes belied the fearsome portrait painted by the dossier, and for a moment Hamilton wondered if he wasn't in the presence of an impostor. Could a man with a visage this mild be the general whose legend had been transported from Kingston to Calcutta and whom even the merchants from Europe called the Tiger of the Mangroves?

Hell, he can't yet be forty, Henry Hamilton would record that night in his diary. Just about my own age. Had Koko been born in a different clime and of a fairer hue, Hamilton would go on to note, they could have been in the same class studying Classics at King's College. Like the consul, Koko could also have picked up employment in Her Majesty's imperial service. Instead, the Chief, who came from common stock, had become the delta's most prominent monarch by spending his youth waging war to unite several small domains and installing himself sovereign over the expansive new realm. His accomplishments make one feel inadequate, the consul concluded in his diary entry for the day.

The foppishness of Chief Koko's manicured fingers, his striking coral bracelets, and the stylishness of his walking stick, on which was carved a menagerie of marine creatures, reminded Hamilton of the famous dandies in his own country. The consul imagined Koko promenading in a top hat down the Strand, wearing a bright brocade waistcoat with a carnation in its buttonhole and clutching a rare edition of Byron's *Don Juan*, but that train of thought was derailed by a glance in the direction of Chief Koko's dreaded canoe boys. Standing about a hundred feet from the parasol, a platoon of the Chief's elite guards, each holding a loaded musket, was eyeballing a company of the Crown's khaki-clad constabulary ranked at attention on the other side of the canopy. The uncompromising gaze burning in the eyes of Chief Koko's men undid Hamilton's casting of the general who had drilled such fierceness into them as a dreamy aesthete. The consul snapped out of his fanciful flights and returned to the reality of the moment.

Chief Koko and Mr Henry Hamilton shook hands firmly. Under a clear tropical sky and on a sunny beach lapped by the waters of the Atlantic, the two men, born at about the same time but on different continents and brought into contact by the impassive deviousness of history, sat down and began talking.

The evening after the boat conveying Hamilton towards his new post sailed out of Plymouth, the consul, tormented by boredom and the ubiquitous pestilence of cockroaches, had struck up a conversation with an old seaman stationed by the boat's safety valve. Over copious swigs of liquor, the sailor regaled Hamilton with stories from the decades he had spent as a crewman ploughing a variety of marine craft across the seas. Punctuating these colourful narratives was the plaintive refrain of the seaman that the years had drained him of wanderlust. He wished for a transfer to a boat plying the other leg of the trip, the one from Tenerife to Fernando Po where his family lived, so he could be assured of spending a few days with his grand-children every month.

Hamilton asked the seaman for his hometown. The old sailor replied that he was a kinsman of Chief Koko. There on the deck, over another bottle of schnapps, the consul struck a deal with the seaman. Hamilton would employ his influence to get the sailor posted to his preferred route. In return, the seaman would tutor Hamilton in the language and culture of the old man's homeland.

Each kept his side of the bargain. During the remainder of the month-long journey, Henry Hamilton learned more every day about his destination than was contained in all of the seventeen worthless files dumped in his lap by the round-spectacled bureaucrats at the Foreign Office. On disembarking at Fernando Po, he was almost fluent in Chief Koko's language – the nineteenth of the twenty-six languages in which Hamilton would be able to claim competence.

After their handshake, the first sentence voiced by Henry Hamilton was an obscure proverb in the Chief's mother tongue, delivered almost without accent by the newcomer whose mission was to impose domin-ion over the general's homeland on behalf of a distant Queen.

I am delighted to be here, said Henry Hamilton. I have done some travelling in Africa but I have never been to this part of the Dark Continent.

My nation welcomes with peace all strangers who come visiting in peace, replied Chief Koko. He waited for the full import of his words to sink in before continuing. Many visitors from your country have told me you don't have as much sunlight in your land as we do here.

Oh, yes. That is in a period that is very cold, much colder than anything you ever experience here. For a good part of the year the sun almost never comes out, and the weather gets so cold you need a fire to keep yourself warm.

If your people spend so much time in darkness, why do you

attribute darkness to this place, where the sun always comes out, rather than to your homeland?

Henry Hamilton frowned. There are many good reasons for that, he said.

Chief Koko shrugged. From my discussions with your white brothers who visited us before you, it is clear that my people and yours see many things in this world with different eyes, he said.

Koko had learned English through his interactions with European merchants but he never spoke it at official functions, so a translator had been made available. Hamilton and Koko chatted on in the Chief's mother tongue, without recourse to the translator. The subjects they avoided were more important than the ones they discussed. Some would later say this duet of omission was tacit acknowledgement from the two men that Berlin had made dialogue redundant long before they met. So Hamilton spoke about his rafting down the Nile, whose delta was a distant sister to the creeks patrolled by Chief Koko's canoe boys. The consul went ahead to describe his almost successful attempt to scale the heights of the Kilimanjaro, and he spoke about how delighted he was to be the discoverer of a river's mouth near the mountain.

Were there no people living in the area? Chief Koko asked.

There is a big village in the vicinity. Two natives who knew the mouth guided me there.

The Chief's brows creased.

But how can you say you found the river's source when others had been there before you?

Henry Hamilton was irritated by the doubts being raised about an achievement that had been gazetted by the Royal Geographical Society. I was honoured for that achievement some months ago in my country, the consul replied.

It will be more interesting to go where *nobody* has ever been, Chief Koko said. The moon, for instance.

The two men laughed, nervously.

Henry Hamilton had been casting awestruck glances in the direction of Chief Koko's walking stick. In response to Hamilton's curiosity, Koko mentioned the names of the creatures etched along the length of the staff. The terrifying distortions wrought on the figures violated every virtue expected of good art in Hamilton's homeland, so the consul couldn't understand why he had fallen under the spell of their artistry. Your walking stick is amazing, he gushed.

I am pleased to know that you appreciate its gracefulness, said Chief Koko. The carver who gave me the staff spent many months working on it.

The Chief began describing the habitats and mannerisms of the fauna carved on the staff. When the verbal safari through the delta that he was conducting for Hamilton's benefit got to the mangrove tiger snarling at the walking stick's head, the consul asked, Does that animal truly exist?

It is a creature much feared in my kingdom and beyond, Chief Koko replied.

Hamilton, a keen naturalist whose childhood hero was Carl Linnaeus, enquired further, Do you know of anyone who saw one recently?

Why?

As far as we know, tigers don't exist in Africa, the consul said.

The Chief smiled. You never see it until the instant before you become its carcass. That is why it is regarded with so much fear.

The consul, dreaming of being the first European to see the legendary creature, was unrelenting. I will try to track down one during my stay here, he said.

We have a saying that only half-eaten corpses know the colour of the mangrove tiger's eyes, Chief Koko said. He pointed the crown of his walking stick towards his chest. The mangrove tiger sitting here, the Chief added, is also one you haven't yet seen.

They both laughed, again uneasily. For a while they said nothing, the only sound coming from the foaming waves of the Atlantic crashing repeatedly against the shoreline.

Hamilton broke the silence with a comment about the clear skies. He noted that the weather would be perfect for cricket and proceeded to give Koko an overview of the game, the almost religious devotion he had to it evident in his animated gestures.

Chief Koko's interest in the meanings of concepts like wickets and runs and over arm bowling was negligible. What intrigued him more were the deeper rituals of cricket, which Hamilton listed out to include fair play and trust. The Chief drew correspondences between those values and the moral principles that defined the practice of age-grade wrestling, his people's favourite pastime. Both men concluded the parallels between their national sports were indeed striking.

There was some more awkward silence. The Chief and the consul stood up and shook hands, bringing an end to the proceedings. Neither of them could have suspected that that first meeting would also be their last. And neither could have known that events triggered by that single encounter would warp the destiny of an entire subcontinent and turn the two of them into eternal enemies, yet both men, as if in common devotion to a creed that mandates the veneration of contradictions, would never stop calling each other friend.

Even after a century following that encounter between the Chief and the consul, when the landscape of the creeks no longer featured palm-oil casks floating downriver or deck-hands loading cargo into the holds of steamships, when the discovery of a different kind of oil in the delta had inaugurated a new age of pipelines and tankers and derricks flaring natural gas skywards, diverse witnesses would keep on testifying to sighting Consul Hamilton and Chief Koko at midnight re-enacting their only meeting on that desolate beach battered by the rough waters of the Atlantic. Fishermen downing gin after trawling with little profit in the polluted waters would itemise the antiquated clothes once fashionable in a previous century that Koko and Hamilton still wore, and market women would lament the anguish on the faces of the two men doomed to continue recycling the same insignificant chatter about wrestling and marine creatures and cricket every night till the wintery end of time. Soldiers guarding oil rigs would pass time by analysing the positions of Chief Koko's canoe boys and the Crown's constabulary, the spectral phalanxes damned for ever to keep glowering at each other from opposing sides of the principal actors. And old women would tell their grandchildren that because those unfortunate combatants and the superannuated translator were implicated by the accident of their mere presence at the seaside summit, they were bound to keep on restaging that spooky theatre as extras to their bosses, like attendants sentenced to everlasting servitude in the courts of ancient monarchs with whom they were entombed. And some historians would go as far as claiming that the meeting between Chief Koko and Consul Hamilton, like the ghostly convocations that followed it, was also a phantom one. Both men had merely been spectators at a public demonstration of their mutual impotence to tinker with the future, the scholars would say, arguing that history's true meeting was the reception organised for Henry Hamilton by the territory's leading European merchants.

The reception was held a week after the consul's meeting with the Chief at the oceanfront residence of John Holt. The warehouse on the premises was the largest in the territory. Mr Holt was notorious for being so taciturn that some people joked that his mouth moved only when eating. He didn't need to speak much. The coin in his pocket couldn't have purchased him a return ticket when in his youth he sailed from England to begin trading in Fernando Po, and the saga of his ruthless rise from an anonymous shop assistant to the mercantile titan whose fleet steamed palm oil to Liverpool and brought back guns and gin to Africa communicated his ambition eloquently enough to all. The most important of his fellow merchants loathed one another, so Mr Holt had to do more talking than he had in a long while before he could convince them to raise the white flag as a banner to war against Chief Koko, their common enemy.

The crickets were chirping in full chorus when the twenty-seven guests began eating. The welcome dinner was enlivened by the presence of Mary Kingsley, a family friend of the Holts who was passing through town on one of her many journeys. The unapologetic woman explorer had grabbed a centre seat for herself in the stag party of the imperial enterprise, and it was the scale of her achievements that silenced the grumbling that at first dogged her activities. Her most rigid male detractors were won over by her distinction of being the first European woman to reach the peak of Mount Cameroon, but whenever her countrymen congratulated her on the achievement, she curtly replied, I was actually the third Englishman, sir.

Though Mary Kingsley had little liking for sweet potatoes, she didn't mind them if they were buttered and browned the way

Mrs Holt ensured her cooks did. As the guests tucked away the buffet of soursop with mutton and potatoes and bananas baked with rice, Ms Kingsley regaled the table with stories about her recent travels way down south in the Ogowe swamps, a place none of her fellow diners had ever visited. The explorer told them about the sword grass trampled into wide paths by hippo herds. Even the sternest of the merchants laughed when she called those hippos the road-makers of the region. And she went on to talk about the incident in which her canoe would have been upturned by a snapping crocodile, if not for quick-thinking by locals standing on the river bank.

The Bengas and the Krus are considerably superior in intelligence to their Bantu neighbours, Mary Kingsley said. I find it laughable when the ignorant lump the whole bunch together as primitive. But that is not to say that any other race is close in abilities to our Caucasian own, Allah forbid an utterance that untutored from me. And I say this without forgetting the frequency with which our people make shocking fools of themselves along the length of this coast.

Mary Kingsley's speech was habitually powered by such contrary sensibilities, generating sentences equally discomfiting as reassuring. Some months earlier, confronted with the paradoxes of her tangled position on native rituals, an official at the Colonial Office had thrown up his hands in exasperation and labelled her the Most Dangerous Woman on the Other Side.

After they were done with eating, the merchants relocated to the smoking room. As usual, Mary Kingsley, who would die young while serving as a volunteer nurse in the Second Boer War, went along with the men. Mrs Holt and the other ladies went into the kitchen for tea.

Over cigarettes, the matter of Chief Koko finally came up. We were informed that your meeting with Koko went on for quite a while, one of the merchants said.

You are the representative of Her Majesty, said another merchant. It came as a surprise that you found worthwhile matters to discuss with such a knave.

Henry Hamilton squirmed.

Are you sure the Foreign Office would be delighted with your conduct? asked a third merchant. Jaw-jawing with that native scoun-drel, as if he were your equal, doesn't strike us as seemly.

I thought this was meant to be a reception, Henry Hamilton protested, not an inquisition.

On the contrary, sir, began John Holt, but Henry Hamilton inter-rupted him. The missionaries are happy about the meeting, the consul said. They want me to convince the Chief to allow them to widen the scope of their operations in his domain.

Mary Kingsley laughed. Traders, not clergy, are the soul of the imperial enterprise, she said. I would be shocked if the distinguished consul didn't know that already.

Henry Hamilton regarded Mary Kingsley. Her eyes were laughing at him. The consul went red in the face.

Remember, sir, she added, without commerce, there would be no Empire.

Berlin has long given us leave to have direct access to the hinterland, Mr Holt said. But Chief Koko is a greedy middleman. Removing him won't be achieved by holding picnics on the beach with him.

John Holt's fellow merchants nodded. Henry Hamilton sighed.

Mr Holt dragged another puff from his pipe. Koko has to go, he said. That is our collective resolution.

Henry Hamilton scowled at the gathering. The merchants glared back. Mary Kingsley's eyes were still mocking Henry Hamilton. The consul felt even more like a fool.

Are you in agreement with us on that? John Holt asked.

Henry Hamilton nodded.

The palaver was cut. Neither heaven nor earth can do anything now to change Chief Koko's fate, John Holt would later tell his warehouse manager. The merchants smoked on in silence and contentment. Mary Kingsley began talking about her ascent up Mount Cameroon and the iciness of the winds that whip around its highest reaches.

Two Fragments of Love

Eileen Almeida Barbosa

I. Graffiti

We met on a school bench. Saladine and Salazar. I was the serious and studious one, you were the artist. You were always drawing – book covers, tabletops, toilet walls: all these were your canvases.

I don't know what came first: becoming your muse, your biggest fan or falling in love with you. Or did it all happen at the same time?

You used to like drawing me from the front, even though I looked better in profile. You never cared much about your drawings once they were finished. They were beautiful. I kept all your sketches of me. And the others; any I could get my hands on.

I always wanted to be with you, though I never really knew why you stayed with me. I was never artistic. But no one loved you more! The years we had were wonderful. Intimate. Colourful. Supporting you was never a burden; it was a contribution to art. I saw myself as your patron, as well as your muse. And what a radiant muse I was.

Although you didn't talk much, I always understood you perfectly, but not from your gestures or the expressions on your ever-reserved face. Simply from your drawings. In that sense, I always thought how transparent you were.

I know, I know, I know. There are no lies or inventions in what you draw. You never expressed a dark thought in your comic graffiti, or a bleak thought when you used bright colours. For a long time I've read you better than anyone. Better than your false friends or your true ones, your fellow artists, your critics, your parents.

That was how, when you drew bolder strokes, I discovered how happy you were, when your strokes seemed to tremble I felt you hesitate, when you used contrasting colours I knew you were comparing us and when your strokes wavered I sensed that you wanted to leave.

I wandered around the city, deciphering the drawings you spray-painted on public buildings, telegraph poles, crumbling walls, or wherever the police let you and the gangs don't bother you.

I followed the trail of renegade, illegal artists, of non-transportable art all around Coimbra. Art for the street, your favourite place. I saw myself everywhere, but in the faded paint of someone drawn only in the past.

Now you draw new faces, eyes different to mine.

I could buy some tubs of paint and cover over all your old drawings, out of spite and fear and anger at being abandoned.

I could empty your cans of paint down the toilet, stop your allowance.

I could weep. Prove my parents right and leave you.

I could sit quietly and hope that it's only a fleeting passion. That in the end you'll choose me.

II. I am Not a Witch

What do you want me to write? What news, when I haven't seen you for all these years?

I will describe for you people you have never seen, streets you will never walk. This is my life now. I leave work, and as I walk I greet familiar faces, acquaintances whose worries trouble me more than yours because I know their relevance, and they spit at my feet.

Their spit settles the dust that would otherwise dirty my white shoes. They bring their children for me to vaccinate. I've learned to love this and I barely remember what it's like to live in a country with running water; television is a myth to me. But I'll tell you how malaria develops, how the scabs on wounds have a special smell that attracts more flies than shit. I want to tell you that I've got tougher. I see young women who've been raped. Women who poison their husbands then regret it come to me asking for antidotes. I'll tell you just what I say to them: I am not a witch.

You want me to write a diary for you, not about my day-to-day life but about the ideas that come into my head. I'll tell you one thing: I learned to sew. I make mosquito nets. I buy metres and metres of gauze; I sew it into big tubes, with a frame for hanging the nets above sleeping mats. When I'm struggling with those metres of white gauze, my mind wanders. My thoughts are random. And with so many metres of white gauze I end up thinking, as well, about brides all dressed in white, about purity and innocence. Above all innocence. Well, I think about the past, too.

Last night, when I was putting the finishing touches to a mosquito net, I was remembering my journey to Spain. I don't know why I decided to disembark there, when I was actually heading back to Portugal. I'd just lost you. The days were like Everests that I had to climb, becoming more and more breathless towards evening, which was when I had to be on my feet, at the restaurant, serving drinks. I never confessed to my supervisor that I felt ill; that I always felt seasick. And what with the pain of having lost you . . . I went ashore at Barcelona and didn't go back on board, not at 6 p.m., nor when the ship's horn sounded.

I spent the days crying. I saw streets I'd never seen before. I imagined us walking in the shade of peach trees. I used paper napkins that I took from the bars where I went to use the toilet. By now, I regretted having spent my savings on you. I had barely any money left. I stole food, too. And the rest of the time, I wandered. The little money I had was for buying batteries so I could keep listening to 'Where is My Love' over and over and over again on my Walkman. And I cried. I wanted to die, but I couldn't summon up the courage to throw myself under one of the cars that passed me by, indifferent. On a park bench, where I'd collapsed, unable to look at the peach trees, a man sat down beside me, took my face in his hands. I saw him through the mist that had fallen over my eyes and thought he had a face like Jesus. He said to me in a thick Catalan accent that he'd seen me wandering around his block for days. What was wrong? I cried even more, I never could stand people pitying me. He hugged me and it didn't even occur to me to think it strange. I slumped into his arms; I cried so much that after a while I was just numb, quite still, doggedly snatching breaths. He said to me: 'Do you want to come to my place for a cup of tea?'

I don't know if I walked or if he carried me, I don't know if I climbed the stairs or hovered over them, until we reached a single person's flat, with books, blank walls, mismatched furniture. A huge fish tank, with the biggest shoal of orange fish I'd ever seen. A sofa welcomed my body and my eyes fixed on the fish tank, finding a certain peace. And I spent six years there. My life has always been like that, I get shipwrecked, then the tide carries me to a beach and to safety. I spend a few days, or years there, then I get shipwrecked again. When my Catalan swapped me for another woman – who was a lot less pretty but a lot more cheerful, the little bitch – I was shipwrecked again, and I fled again.

I thought I'd found you on a Greek island, but it wasn't you. And then I came here and saw people in a much worse state than me, I found some perspective. And I lost my expectations. Just like that.

Folks here don't bother much with expectations either. The average lifespan is so short that they have children as teenagers and are old by the time they're thirty. They don't use coffins and each grave serves for two or three, stacked up. They are buried in their clothes.

I often think, too, about how short my time on this planet will be. But do you know what? There's a force, some kind of force that pushes me along, pulls me out of bed in the morning, dresses me and compels me to try and save these poor wretches.

I went to the capital once. I didn't like it. It seemed like the whole city was covered in a cloak of sleep. In parks, in cinema aisles, behind the barred windows, the homeless and the middle classes, little old men and young girls, teachers and businessmen: they were all half-asleep. In air-conditioned offices, not even a fly buzzed. The city had been besieged for longer than anyone could remember, and outside, those still surrounding it blinked in confusion. They didn't feel angry any more, they no longer craved blood. The languid air seemed to be fading the green of the trees, and very slowly withering the general's moustache to the point that he no longer seemed terrifying.

There was a certain spirit, drab, washed-out, neither black nor white nor any colour at all. It felt like a landscape-poem, an elegant melancholy sometimes, a lump in the throat, a knot in the stomach, a burning sensation in the eyes.

But no one was alert enough to notice. I came straight back and never returned. It seems like the siege ended a long time ago but nothing changed. Me? I don't cry, I don't gesticulate, I don't sing, I live, but not much. And the kindly breeze lifts the hair from my forehead and dries my sweat. I drag myself through the day and, with luck, I get to midday, with faith I get to midnight and the worst will have passed and the next day will dawn blank and white. But there are no colours, so the white will barely stand out against the hues that cover me from skin to pupil, inseparable, like nail and cuticle.

Right, that's enough for my first letter, I think. This is the life I'm leading, here in this place where I flung myself or where I washed up. Tell me about you too.

Lots of love,

From your Saladine

Translated by Lucy Greaves

from the forthcoming novel *Blackass*

A. Igoni Barrett

Why Radio DJs Are Superstars in Lagos

At Ikoyi passport office, Syreeta waited in the Honda as Furo went in. When he returned minutes later with his new passport grasped in his hand, she reached out for it, and after reading the identification page, she handed it back and asked how come his surname was Nigerian. Furo's answer:

'I've already told you I'm Nigerian.'

'But you're white!' exclaimed Syreeta.

'So you mean I can't be white *and* Nigerian?'

'That's not what I'm saying. I'm asking how it happened.'

This question had been expected by Furo for some time, and over the long weekend he had thought through his answer. He'd considered saying he was mixed race with a Nigerian father and a white American mother, but while that explained his name and his black buttocks, it raised other questions, the most irksome being a white extended family and his lack of ties to the US embassy in Nigeria. The second story he'd considered was that his white family had settled a long time ago in Nigeria and along the line had changed their name, but on further thought that idea seemed absurd and so he discarded it. Nigerians readily adopted European and Arab and Hebrew names. It never happened the other way around.

The story he settled on appeared to him the most plausible, the least open to rebuttal – it answered every question except that of his buttocks. But then, he told himself, nothing in life is perfect. To Syreeta he said:

'I don't like talking about it so I'll just say this quickly. My parents are Nigerians. They lived in America for many years, my father was born there, and while they were over there they adopted me. My mother couldn't have children. They returned to Lagos while I was still a baby, and they quarrelled when my father married a second wife. My mother took me away, we moved to Port Harcourt, and I haven't heard from my father in nearly twenty years. My mother passed away last year. I came to Lagos and got stranded. Then I met you. That's why I have this name. That's why I have nobody. Now I'm hungry. Can we stop somewhere to eat?'

'Of course,' Syreeta said, and after she faced forwards and guided the Honda on to the road, she added in a voice hoarsened with awe:

'I didn't know it was possible for black people to adopt white people.'

And so it happened that Syreeta stopped over at the Palms to buy lunch at the café where she and Furo had met six days ago, and by three o'clock they were back on the Lekki–Ajah highway, in after-work traffic, headed towards her friend's house in Victoria Garden City.

Seated beside Syreeta as she steered the Honda through traffic, Furo realised why radio DJs were superstars in Lagos. The car radio was tuned to Cool FM, and many times on the drive from Lekki to Ikoyi to pick up Furo's passport and back to Lekki for lunch and on to Ajah to visit her friend, Syreeta had danced in her seat and squealed with laughter at the music selections and the lisping banter of a host of DJs who seemed never to run out of something to say. With the Honda now stuck in a monster traffic jam on the outskirts of Ajah, Furo began to think that for the millions of commuters who spent hour after hour and day after day in Lagos traffic with only their car radios for company, these feigned accents and invented personalities became as dear as confidantes. The more he thought about it, the more he was struck by blinding flashes of the obvious, a whole rash of ideas marching into his head to the beats from the car radio. Persistent power cuts in Lagos, in the whole of Nigeria, meant that battery-operated radios were the entertainment appliance of necessity for both rich and poor, young and old, the city-based and the village-trapped, everyone. Radios were cheap to buy and free to use, no data bundles or subscription packages or credit plans, and they were also long-lasting, easy to carry around, available in private cars and commercial buses, and most important, they were independent of the undependable power grid. Mobile phones even came with radios, as did MP3 players; and computers had applications that live-streamed radio; and thinking of it, the recharge-able battery lamps that everyone owned also had radios built into them. Then again there were those new Chinese toys for the tech-starved: radio sunglasses, radio caps, radio wristwatches. It was endless. Radio was deathless. Radio DJs were superstars.

Furo lost interest in this line of thinking when the DJ cut the music to announce that it was time to pay the bills so don't touch that dial. After several minutes of jolly-sounding jingles, most of which seemed aimed at schoolchildren and petty traders, a new Tuface single was introduced by the DJ, and as the song sprang from the speakers Syreeta flung up her arms and hooted with joy, and then glanced over at Furo with a wide grin.

Syreeta showed a clear fondness for local music. Pidgin hip-hop, Afrobeat electronica, Ajegunle reggae, highlife-flavoured R&B, even oldies' disco crooned to a lover named Ifeoma. Nigerian music domi-nated the Lagos airwaves, and Syreeta seemed to know the lyrics to every song. Rihanna's anthems might be enjoyed, and Drake's rap acknowledged with sporadic nods of approval, but when P-Square warbled, Syreeta hollered back. Furo also listened to Nigerian pop – he even had two P-Square songs in his old phone – though he couldn't say he had a particular taste for it. But now, hearing Syreeta sing along to lyrics that preached money and marriage and little else, he found himself hating P-Square a little.

The song ended, the DJ resumed his adenoidal chatter and Syreeta said, pointing with a finger straight ahead, 'See where those buses are turning – and that LASTMA man is just sitting there looking! OK now, I'm going to follow them.'

Furo stared through the windscreen at the congested road: in the confusion that met his eyes he couldn't find what Syreeta was pointing at. The road should have resembled a Mumbai train station at rush hour – lines and lines of stilled cars stretching into the distance, armies of hawkers darting about in rag uniforms, the air sluggish with exhaust fumes and exhausted breaths – but it didn't, it had a chaos all of its own. It looked exactly like after-work traffic in Lagos was supposed to look. A sprawling coastal city that had no ferry system, no commuter trains, no underground tunnels or overhead tramlines, where hordes of people leaving work poured on to the roads at the same time as the freight trucks carting petroleum products and food produce and all manner of manufacture from all corners of Nigeria. The roads were overburdened and under-policed, and even in select areas where road expansion projects were under way, the contracted engineers worked at a pace that betrayed their lack of confidence in the usefulness of their labour. They knew as well as the politicians that Lagos was exploding at a rate its road network could never keep up with.

The cars ahead revved and spat out smoke, the Honda rolled forward inches, and finally Furo saw the reason this section of the road was gridlocked. Metres ahead, in the middle of the highway, an excavator was breaking blacktop and scooping earth, and at the spot where it heaved and clanged, a new roundabout had been partitioned out with concrete barriers that narrowed the road into a bottleneck. A small band of touts, led by a cap-wearing man, whose white goatee caught the sunlight, had pushed aside one of the barriers, opened a path to the other side of the road – which was free of traffic – and they collected money from any car that squeezed through the breach. It was mostly minibuses that turned off to disgorge passengers and rush back into town, but a few private cars also took the opening. A state traffic warden sat on the tailgate of a Peugeot wagon adjacent to the breach and calmly watched proceedings. His crisp uniform shirt, the yellow of spoiled milk, was tucked into his beef-red trousers, and his black boots gleamed as he swung his feet back and forth.

Furo turned to Syreeta. 'I've seen the opening. Do you want to turn around? Aren't we going to see your friend any more?'

'We are,' Syreeta replied. 'See where the petrol station is? VGC gate is right beside it. I'll cross over and drive by the side of the road till we reach the gate. If I stay here I'll have to go far ahead, I'll have to follow this traffic till after Ajah junction, then turn around and start coming back. With this go-slow, that will take us at least another thirty minutes.'

Furo was tired of sitting, his buttocks ached, and yet he wasn't eager for Syreeta to take the shortcut. He felt too conspicuous to break laws openly.

He spoke. 'I don't trust that LASTMA guy.'

'He won't try anything,' Syreeta responded, and turning to smile at Furo, she added in a teasing tone: 'You white people fear too much.'

Furo didn't return her smile. 'I still think it's safer to stay on the road.'

Of course Syreeta ignored his warning, and after she forked over two hundred naira for the illegal toll – special fee for special people, white goatee said with a brooding glance at Furo – and drove through the breach, of course the traffic warden jumped down from his perch and bolted forward to accost the car. Syreeta tried to drive around him, but the man was nimble for his size and he also seemed to have no regard for his life. When finally he leaped on to the bonnet and bumped his forehead against the windscreen, smearing the glass with sweat, Syreeta braked the car to a stop, wound down her side window, switched off the ignition and removed the key, then stuck out her head. 'Are you crazy?' she yelled. 'Do you want to break my wind-shield? What sort of nonsense is this?'

The traffic warden slid off the bonnet, dashed to Syreeta's side and grabbed the steering wheel through the open window. 'Your key,' he puffed, and glowered at Syreeta with his sun-darkened face only inches from hers. His chest rose and sank with each breath.

'Are you joking?' Syreeta snapped. 'I'm not giving you my key!'

'Give me your key, Madam,' the traffic warden said again in a voice whose threatening tone had jumped several notches, and his knuckles bunched on the steering wheel.

'No,' Syreeta said, and shook her head in emphasis, leaned back in her seat, calmly returned his stare.

'You this woman, I'm warning you o, give me the key!'

'Why?' Syreeta shouted back. 'Oya, tell me first, what did I do?'

'You don't know what you did, ehn? OK, I will tell you after you give me the key. Just do as I order. Obey before complaint.'

'No fucking way,' Syreeta said.

'You're looking for trouble.' This said quietly, his tensed forearm trembling through the window. Vapours of cold air wafted out of the car into his shiny face.

'You're the one looking for trouble,' Syreeta said. 'Didn't you see other cars passing? How come it's me you want to stop? You think you've seen awoof? You better get out of my way if know what's good for you!'

'If you move I will show you!' the traffic warden growled in warning, at the same time shoving his second hand through the window to grasp the steering wheel. His flexing muscles seemed prepared to wrest out the steering wheel, and his expression showed he would try, but Syreeta, to Furo's growing wonder, didn't appear in the slightest bothered by the suppressed violence of those arms in front of her chest. With a mocking laugh she averted her face, stared straight through the windscreen, ignoring the traffic warden. It was a deadlock.

Furo knew there was nothing he could say to defuse the situation, and nothing he could do in his broke state, but still he felt compelled to act. He leaned across Syreeta, met the traffic warden's hostile eyes, and said in a beseeching tone, 'Excuse me, oga,' but Syreeta whirled around and shushed him with a curt 'No.' He settled back in his seat. Syreeta was handling this all wrong. She should be ingratiating herself to the traffic warden, not provoking the man to arrest her. With her car impounded she would pay a fine many times larger than the bribe that had prompted the traffic warden to pick on her, while he, for all his exertions, would get nothing except paperwork to fill.

The traffic warden broke the silence. 'Answer me, Madam,' he said, and Syreeta did, she turned her face to the window and told the man in haughty tones that she would have his job for the embarrassment he was causing her. Furo rolled his eyes in exasperation at her words. But surely she must know what to do, he thought. Nobody who had lived in Lagos more than a week could remain ignorant of the survival codes, and yet Syreeta flouted rule after rule. The traffic warden had begun shouting the threat Furo was waiting for – he demanded to board the car and lead Syreeta to the nearest LASTMA office. Bureaucratic hellholes, LASTMA offices, and if the traffic warden made good his threat then Syreeta would be lucky to retrieve her car before the month's end. And only after paying a heavy fine and settling the bill for mandatory driving lessons and a psychiatric evaluation, this last a precondition for allowing her back into the madness of Lagos roads. Furo felt he had to warn her, and he opened his mouth to do so, but Syreeta spoke first.

'Furo, I'm sorry, please get down from the car.'

He tried to catch her eyes. 'This is not the best way—'

'I know what I'm doing,' she cut him off, her right hand cleaving the air in time to her words. 'I'll deal with this idiot my own way. Just get down.'

Sighing in resignation, Furo reached for the door handle, and the traffic warden released his grip on the steering wheel and sprinted around the car's front. As the man grabbed the door and yanked it open, Furo looked at Syreeta. 'Should I sit in the back?' he asked. 'I don't mind following you to the LASTMA office.'

'No need,' Syreeta said. Then she noticed the anxiety on Furo's face, and her expression softened, she curved her lips in a smile intended to reassure. 'It's OK, I have this under control.' She cast a look around. 'But there's no place for you to wait around here,' she muttered, as if chiding herself. 'Oh, I know. Why don't you walk to VGC? Go inside and wait for me near the gate. I won't be long.'

Behind Furo the traffic warden snorted with derision, and Syreeta threw him a vicious look. Furo spoke quickly to forestall the attack gathering in her face. 'If that's what you want,' he said, and climbed down from the car, then stood watching as the traffic warden clambered in and slammed the door. He heard the harmonised clicks of the car's central lock, followed by the whirr of Syreeta's side window closing. When Syreeta and the traffic warden turned on each other with furious faces, Furo spun around and strode away from their muffled yapping.

Avoiding the curious stares of the pedestrians he passed, Furo walked quickly to the filling station, then cut across its concrete expanse and approached the double gates of Victoria Garden City. Two lines of cars flowed through the estate gates, entering and leaving. In front of the entry gate, right beside the sleeping policeman, stood a uniformed guard. Hands clasped behind his back and feet spread apart, he eyeballed each car that clambered over the bump. He raised his head as Furo approached, and his shoulders stiffened, his features gathered into a scowl. Furo realised there was someone walking behind him. A man wearing black jeans and a white T-shirt, his hair cornrowed, a rhinestone stud glinting in one ear. Furo turned back around, and slowed his steps to a shuffle, unsure if he should walk past the guard or state his business. Deciding on the action least likely to cause offence, he halted by the guard and said, 'Hello.'

'Good afternoon, sir,' the guard replied with a smile. 'Are you here to visit?'

'Yes,' Furo said.

'I see, I see,' said the guard, and ran his hands over the front of his epauletted shirt, smoothing it out. He ignored the cars entering the estate; he stared hard at Furo's nose. 'Who is the person you want to see?'

'I don't know her name . . . she's the friend of my friend,' Furo said. 'Well, actually—'

'I see, not a problem,' the guard interrupted, and threw a suspicious look at the cornrowed man waiting behind Furo. 'What is her house number?'

'I don't know,' Furo said. 'The thing is, I'm supposed to—'

'Not a problem,' the guard said and wrinkled his brow in contemplation of the problem before him. At that moment the cornrowed man made an impatient noise in his throat, and then he moved forwards, muttered 'sorry' to Furo, and said to the guard, 'I'm going to Mr Oyegun's house.'

The guard aimed a hard stare at him. 'Can't you see I'm attending to somebody?'

'I'm in a hurry,' the cornrowed man said, his voice urgent. 'Mr Oyegun is expecting me. I know his house, I've come here before.'

'Respect yourself, Mister Man!' the guard barked at him. 'Or you think anyone can just walk in here anyhow? Who are you anyway? Move back, move back – can't you hear me, I said move back!' He flapped his hands in the chest of the cornrowed man, drove him back behind Furo. 'That's how we Nigerians behave, no respect at all,' the guard said to Furo with a grimace of apology. Lowering his voice, he asked: 'Do you have your, erm, friend's phone number?'

'I was trying to explain,' Furo said. 'I'm supposed to wait for someone to pick me up here. If you don't mind I'll just stand in that corner.' He pointed to a spot just inside the gate.

'Oh, I see,' the guard said, nodding his head. He waved Furo in. 'Not a problem at all, you can go inside. Should I bring a chair for you?'

'I'm OK,' Furo replied. He passed through the gate, strode a few paces to the road's grass shoulder, and turned around to face the road. The cornrowed man had moved forwards, he was speaking with the guard, who shook his head with vehemence and remained standing in the way. The cornrowed man flung up his hands and uttered something in complaint, then with a stony face he pulled out his mobile phone, dialled a number. After repeated attempts at reaching someone on the phone, all seemingly unsuccessful, the cornrowed man again spoke to the guard. The guard ignored him, he stood with his fists clenched and his boots planted apart, he glowered at passing cars. The cornrowed man gave up talking with a gesture of dismissal. Pocketing his phone, he whirled around and stalked off, and the guard glanced over at Furo. 'Are you sure you're OK, sir?' he shouted across. 'You're sure you don't want a chair?'

Syreeta drove through the gate barely three minutes later. Furo started to raise his hand, but let it fall when he realised she'd already seen him. She pulled up, and he climbed into the Honda's chill, which was spiced with a whiff of the traffic warden's sweat. The skin over Syreeta's cheekbones was stretched tight, a vein beat in her temple, and the car radio was off. Furo knew better than to ask about the traffic warden, how she had got rid of him so quickly. He held his gaze away from her face; he stared through the windscreen. Road signs whizzed past. *No honking. No hawkers. No litter. No parking.* No okadas and danfos. The quiet through which the car sailed was deeper-rooted than the fact of the silent radio. No crowds, no roadside garbage, no traffic jam, no noise.

The Lagos he knew was far from this place.

from the forthcoming novel

Our Time of Sorrow

Jackee Budesta Batanda

The bell announcing prayer time rang earlier than usual and more urgently this time. The bell was an old tyre rim tied to a mango tree branch dangling close to the ground. Its persistent ringing reminded me of the numerous times the phone in the vicar's office rang. I had learned to tell the time by listening to the sounds in the night. The way the trees whistled meant that it was still early and although my brain had become accustomed to the bell ringing at a certain time, my body was still weak. I didn't feel like praying today or ever again. I just wanted to remain lying on my mat, between the other sleeping forms, listening to the sound of their breathing and snores, and waiting for the End of the World. I tried to imagine what kind of dreams they had when their souls visited the land of dreams; instead my thoughts kept drifting to my own dream. It had been about Mzee Turomwe who doubted and would be killed. In my dream his head was dangling before me, his mouth wide open as if he had managed one last protest before his head was severed. His eyes kept winking at me, and then his mouth twitched into a smile before resuming its mournful countenance. I had opened my eyes to find myself on my sleeping mat and failed to get back to sleep again.

I had difficulty sleeping after I had crept out of the banana plantation ahead of Byaruha, who followed me much later as planned so as not to arouse suspicion. We knew we were treading on dangerous ground. During one Mass, Owa Puroguramu had announced that the Blessed Mother had banned sex because it made us impure. We were the brides of the Lord Jesus, and we had to keep our purity if we were to go to heaven. That had been the day marrieds were separated and banned from further sexual liaisons. I had not bothered about the purity because I never cleansed myself enough. In any case, none of the penance I performed could rid me of my original sin.

Byaruha had singled me out long before the prohibition on sex was announced. He said he would cleanse me of my sin and then I was too scared to know any better. I also gave in because he was one of the inner circle of police also known as the 'Blessed Ones' and I believed he had the powers to cleanse me. He had broken my virginity and since then had continued having privileges with my body.

I never stopped him. This was not as bad as the sin I had carried with me from birth, which made everyone stare at me as if I gave off a rotten stench. I was the love child of a married woman and a priest, a taboo within the community. I was blamed for every bad thing that happened, because of the 'demon of seductive temptation', they said, that had led to my birth. The visionary singled me out for exorcism, the day Ma and I joined the Movement. It seemed the demon that possessed me returned in another form and I did not chase it away. I gladly welcomed it back and let it repossess me. Byaruha seemed to know. I still had to do penance for that sin I had no hand in creating. I had accepted Byaruha's intrusions on my body as a purging of my sin and had come to accept the sex as I had learned to carry the demon which had settled in my body from the day of my birth.

This morning I did not feel like seeking the grace or face of God. I wanted to lie in contentment with my little demon and listen to the voices that the woman who lived in a little store by the chapel had told me about. She was a closely guarded secret, only a few people within the community knew about her. It was my job to feed her and I had nicknamed her the Secret Woman – I didn't know her name. The voices, she had said, communicated to us from beneath the earth, if we only learned to listen to them. These same voices had predicted Mzee Turomwe's murder.

I started to move as the others woke up slowly from their fits of interrupted sleep. We were being called to the House of the Lord, and no one ignored the summons. I sprang up, threw my thin blanket aside, rolled my sleeping mat and joined the others heading for the door. We rushed to wash our faces, to rinse the sleep from our eyes and the dreams from our heads because lateness was a mortal sin. The bell could be the sign we were waiting for that the end had come. We wouldn't want to be left behind. We brushed against each other but only nodded greetings as we scrambled for the door like people rushing out of a room on fire.

By the time we entered the chapel the elders and visionaries were already assembled. It was a large rectangular room. We usually sat on the cold cement floor when we were not standing. The wooden blinds were shut to keep out the early wind and the spirits that would still be loitering about at that time of the morning. We immediately took our places on the floor – children in one corner near the altar, while the rest of us took the remaining places. The guards leaned against the walls. We were told they were there to protect us from any attacks by the evil one. They were like archangels in heaven. The Bishop of our Blessed Virgin, Owa Puroguramu, the vicar and the parish priest. The other elders and visionaries, also known as the apostles, twelve in number, sat behind the altar where the statue of the Blessed Mother carrying her son, and statues of the Holy Family stood. They sat on the only seats in the room, looking reverent, their hands on their laps.

The bishop was rarely seen at these Masses. We only saw him when an exorcism was taking place, and this was mainly when new members joined the Movement. His presence here also meant there had been another vision from the Blessed Mother. We sat in silence and waited. The vicar stood up and conducted the morning Mass as he did each day. This time he moved towards us sprinkling holy water, which fell on our faces, first stinging us with the cold and later rolling down our foreheads. It was a cleansing carried out before the Messenger stood to deliver the message from the Blessed Mother to ensure that the message fell on holy ground. With the sprinkling of holy water completed, the vicar returned and took his seat and waited for the Messenger. Owa Puroguramu had indeed received another message.

When she stood up we bowed in silence before raising our faces.

'My children, do not despair. These are the last days, and only those who follow my teachings and listen to my message shall survive the

terror. Pray and fast unceasingly that you may not be left behind. Pray
against the demons of doubt. Pray and fast. Keep yourselves pure at all
times. Many will fall but stand firm. You are my chosen ones . . .' Her
voice receded, and she started mumbling to herself as she was rocked
by spasms. Then a small murmur started at the back of the gathering
and picked up slowly as we all started praying out loud.

Even after the declaration of the communal fast, I still prepared the
special meals. The fast was meant for the rest of the congregation who
were not in direct communion with God; everyone except the vicar, the
bishop, Owa Puroguramu, the twelve apostles and the Blessed Ones.
For their sake the rest of us had to fast in order to get closer to him. The
regular fasts were on Monday, Wednesday and Friday. This time the fast
was for all the seven days of the week. We were to drink only water.

I peeled the bunch of *matooke* and wrapped it in banana leaves before
placing the load in a saucepan and pouring water round the bundle and
putting it on the fire to steam. I put the peelings on a woven tray by
the door. The kitchen cleaner would carry the peelings to the rubbish
pit later. Next I poured rice on another woven tray, cleaned and sorted
the rice before putting it to boil, and set about preparing the sauce:
eshabwe, beef, beans and *dodo* vegetables. This made me forget the rest
of the world for a time, as I concentrated on the meal I was preparing,
careful that nothing burned.

I later set the dining table in the house near the chapel, where the
elders always had their meals, wondering why they would eat food
when they had ordered the rest of the congregation to go without for
a week.

I carried a meal to the Secret Woman and entered without knocking
on the door. A damp smell filled the room. She crouched in her corner.
Her long hair was uncombed and wild, and it seemed like she had been
pulling at it. Her eyes looked through me as I set the food down before
her and sat waiting for her to eat or to start talking. We sat in silence,
listening to the sound of each other's breath. She stretched her hand
over the food and clasped my wrist, holding my gaze as she turned my
palm over. I dropped my eyes.

'He does not believe you,' she spoke.

I stared at her.

'He told you not to mention me to the vicar in your confession. He's right. Every man has a secret that must be guarded. Even the vicar who listens to your sins every Thursday has his own secrets. His own sins. But he does no penance.'

'You should not talk so,' I whispered.

She laughed softly in response.

'But I can. I should. They say something ate my brains and held my tongue. He told you last night. Yes! Something ate my brains and put something else there instead. But you are special. That is why my tongue is loosed when you come in here. You are special.'

I tried to disengage my hand from her grip. This was the first time someone was telling me I was special. It sent warmth through my body. I smiled – a shy smile that started slowly and took over my face. My other hand went to my cheek. I saw my smiling face in her eyes. She did not let go of my hand but tightened her grip.

'No, I'm not. There is a demon that sits in my body. I carry it like the memories in my head.'

'That's what they tell you. But what do you tell yourself?'

'I have paid for all my future sins,' I heard my voice say.

'You should learn to smile more often,' she said.

'But what is there to smile about?'

'The man. You have started to love him. You feel a burning in your heart when you see him.'

I looked at her and dropped my gaze because her eyes were searing through mine, reading secrets I did not want revealed. It was wrong that she would read me so well. It was wrong to start to love the man. It was wrong.

'I am not special,' I mumbled. 'I am a child of sin.'

'We all are children of sin. And we all have secrets.'

'No,' I burst in. 'The apostles do not have sins. They are God's messengers.'

'Ah, but they have the biggest sins and secrets too.'

'I have to leave,' I said.

'Nothing ate my brains,' she replied letting go of my hand. 'I see things and hear many things. The man who doubted was not at the Way of the Cross?'

I had forgotten about Mzee Turomwe. I had not searched for his face during the Mass.

'He was.'

'Hmm . . .'she grunted and spat on the floor. 'His life left him. Look again.'

I stumbled out of the room. This time I had not cajoled her to eat. She had taken over the conversation. How could she accuse the elders? They were in direct communion with the Blessed Mother and received messages from her. They had the powers to punish and pardon any of us. We led a life according to the visions passed on to us through the apostles.

When Byaruha and I met in the plantation that night, I asked him.

'What's your secret?'

'What do you mean?'

'We all have secrets. Those little sins we polish and pretend are harmless. What is yours?'

'You,' he said. 'You are my secret.'

'Why doesn't the Blessed Mother punish us?'

He did not answer me.

The closed meetings intensified after the declaration of the fast. The apostles, the bishop, the vicar and Owa Puroguramu spent hours locked in the meeting room, only taking a break to eat the meals I prepared. It made the air around the place thick with anticipation. It reminded me of the time in the mid-nineties, when Father Romaro left the Movement, a few months after Restetuta, the first deserter had left. Restetuta, a widow, had been the first person to leave the Movement enclosure and walk down that winding dirt road out of the imprisoning fold of the compound back to the one-street town that stands on a roundabout. Nothing was done because the Movement did not consider Restetuta a threat. The departure of Father Romaro, one of the apostles, shook the foundation of Movement. Meetings had been held for days. Only then, the elders had not raised their voices at any time. It was obvious that something was amiss. We had not been told what the matter was but from the little Byaruha said, it had to do with Father Romaro's disagreement with Owa Puroguramu over the vision, which ordered the followers to sell all their property and give the money to the Movement. Father Romaro's argument had been that when Jesus walked this earth thousands of years ago, he had not requested people to sell their property and give him the money. The meetings had been held to discuss the matter at hand and to bring him back to his senses. They had yielded nothing and Father Romaro had addressed us in the church, asking those against the selling of their property to return with him to the main church. Only a few people had followed him, while the rest of us had looked at them in sympathy. Sorry for them, that they were returning to the world of sin. That the End of the World would pass them by while we ascended to glory to sit at the right hand of Jesus Christ, our Saviour. We had pitied them. After all, Owa Puroguramu had warned us of the fickle ones who would lose their faith in favour of worldly riches. They had not understood the meaning of separation, of oneness, of humility and sacrifice. Of nothingness in exchange for eternal life.

Owa Puroguramu called us to Mass after the deserters left and asked us to pray for their damned souls. For the souls of those who had been fooled by Father Romaro. As for him, she declared that he would not live to see the end of the month of July. He would die, his bowels would burst open, and no one would come to his aid as he lay writhing in pain, pleading with the Blessed Mother to forgive him. He would bleed to death because it was already decreed in heaven, and nothing could change that. He was not meant to enter the Year One of the new generation. He would be like Moses who was not allowed to enter Canaan, the Promised Land. Like Judas Iscariot who died in an open field. Father Romaro would die in an open field and grass would grow on his remains. She had asked us to join in cursing Father Romaro and damning him to a painful death.

Father Romaro had lived beyond the month of July. He still lives.

These meetings now were different from those held before Father Romaro's departure. They were more strained and silent. Even Byaruha could not tell me much except that something serious was being discussed. The rest of us kept on praying and fasting as ordered. Even the sick were ordered to fast. They were told that if they did not intensify their prayers, then Sitani would come and steal their souls. We had to recite the scripture: *the thief cometh not, but for to steal, and to kill, and to destroy: I am come that they might have life, and that they might have it more abundantly* – John 10:10. The sick had to pray harder than everyone else so as not to miss Paradise and to build a shield against the thief.

After four days of intense praying and fasting between our chores, Owa Puroguramu called us to a special Mass at 4 p.m. We shuffled to the church still sweating from the pineapple fields, banana plantation, cattle sheds and other places where we had been working. The visionaries and apostles were already in the church. While our skin was ashy, the skin of the apostles and visionaries was shining in the light. Their eyes were bright. They were already seated as always on the bench at the front of the church, looking as if they had just left the presence of God. It made us more conscious of our own sinful nature – our inability to commune directly with God. We took our rightful places as the archangels, as the Sunday church guards were known, positioned themselves at the doors and windows. From the way their eyes darted back and forth round the room, it was evident they were conducting a head count.

After a few prayers and singing, Owa Puroguramu stood up.

'My children,' she started, 'there is evil that has infiltrated our Movement and it pains my heart to see us come to this.'

This time I was sure she was going to point me out as the cause of the sin. It was like I had been waiting for this time to come since the closed meetings started.

'We need to pray harder than before, to get rid of Sitani in our midst. The Blessed Mother is grieved with your lack of belief in her messages. She cries for you the chosen ones. Her back is turned to the world, but to you she beckons you to come join her.'

A child coughed as we waited for the message. Owa Puroguramu continued softly, trying to mask her anger.

'Someone pushed Sitanish writings under my office door.' At this point she waved a Picfare exercise book, contorting her face as if the book emitted a sickening odour.

'Why do you doubt the work of God's chosen? Why are you threatening the wrath of the Almighty one upon us? He has had mercy and sent the Blessed Mother and Jesus Christ our saviour to warn us of the impending suffering to the rest of the world. He did so because he loves you. He does not want you to perish. But now you doubt him and threaten to make him turn his back on us.'

We were quiet as we stared, wondering who had caused this outburst.

'Don't you remember Sodom and Gomorrah? How Abraham interceded with God on behalf of those two sinful cities? How we have taught you the way of the righteous and still you doubt. The end time has not come because of God's mercy. He has listened to your prayers and fasting. Because you have interceded for today's Sodom and Gomorrah, he is giving more time to the world. He wants more people to enter Noah's Ark and survive the suffering spelt out in the Book of Revelation. But you still doubt his mercy and goodness.' She waved the book, 'You reward our merciful God with this, asking for the return of your property. This is Sitani at work and we must get rid of him.'

At this point, the visionaries stood and walked towards us. They each carried plastic bowls and twigs, which they dipped in the holy water and sprinkled on us to cleanse us of the Sitani sitting in our midst. One of them emptied the contents of her bowl directly on my head. As the water washed over me, I shivered for a second because the sudden coldness attacked my skin. I rubbed the water from my eyes and kept my head lowered on the ground. I remembered the woman's assertion when she said I was special. But this reminded me of my original sin that followed me wherever I went.

Alú

Recaredo Silebo Boturu

Time and weather did not dawdle, between thunderstorms and too much sun, the falling raindrops ringing out harmonious melodies as they hammered on the zinc roofs, a pitter-patter that filled the space. Time ran on ahead, it almost flew. Days and nights came and went. Alú kept growing. People said his birth had not been easy, that the boy had come into the world with little help from anyone. Life is unpredictable, and Alú's mother was still in her native village when her waters broke. Since there was no clinic and no midwife, she was forced to rely on the wisdom of an elderly woman, an aunt of her mother, who was known for helping those women who defied the odds in their attempts to bring a child into the world.

The old woman boiled up leaves and bark offered by the forest to remove the dried blood and did not charge a single *franc*. It was an arduous task. I cannot say exactly what the old woman did since, if truth be told, I do not know. What I do know is that it took several slaps before the baby began to bawl, before the first blast of air, burning though his little lungs like fire, finally offered itself to this life, this world.

Alú's town was bordered on one side by the sea and on the other by dense, dark forests. There were afternoons when it was possible to make out the humpbacked form of a rainbow impregnating the belly of the earth and the depths of the sea. The child would stop to stare and ask:

'Mamá, what's that?'

'It's a rainbow.'

'What's a rainbow?'

But no answer ever came. If Alú persisted, he was told not to ask so many questions.

Alú's mother, like the other mothers, the fathers, the uncles, the aunts, the grandmothers, the grandfathers and the big brothers found it difficult to explain to their children, their grandchildren, their nephews, their nieces, their little brothers and sisters what exactly a rainbow was and how it came to be. Some did not know. Some knew but did not take the time to explain. This was why they were irritated by the insistence of the little children who had to content themselves with knowing that, on certain afternoons, a rainbow would appear, and when it did, was beautiful to behold.

Alú also enjoyed watching the sun as it rose and set. It seemed to him to be one of the finest spectacles that nature offered to delight her children. He found the shifting colours of the sun's ever-changing faces infinitely poetic. Often, he would watch and think to himself, not bothering to ask anyone for an explanation since, as likely as not, no one would give him an answer. Sometimes the sun would set slowly, slipping behind the mass of earth that rose to form a triangle and seemed to hang, suspended in space, a mass of earth that seemed to follow the walker wherever he went. This mass of earth, I should have mentioned earlier, was the Pico Basilé. This feeling of the mountain as a constant companion from the moment you arrived on the island was spectacular. Alú knew, because he had been told, that in its day the Pico Basilé had been much bigger and had been sundered in two by the eruptions of nature. Now, the two great mountains faced one another, though the second peak towered over another country and the two were separated by a stretch of sea. At other times, Alú would watch as this same sun, depending on the evenings, silently plunged like a diver into the depths of the sea.

The Pico Basilé was covered by a green mantle. It was, as I have said, a wonderful sight to behold when the clouds permitted, since often they would laze peacefully over the encircling trees, resting on the lush green foliage, forming undulating lines like a quivering froth of bubbles shrouding the peak in an impenetrable mist. The belly of the mountain concealed many mysteries. Alú had been told that the volcano was extinct now, that it could no longer spew lava, that hidden in its belly lived a bird incapable of surviving in any other place in the whole round world.

These and many other details made Alú realise that he had been born in an exceptional land ringed about by seas, a place that was mysterious and unique. Even as a boy, Alú felt that if sociologists could rise above the politics of monolingualism and dedicate themselves to analysing human behaviour – *our* behaviour – they would go down in history. Through their books and their theses, they might teach humanity not to create breeding grounds for rapacious minds, censorious minds, malicious minds, they might teach humanity not to produce people with dull minds, with dead minds. But, he also believed – as I have already said, he was a boy with a very particular way of seeing, thinking and reasoning – that as likely as not they would die of starvation because here people, many people, were forced to live through corruption.

Alú was nicknamed the 'witch child'. Not because he disappeared from his bed at night using some magical power and caught a Boeing to other latitudes to live his other life only to reappear at dawn to live his everyday life. No, I am not referring to the type of witch who lurked in the subconscious of Alú's neighbours. Alú was a child like other children; the colour of his hair, the colour of his eyes was no different to his friends. There was nothing to distinguish him physically from the others. He played with other children. He went to the same school they did; the only difference between Alú and the other children was that he took the time to question while those around him never stopped to wonder at the why of things. This is what made the boy different from others: his way of seeing, thinking, reasoning and doing things.

You already know that the boy's first name was Alú. This was followed by his father's surname and then his mother's surname. Out of respect for the boy, I reserve the right not to tell you these surnames, since you would be able to find him on a map and since most of us here know each other, you would be able to track down his parents, his neighbourhood, his town . . . So let us just stick to his first name, Alú.

There is something you do not know, or perhaps you do but I will remind you: many years ago, there were men who believed themselves to be greater and more intelligent than others and they decided to journey miles and miles, carrying with them a cross. They rowed and they rowed until they came to some remote countries where, with neither permission nor compassion, they plundered the lands of foreign peoples, their seas, their forests, their names, their surnames, plucked out their personalities, stripped them and gave them different clothing, indoctrinated them so that they abandoned their traditions and their culture. And since that time, the people in Alú's town have not had African names, they are ashamed of their names and instead they bear contaminated names, and with these Christian names, the people were forced to take the surnames of their father and their mother. In this small patch of land surrounded by the sea on all sides, it was rare now for a father or a mother to give their child a typically African name. Was it an act of courage or a matter of principle that led his parents to decide to call him Alú? No one ever asked the boy who had chosen his name.

If I could meet with Alú today, or with his mother or his father, I would ask. I would ask the question because it is rare to come across an African child with an African name. The men who arrived on our shores were white – I forgot to mention this earlier – white men with thick beards. Whether because it was the fashion or whether it was for want of time or want of a pair of scissors, the white men all had beards. They claimed they found the Negroes naked but for animal hides covering their private parts. But these men themselves were not wearing suits by Cristian Door, Sahara, Bescha, Luis Buitoton, Maximo Dutin, Atmosfera, or whatever they're called . . . No, they were not wearing anything of the kind.

The years passed, the travellers left us their languages, their cross, their diseases . . . and what else? We fought in order to gain our independence only to become prisoners of our own brothers as dictatorships flourished in abundance. All these things Alú knew. All these things he shared with his little friends. Years passed, some dictatorships fell and others appeared dressed in other colours, other smells, propped up by the West and by feeble citizens. Little by little, people began to believe that everything that was imported was good. They began to abandon their own names; this was why Alú's friends had names like Giovanni, Ronny, Frank, Charlis, Yarni, Jerry, Mark, Robert, Richard, Efren, Nick, Eduard, Aitor, Michael, Steyci, Ares, Cris, Cristian, Axel, Yanick, Edgal, Andy, Aaron, Brus, Dona, Leyre, Eiza, Shakira, Melc, Nancy, Nurcy, Soraya, Dalia, Leyda, Marylin, Dorothe, Gimena, Sandra, Leonel, Leny, Fructu, Simpático. We could fill pages and pages with imported names. None of Alú's classmates had African names though all of them were black – well, there were a few half-castes. Alú took pride in his name and when his classmates mocked him, he would tell them his name was unique, that it was his. Once, the children here were called Boiye, Besaha, Besako, Bohiri, Rihole, Ribetaso, Boita, Riburi, Wewe, Motte, Rioko, Wanalabba, Sipoto, Bula, Laesa, Bosupele, Borihi, Rioko, Bosubari, Mome, Rimme, Momo, Obolo, Moretema, Sobesobbo, Bosope, Nta, Pudul, Zhana, Zhancuss, Tenzhul, Mafidel, Masse, Pagu, Massantu, Madesha, Madalam, Guttia, Magutia, Chitia da boto, Obama, Ada, Chicanda, Abuy, Mokomba, Masamdja, Molico, Ichinda, Ulangano, Mondjeli, Eboko, Beseku, Upinda, Motanga, Ikna. These days, you could count the number of children with African names on the fingers of one hand. I don't think I mentioned: the name Alú means 'night'. Poetic, isn't it?

Nothing and no one could stop the takataka of time, no event, no eruption; it moved on, sometimes listlessly, with Cyclopean strides. It walked, it swam, it flew. Days drowned in the torrent of time, and the nights drew in, filled with mystery, with silence, with sound, and left again. Still Alú lived in his neighbourhood; still he had a particular way of seeing, of thinking about things. Every day, he tried to savour a sawa-sawa, his favourite fruit. Alú kept growing.

Alú grew out of his bostololo trousers, so too did his curiosity. Though, like his parents, he had never left his island, he could not understand why in this town people had cut down the trees despite knowing full well that the opportunistic sun would make the most of this to rain its fire upon the earth. From November to March, the heat was stifling. Successive mayors had brazenly ordered the trees felled. This was something Alú knew because he had been told. And it made him think, think, think, ponder, ponder until a wave of sadness flooded his being. One of the mayors with a very particular approach to civil hygiene went from barrio to barrio in a hard hat carrying a chainsaw. Every tree in the town was felled.

But this affront to life on the island did not change the fact that every day, every hour, a new baby was born and, although it should have been cause for celebration, often the birth of a child was tinged with sadness. Though Alú tried to paint a smile on his lips in spite of this paradox, his heart bled to see mothers and fathers break down at the loss of a child, to see grandmothers shattered by grief when a grand-child died of typhoid fever, of mosquito bites and tropical diseases that had been eradicated in other tropics.

From the outset, we have talked mostly about Alú, but the boy also had a mother and a father. A mother like so many others in the town who would have put her hand in the fire for her children. One of those mothers who would do anything, give anything, so that her children did not have to bear the burden of everyday life. Do not think that all of Alú's little friends lived with their parents. Some lived with uncles, aunts, with stepmothers, stepfathers, grandfathers, grandmothers, with older brothers or sisters. In some cases, they lived with people with whom they had no blood ties.

Alú's mother was not a poet or a witch doctor, a teacher or a nurse, but she was an inspiration to her children and her neighbours. Sita Konno was a woman with great charisma; a good person prepared to shoulder every burden life put in her path. To Alú, his mother's commitment to the community seemed magnificent; it inspired him. Sita Konno helped to build the community. Engraved on Alú's memory was something that his mother had once said to him and to some other friends his age.

It happened on an afternoon not unlike yesterday afternoon when the sun sank slowly to hide behind the mountain. It was one of those afternoons when Sita Konno invited children in to eat *fuludum*. And when the boys' bellies were full, she began to feed their souls. Knowing his mother as he did, Alú could tell that something was amiss. Though she tried to hide it, he could see her face was lined with worry. Secret thoughts teemed inside Alú's head but he did not have the courage to ask his mother. Sita Konno had decided to speak; she had been waiting for her son to grow so that she could tell him what she had never dared to relate. For many years, the boy had been curious to hear about his grandparents. On that afternoon, Sita Konno said this:

'Our ancestors never learned to read or write; they taught us through stories, through fables and legends. I did not have the good fortune of growing up with my grandparents. Time was, people would sit around the kitchen hearth and tell children fables, legends and stories to teach them the difference between black and white, good and evil. They told their children stories in order to feed their souls, so that they might grow to be competent human beings. Then, as now, in our towns, our neighbourhoods and in our houses the voices of women went unheard. Many women's voices were stifled. If I dare to speak today it is because I remember that I was once a girl, because I know that one day you will be fathers and grandfathers. I want my mother's story to help you open up new pathways, help you to move always towards the horizon. I want you to fight to be happy; I want to shrug off the weight of this ghost that is devouring me. And so, for the first time, I want to tell my story because in the village where I come from, when a tree falls we use it to make firewood.

'My mother was scarcely older than a child, she was living happily with her parents in a tiny village. They had nothing but my mother told me that they were happy nonetheless. As a girl, I often asked my mother how she could have been happy if they had nothing, if she never even had a doll. And my mother would always say that happiness does not depend on whether or not you have material things. She used to say that happiness was an act of will repeated every morning, every evening, every night. That it was a daily struggle unrelated to the waves we had to face.

'My mother was only fourteen when she lost her parents to an epidemic of cholera that swept through her village. My mother told me it was a miracle that she survived. I don't want to upset you, so I won't tell you the devastation my mother saw with her own eyes, but I will tell you that she lost her parents, my grandparents. Can you imagine how many people lost their parents, their children, their mothers to diarrhoea? Countless.

'My mother told us that she was forced to move to the big city, there to weave new dreams. She had to move to the big city where everything was different, where there was no sense of community, where there were big cars, big houses, where people had learned to live with rats and cockroaches. She had to fight off her old ghosts, had to forget the love of her parents if she was to fashion new paths, new dreams.

'Make no mistake, even my mother had dreams.' Sita Konno picked up a plastic cup, opened a plastic bucket, dipped the cup into the bucket, drew out water and took a sip. The sun by now was fading; *tik* went the light switch that Sita Konno flicked and the bulbs began to glow.

Translated by Frank Wynne

Mama's Future

Nana Ekua Brew-Hammond

Mama was on her deathbed. She had been there for nearly a century, and for almost as much time, a cavalcade of PhDs and MDs had theorised about what exactly was killing her.

Some said poverty. Others, corruption. Another strand blamed her penchant for foreign lovers.

If only she hadn't been so easily flattered, was the prevailing prefix to a frustrating ellipsis of what ifs. Yet another school posited, *She never got over the loss of her kids.*

The only thing they could agree on was that her time was near. And so, her children – the ones who had been taken, and the ones who had left – were located and summoned to say their goodbyes.

They came from North, South and Central America, Asia, Europe, the Middle East, and Oceania, joining the only sibling who had stayed home. For the first time since their youth all eight of them were in the same room, and as they waited to be invited into their mother's chamber, the interaction between them was wary, competitive, and nostalgic.

'Six hundred years and nothing's changed,' Musa said to none of them and all of them, when they had run out of catching up.

'Well, there's a new jet,' Aesop quipped. They all had to laugh.

Their mother had sent a private jet for those who had been able to catch the ride from London. Currently, it stood parked on the dirt road outside, dwarfing the now crumbling mansion they had grown up in and drawing squatters seeking shady respite from the sun.

'Vintage Mama.'

The laughter faded to wheezing sighs of reflection. *Oh, Mama.*

* * *

At her height, Mama had been the richest, most sought after woman in the world. Suitors would come from China, Vijayanagara, Arabia, England, Portugal, the Netherlands and France for the privilege of a glimpse, and she would keep them waiting in the courtyard while she and the kids spied them from her window.

What do you think he's brought me this time? She would ask the children, excited.

Silk! Spice! Horses! Jade! Velvet!

The kids were her audience and her wardrobe attendants.

Yauwii would make a mess; strewing embellished caftans next to silk robes on top of yards of kente. Mama would slip into or wrap herself in each swath and prance in front of them. The look that received unanimous approval graduated to the consideration of jewellery.

Heben would bury her arms in Mama's trinket box and pull out fistfuls of gold, diamonds, ivory, jade, amber and garnet for Mama to try. When the decision had been made – and Mama's White Crown had been fitted on her head, her arms weighted from shoulder to wrist, her fingers glittering, her ankles tinkling with charms – she would sink on to her gold palanquin, rising on the shoulders of her slaves to be carried to her guests.

Now that she was among the poorest on the globe, Mama had not adapted to her changed station. Her home was a shrine to the past, the fossils of her youth poorly preserved, but displayed all the same.

Mama still wore only custom-fit, painstakingly loomed ensembles; imported, mass-manufactured pieces were cheap to her. She ate free-range, cage-free, organic-fed, fresh-killed meat for breakfast. 'Eating out' meant food that had been flown in. Chicken from the United States. Rice from Thailand. Luncheon meat from Japan.

She bled what money was left, after her lovers had stolen what they hadn't been able to dupe her out of. And she had become a flagrant borrower. When she came around, people either scattered – not wanting to be guilt-tripped into giving – or they made an ostentatious show of their charity.

For her part, Mama did not consider one penny of it to be *aid*. Those who gave her could call it what they like, but as far as she was concerned, it was *owed*. They had built empires on the backs of her children and the bulk of her wealth. Anything they gave her was remittance.

'Your mother is ready to see you.' An aide emerged from the carved wooden door that shut them out of Mama's room, not moving to the side to give them way. 'She wants to meet with you individually, before she speaks to all of you.'

Apprehension knotted Ananse's stomach. Mama had not seen all of her kids in millennia, and he feared emotion could confuse his promised place as her sole heir. A promise he had earned.

He was the one who had kept vigil with the flies at Mama's bedside when Johan, Elizabeth, and Philip had kidnapped Aesop, Temisha, Xiomara and João. He was the one who had nursed Mama from the brink of death after Victoria, Jules, Alfonso, Luís, Vittorio, Léopold, and Wilhelm had carved her up at the Berlin Conference, leaving her for dead.

Ananse had watched Mama drop to her knees when she was forced to sell herself at whatever price buyers set for her bauxite, cocoa, copper, diamonds, gold, rubber and oil. And he had colluded with Mama to hide a reserve of her commodities in the Future, where only they could find it.

His brothers and sisters had left.

Ananse started to push past the aide, but the young man stopped him. 'She wants to see Temisha first.'

Temisha swallowed the spit of insecurity as Ananse and the rest of their siblings watched her disappear behind Mama's closed door.

Temisha gasped. No child should see her mother like this.

The old woman lay in between states, a shrunken memory of herself. A brigade of flies covered the mosquito net that shrouded her bed like so many polka dots, as if they could smell her impending death.

Despite the gruesome scene, Temisha sniffed a smile at her mother's stubbornly fabulous presentation.

★ ★ ★

Mama was pancaked and rouged. False eyelashes fluttered from her kohl-rimmed lids and a wig that appeared to be from the private collection of Diana Ross and the Supremes sat on her head.

She wore a robe with an elaborately embroidered neckline that managed to complement and mock the necklace her jutting collarbone had become, its pattern in eerie harmony with the lesions tattooed all over her skin. Someone had adorned her with the few gems she hadn't sold off, gold cuffs exploiting what was left of her wrists, the diamonds at her lobes threatening to split the skin in two.

'Aminatu.' Mama whispered the name she had given Temisha at birth. The one her captors had added to their booty the day she stepped on to the ship.

Temisha's voice wavered. 'I'm here, Mama.'

'Yes. You are.' The old woman drew a laboured breath that said more than words. 'I never asked what happened when you left me.'

When you left me?

The first time Temisha had returned home, her mother had put it the same way, casting herself as some kind of jilted lover. Mama had also criticised her hair – then it had been dreadlocked – and berated her name.

What kind of name is Temisha? You Black-Americans and your Shanequa, Shaqueeda. Sha. Sha. Sha.

Mama was so focused on the 'sha' she didn't hear the 'Temi'. *Temi*lade. Ife*temi*. Eyi*temi*. She expressed zero desire to know or understand what happened then, choosing instead to pick out the differences between them.

Now, in what could be the last moments of Mama's life, Temisha didn't want to dig up the bodies. She had written spirituals, poems, books, scripts and essays about all she had been through. Mama could check her website for the details.

But of course, Mama prodded. 'Aminatu, I'm waiting.'

'I didn't leave you, Mama.' Temisha heard the *Boulie* in her voice, when she wanted to sound like the High Street Mama respected. Why, at this stage of her life, did Mama's acceptance still mean so much?

'I was plucked, Mama. Like a grey hair. And I was raped. Passed from one man to another from the centre to the coast, from the ship to the other side.

'I was flogged and I was lynched. I was bred and I was brainwashed.

'I broke tools and fell sick, prayed for weevils and locusts to destroy their precious cash crops, and I started insurrections to survive. I founded advancement associations and advocacy groups. I joined fraternities and lodges. I sat in at lunch counters and marched up and down streets.

'I filed lawsuits and I wiled out. I rotted in prison for crimes I committed and offences I was framed for.

'I went to war for my kidnappers, and went to war on myself. Shot heroin. Smoked crack. Sniffed coke. Numbed the pain with Mary Jane. Ate and drank myself to diabetes.

'Climbed corporate ladders and rose through Union ranks. And each time, I hit my head against their glass ceilings, suffering concussions with the contusion-marred egos to prove it.

'I led gangs and menaced streets. I minded my business, and I was shot for standing my ground.

'I gave my life to Jesus. Studied the Quran. Recited mantras. Practiced Baha'i. Sacrificed to Yemaya. Created my own holidays and traditions.

'I've had so many names, Mama. Nigger. Nigra. Coloured. Negro. Black. Black-American. Afro-American. African-American. Nigga. Now, the only one I answer to is Survivor.'

When she finished speaking, the room was a balloon of *saudade*; and Temisha felt deflated. 'Did you make me come all this way to tell you what happened, Mama?'

'I wanted you here to bless you, Aminatu.'

The old woman struggled to sit up under the net, and the flies stirred.

'During the day, it's flies,' she complained on a momentary tangent. 'At night, it's mosquitoes. Like they are shift workers. I don't understand it. This net is treated.'

'You don't need a treated net, Mama. You need to keep yourself clean and work out an effective water and sewage system so the flies and mosquitoes won't have anywhere to breed.'

'Temisha.' It was the first time Mama had called her that. 'When you lef—. When you were taken from me – you carried my strength with you.' She shrugged. 'You needed it more than me then, but now, I need it back; and I am willing to pay you for it.'

Temisha raised an eyebrow. Ananse had assured them Mama's faculties were sharp, but delusion suddenly seemed to be infecting her speech.

'I sealed some of my riches in the Future for you,' she kept talking. 'Diamonds. Gold. Oil. Natural gas. Not in the amounts I once had, but enough for a smart person to do something with. I need you to go to the Future, and use what I left to make my legacy great again. *Promise me.*'

Temisha wasn't sure what her mother was asking. Either way, Mama didn't wait for an answer.

'I want to see Xiomara next.'

Temisha held the door open for the sister she had been chained to for part of the march to the ships.

That they were both enslaved should have bonded them for ever, and to some extent it did. But they had fundamental differences over the best way to carry the history. To Temisha, Xio (and their brother João, for that matter) was too cavalier about the impact of their enslavement. Xio felt Temisha had allowed it to swallow her.

One specific point of contention Temisha had was that Xio did not correct her children when they referred to themselves as 'Afro-descended', 'Garifuna', 'Creole', or 'Mestizo' – anything but Black.

'Why should they call themselves "Black" when they are mixed blood, Temisha? You Americans and your one-drop-ruled identity. It's dishonest, and it lets our captors off the hook.'

'You are the dishonest ones. No matter how light, or bleached, your skin, how straightened your hair, how straight your nose, you are African.'

'You Americans have to own the discourse on everything.'

'If you don't own, you are owned.'

When the door shut behind Xio, Temisha wished for a moment she could be one of the flies on Mama's net.

Xio entered Mama's room singing the lullaby Mama used to serenade them with.

'*Wá wá . . .*' she began, and the old woman joined her. '*Wá wá . . . Quietly, listen to me. My child, don't cry. Don't cry, my child. Mama is here. Don't cry, don't cry for your mother.*'

They let the lyrics hang in the air between them, reflecting separately on the memory.

'Even when you were far from me, you felt near,' Mama said, blowing air on the damp silence.

Xio reached under the net to thread their fingers together. She didn't feel the same way.

'I held on to what I could, Mama, but I am different from what I would have been, and I know that. It's just how it is. I am yours, but I am mine too.'

Her mother began to cry. A Nile of blood ran from her eyes because it hurts when a child's path leads away from you.

Xio lifted the net fully and crawled in next to her mother; rocking her as she ached to be rocked. It was odd, Xio thought, and magical, how the old became babies again. '*Quietly, listen to me. Mama, don't cry. Xio is here. Don't cry, don't cry for your daughter . . .*'

The old woman shook her head stubbornly. If she were standing, Xio was sure Mama would have stamped her feet. 'I delivered you. Now, I need you to deliver me.'

Xio smiled as she blotted her mother's tears with the hem of her dress. Only Mama would make such a demand. 'Mama, I love you,' was all she would say before calling Musa to take her place.

Mama's firstborn son adjusted the loosened net and tucked it under Mama's mattress to secure her from the flies. He noticed the tattoo – a small Chinese symbol – emerging through her tear-streaked make-up. He was not ignorant of China's growing influence over his mother. No one was, the way the two of them were carrying on. China was laying roads and erecting businesses all over her. But Musa couldn't believe Mama would take his mark on her face.

'Haven't you learned from your mistakes, Mama? Do you really think China will save you?'

'If you care so much what happens to me, Musa,' she said, 'mind your business.'

In other words, China was doing the business of saving her that Musa was not. Mama had a way of making her problems other people's fault.

'Mama, I am not the reason you are in this state. You are.'

'When I needed you most, you and your siblings abandoned me.'

'You were unable to take care of us, Mama. You squandered our inheritance. We didn't know when our next meal was coming. We weren't being educated. You expected us to stay and suffer with you through that?'

'I expected – and expect – you to stay and help me rebuild, the way Ananse did.'

'Mama, what has Ananse rebuilt? Mismanagement? Corruption? Famine? Poverty? A haven for flies, mosquitoes, all manner of communicable disease, and fundamentalists? If so, he has done a masterful job.'

'Is this how they talk to mothers in the country you have run to?'

Musa suppressed an exasperated chuckle. *Oh, Mama.*

'Mama, I love you too much to lie to you. Things have to change now.'

'I can't do it by myself, Musa. I need you and your siblings.'

'What do you want from us, Mama?'

'I want more than the money you give to assuage your guilt. I want you to come home and take care of me till you find the Future.'

Musa nodded, patronisingly. 'Yes, Mama. Yes. Temisha told us all about the treasure you buried in the Future. Where exactly is the Future? Does Ananse know?'

Musa strode to the door and peered out to shout.

'Ananse! Do you know where the Future is?'

Ananse took his opportunity to enter the room. He knew from Temisha and Xio that their mother had revealed the hidden fund, but he couldn't determine how much detail the old woman had shared. Had she told them exactly how much was in the Future?

'Musa, I wanted this conversation to be between you and me.'

'Mama, the closed-door conversations have to stop. It's time for transparency.' He called his other siblings into the room.

In her youth, Mama would have put ginger in Musa's anus for defying her this way, but the Past was now the Present; and these kids were the key to her Future. She saw pity and sadness and distance in their eyes. She needed to remind them of who she was. Who they were by extension. They needed to have faith in her again.

'I wasn't always on this bed,' she said. 'It is imperative that you don't forget. Otherwise, you will miss the Future.'

She continued, 'I don't mean the Immediate. I'm talking about the Long Term – where I hid a reserve for all of you.'

Ananse took the opportunity to assert ownership. 'Mama, I remember the moon as our only witness as we dug to the Future. I will never forget because I was there.'

'You left early, Ananse. Remember? I made seven more hiding places.'

Ananse felt his scalp catching fire. After all the time he had invested in Mama, his portion was to be equal?

Aesop gave his brother a consolatory clap on the back. 'The Future belongs to every soul blessed to meet it, and every soul able to seize it.'

'Mama, you can't expect us to go on some kind of scavenger hunt for you. We've made lives elsewhere,' Xiomara reminded her.

'Elsewhere is for strangers, and that's what you'll always be anywhere but Here. The hunt is for you and me.'

'How do we get to this Future?' Yauwii asked. Once upon a time, the kids had accused her of loving Yauwii most, but what mother didn't love the child who humoured her without making her feel humoured?

'You dig until you find it.'

'That's it?' Musa snorted. 'Simple as that?'

'No,' Mama shook her head. 'Hard as that. But you've done harder.'

from the forthcoming novel *Azotus, the Kingdom*

Shadreck Chikoti

The Occupant

For many years Kamoto had not thought of going outside. The world outside offered him nothing that he could not find within the confines of his own home. He always had enough air to breathe and food to eat. Even if he fancied connecting with distant places, he was happy to do so through the convenience of the Telecommunication Curtain – the TC – he had in his living room.

On rare occasions he would get a chance to peek through the front door. This usually happened when the Room Service girls showed up to deliver things like food, groceries or clothes. Or when they came to clean the house and appliances. Since it was he who had to open the front door in order for the workers to come in, on more than one such occasion he caught himself peering through the door. But neither the need nor the thought of exploration ever crossed Kamoto's mind.

But recently, Kamoto had made the habit of going out at dusk to watch the sun go down. Even though he could watch this natural phenomenon on the screen of his living room TC, it did not take him long to conclude that it was in too many ways unlike the real thing. The actual sunset appeared to him to be much bigger, much brighter, much more varied in its display of colours. Untamed.

Today, he found himself carrying a chair outside to sit while he watched the sun slowly descend beyond the mountains. Sometimes, it seemed like the sun was heading for the yawning mouth of a cave which dominated the face of the largest mountain. The range of mountains in the distance had the effect of creating what seemed like a boundary of all that existed, almost as if this was the very edge of the world.

Each time Kamoto came out to watch the sunset, he felt altered but he had not found the right words to describe it. The best he could come up with was that his heart felt lighter and he breathed much easier.

He sat with his legs stretched in front of him, occasionally lifting and suspending them in the air for a while before bringing them down again.

A flock of birds – crows – flew across the sky above him, cawing as they went their way towards the direction of the sun. They'd been doing this every day he'd been outside at sunset and now a week had gone by. He figured that the birds were returning to their nests, and that his house just happened to be on their route. There was only one day when the birds had veered slightly to the west of where they usually flew.

Why had he not come outside more often? He wondered? But as quickly as the question had been asked, he decided that it was the wrong one. He rephrased it: Why have I spent my whole life indoors? But still he could come up with no answer.

The clouds had a shiny silver grey lining against the backdrop of the blue skies, giving the birds a domain in which they played freely. On the ground below, the trees were big enough to compete with the grandiosity of the mountains. The intricate details of nature's beauty made him feel he was at one with his surroundings.

His neighbour's house, directly in front of his own, was a large dwelling surrounded by a picket fence. Matching the white of the fence was the paint of the metallic doors of the house, as well as its white walls, rising up to a bright red roof that consummated it all like a burning flame. The roof made the house stand out. Presently there was one large bird contentedly perched on the satellite ball that was on the rooftop.

For the seven days that he had now been coming out, Kamoto had not seen anyone come in or out of the house across from his. He had not even heard so much as a ruffle or whisper to signify that the house was inhabited. Perhaps that's why he had not really noticed it there. Perhaps this explained why he had not noticed all the other houses, for he now saw that there were several. But with all the trees in the area, the other houses would have been impossible to see from indoors.

By now the sun was beginning to dip beyond the mountains, so Kamoto decided to get on with taking stock of his surroundings. He got up from his chair, stretched his limbs and neck to relax his muscles, and came down the steps of his front porch to get a better view of his house. He walked further out from the facade, far enough to get as wide a view of his roof as possible. And his expectation of a touch of uniqueness in the design of his house was quickly disappointed. His roof was as red as his neighbours', his house was just as large, and a large satellite ball, similar to that of his neighbour, sat on the rooftop. Electric bulbs lit the sides of his roof, bright enough to give light to all sides of the house. He followed the illuminated path to the back of the house where a surprisingly wide yard welcomed him, with neatly cut grass flanked by a colourful array of flowers growing on all sides.

Two birds chased each other in excitement around this pristine garden, taking off from and landing on one branch after another. While his eyes followed them on their random trail, his sight was led to the back wall of his house and he was shocked to find that there were neither doors nor windows on that entire wall. As the birds flew further out towards the edges of his fence, he noticed rocks, big boulders sculpted and arranged in a pattern of deliberate design, with one boulder shaped like a canoe. The rock structure was coming out of the ground. There was a water pipe which ran across the surface of the rock, drawing water from some source beneath and continuously pouring the water out again into the fountain that bubbled in front of the rock.

Further out into the very back of the yard, he saw more large trees, good for shade. He would have examined his house further, but the darkness that was quickly descending around him made him think better of the idea.

Tina had been watching Kamoto with keen interest the whole time. The oversized dark-green leaves of the trees in front of the picket fence of the house across the road afforded Tina a perfect spot from which to observe everything Kamoto was doing without being seen herself. Tina was sure that Kamoto had seen her when he got up from his chair and started down the front steps of his house and walked towards his fence. She had no choice but to stay put until she was sure that Kamoto had not seen her, hoping against hope that her cover had not been blown. She was just about to resign herself to the prospect of getting caught when Kamoto reached the fence and turned around to admire his house. What she felt after that was more than relief. It was gratitude.

As Kamoto strolled towards the side of his house to go into the back yard, Tina became more curious about him. Seeing an Occupant outside was enough of a shock, but seeing one acting as freely outdoors as they were indoors was unimaginable. Maybe Kamoto had been doing this for a long time, she thought, perhaps at night when everyone was asleep. But she decided that was mere guess work. So she just continued to watch.

While Kamoto was surveying the back of his house, there was not much for Tina to see. She dipped her hand into the left side pocket of the small green bag that hung securely across her shoulder. After fingering the inside of the pocket for a few seconds, she pulled out a small metal device and a glass pad. She proceeded to attach the device on the tip of her forefinger. The thought of taking notes of the observations she was making of Kamoto made her feel in control, but just as she was about to turn to a blank screen on the glass pad, that sense of control gave way to alarm. She quickly pulled off the writing device, and put it back in her purse, together with the pad. She was feeling the beginnings of a sneeze, and as numb as her legs had started feeling from squatting behind the tree for so long, she knew she could trust one hand to steady her and another to cover her mouth and nose in the now-more-than-likely event.

As she waited for Kamoto to emerge from behind the house, Tina turned her thoughts and questions inward. Was it right for her to be stalking him this way? Didn't Occupants, like all the subjects in Azotus' kingdom, have the freedom and right to wander around outdoors even if no one else found it worth the bother? Tina pondered these questions briefly, but concluded that if Kamoto had the right to wander around outside his home, then she likewise had the right to watch him from her stake-out spot, even if for no other reason than to satisfy her curiosity. She finally sneezed. It was loud enough not only to break the trail of her thoughts, but also to be heard across the street. She knew that what little camouflage she got from the leaves was about to be undone by the sneeze. She looked up to see if there was any movement at Kamoto's house, only to find that he was now back on the front porch, about to enter. And, as if startled by a sudden noise from behind him, Kamoto turned abruptly and Tina feared the worst. The panic returned, but was gone just as quickly, for Kamoto looked down when he turned, examining the leg of his chair, which had apparently snapped with a cracking sound, giving Kamoto reason to pick it up and carry it the rest of the way. Tina knew it had been another close call, perhaps a signal for her to go home.

Tina looked at the front door of Kamoto's house and noted the house number, G8. She was about to pull out her glass pad again to record the number but immediately thought better of the idea after an unpleasant memory flashed before the screen of her mind. She had once written down the number of another house, AC52, because she heard music coming from inside while she passed by; music she had never heard before and she thought she could use the house number on her TC to identify what the music was. But she was amazed when her supervisor had quizzed her about it.

'I was on duty distributing food to Occupants, and I wrote down the house number so that I could know where to pick up from the next day.' She had difficulty convincing the supervisor with this excuse, and he did not seem to buy it, but it was the best she could come up with. It wasn't necessary for Room Service personnel to write down the numbers of the houses where they had distributed food. No one went to any house for any reason without being given instructions to do so from their superiors. It was Azotus' way of running an efficient system so that every Occupant would have everything they needed at exactly the time and in exactly the way they needed it. Tina knew that she should have come up with a better answer.

Tina rose up and briskly walked back to the gravity mobile she used to run errands and carry out her usual Room Service duties. She had parked far away from Kamoto's house. She had not noticed it becoming dark. This was not surprising, as the lights in the streets were bright enough to make one forget when the real light of the sun had ended and the artificial light of the streets began.

The Central Square, especially, located right in the mid region of the kingdom, was known to have the brightest lights. It was there that Tina reported for work at the Department of Room Service, and it was from there that she and other Room Service workers received their instructions and directions about what items needed to be delivered to which homes.

She drove off, exhilarated by the thoughts that her stakeout had sparked in her mind. She did not know anything about Kamoto, and this left her with more questions than answers. She was anxious to get home and she thought of flying her gravity mobile but decided against it for fear of attracting attention. One had to have a good reason to fly. She chose to drive faster instead, but not enough to put her at risk. She drove through the woodland that was at the end of Kamoto's neighbourhood and joined the road that went uphill. There were a few cars. Right after going uphill, the road descended steeply, requiring one to have a foot on the brake pedal all the way down into the valley below. She turned east and joined the highway, speeding towards the woodlands that lay beyond the glistening lights of the high rising scrapers that formed the luring skyline of the City Square.

When she reached home she went straight to her TC, opened the file for House No. G8. The file provided live video footage of Kamoto's house. Kamoto himself was sitting quietly on the couch in his living room, watching a video on the TC that dominated the northern wall of the room. He looked tired, with his legs stretched in front of him, resting on the coffee table that matched the couch and the drapes. In his hands he held an object which Tina could not identify as she watched him on the video feed. She knew better than to jump to conclusions about what the object was, because things on the curtain did not always appear the way they were in real life. So she was not surprised that Kamoto's black beard, which she had just earlier seen to be neatly shaved to a single-lined sideburn running down and around his chin, now appeared grey. His face, compact and sturdy and full of life, now looked slightly elongated and sickly. Even his complexion, a smooth and natural dark brown, looked slightly pale.

Tina tried to be even more observant of Kamoto on the curtain than she had been when she saw him in person earlier that afternoon. But there was nothing interesting about what Kamoto was doing; he was simply slouched on a sofa, staring blankly at the screen on the wall. Tina found this frustrating, especially since the camera that enabled her to view Kamoto was facing away from the screen, making it impossible for her to see what he was watching. The cameras had been positioned in this way so that no one could see what another citizen was watching for personal entertainment. Not even the Super Curtain that ran the Central Square could access such intimate details about the activities of the Occupants.

She switched off the TC and headed for the kitchen to make herself a meal, a privilege that she had as a Room Service agent. Tina made herself soup and a sandwich, then she sat down in the kitchen to sift through the events of the day. All she could wonder about was what Kamoto was looking for when he went for a walk around the premises of his house. But was it right for her to be spying on an Occupant like that? At that moment, it occurred to her that subjects of the kingdom, especially Citizens, had taken their freedom for granted for so long that they no longer felt the need to exercise it or the need to explore why freedom should be exercised. In fact, she realised that most of them did not even think of themselves as free, because even though they were free, they did not know enough about bondage to go beyond *being* free, to reach the place of *feeling* free. Freedom had become common-place, and therefore meaningless.

The Professor

Edwige-Renée Dro

The marquee was set. Waiters and waitresses wearing the blue and white colours of our uniforms weaved around, carrying hors d'oeuvres and champagne flutes on trays. Here and there, I spotted an old teacher and waved from a distance before making out that I needed to speak to someone else. But there was only one person I was waiting for and that was you. I wouldn't have come otherwise. Ever since the reunion was advertised on Facebook, I had known it was just an exercise in boasting. Reunions always were, and one where even old teachers and headmistresses were invited was taking the art of boasting to another level. Yes, mention was made of the fact that funds would be raised to bring the library of our *lycée* up to the standard of a library of a *lycée* of Excellence . . . but still. So I came, because I would then be able to share my suspicions about the reunion with you. A few times I had thought about calling you and then decided that the element of surprise would work best. But for an hour I'd been participating in conversations I had no interest in and you were nowhere in sight. So I decided to mingle. Parties were not your thing anyway so perhaps you had decided not to turn up. And if that were the case, I would visit you at home.

'Ah, Essien! There you are.'

'I hope you're not about to give me a job, chieftain,' I groaned inwardly but managed to keep a smile plastered on my face.

Chantal has always been the bossy one of us girls and I had been trying to avoid her lest she roped me in on some task. Apparently the reunion was her idea. But then again, only Chantal had the persuasive power to gather together 120 girls living on at least three different continents.

'Well, it's not really a job. By the way, how's you, Mrs Professor?' she planted a kiss on my cheek. 'And don't fear,' she waved her hand as if swatting away a fly, 'my lippie doesn't stain. Do you know how long I've been waiting for a lippie that doesn't . . .'

'Please tell me I didn't spend close to a thousand pounds on air fare to hear you talk about a lippie that doesn't stain.'

She cackled. 'Oh, Gabrielle Essien, always as cutting. Anyway, here's the job. I see a cluster of teachers forming over there and that's no good . . .'

'So I'm supposed to go show them that this reunion is to break all barriers.'

She blew me another kiss. 'That's why you were always my favourite deputy.'

I was just glad for the excuse to enquire after you and once all the salutations were out of the way, I quietly asked one of your colleagues where you were.

'Jacques?' he frowned.

'That's the only Mr Sylla *I* got to know, Sir.' I smiled.

'No, I know who you mean. It's just that Jacques is dead. He died a couple of years ago,' he shrugged.

I stared at him, wanting to ask more questions but the logical side of my brain told me he could not help. No question was going to bring you back. And despite the fans whirring overhead and the sea breeze, I felt hot.

'Anyway, we've heard you're now a professor in some big British university.'

Was Reading a big British university? And I was a lecturer.

'I'm sorry, Sir. I must . . .'

I turned and hurried towards the exit. I walked as far away as my wedge heels would carry me on that sandy beach and found a rock I could sit on. Even though I could still hear the music, I knew I wouldn't be going back.

I lit a cigarette, for once not caring who saw me. The tears I had been holding in now fell. I wiped them with the back of my hand and put on my sunglasses. I took a drag and wished I was smoking with you, like that day in Paris. It wasn't something I would have done with any of the other teachers, even those who smoked. They would have had their little word to say, along the lines of why a good girl like me shouldn't be sucking on a cigarette. Well, if anyone dared to spout such things today, they would get theirs. Having the odd cigarette was something I have been doing since I was sixteen and I wasn't about to stop now. I confessed this secret to you the day one of the girls was expelled for smoking.

'Trying to knock it out of you, hey?' you'd smiled, but you also shook your head at the heavy-handedness of the administration.

Unlike the other teachers, you did not think a satisfactory conclusion had been reached just because you'd shaken your head. You saw the headmistress and our friend was allowed back in class but not until after being subjected to a pep talk on the responsibility upon her and the rest of us to uphold the values of our *lycée*; values of rectitude, civic duty and camaraderie. We were the future elite of Côte d'Ivoire.

The next day in class, you told us about those giants of French literature fuelling their imaginations with opium. And while the rest of the girls contented themselves with making surprised sounds before resuming their ever present bored expressions, I hung on to your every word.

'Baudelaire, Gautier, Rimbaud, Lamartine; all these people, they did things,' you mused and your eyes lit up.

'It's not all about flowers and love, you know. Look for the symbolism, girls!' You banged the table and my heart leapt at your passion. It was your love for and knowledge of your subject that made me passionate about French literature. You made it interesting and fun, and soon I was trawling bookshops for the works of those men and women instead of spending my pocket money on clothes and make-up like all the other seventeen-year-olds. And just like you, I fell under the spell of their work.

'Do you think it could be the opium?' I once joked as we made our way out of school, you to your car and me to my chauffeur.

'*Pourquoi pas?*' we laughed.

From that day on, we just needed to say 'opium' and we knew. We sometimes wondered who would turn the face of our own Ivorian literature upside down.

'What about Bandama? Or Venance?' you would ask.

'Huh, interesting but don't you think there is too much militancy in their books? Not subtle enough.'

'Adoras then.' You replied with a shrug of the shoulders, and we laughed some more. Books about dashing young men saving terrified little women were not what we considered literature.

I have a daughter now. She is only two years old but I sometimes wonder what I would do if I were to find out she was having such intense chats with her teacher. Would I think it totally innocent or would I see something behind it? I mean, I used to know which class you would be teaching at every hour of the day. I also knew when you were off. I sometimes went to your house and we chatted. I telephoned you. We had such easy conversations. But we only ever limited ourselves to talks about literature and my ambition to open a literary salon one day, when I was older.

'Why not now? Why wait till you're older? How old is "older"?' You would ask with such an earnestness that I felt emboldened.

If you hadn't been around, I wouldn't have found an outlet for my thoughts and ideas, save for my diaries. These were not the kind of conversations we had in my house. Maman and Papa would've laughed at the thought of a literary salon where people debated, wrote and performed poetry. Their ambition for me was to go into the law. They would have preferred it if I had had an aptitude for the sciences of course. But with your encouragement, I went ahead and set up a poetry club. It didn't quite catch on and I soon gave it up when, after three months, numbers didn't go up to more than three.

I didn't stop writing, though. I wrote poetry, not about the ills of colonialism but poetry on love, ambition and sex and showed them to you. I liked that you didn't raise your eyebrows and I liked that you didn't bat an eyelid. Even during lessons, I found a way to communicate with you. My essays were a code to tell you what I'd been reading. And you appreciated it.

'It's always a joy to read your work,' you would say and I'd beam, for it was my intention that my work should set the standard. I knew the other girls invariably wrote about those writers we had already studied. So I had to be different.

I also think we loved one another. We never said anything. Not while I was your pupil anyway. But do you remember that time in France?

I invited you to come see me when you told me you would be visiting friends in Lille over the summer holidays. You came to the Sorbonne, which you had recommended to me as you'd also done your *maîtrise* in French literature there.

It felt so good to see you, especially as five years had passed. Sure, we called one another, but on that occasion, it felt good to meet up. We strolled the streets of Paris, unfazed by the hordes of people who always took over the city in June.

I took you to my favourite café in Montmartre where we sat on the metal bistro chairs outside – we both had coffee and you had an almond croissant – and lost ourselves in people-watching. We shared a *Gauloise*, passing back the cigarette after each drag. Even though there was a new packet lying beside our coffees we didn't think to light another cigarette.

'I'll share with you,' you'd said when I held the packet open to you, so that was what we did. You took that first drag, sighing as you did so. I imagined your eyes closing behind your sunglasses.

'Why does the first drag always taste so good?'

'Especially when you haven't had one in a while.'

You clicked your fingers in agreement.

You noticed that I didn't have any of the croissant.

'I don't want to get fat.'

'If you're worried about fatness, what about me?' you patted your stomach.

I turned towards you then, 'You're not fat at all.'

'Middle-age spread then.' You smiled and even though your sunglasses hid your eyes, I felt them dancing behind the mirrored lenses.

With any other man, I would have felt the need to fill the silence with chat, any type of chat. With you I enjoyed the companionable silence. And there wasn't that need to do something, anything, just so we could say we were doing something. Even when we finished our coffees and our cigarette, we whiled away a few minutes just sitting there. Every once in a while you would comment on a building that wasn't there in 1975 and I would realise then how old you really were. In 1975 you were finishing your first degree. In 1975, my father was fifteen; my mother was twelve years old.

I did not share those thoughts with you. You were fully aware of the age difference between us. In fact, while we were sharing the *Gauloise*, you mentioned how those passing by would think what a cool father I had to be sharing a cigarette with. I looked at you then and you turned your head towards me. You lifted your sunglasses and raised an eyebrow.

'Hey, we could do it like the French,' you said, your eyes dancing with what seemed to be mischief, and thus closing the gap you'd opened with that comment about me sharing a cigarette with my father. 'Oh my goodness!' you sat up and started pointing at something across the road.

'What?' I asked.

'That bookstore.' You jumped up, taking my hand in yours and we crossed the road. 'I used to spend my days in that place.'

'I thought every African student had to work like a little demon?'

'No. These were the days Côte d'Ivoire was competing with Singapore. The government was sending every student at least a million French Franc . . .'

And again, I would be reminded. The French Franc went out of circulation when I had started university and I only seen one at *Le Musée de la Monnaie*, but you'd touched it and handled it.

'The guy who owned this place used to let us sit in there with a cup of coffee and just read to our hearts' content.'

It did look like the sort of bookstore where one sat to watch the world pass by. Although it was in the main square, stepping inside felt like shaking off the madness of Montmartre. Shelves and rickety tables groaned under the weight of books. The floor shone with the number of people who'd walked through its doors. Shabby sofas and armchairs were placed in the alcoves. A benevolent member of staff walked up to us and asked if we needed any help.

'We are browsing, thank you,' you told him and to me, you said, 'Come on, darling.'

My heart melted at that. Thankfully you'd let go off my hand by then.

'Oh, look, the new owners haven't made many changes. Here is the rare books section,' you continued, unaware of the avalanche of emotions you were causing in me.

It was from that section that you got me a collection of stories by Balzac and I gave you some poems by Jeanne Duval.

'Do you know, people said she didn't write? But obviously . . .' You held the tattered booklet out to me as proof.

'Maybe they didn't want to take the star away from Baudelaire. Besides, imagine the time she used to live in. Not only was she a woman, but she was Black.'

'Hum,' you agreed with me. 'She was also the woman Baudelaire loved the most, you know.'

'I know,' I winked. As if I wouldn't know such a thing.

That was when I told you I loved you, and I was so glad when you didn't look at me with shock or worse, pretend you hadn't heard me. Or say something about how young I was and therefore couldn't possibly know what I was talking about. Because I was twenty-two then, not a seventeen-year-old who didn't know her mind.

But you said, 'I love you too,' and brushed my cheek with the back of your hand before pulling me into an embrace. 'But I'm fifty-five, *ma chérie. Un vieil homme*,' you'd sighed.

I smiled and burrowed my face against the material of your *boubou*, smelling your spicy eau de cologne. You were not old at all, not for me. But I didn't tell you that. We pulled away from one another. You planted a kiss on my forehead. The same member of staff who accosted us before rang up our books and we left the shop, with you holding my hand. We stopped by the entrance to the store. We looked into each other's eyes, wondering whether to kiss or not. In the end, we didn't. We just smiled at each other and went to a bistro where we did it like the French, consuming alcohol at lunchtime, that is.

Do you think it was because we didn't want to break the magic? Relationships tend to complicate everything after all. And I don't think it was a coincidence when you telephoned me a year later to tell me you had met someone.

'Wonderful.' I said and I really meant it, even if my voice choked up a little. 'Does she like Baudelaire?' I teased and was strangely relieved when you said no.

'She has more of a scientific mind. She's a doctor who doesn't understand literature,' you replied and went on to ask if I had met someone.

'No.'

After that conversation, I had sat at my desk in the little studio I was renting in Montmartre, holding the telephone and instinctively knowing that this call would be our last. It wouldn't have been fair of me to keep calling you when you now had someone in your life. You had been a single man for such a long time that I didn't want to give the poor woman the impression that you were still holding out a candle to some lost love.

'Find someone. Be happy.' Your voice had trailed off. I had known that we were saying goodbye to each other.

'I'll find someone,' I promised. And I did.

His name is Martin and we both moved to England after my *maîtrise*. He also just doesn't understand my obsession with nineteenth-century French literature, especially as I have set up a thriving literary salon. We drink wine, smoke cigars or cigarettes and we read poetry, ours and our heroes'. Sometimes when someone says something witty, I find myself thinking about you and almost ache that you are not there because you were the one who sowed the seed in me. You introduced them to me.

from a novel in progress

New Mom

Tope Folarin

The most confusing period of my childhood began when my schizo-phrenic mother left us and returned to Nigeria. Her sickness had come on so quickly – had wreaked so much havoc in our lives – that my brother and I weren't really traumatised by her departure; when she left, we simply felt wounded and relieved. I was only six years old, and my brother was five. I had just started the first grade and I was having a hard time understanding how a family could be a family with-out both a father and mother.

In her absence, my father assumed the guise of a superhero. He kept hunger at bay by working longer hours as a mechanic at various shops across Northern Utah. He fought off the forces of sadness by laughing at everything, no matter how bleak or obscene. He vanquished our fears by telling Tayo and me that he would always be there for us, no matter what. And he taught us the meaning of kindness by never once uttering a negative word about our mother.

For many days we lived this way, my father laughing, dancing, work-ing, teasing, praying. He told us that Mom was receiving special care in Nigeria, and that she was getting better every day. Tayo and I imagined tall, good-looking doctors standing over her with notepads and clip-boards, almost like the doctors we'd seen on TV (unlike the doctors on Dad's favourite show, *M*A*S*H*, our imaginary doctors were black, and they spoke Yoruba to each other as they attended to Mom).

In the weeks following Mom's departure, though, my brother and I began to notice a change in Dad. He seemed less confident than he'd been before. He maintained his habit of chasing us around our little apartment before leaving for work each morning, but now instead of tickling us at the end he hugged each of us fiercely, and he didn't let go until we tapped him on the shoulder and called his name. He still told us he loved us at least twice a day, but the way he said it sometimes made us feel as if he were saying it for the last time.

Sometimes, when we stood by his bedroom door, we heard him praying quietly, insistently, begging God to make Mom right.

One night, after Mom had been gone a month or so, my father tucked Tayo and me in and closed the door without saying a word to us. After a few minutes we heard him sniffling in the living room. Tayo got up and walked to the door, and I followed. When we reached the living room we saw Dad sitting on the couch with his head in his hands. Tayo tapped his shoulder and Dad looked up at us. His eyes were red, and his moustache was wet. He shook his head slowly. I suddenly felt very queasy. 'Mom isn't coming back,' he said. I looked down at his feet. He'd been wearing the same pair of socks for four days; I knew this because his big toes were sticking through each one. 'She is just too sick. This country's no good for her.'

We tried to get more information from him, but Dad began to speak in riddles, as he often did when he didn't feel like giving us any more information. When we asked him why America was no good for her, he told us that we had eyes at the front of our heads for a reason. When we asked him what he meant by that, he told us to go back to sleep.

Tayo and I returned to our bedroom and sat on our beds.

'How can Mom still be sick?' Tayo asked. 'She's been gone for ever.'

'Yeah,' I agreed.

Tayo kicked the air, and his foot fell back to the side of his bed with a soft thud.

'I'm scared,' Tayo said.

I just nodded.

In the days that followed, Dad stopped playing with us, and he sent us to bed early each night. Afterwards, he would stay up and yell at the telephone – we knew he was talking to someone in Nigeria whenever he did that. We could never make out what he was saying, but we wondered if he was speaking to Mom. We wondered if Mom was

trying to convince Dad that she needed to come back. If Dad was telling her to give America one last chance.

In time, Mom's absence became the most prominent aspect of our
lives. Dad stopped talking about her, and he encouraged us to do the
same, but we could tell that he missed her. Sometimes he'd slip up and
tell us to ask Mom what she was preparing for dinner. Other times,
when we passed by his bedroom on the way to the bathroom, we saw
him fingering some of the items she'd left behind. Her purse. Her
records. Her colourful head wraps. Her purple flip-flops.

Tayo and I continued to speak about Mom, but we always whispered when we did so, like she was a secret that only he and I shared.
Like her life was a story we had made up.

One spring morning, maybe six or seven months after Mom returned
to Nigeria, my father strode into our bedroom while Tayo and I were
getting dressed for school. He sat on Tayo's bed, which was closest to
the door.

'Come here,' he said to me.

I joined Tayo and my father on the bed.

'I know you guys miss Mom very much. And I know you guys want
to talk to her. But she can't talk to you now. And it's possible you
won't talk to her for a very long time.'

'What do you mean?' asked Tayo.

'Let me finish,' Dad said. He smiled and then he coughed. He took
off his glasses and rubbed his eyes.

'You guys are both young, but there are certain things that you need
to know. Life doesn't always go the way you want it to, but God
always has a plan for us. And it's not our job to question His plan. Do
you understand?'

'Yes, sah,' we both said.

'Good. Things are going to change from now on. And it may be
difficult in the beginning. But everything is going to work out.'

With that, Dad reached into the front pocket of his overalls and
pulled out a small picture. He gave it to me. The lady in the picture
was beautiful – she had a round nose, deep dimples, and bronze skin.

I did not know who she was.

'This is your new mother,' my father said, solemnly. 'I am going to Nigeria to pick her up next month. She is from Lagos, like me, and she's ready to meet you guys.'

We couldn't believe it. We hadn't expected anything like this.

'Who is she?' I asked. 'And what about—'

'Everything is going to be fine. Don't worry. Finish getting dressed.'

He got up and left the room.

Tayo began to cry. I moved closer to him and rubbed his back. And then I began to cry as well.

Dad flew to Nigeria two weeks later. He left a picture of our new mom for us, and I spent hours after school looking at it. I tried my best to see this stranger as a member of our family, but it was hard. I couldn't imagine her preparing moin moin the way my mother had when she felt like cooking. I couldn't imagine feeling as safe in her arms as I'd felt in my mother's arms, even when I knew she was only holding me so she could pinch me up and down my back and legs.

I missed Mom, but I was still scared of her. This was the only reason I was willing to give my new mom a chance.

My brother and I stayed with an older white couple while Dad was gone. They lived in a large red brick house on the other side of town. Dad dropped us off on his way to the airport, and after introducing us to them he rushed back to the car and waved goodbye before revving the engine and speeding off. Tayo and I stood on their porch waving even after his car had disappeared from view.

The old lady stood there with us, her hands on our shoulders. I'd never seen her in my life. She was taller than Dad, and I remember being fascinated by her long, silvery hair. She was the first old person I'd seen with long hair. I'd always thought that people couldn't grow long hair after a certain age.

She gave Tayo and me a hug after Dad disappeared, then she stepped back and stared at us for a moment.

'Welcome to my home,' she said. 'You can call me Missy.'

She smiled, and then she turned around and walked into her house. Behind her back, Tayo rubbed his arms like he was trying to rub her hug away. I glared at him and he stopped.

I'd never lived in a white person's house before, and everything I saw inside assumed a special meaning. In the corner of their living room a tall grandfather clock stood staring at me. I heard it ticking under its breath. There were pictures all over the walls, and the people in them looked so happy that I wanted to step into the pictures and sit with them, so I could smile at whatever they were smiling at. Tayo rushed across the room and picked up a small globe that was sitting on a side table next to their dark leather couch. He stared at it as if he expected the miniature people inside to wave at him. I glared at him again but then I looked up to see Missy smiling as she wooshed by me. She took the globe from his hands and showed him how, by shaking it for just a few seconds, he could initiate a small, furious snowstorm, a beautiful blizzard encased in glass. I was jealous as I stood there by myself, watching Tayo shake the globe again and again as Missy nodded her approval. Yet I was happy, too, because I could still smell her. Her scent had remained with me after she rushed by to show Tayo the secret of the globe. She smelled like something soft, like my mother's favourite perfume.

That night, after a dinner of fried fish and rice, the old man showed us our room. I could just make out the fading striped wallpaper in the dim light. The dry carpet scratched my bare feet. The beds were small and thin. Tayo and I stared up at the man, and he smiled. He had a thick white moustache, and he was missing a few teeth.

'You think you guys will be OK here by yourselves?' he asked.

We nodded.

'Let me know if you need anything. You can call me Mr Devlin.' He rubbed my head. 'We're happy to have you. Your father's a good man,' he said. Then he closed the door behind him.

Tayo and I didn't say a word until we had changed into our pyjamas and I flipped off the light.

'When do you think Daddy's coming back?' he asked.

'I don't know.'

'Soon?'

'I don't know.'

'Do you think he'll come back with Mom?'

'I don't know.'

'What will happen to Mom if he comes back with a new mom?'

'I don't know.'
'Why don't you know anything?'
'I don't know.'
'Tunde!'
I laughed.
'I hope he comes back with Mom, but I like it here,' he said.
I paused for a moment.
'Me too.'

A few days after we'd moved in with the old couple I mentioned to
them – over a big dinner of turkey, stuffing and green beans, food that
I'd only seen on the television before then – that I loved to read books
about karate. Missy leaned over her plate and asked me if I had ever been
to a karate class. I told her my father believed that karate was violent, that
he had told me he would never allow me to learn. She smiled widely at
me. The next day she picked me up from school and took me straight to
a karate studio, and for two hours I kicked, punched, screeched and had
a wonderful time. She took me to karate class every day after that, and
when I wasn't practicing kicks and punches around their house, Tayo
and I played together in their den, which had a massive TV with dozens
of Disney movies stacked in neat piles on top.

It seemed like Missy and Mr Devlin loved us from the moment we
arrived. They took us to movies and puppet shows and bought candy
for us. They taught us nursery rhymes and fed us strange foods that we
learned to love. We went to church with them on Sundays, and they
held our hands as we sat on the hard pews. Missy hugged and kissed us
more than our parents ever did, and I sometimes wondered if she were
actually my grandmother, if maybe we had other white relatives that
my father had never told us about.

As our days became weeks Tayo and I missed Dad more than we
could have imagined, especially when we didn't hear from him. But we
couldn't believe that we were living such joy-filled, impossible lives.

After we'd been living with them for about a month, though, Missy
and Mr Devlin began to treat us differently. They began to send us
straight to bed after dinner without reading to us. They began to ask us
odd questions.

'Did your Daddy tell you when he was coming back?' Mr Devlin asked, his bushy eyebrows making him seem for all the world like a cartoon character come to life.

'Did your Daddy say anything about what he was planning to do in Africa?' Missy asked, peering at us like one of those angry witches from our favourite Disney movies.

I nodded emphatically at this question and showed them the picture of our new mom. Missy looked at it for a long time before placing the small picture back in my hand.

'Who is this?' she said.

'That's our new mom,' said Tayo.

Missy's eyes grew wide. She touched Mr Devlin's side and they stepped away from our bedroom. They began to whisper to each other. I could not hear much, but I heard Missy say 'no divorce' and 'good woman'. After a few minutes they came back. Missy smiled kindly at me.

'I'm afraid that your father lied to us,' she said. 'He lied to us about what he was doing in Africa. He lied about how long he would be there. I'm afraid that you and your brother can't live here any more.'

The following morning, Missy woke us up early and drove us to a tall white building a few blocks away. She held our hands as we walked inside and asked us to sit on the couch near the door. She went to speak with a short lady with black hair who was standing behind a big wooden desk on the other side of the room. She occasionally pointed to us as she spoke with the lady, and then she walked back to us, kissed each of us on the forehead, and left. She drove away.

The short lady with black hair was nice, she allowed us to play with the toys that were scattered about the room. Tayo and I couldn't answer any of the questions she asked us. That evening she drove us to another house and introduced us to a younger white couple. The woman with the black hair told us that they were our foster parents, that they would take care of us until our Daddy came back.

Dad returned from Nigeria two days after we moved in with our foster parents. He simply showed up one afternoon after school and picked us up.

'Daddy, what about our foster parents?' I asked as we entered the car.

'Don't worry about them,' he replied, gruffly. 'I am your father, not them.'

We drove in silence for a few minutes, and then Tayo spoke up from the backseat.

'Is our new mom at home?'

'No.'

'Is she coming to join us soon?'

'No.'

'What about Mom? Is she coming back?'

'No, and don't ask me any more questions about her. Don't worry about her. Kick her out of your memory.'

Dad looked angry, so we listened to him.

Things went back to normal. Dad never told us why he was late returning from Nigeria, and he didn't mention anything about our new mom again.

My father changed jobs a few weeks later, and then he changed jobs again. We saw him even less than before, but he began to talk to us for long periods of time at random moments; sometimes after we'd finished our dinner, sometimes before he left for work, sometimes after he'd tucked us in.

'I have big dreams for both of you,' he'd say. 'You guys are the only reason I am still in this country. I should have left a long time ago, because I don't have any opportunities here. No one takes me seriously. But whenever I think of leaving I ask myself what the both of you would be like if you grew up in Nigeria. Here you can become leaders. I don't know what would happen there.'

We always nodded, but I can't say that I really understood what he was talking about. My father claimed that I had been to Nigeria before, but I had no memory of the trip, and Tayo had never even left Utah. Nigeria, to me, to us, was merely a chorus of scratchy voices over the telephone, a collection of foods and customs that our friends had never heard of. It was a place where everyone was black, where our cousins spoke a language we couldn't fully comprehend. Where our mother lived.

But somehow I knew that my father was right. And I was glad we were living in America. In Utah. I never wanted to be anywhere else.

After Dad tucked us in, Tayo and I would stay up and read to each other. We waited until we saw the thin patch of light beneath our door go dark, until we heard Dad's soft snores rattling down the hallway. Then Tayo would reach under his bed, pull out our emergency flashlight, and walk over to the single, tall bookshelf on the other side of our room.

We had dozens of books. My father never bought us toys, and he always claimed that he was too broke to buy us new clothes, but somehow we each received at least three new books each month. Most of our books were non-fiction – short biographies, children's encyclopaedias, textbooks – because Dad was convinced that novels were for entertainment purposes only, and he always told us that we would have time for entertainment when we were old enough to make our own decisions. So Tayo and I would huddle in a single bed, his or mine, with a biography about George Washington, or a book about the invention of the telephone, and each of us would read a page and hand the flashlight over.

We eventually grew tired of these books, though, so we began to make up our own stories. Actually, Tayo made them up. Even though Tayo was a year younger than me, even though he looked up to me and followed me in every other part of our lives, he was a much better storyteller than I was. He was almost as good as Mom.

He always began:

'Once upon a time . . .'

'There was . . .'

'There was a large elephant with a long purple nose and polka-dot underwear . . .'

'That liked to run . . .'

'That liked to run all over the valleys and desert, and the elephant had many friends, giraffes and leopards, and a cranky orang-utan that always wore a pair of bifocals like Dad's . . .'

We'd continue in this manner, sometimes for hours at a time, until Tayo fell asleep. Then I'd pull the flashlight from his hands, place it back under his bed, and snuggle in next to him until I fell asleep as well.

★   ★   ★

One Saturday morning, as Tayo and I were playing basketball on the concrete courts behind our apartment building, laughing, shouting, and leaping, Tayo stopped dribbling and looked up at me, his eyes shining, hopeful.

'Don't you wish Mom would come back?' he asked.

I didn't know what to say. I took my status as older brother seriously, and I knew that Tayo would probably mimic whatever I said. I wasn't sure if it would be OK for me to tell the truth, or if I was supposed to say what Dad would say in this situation. I chose something in the middle.

'Sometimes,' I said.

'I do all the time,' Tayo said. 'I want her to come back now.'

And a part of me agreed with him. I wanted her to come back, I wanted everything to be the way it had been before she got sick. Before she left us.

But the other part . . .

Looking back, I think I was open to the idea of a new mom because there was a part of me that was ready to consign my mother to memory. I wanted to install a false version of her in my mind. I wanted to forgive her by forgetting her cruelty, the pinching, the slapping, the screaming. I wanted to forgive her by forgetting her.

But now, Mom, I remember your hugs. They were warm and tight. When you wrapped your arms around me I always felt as if I were home. And your food was delicious. Even when you stopped cooking, even when you would only warm up a few pieces of frozen chicken in the oven and open up cans of beans and corn for dinner, your food tasted as if you'd spent hours preparing it.

And your smiles, I'll always remember your smiles. They were rare and lovely, like priceless coins from an ancient kingdom.

No Kissing the Dolls Unless Jimi Hendrix is Playing

Clifton Gachagua

Posters with the face of a grinning girl with red hair are all over the city's walls. A family of three who have found a home outside an Indian café stitch the posters together into a curtain, her face watching over them. Her name has become infamous. Seventeen murders in the ghettos, no MO, no evidence, and somehow the murders all happen at the same time in the five different ghettos.

The poet has come home to roost. He is in love for the first time after a very long time. He spent the night out with a girl in a leather dress the colours of collage frangipani and a long face under red hair and Bengali bangles and heavy chains stretching from her nose ring to an earring, a girl who would otherwise be living in a hefty loft in the UK with another poet with no medical cover to boast of. A girl who held his hand through the city and showed him her blue blazoned red tongue and the weapons she carried in her nightmares.

He puts something on the record; he's not sure what it is, as long as it is not silence. Love likes noise. He lives alone now. Once in a while he will miss them, the other poets. They fucked indiscriminately and with few inhibitions, smoked and listened to vintage radio podcasts playing *zilizopendwa*. There were debates about Them Mushrooms. Of course everyone knew, they were all there when it happened, that Them Mushrooms had failed in that event of '67 to keep the noontide in its place. The water had come all the way to their feet, bringing with it the dead bodies of children and chihuahuas from the Italian villas off the coast of Malindi. No one could write poetry after that. They went back to smoking, fucked less, let silence replace Them Mushrooms;

their fathers' favourite musicians had failed them. They listened to their bodies more, the silence of metabolism, spent time fixated on the now obsolete. They all had penises the size of semicolons and made a show for everyone who came to visit. The sky was not enough for them so there were the octane tanks hidden in the boiler. How many ways octane helped them re-enact what Marijani Rajab must have felt when he made *Zuena*, and, more importantly, would *Zuena* ever come back to him? Their poetry came down to that important question: would the dead lover ever return?

They smoked and smoked and danced to the old tunes better than their fathers ever could, twisting waists and shifting disks in their spines. Koffi Olomide's *Andrada* and *Effrakata*, first slow then fast, slow then fast again, a recital about dead children as intermission, then the climax. They imagined dance-fucking their own mothers in those fallen hours of the night when it was possible to see certain constellations when you lived next door to the equator, and in this regard constellations of both the southern and northern hemispheres. They had forgotten lung cancer. They worked in advertising and owned holiday homes in Shela and Pate and failed to train chihuahuas to sit, roll, stay, jump, do not poop on people's lawns. Some anti-smoking campaign display-glass lungs full of dead babies and filters were enacted next to strip clubs but the poets knew nothing would ever stop them from smoking.

After a while they all had to leave his loft and find another place for their semicolon parade. That was then.

Dik Dik remains one of them. *One of them* is a phrase he carries with him around his neck, it's something his mother could never and will never offer him, a place where his bow-legs meant nothing, when all he ever wanted was for her to stick out her tongue.

He sits alone in the middle of his living room and thinks about the girl with the red hair. He readjusts a register.

Long hallways of palm frond alloys, boulevards of thick baobab, dead children, flying dragonflies, cheap foam life-size GSU and imitation art line Kenyatta Avenue. *Beautification* programmes. Meja Mwangi, last seen here a long time ago, disappears into Sabina Joy with an amputee prostitute who offers him an hour's worth of conversation in Gikuyu – no longer spoken here – for ten times the normal rate. She holds his hand tight and smiles like two moons, blush on the cheeks. He disappears inside her, never to be seen again. Some people will stalk his grave and spend fifty years waiting, fasting, praying. Cyborgs will find them there and eat their intestines alive. *Alive*. Pick, roll, unfurl them in their hands like cashew nuts. He will never come back; the sons will never come back to their mothers. The mothers have forgotten they ever had sons. If they meet in the Matrix Way they will greet each other like strangers, probably sleep next to each other, tired and outworn, and they will kiss with their eyes closed.

The prostitute comes back and the night is on her lips and anyone who asks to kiss her she says yes. What else can she say but yes? Because yes is a sacrifice to all those young twenty-somethings and taxi drivers who have the world in front of them and the government so up their assholes it tastes like the Year of the Colon.

She comes back with those dark lips the colour of night and she is blowing kisses to the night and right there at the equator there is a kind of magnetic borealis – a migration of evolving nova from the 456 regions to the Near Death Kentucky Fried Chicken Canto regions, where it says Dante was just looking for the devil to fuck his ass. She is dying and her body is in this experiment of reverse engineering and she is tearing into ribbons of primary colours – wait, wait, are these wings? – no, they are not wings, they are the roads she must take to get home but as soon as she steps on to the curb they disappear. She goes back to the house, kisses him on the forehead, no eye contact, and he remembers his mother. She just wants someone to accept her love.

She walks out into the street.

A man with an eye patch on his nipple and a single eye on his other nipple pinches himself to look at her. He feels a chill, goosebumps spread across his body – he has not yet learned how not to arouse himself whenever he pinches his nipples. He is a work in progress, he reassures himself.

She sees Dik Dik clear in her closed-eye vision when she finally falls asleep.

He has seen the way many men fall into the night of that smile and never come back so he simply looks at her from the corner of his eye.

For her this is enough. She says her name is Chromosome-1972. He has read on a banned billboard the short history of seventies chromosomes so he does not ask her anything else, he is playing it cool – some genuses don't take too lightly to old-age categorisation. *Short history* and *early death* appear together in conversations. He does not offer a smile.

They are at Aga Khan Walk, and the blind man is singing. Dik Dik lets her know he loves the blind man. He doesn't say what he really means is that he loves his father. She knows this. She shows him her tongue and he sucks some colour from it. His tongue is darker, the contrast of colours not as sharp. No one can save him.

The blind man sings in a baritone. He has long stopped singing in semi-quavers. He finds the deepest voices and re-enacts dead street children who would have grown up to give Pavarotti a run for his money. He points his walking stick up, demands that God shut up and the city goes all quiet and he sings the most beautiful ballads, only he is also deaf and Dik Dik and Chromosome-1972 stand there marvelling at such talent.

They are deaf.

The city is collecting deaf people in blue rooms; the governor wants to know what the gods are saying.

'What do you think he sees?'

'When he sings or when he dreams?'

'Difference?'

'One is about wavelength, the other is that I'm so damn hungry can we get out of here and get some food?'

Leaving a trail of their favourite love song of distant gunshots, ambulance singsongs and dead children crying behind them, they walk into Mocha Cola where blown-up balloons smile and stick out their tongues to them. Their tongues are made of old turntables, each taste bud a record with a spindle so that, in addition to the love songs, there's all this beautiful music inside and Dik Dik and Chromosome-1972 just want to stick out their respective tongues and kiss some dolls. They kiss some dolls.

On the wall, on this big red poster, is a warning in bold letters: NO KISSING THE DOLLS UNLESS JIMI HENDRIX IS PLAYING. A grinning Chinese man stands below it.

Dik Dik wants to order French fries and some old love songs on the machine. She wants to offer her services to the brotherhood of man and the cleaning of dishes with no pay. Two hours after their meeting they have fallen in love, he knows because she is sticking out her tongue and showing him how many flavours of candy are in the register of her mouth. She's showing him only, not the Chinese man. Soon they fight for a short while about the range of colours on her tongue and he agrees that she makes better sense. He is Mr Sinister, hates the primary colours. Truth is he is wasting time for some JIMI HENDRIX. The calendar at the main lobby states the date as 1/2/1972, and the calendar in the kitchen says it's 1/2/1967. He's not sure if this is an elaborate joke. Maybe they have run out of a register. In a Nairobi filled with disreputable fried-chicken-and-cabbage-sandwich Ssebos hiding guns and lipstick under the white meat of genetically modified chicken and drunk clockmakers who can he believe? He decides to walk into the kitchen and do the dishes if only to prove to her that he can be romantic. To really drive the point home he tells her of this dream he had of transgenders plaiting cornrows on dolls from the one and only most expensive doll shop in Nairobi and possibly all of East, Central and South Africa – The Most Superficial David Foster Wallace Dolly Dolls Shop.

Nairobi, unlike any other city on earth, is a city of visiting poets, men possessed by the love of other faraway places and Samburu festival dolls – Madilu System, Kanda Bongo Man, Les Wanyika, Fundi Konde, Mbilia Bel, Dik Dik's long dead absentee father, the man with ears and habits like a September Playboy bunny – all these are poets. Dik Dik is a poet, he has thought of his father as homunculus, as atypical, primitive, strange, as absent and as human, as a man possessed with the ability to discern temperaments in dolls of the same gender and age, as a transgendered doll. But on this night he's thinking of nothing but kissing this girl and possibly hot dogs later in the park. Possibly dog meat.

He still wants to go back to that park despite the frenzied woman who waits there for boys like him, singing siren songs, songs not so unlike those of the blind man.

Dik Dik pauses. Chromo | Domo – what he imagines to be a funky sexyname he has developed in the rush for her acceptance – pauses too. She does not pause just because he does, no no no. So the lovely couple under a blue umbrella and yellow scissors take a pause. They are so in love with each other a bridge somewhere falls apart at the beating of a butterfly. He takes out an octane tank and gets her to take three puffs in quick succession. He decides right there this is the only girl he will ever show his octane tank.

They walk on to Short Lane just when two mellow young boys say goodbye to their ailing mother who is going out to beg for coins from the big and rich Somali men who now own the city and talk in the language of appreciating dollars. Dik Dik grew up with Somalis, fought with them. He wanted to be them. He loved among them.

Nineteen seventy-seven. He tells her the story he has not told any other girl.

A Gikuyu man spanks a Somali woman. There are unconfirmed rumours that it was a Somali man in a buibui. A Somali man pulls out a sword. Innards the colour of reparations denied and the smell of secessionists spill out into the September sun and into the blocked sewers. Red ceases to be a colour, it becomes everything they know. They are happy to kill and risk being killed in this sweet intermission. War breaks out. No animals spared.

He tells her he was once happy, she smiles and believes the lie, loves him just a bit more for lying. He says he will never forget her name.

She cuts some of the red hair and offers it to him. He puts the hair in his mouth.

The young boys approach them from the darker recesses of the alley; the younger one takes out a tube of hallucinogen and gives it to the other one. Dik Dik gives them a taste of his gin and tonic, a bit of the red hair – if she can belong to him she can belong to them – blesses them in the long way of the cross, a technique he has come to acknowledge as more meaningful than what they taught him to be the truth in catechism classes at an age not so different from the kids he sees in front of him. The initial way of the cross as trailed by the index finger and a reverse of the same, with three insistent kisses on the lips in the fashion of Serie A footballers. It's all he can do in a city like this. The young boys leave without saying a word, not even their eyes are capable of language. They retreat, eyes fixed on the couple.

A giant drive-in cinema shows an Indian film, no cars in the lobby, say, for a woman who sleeps under the tower with her two infants, the older one teaching the other how to cheat at thumb finger sucking. Children in the rows of houses both in the Residentials and ghettos can watch the fuzzy images of Bollywood in the drive-in; this is how from an early age they learn Bhangra. The governor discovered this, and, in a new taxation programme, made sure children paid entry fees. The question of where they enter is yet to be resolved. Kenya, 2067. Happiness index better than anywhere else in the world.

Dik Dik remembers coming to the city as a child, in search of the orchestra of night and smiling lips: drive-in cinemas; white-chested crows; amputees with placards telling the history of their bad luck; wild pigeons; old women walking so slow they turn into scarecrows, maybe one of them was his grandmother, for he's made sure her grave at Langata Cemetery is empty, so she must be out there, roaming the streets of Nairobi, going around saving the children; the man with long nipples – his father.

The night has a language of empty parking lots, headlights, car horns, incidental white lights on the top of most floors of tall buildings, live bands in famous tourist joints – *Miller's Guide to Nairobi*, 2nd Ed, 2067 – rooftop pools illuminated by the light from the eyes of long-dead street children. White skin looks beautiful there, like a Standard Chartered banking hall. Bodies come out of nowhere and occupy the empty spaces.

Dik Dik walks into an alley. Some children are born with congenital heart disorders, holes in the walls of the heart as big as black holes, but he's special enough to have been born only with bow-legs. The country missed the World Cup because of these bow-legs. A distant muezzin affirms his belonging to another world, but in a language he will never understand. *Come here, child.* Be good and be gone. Dik Dik tiptoes. Slowly, slowly. Dik Dik tiptoes. Midway through a whistle – John Coltrane, Carnegie Hall, a lost time – he stops and the language of the arrangement of his bones in the general order of the skeleton appears to say hi to a cobbler in red and green. He smiles, nods back and reaffirms a longstanding discount, 'You will always have a home here.' The cobbler's smile is so wide Dik Dik can make out pools of saliva in the gorges of the man's toothless gums. A three-headed mousebird untucks its head from under his apron, he pats its crest and tucks it back, smiles to Dik Dik by way of an apology. Dik Dik needs no shoes owing to the size of his feet. The size of his penis begs to differ.

What is home if you don't have the right size of shoes to take you there?

Dik Dik walks into Marienbad, says 'Good morning, M'bad.' The people laugh with their mouths closed, in the burrows of their smiles and creases are incomplete guides to difficult museum pieces.

He kisses each man, slowly, takes time to get the tilt angle just right, just the right amount of aftershave, just the right amount of tongue. JIMI HENDRIX is playing.

Conversations circle around modern architecture. Ah, Nairobi is a riot in July. The sun is out, Hartlaub's Turacos play in certain gardens. Dead children come out to sing the anthem. So much sun in this city. Wounds fester. Everyone is happy with the government and the children of diplomats are happier with the dollar rate.

Dik Dik had dated the son of a diplomat not a long time back, he tells them. South Sudan. They toast: here's to wishing for places much further from the Greenwich Meridian.

There was the *her* – cinematography and choice of costume notwithstanding – he met along the sands of Casablanca. He forgave her for so many things, pretended not to notice other men (and women), as long as she agreed to sign a memorandum stating their memories would not be erased by the happy men at immigration. Casablanca had old men who reminded him of a rundown smoking zone on Koinange Street, but he stayed there for years, long after his parents had left the place and long after they'd stop sending him postcards. He understood the postcards to be a form of their nostalgia, so he forgave them – it was enough that they suffered. He wanted to be near Europe, in Lampedusa, near the cemetery of sunken boats, in commune with so many West Africans he could dream dreams where he spoke with an accent and impressed the women almost enough to make them smile but not enough to take them home.

In the end he left and immigration said the memorandum was a forgery.

Casablanca stayed with him. In a certain dream Dik Dik can smell the loins of a woman who has travelled from Syria through Jordan though Tunisia to Lampedusa only to die on the shallow shores of a European beach. The morning after a child smiles at the shallowness of the shore: she knows it's easy to conquer the ocean, for her, on this other side; no other truth will be truer than the ocean being conquerable and distance being nothing more than the wet lips of a generous lover between her legs.

Chromosome-1972 calls, says as way of salutation: 'What Chromosome sees in the eyes of the goat.' He's tired but humours her. She's dialling him in her sleep again. He knows what goat she is speaking of but does not stop her when she goes into the details of its appearance. Finally she returns to the eyes of the goat. They are far from perfect spheres, she explains. What she means is that she felt something in the way the goat looked at her. It's the same way children born long ago would look at you with tilted heads, thinking: 'asshole'. It's the same way he looks at her, not entirely trusting her love and all the tongue she offers him, the dead colours, the dead children she brings to life when she licks his anus and tells him *it's OK, you don't need to be afraid, there no shame in enjoying anal.* She's saying *goat* but he hears *ghosts.*

A beep goes off and he notices his register is running low. He dials for the police and gives them her address.

Talking Money

Stanley Gazemba

Mukidanyi stood in his doorway and watched his elder brothers as they walked towards the compound gate. His eyes were flaming red. The three of them had almost come to blows.

'Go on, get out of my compound, you two!' he shouted after them, waving a thick index finger at their backs. 'I don't need your help here, hear? I don't need anyone's help at all! This is my household, and I will run it as *I* deem fit, understood?'

Ngoseywe, the elder of the two, stopped and turned, leaning on his walking stick, the patched old greatcoat he wore hanging about his tall thin frame like a scarecrow's weather-scoured sacking.

'You say you don't need us?' he said softly, stabbing his finger at their younger brother. 'Today your head has swollen like that of a child-heavy toad in the ploughed field, hasn't it, *ndugu*? Well, you will need us some day,' said the old man, with a slow nod, wiping at a line of spit snaking out of his trembling mouth. 'Yes, you will eat dirt, I tell you; and you will send for us.' Turning, he went on slowly out of the gate.

'*Jinga sana!*' shouted Mukidanyi after them, waving his fists. '*This* here is my land, and I am going to do damn well what I please with it!' he exclaimed with a loud click of the tongue, spitting angrily in the grass.

So great was Mukidanyi's fury it could only be assuaged after he had picked up a water pot left lying outside and dashed it against the wall.

And as he lumbered back into the house, his neighbours, who had gathered on the path outside the compound, shook their heads and one by one retreated to their own compounds. In that terrible rage no one dared approach him.

Later that night, after the children had gone to bed, his wife Ronika came up to where he was warming himself in the main room and sat down on her little stool, drying her hands nervously on the edge of her worn *lesso*.

'Mukidanyi, my husband. You must listen to what your brothers are telling you,' she pleaded. 'Ngoseywe and Agoya have a point. No one can stop you doing what you please with the land, but still, selling it off needs consultation. Maybe you should think of leasing it for a period of time instead.'

She watched him, awaiting a response. But he said nothing.

'Mukidanyi, I am speaking to you,' she carried on, emboldened. 'Do you even know those people you want to sell the land to? Eh? You know that hardly anyone in this village does business with the Galos. Their money is not good; we don't know where they get it from. You should not turn a deaf ear to what everyone tells you, Mukidanyi.'

All this while Mukidanyi was sitting still, his gaze fixed on a point on the wall in front of him. All of a sudden he sprang to his feet, his hand reaching up into the smoky *jamvi* ceiling where he kept his hippo-hide whip.

The woman's screams rang through the village as the blows fell, shattering the still of the dark August night. It was only in the small hours that her whimpering finally died down.

Galo's large four-wheel-drive turned into the compound and drove up to the huge *msunzu* tree, startling the cows tethered to the scarred tree trunk with the deep roar of the motor as it was turned off. Mukidanyi came out of his house and went to meet his visitors. He was dressed in the long *kitenge* shirt that he kept at the bottom of the clothes trunk reserved for special occasions, his shepherd's hat set at an angle on his rounded head.

'*Karibu sana*! You have kept me waiting longer than we agreed, *Bwana* Galo. For a while there I thought you would not come!' he said with a bright smile, glancing at the heavy watch on his wrist though it had stopped functioning long ago.

'Ah, good day to you, Mukidanyi!' said Galo with an equally bright smile, climbing out of the vehicle. 'You know I am a terribly busy man, *bwana*! Sometimes I even forget my appointments!' He was a stout man, round like a barrel, with a dark chubby face which shone like that of a well-fed hippo. Galo was in the company of a thin bespectacled man who Mukidanyi had never seen before, and who wore a stiff smile that didn't quite reach his steely eyes. He was dressed in a crisp *karani*'s suit and carried a leather attaché case.

'Well, at least you came then. I don't think anything is lost.'

After the introductions had been made, Mukidanyi bade them welcome into the house but they declined. And so they set off for the portion of the land that Galo was eyeing down by the river.

As they surveyed the land Mukidanyi walked alongside, chatting them up.

'You have seen for yourself. A fine piece of land,' he said after they had returned to the shade of the *msunzu* tree.

'The fertility of the land is certainly not in doubt,' said Galo, taking out a crisp, perfumed white handkerchief. 'It will certainly grow good Napier grass for my cattle. What I am worried about is how my truck will access it to collect the fodder. The road here seems rather narrow.'

'Ah, that is a small matter, my friend,' said Mukidanyi enthusiastically. 'I can organise a band of boys to clear the bush along my fence. I wouldn't mind felling the trees along that side.'

'Well, if you can organise the work gang for me, I will be most willing to negotiate their pay with them,' said Galo.

'That I will, *bwana*! Just leave it to me.'

'In that case then I suppose we negotiate.'

Mukidanyi had expected it to be a long tussle in which either party would tug back and forth, something he was well prepared for, given his experience buying and selling cattle at the local market. He was surprised when the wealthy man accepted his opening offer of half-a-million shillings, which he had sprung out of the blue, as was the haggling custom. Really his intention was that they pull and push to roughly half the figure.

And he was even more surprised when Galo's slim accomplice rose and went to the car and returned shortly with another black leather briefcase. The slim man donned a pair of spectacles and opened the case. He took out a stapled sheaf of papers and scanned them briefly, entering some figures in the blank spaces with his biro, before passing it across to Mukidanyi to sign.

'You can put your sign at the places marked with an "X"' said the man in the crisp Kiswahili tone of a cultured man who spent his days in a neat office.

Now, the truth was that Mukidanyi had never been to any classroom to speak of. The few occasions his father, Kizungu, had attempted to take him to the local school he had jumped out through the window and dashed across the yard, hopping over the school hedge and away to the marshes down by the river where he passed his day with his friends playing *simbi* and roasting maize that they had carried off someone's farm.

But that was not to say that the lack of a classroom education had denied him much in life. For soon after he came of age and graduated from the marshes and got married he moved to the local cattle market, where he perfected the art of buying and selling, mastering the steadfast stare with which you arrested the buyer and the firm handshake that rattled the shoulder, and which sealed a deal like nothing else he knew of. Thereafter he left the market and passed by the butchery for a cut of beef before retiring to laugh off the day's good fortune with his buddies at the beer halls, stealing pinches at the rump of the fat proprietress, his day ended.

But right then, confronted with the papers needing his signature, he faltered. Perhaps Ngoseywe and Agoya were not so bad to have around after all.

The slim man promptly surmised the cause of his discomfiture and rushed off to fetch an inkpad, to which Mukidanyi applied his thumb and transferred the prints to the places the man pointed out. It was the routine he was more accustomed to whenever he went to the local tea *banda* where he delivered his little crop of tea for the monthly pay, and even at the bank in Kakamega for the end-of-year bonus.

The messy paper business done with, Mukidanyi was even more surprised when the slim man opened the briefcase and directed it his way, exposing the contents to him.

Mukidanyi had handled a bit of money in his cattle trade, but he had never seen that much money all at once. Inside the leather case, stacked in neat rows, were bundles and bundles of money in used bills that were held together with rubber bands – just like in the bank at Kakamega.

'Your half-a-million, Mukidanyi,' said Galo coolly, as if he was offering fifty shillings for a kilo of meat at the local butchery. 'You can count it. Take your time.'

'. . . Well, won't you count it?' said Galo, his brow slightly raised after a length of time elapsed in which Mukidanyi just sat there staring at the money in the case in his lap. 'We really need to be getting on our way for some other business.'

'Ah, I don't think there is need,' said Mukidanyi nervously, passing his trembling hand over the top row. 'Ahm . . . I trust you, my friend. I don't think you would lie to a clansman, Galo.'

'Well, in that case, then I suppose you release us. Still, just in case anything comes short in your counting, I will be very willing to come back and settle with you,' said Galo with a confident smile. 'I will tell you when we will be going to Kakamega to sort out the transfer and title deed at the survey office. Good day to you then, and looking forward to us being good neighbours!'

Long after the two visitors had climbed in the car and left Mukidanyi sat there under the *msunzu* tree, clasping the black briefcase in his lap. His gaze was fixed on a point in the distant hills, trained on an object in the periphery that only he could see. And then it occurred to him that he was holding money – lots of it – in his lap, and he stood up and rushed into the house, his heart thumping in his chest, dry throat craving a drink of water. He didn't eat anything for supper that evening.

It was later in the night after they had gone to bed that he uttered the first words to his wife Ronika, who had stretched out next to him in their narrow termite-infested wooden bed. Twice he had woken up and lit the lamp to make certain the briefcase was still there, chained to the bedpost with the rusty chain and padlock that he usually used to secure his old bicycle to the trees at the market.

'Ronika!' he whispered after the usual night sounds had died and the night had matured to silence. 'Can you hear me? What time is it?'

His wife turned over and sleepily opened one eye. 'Just how do I know a thing like that at this hour?' She was still bristling from the lashing he had given her the day before.

'I meant, is it nearly daybreak?'

She squinted at the parting between the thatch and the top of the wall and shook her head groggily. 'Unless you are dreaming, Mukidanyi, but this seems like the middle of the night to me – the hour for witches. And so, unless you are one yourself, I think you had better go back to sleep.'

'Well, I was just wondering how soon the day will break so I can take the money to the Post Office in Mbale.'

'Break it will, if you don't rush it by refusing to go to sleep.' And with that Ronika turned over and resumed her soft snoring, pulling the patched old blanket up to her ears. With an uneasy shrug Mukidanyi too turned on his side and, drawing the old nylon shirt that he slept in closer about him, squeezed his eyes shut and tried likewise to work up a snore.

It was as the downy wing of sleep was starting to spread its shadow over Mukidanyi's pillow that he woke with a start, blinking rapidly in the dark. He was certain he had heard voices, and they sure hadn't been dream voices. '*Ronika!*' he whispered, nudging his wife in the ribs sharply. '*Wake up!*'

Of all his shortcomings, Mukidanyi couldn't be accused of sleeping like a corpse. He had always slept with one ear open, and would spring awake at the slightest stirring in the cattle *boma* outside.

'Now what is it?' said the audibly irritated Ronika. 'Just because you have money in that briefcase does it mean we'll not have a night's sleep today? What is wrong with this man!'

'*Shhhh . . . ! Ronika, listen!*' he said with a note of urgency, cupping his hand over her mouth. '*Please be still. I am not imagining this!*'

A length of time elapsed in which a pack of dogs in a homestead across the valley engaged a chicken-stealing mongoose in a shouting match. And then in the ensuing silence the voices that had woken Mukidanyi returned, tinny and playful, like a couple of school children chatting along the village path on their way home from school, albeit strangely disembodied.

'This place is nice . . . I like it very much,' piped the first voice.

'Indeed. It is much better than our old place,' said the corresponding voice.

'*Magu!* It is very warm here close to the fire. We will grow fat in a couple of days . . . *magu!* . . . *magu!*'

'*Magu!* And our new hosts are kind-hearted people too!'

'Yes, they welcomed us very well . . . at least here we'll have space to play . . . *magu!* . . .*magu!*'

Mukidanyi had frozen stiff beside his wife in the bed as they listened to the strange conversation, his whole body covered in sweat. Beside him, his wife was none the better for fright, her bony hand clasped on his wrist, bosom heaving. The strange voices were coming from right underneath the bed where Mukidanyi had left the briefcase.

In the morbid silence that had descended they waited, their breath held. But the voices did not come again.

'You heard that clearly, didn't you, Ronika?' said Mukidanyi at length, still speaking in a whisper, letting out his breath slowly.

'I did, Mukidanyi,' said Ronika, letting go of his wrist. 'My ears are fully awake.'

'Who were they?' said Mukidanyi in a frightened child-like whisper.

'You ask who they were, do you?' said Ronika in a shrill voice, sitting up in bed. Her breath was whistling through her teeth in the tense darkness, her tone scolding. 'I will be damned, but *those* were certainly *viganda* spirits speaking. I have no doubt in my mind about it. I have heard of these things before, but today was really my first encounter with them. Light the lamp, I say!'

'But . . .' Mukidanyi's hands were shaking as he groped about for a matchbox and put a flame to the sooty tin lamp on the rack above the bed.

'Yes, now you will listen to people, Mukidanyi. Now you will listen, I tell you!' said Ronika, springing out of bed and moving to the far end of the room. There was a wild look in her eyes, her face slick with sweat.

'That was the money in the briefcase speaking, you mean?' Mukidanyi was shaking.

'Go on, take it!' snapped Ronika, a note of hysteria in her voice.

'Take your millions, Mukidanyi, go on . . . do not now be afraid of it, big man who is hard of hearing!' She was adjusting her *lesso* around her waist, her lined face set as if she was going to fly at him and wrest him to the floor. 'I warned you about the Galos, didn't I? Eh? Ngoseywe and Agoya warned you too against this, didn't they, big man? . . . And what did you do . . . eh? Tell me, what did you do?'

'Come on, Ronika,' pleaded Mukidanyi, backing into a corner, scared of touching the briefcase. 'We are not even sure about this.'

But the briefcase confirmed the grim news for him shortly.

'Now they are talking loudly,' complained the voice inside, stifling a yawn. 'I don't like their shouting! It was better with the silence.'

'I don't like it either. I wish they could stop. It makes me hungry,' answered the other.

'*Nyasaye goi!*' exclaimed Mukidanyi, throwing his hands on his head. 'What madness is this!'

'He-he-heeeee!' laughed Ronika hysterically, her eyes glowing angrily. 'Mukidanyi, son of Kizungu, now you have seen it with your very eyes, haven't you? Eh? Now you have dipped your finger in the wound and ascertained for yourself, eh? Today you will learn about the people of the world, I tell you, today you will know!'

In the end she had to physically drag Mukidanyi to the briefcase and force him to unlock the padlock and free it from the bed frame.

'*Out!*' she snarled, hurling the briefcase out into the night and sending him after it. 'Go on with your devil money this very minute . . . find somewhere else to keep it but not in this house, you hear?'

The children, who had been woken by the raised voices, huddled together in a corner, puzzled. They had never seen their mother that agitated, or their father that scared.

It was the longest journey Mukidanyi had ever undertaken in his life. That couple of hundred yards from his compound to the Galos' seemed like a mile with that scary case that got heavier and heavier in his hand with every footstep he took. All around him the night swam with unseen creatures, their formless bodies squirming in and out of his way as if they meant to entangle him in their many scary octopus arms. Occasionally he tripped and as he put his palm to the ground to right himself, struggling to keep the heavy briefcase in his grip he felt a slick tendril snaking out of the darkness and coiling around his ankle, tightening in a bloodsucker's grip. In the scary moment in which he wrestled with the unseen demon he felt the hold tighten, the razor edge biting into his flesh, but without drawing blood. And yet for some reason he just couldn't let go of the case and turn tail, for his leaden feet seemed set on doing the entire journey to the Galos' and nothing short of that.

It was a big relief when he finally saw the electric light the Galos had installed at their high wrought-iron gate looming in front of him. The moment he approached the gate two huge hounds came bounding out of the flower bushes, their teeth flashing.

'I say, Galo, open up for me!' shouted Mukidanyi. 'It is I, Mukidanyi!'

There was a moment of silence before a light went on in one of the windows of the double-storied brick house. All this while the dogs had been snarling at him from a distance but now as he attempted to rap on the gate they both lunged at him, clinging on to the metal grille, a manic glint in their shiny eyes.

It was as he was almost giving in to the hysteria and tossing the heavy briefcase over the gate that he saw a bright light flash from the direction of the partly hidden front porch, the powerful beam seeking him out and playing around his chest and legs.

'Bayaa, Mukidanyi, what brings you here at this hour of the night?' said Galo, drawing closer, his bedroom slippers slapping a pata-pata rhythm on the baked brick drive. 'Anything the matter?'

'Still your dogs, Galo. I am not a thief or a witch that they may tear to pieces,' shrieked Mukidanyi breathlessly. 'And yes, something is the matter. I changed my mind about selling the land. Here is your money.'

Before Galo could take in what it was all about Mukidanyi had dumped the briefcase at the gate and taken off into the night like an arrow. And he wouldn't stop to catch his breath, not even when he banged his head on low hanging branches or knocked his toes on outcropping roots on the path, opening up flesh painfully. All that preoccupied his mind was getting as far away from the storied brick house as he could.

Day and Night

Mehul Gohil

The kitchen was dark and I didn't see Daddy pick an orange from the bowl. I dropped big red Eveready batteries into the torch. Daddy said, 'On it'. My thumb slid forward. Yellow light streamed out. I manoeuvred the light beam around the blender and the fridge and the microwave then focused it on the orange. Daddy's strong fingers were holding it from the very bottom. They turned and the orange turned. I had once seen those fingers squeeze all the orange juice out of the fruit with just one squeeze. A dirty grey patch gradually came into view. Daddy continued turning and the dirty grey patch disappeared.

This is how, at the age of six, I learnt of the existence of Earth's rotation.

The Night. The Sleep. The dreams and Rapid Eye Movement. The leg jerks in-between.

At half past five, the first bird sings. After all these years, the song still sounds the same. A slight variation in the melody perhaps; a slightly different tone maybe. Because this is another bird, another life.

The Day.

I am sitting up on my bed. My hands are on my bow-legs. My fingers are playing with the hair on my thighs. My head is empty and light this morning. I am looking at my fingers and seeing how I have grown – the hard and strong bones in them now. And seeing how small and soft they are in my memory.

I am putting on my black trousers and fashionable striped shirt. I think they have a name for this kind of shirt but I don't know what it is. I just know it looks good and everyone's wearing a variation of it. Including my boss, who's an early-twenties retail prodigy. He's short and has baby fat glowing from under his fair skin.

I'll call him Striped Shirt. He owns Organic Body Building.

I am at the Sarit Centre branch of Organic Body Building. Striped Shirt's complaining about the lack of reports. He calls me a fizzy drink. That I start off great and then begin exhibiting properties of diminishing returns. That I switch off my phone. I tell him I got robbed but he tells me I'm always getting robbed. He says I am a 'Head of Department'. I say I should be given a car because if you expect me to take Cabanas to Mlolongo matatus, expect me to get robbed.

'That's not the point,' he says. 'Reports have to be mailed. I, Striped Shirt, have to keep an octopus eye on things from my laptop. I, Striped Shirt, should not be bumming around branches, doing low life, shelf attendant jobs. That's your job. To coordinate operations at the bottom two levels of this organisation's hierarchy. I need reports to know if this is happening.'

I tell him nothing's going wrong, there are no stock variances straying out of bounds, the negative stock levels are under control, no pending transfers in the transit warehouse.

A 'pop-up window' appears and I maximise it. There are lines of transactions listed in chronological order. Most are simple POS entries. Others are 'IMs' or 'Inward Movements'. There are 'CNs', 'STs', credit notes and stock adjustments. The list of transactions is the complete history of a particular item. I am good at translating this history into layman's language and telling everyone what's going on. In fact, I am the best at this in Organic Body Building. I can mystically conjoin the information in 'Stock Queries' and 'Sales Reports'. I am the SAP guru.

But the truth is stock auditing at Organic Body Building is a boring job. It's a prison of files arranged alphabetically – Assorted toiletries, Baby foods, Body building, Body care, Bulk items, Confectionary and so on until Teas.

★   ★   ★

I am going at a line of 250gm Xanthan Gum packets with moon walking fingers: two, four, six, eight. Then Tetra Paks of Rice Dream milk, two outers, four outers.

Seventeen tubs of Whey. I scour my inventory reports and compare and contrast shorts in Yaya to excesses in Galleria. Calculate inventory movements and set limits to the frequency of containers coming in for Organic Body Building. Cut out slow movers. And all this is only the tip of the Organic Body Building iceberg.

I can mention the story of the twenty-five kilo Deluxe Muesli bag that came out of the Maersk. A Goods Receipt was done without a prior check and it was received at the Westgate branch. A Ku Klux Klaned, Karen suburb-born, Mzungu White British Bitch bought it. On reaching home, she screamed out her fucking ovaries. The bag had four dead rats in it. She came back with reporters and a seven foot Cholmondeley guy. Their faces looked so fucking concerned. But fuck it; I have been doing this for four years.

After four years I can float into daydreams whilst playing with the SAP. Like taking myself to the last day of the 1989 Safari Rally. April 4. This was the one Miki Biasion won. I pronounced him Miki Bison, after the animal. Spectator cars were lined up on the footpaths along Uhuru Highway. We were parked on the hilly stretch that overlooks the scrap metal sprawl of the railway yards. The sky was blue and stainless. It should have been a great day but it wasn't. Daddy was not happy. He was an angrier Daddy, the one looking straight out of the window. Not even knowing what he was looking at. Moving his lips and talking to himself in whispers. I was sorting out these – what can I call them – playing cards – each one had a picture of a species of fighter jet on it with details below about size, speed, wing span and other random aeronautical jargon – they were all mixed up – when the shadow of a man slid past us and Daddy gave a start. Miki Bison's car zoomed past with a roar. I quickly looked through the back window and saw a nude brute walking down the Uhuru Highway hill. It was a total surprise for sure.

Then I come to the end of another dull working day. Orange skies fireball across car windscreens. Downtown becomes an underwater metropolis – all the cars in traffic become submarines caught in the rip of the highway currents. And from left and from right thousands of people come and gather at the edges of the rip, waiting for their turn to cross the highway, and when they do they move like majestic shoals of multicoloured fish. Some are attired formally in their grey-scale suits and well-heeled toe-fins. Others have dyed the plaited scales of their hair a scareberry blue colour; their frocks breathe and flap like gills in the wind. Sometimes matatus manoeuvre rudely around them and this upsets the natural flow of the rip. Giant bubbles rise up from the highway and, when I look through them, Nyayo House is bent. Deep bass pop songs thump out of cars, matatus, buses, so it seems a pissed off whale hides underneath the sprawling grass of nearby Central Park; great coughs booming out from the undergrounds of its lungs. Dim violet skies cool across windscreens.

Dinner in the night and Daddy is sneezing. I thought he had recovered from a cold just a month ago but he's sneezing again. I eat my *dal bhat* alone. Who cooked this? The other two are not in the house. It might be a bad night if they don't come in peacefully.

Something of the day remains. A tiredness devised by that entire stretch of workday boredom. And now it depends on the talents I was born with – is it the talent of hard work or the talent of sloth? My fight with myself begins. I want to write. All I have ever wanted to do in life is write, whether I write good or bad. I like to believe I was born to do this but the greatest talent God gave me is the sloth one.

I fight with myself. I make plans. I am going to read a chapter of Michael Herr – helicopters and napalm and naked Vietnamese girls walking the Phan Thiet beach.

Then I am going to have a shower. Then I am going to put my laptop on the desk.

Then I am going to pull the chair to the desk. Then I am going to boot the laptop and write.

This is the plan – Herr, napalm, shower, desk, laptop, write – I convince myself. In the shower I feel it's really going to happen. The water is hot. Steam all around. And when I come out I feel I need to relax by lying down in bed and reading another Herr chapter: *There were times at night when all the jungle sounds would stop at once . . .*

I hear Daddy sneeze again, his soft muffle coming from the other room, through my door and into my wet ears. A depression buzzes through me and for a nanosecond I feel a resolve arising inside me. Maybe I'm going to get up and go to the laptop.

Then the brief depression passes but something else pains in compensation. I want to mould the litfest finale into the shape of a black hole. The idea has been growing inside my head for many days. Increasing in weight, increasing in pain. I need to give birth but my goddamned talent of sloth traps me in bed like a rock underneath mighty Elgon.

I decide it's many hours that make a night and I can still get up at 2 a.m. I'm going to sleep for a few hours. And I don't bother to switch off the lights because I am thinking keeping them on will stop me drifting into dreams; the constant brightness will wake me up soon.

I flip-flop in bed. I look through the parting of the curtains and see what I think are stars in some constellation. I used to know the name. But the light is on and the sky is simply black. When we finished with the orange, Daddy spelled out the various arrangements we saw in the high sky. The following day I saw the face of the setting sun whilst standing in the kitchen and saw the very clear edges of the sun's circle. I looked right at it until it sank into the horizon. Maybe that's why I can't see the stars properly tonight . . .

My God, it's Friday morning. My fingers are again playing with the hair on my thighs.

I am again putting on black trousers and a fashionable striped shirt. I am going to wear a tie today. I see my laptop unopened on the white desk. I failed again. But I am not angry. Tonight, I will try again.

I crack two eggs and half fry them, constantly looking at the wall clock. I'm checking if there is enough time to eat well and get to the biometric clock-in device before nine o'clock. The yellow eyes of the eggs shiver inside the white oval. That's how I like it – a mix of crunchy brown toast and leaky yellow yolk in my mouth. I am suspicious they are looking closely at my clock-in reports because after this many years on the job I know the tricks of stealing 'company time'. Like standing next to a newspaper man outside the mall and reading the day's headlines off the broadsheets draped over his moving arm. But I'm washing breakfast down with a hot coffee then brushing my teeth and then adjusting the hair a little more with a comb. There are so many mornings in life exactly like this.

How about questions: Like how many expired tins of Nanny Goat Milk does it take to push Striped Shirt into taking it out of his system? And how worthy do I look as I stand there watching him flex his circumoral muscles and spit, knowing how much fun I'll have gossip cunting with the other staff after he's done and gone?

Where are the PDQ rolls for the credit card machine? How can these indigenous-bred cows simply take this shit from us sophisticated *dukawalla* types and not walk out, en masse? How did these cows get born with such extraordinary levels of tolerance? Could it have been the lady with the big black purse, the slightly fat lady?

Did she pilfer the Hydroxycut by putting it into that big black purse of hers? And can we transpose the expired Alpen to fresh bulk?

Then I come to the end of another dull working day. Crepuscular Nairobi rolls across windscreens. A dark figure ahead cavorts with an invisible lover called air. There's traffic but the number of times a wheel turns Fridays means it's slowest traffic, the couple of snail hours of wasted life, listening to same old, seeing same old. I know her number plate, her previously plain face now looking uncommonly sexy. I have never talked to her. And I speculate on whether the change of day into night means it's now another world. Whether the night-time insects that now crawl out are different from the daytime ones – migrating butterflies being replaced by the crickets, a family aroused out of its torpor by the darkness, coming to claim the world with fellow collembola. Maybe the night-cooled concrete inside the billion buildings bends them into shapes different from those in the day. How about myself and her? Perhaps we are programmed to live in dream-world and become imagination itself. And Rapid Eye Movements blossom. Maybe this is how it's supposed to be but we invented night lights and so we'll never know and maybe we'll have to console ourselves with only half and quarter chicken junk food dreams. My car moves up and she is now opposite me, on my left, and I look at her and she, just like that, also turns and looks at me. And beyond her is the other woman, the cavorting woman, who's slowly changing postures on the footpath, the utterly naked woman, with very small breasts and overgrown pubic hair. But she in the car looks at me, not her. The neon Nairobi night jazzes across her windscreen.

I attack the laptop wearing a complete work uniform – the striped shirt and black trousers. Belt, shoes and socks. I am not going to remove my wallet, mobile phone and receipts which are all stuffed into one trouser pocket. The collection is visibly bulging because the other trouser pocket is torn and everything had to be kept in this one and it has pinched my thigh all day long. I am going to leave the pen, on my shirt pocket, clipped on. I am trying again.

Daddy has a full-blown flu now. He's struggling with the stuffy nose and shaking *kaboom* every time he sneezes. He has to retire now. I keep telling him it's my turn to take care of things. But this man was born with the talent for hard work. After he showed me day and night in the torch-lit kitchen, I went to bed and read myself 'The Three Little Pigs' (as I sucked an Eveready) and fell asleep and wafted into a wholesome dream; Daddy washed the dinner dishes and whistled up a salad out of the orange and the few fruits left in the bowl and put the creation in the fridge. When I woke up the next morning, I tasted the cold grey patch of the orange in the salad and it tasted sour and acidy. Just like the Eveready battery. It's my turn to take care of things but I hate my job and all I want to do ever is sit in front of the laptop and write.

A paragraph comes out: *Now imagine you are landing into Nairobi on a night like this.*

From the windows of the Boeing you see the orange-red beacon flickering on the wing. And below is the entire night of the capital, moving and shimmering with countless stars. The nose is tipped and the Boeing body is diving in. Your eyes are ranging over this whole assortment of switched on tube lights and turned on TVs, trying to peek further into the underlying life of the litfest world and hoping, before the undercarriage hits the fine tarmac, to spot through an open window, in a split second, the steaming beef and vegetables being scooped out of the pan.

Then I don't know what to do.

I think about tomorrow.

I think about how the seven o'clock sun will blaze across the sky as I drive eastward along Mombasa Road and onwards to the Organic Body Building warehouses at Mlolongo. Where Striped Shirt . . . ah! Fuck him. I don't want to think about him or his organic body buildingness.

I think about how, like an uncaged something, I'll move into my car after clocking out. The great remains of the weekend waiting for me. The leather of the steering wheel burning my palms. It'll be a sky blue Saturday. And it'll be a complete coincidence – a plane indeed landing. I'll see it floating in from my left side where the national park expanse is. And this is it – as my car moves forwards, the plane moves in from the left. I'll slow down and look up through my windscreen and I'll get to see it from exactly underneath for a second or two. The hot silver metal of its undercarriage, the landing gear tyres, the smoke coming out from its turbines and the oil boil sound of its whoosh-thunder as it glides past. The zenith sun blindingly revealed.

I think about how the traffic will stretch from Bellevue to Nyayo Stadium. I'll look into my side mirror and I will see that my fingers look like Daddy's, my slim nose looks like his, my curly hair is his. I think I am Daddy.

I think about a yesterday.

Yesterday, I read a volume of Ladybird Educational in the Aga Khan Nursery School library. I came home and told Daddy I was very confused. Some guy had written, 'the Earth rotates'. I told Daddy to look outside and tell me if he thought the earth was rotating because I couldn't think it that way. Then at night Daddy took me to the kitchen.

from a novel in progress

The Score

Hawa Jande Golakai

Dawn snuck up out of nowhere. Across the grass, patches of morning gold swelled and merged, creeping over stretch by stretch of dewy lawn. Blinking as rays striped across her face, Vee swallowed hard and picked up the pace. She squatted and examined the dead man's feet. His shoes were relatively clean, bar disks of dried mud and grass jutting off the back of the soles. Flecks of mud spattered the bottom inch of his chinos. She leaned closer and took a picture with her phone. Gingerly, Nokia pinched between two fingers, she inched up the cuff and peered up his hairy leg.

A flurry of gasps made her jump.

'*Hai, wenza'ntoni!*' Zintle yelped.

'You frickin' crazy?' Chlöe growled.

'What I should do?' Vee hissed over her shoulder. 'Y'all got a better idea?'

Huddled and wild-eyed, Chlöe and Zintle stared her down in silence, ample bosoms undulating in unison. Zintle tightened her grip on Chlöe's arm, chunky fingers digging trenches of red into Chlöe's milky skin.

Dah helluva mark dah one will leave, Vee thought, wincing.

'We're not supposed to touch anything. And you're touching things!'

'I touched one thing!' Vee wobbled as she got to her feet and reached out to steady herself. Her flailing hand grappled over dead leg, which sent her stomach contents into a slow roil. The man's body, strung by the neck to the coat hook, took up a gentle pendulous swing, the fabric of his chinos and leather of his shoes making a low, eerie rasp against the grainy cement wall. Chlöe and Zintle shrieked and leapt away. Vee toppled onto her butt, scrabbled in the gravel till she found her footing and scurried over to them. Together, the circle heaved in harmony.

'I've never seen a dead person before,' Chlöe whispered. 'No, I mean I've seen a *normal* dead person before. At a couple of funerals, when they're clean and stuffed and make-upped. But not like this.' One hand knuckled to a cheek, she moved it in frantic circles against her skin, a sure sign she was freaking out. 'Not, like, a brutal murder.'

Vee sucked her teeth, a biting '*mttssshw*', cut short considering the sombre atmosphere. 'Dah wha'tin you call a *brutal murder*? It somethin' like a very orange orange?'

'Acch man.' Chlöe rolled her eyes. 'I mean . . . you know . . .'

'I've been to hundreds of funerals,' Zintle breathed, then stopped, mouth agape. From her expression, this was clearly a new one for her too.

'Exactly. Who's seen *this* kinda thing happen every day?'

Vee held her tongue. In her time, more recently than she cared to recall, she'd seen far too many abnormally dead people. Shot, hacked, diseased, starved . . . And once, bloated flesh piled high enough to darken the horizon of her young mind for months, years even. In comparison, this hapless soul had gone with reasonable dignity.

She averted her eyes, the violence of her heartbeat reaching up her chest like a clenching hand, closing her throat. Now was not the time to let an acute phobia of dead bodies run riot. The dangling man had her property. Every time she looked at him, her eyes were drawn to his neck, a thickened, bruised pipe wrapped in purple fabric. Her flesh tingled and shrank, drawing her face tight. She had to think clearly and quickly. Neither was happening.

'Why isn't anyone coming? Why the hell's it taking so long?' Chlöe whined.

Zintle turned her back to the scene. 'They're coming. We called them, so they should be here soon. But you're right, it's taking forever.' Eyes fixed to the gravel, she smoothed down the front of her maids' uniform and shuffled her feet. 'I want to leave this place.'

Chlöe clucked sympathetically. 'It's OK if you want go back to reception. We can all wait there.' Vee whipped her a withering look. 'Or maybe hang around with us a bit longer. Please. It'll look weird to the police if we're left alone with him, when we're the ones . . .'

Vee fired another eye, sharper still, watched Chlöe taper off to a biting of her lips.

Situation was bad enough already. Why help it escalate from strange to outright damning, which it sure as hell would when the police inevitably found out exactly which guest had been present when the body was found. The less incriminated she looked, the better.

'I can't keep working here any more,' Zintle repeated. 'Too much bad luck.'

Vee softened. The last forty-eight hours had been rough on all of them, but Zintle had borne the brunt. If she heard the phrase 'excelling outside of one's job description' ever again, she would think of hospitality's unluckiest ambassador.

Zintle's face contorted. 'Ugghhnn, I feel sick.' She doubled over, clutching at her stomach.

Chlöe's horror magnified. '*Sies* man, don't throw up.' She rubbed a soothing hand over the maid's back. 'If I see or even hear someone throw up, it makes me sick too.'

'I . . . uuggghhnn . . . won't vomit . . .' Zintle compelled herself, gulping air like a landed fish.

'Oi. Can you not say "vomit" either? It's not helping.'

Vee edged closer. The man's eyes were shut, tiny slats of the whites just visible when she crouched. She'd always thought the popular strangled expression was one of bulging, terrified eyes, shot through with harried blood vessels. Tongue drooping over toothy grimace for effect. Nothing like that here. Facial muscles slack, expression . . . not peaceful, or particularly anything for that matter. Just gone.

She inhaled and clamped her airways before creeping even nearer. Once upon a time in a faraway lab somewhere, super-nerds had taken time to ascertain that the soul allegedly weighed twenty-one grams. They probably hadn't bothered identifying its odour, but some process made the human body smell torturously different after death. Not decay exactly; this man had been gone a mere matter of hours. But there was that subtle yet unmistakable turn after the flesh and spirit parted ways, the thing she could stand least of all. She stared at the noose around the man's neck, throbbing alternately with regret and then shame for feeling such regret.

'Don't even think about it.' Vee whipped around. Eyes narrowed, Chlöe stared her down over the head of a wilting Zintle, now snuggled in her bosom.

'I wasn't,' Vee snapped. Maybe a tiny, foolish part of her was. But if she removed the scarf . . . hide it where? And explain the absence of a murder weapon how? Massive shitstorm potential.

The silk had been knotted twice then twisted completely along the length stretched around the neck. The noose closed in a third knot at the back of the head, where the loose material had been fashioned into a loop of sorts, easily slung over a worthy hook. Under the substantial weight, the workmanship of the coat rack was literally holding up. The tips of the man's shoes barely touched the ground. Breath held again, Vee zoomed her phone's camera and snapped a close-up of the garrotte. She stared at it for a long time, nonplussed.

A triangular tip of white poking out of his pants caught the corner of her eye. She exhaled shakily. A furtive peep over her shoulder ran smack into Chlöe's glare, drilling a hole through the back of her head. Answering with silent plea, Vee deftly slid the object from the man's pocket and stuck it in hers. She turned her back on Chlöe's widening eyes and frantic head-shaking.

'They're coming,' she said.

Three older men, flanked by two strapping groundsmen in blue work jumpsuits, trudged across the expanse of grass. The groundsmen were no less wild-eyed than they had been when, short of two hours ago, they'd come across the florid-faced white man strung up outside their workroom door. They hung back with a couple of the older men, wildly gesticulating over what Vee felt sure was a colourful extrapolation of a story they'd told several times already. The last of the group, hard-faced and decked in a trench coat that was absurd considering the building heat, made a beeline for them. Is it a coincidence that the police look the same everywhere, Vee wondered, or do they follow an international manual? A surge of weariness cut through the shock, overcame, left her feeling like a jaded witness in a cheap private-eye novel until the policeman tripped on the downhill verge of the lawn and nearly fell. She turned away to hide a giggle.

A crowd of gawkers, guests and staff from the lodge, was in full fluster by the time the officers had questioned them. The single crime-scene technician, whom Vee had anticipated would be an entire team working with scientific flourish, simply clicked away at different angles on a basic Kodak and cut the body down. Another stab twisted under her ribs as the massive pair of scissors worked through her silk scarf.

Chlöe sighed. 'I feel cheated after all these years of watching *CSI*. We could've done that. Well, not take the body down *ourselves* but . . .'

Vee tuned out. The best bit was kicking off. The cops formed a scrum of whispers for what felt like forever. They pulled Zintle, sobbing by then, aside. Head down with hands clamped under her armpits, she seemed to be speaking in fits and bursts. She shook her head and shrugged a lot. As the probing wore on, she stole guilty glances over her shoulder at Vee and Chlöe. One of the cops snuck a comforting arm around her shoulder and leered down the front of her uniform. Finally, Hardface Trench, who was clearly in charge, broke the huddle and set about creating another expert beeline. He had thrown off the coat, revealing a crisp blue shirt and pants of a brown so similar to his complexion that from afar he looked naked from the waist down.

'Ohhh, Gooood . . .' Chlöe groaned. Vee steeled her spine and set her expression to 'concerned but oblivious'. In the pockets of her jeans, her fingers began to tremble as they stroked the rectangle of paper.

'What's your name, ma'am?' Hardface looked directly at Vee.

'Voinjama Johnson.' She let him blink, purse his lips, mouth the name soundlessly many times as he scribbled in a battered notebook, and offered no help. She wondered what highly revised version he'd put down. Probably just Johnson; most people went with Johnson.

'It's my understanding you know this man.'

'No, I don't.'

'Hhhmmph. He's one . . .' He squinted, flipping at leisure through the notebook.

'Gavin Berman,' Vee blurted.

Hardface stopped and raised his head very slowly. 'You just said you didn't know him.'

'You asked if I know him, not if I know his name.'

The policeman's head reared a barely perceptible inch as his eyes hardened. His body language computed a rapid adjustment from 'the easy way' to 'the hard way', now clearly the only option on offer. 'Would you mind coming with me so long? So we can work out how everyone here knows everyone else, which you seem to know a lot about.' His arm executed an upswing as if to shepherd her along the path. Neither Vee nor Chlöe, crowded to her back like a fledgling to its mother, fell in line. The arm dropped. He flicked his head in the direction of the front entrance and abruptly strode off, a contemptuous click of his tongue slapping the morning air.

'Find Lovett now. Start with that blonde's room, then his,' Vee whispered to Chlöe. 'I doubt they've left yet. And call Nico.'

'I thought we weren't calling Nico!'

'Change of plan,' Vee muttered.

Vee rotated kinks out of her neck and shoulders as she trudged down the hall to the managing editor's office, apprehension stirring up her breakfast. She really wasn't up for it this morning. Investigating for *Urban* magazine had been one thing, but wading through the innards of the *City Chronicle* beast had so far proved a different adventure altogether. Yeah, definitely Jonah in the belly of the whale level of wading. Nico Van Wyk captained his ship using strangely different coordinates, ones she had yet to decipher.

'Bugger off,' he barked in answer to her knock. 'Unless it's Johnson.'

The office was cool and furnished with austere, practical taste, a man's space. *Chronicle* was close to the top floor of the office building, the room swept through from a perfect angle by breeze. Envious as always, Vee thought of her cubicle next to a sealed-off window.

'Overtaking specific projects without permission.'

She blinked. 'Beg your pardon?'

Rifling through the filing cabinet behind his desk, Nico didn't turn or look up. 'Seat,' he pointed. Vee considered declining, thought better of it and sat.

He pulled a sheet from a folder and sank into his chair. He vigorously massaged his face with both hands before dragging them over his head, buzzed short of honey-brown hair to downplay the balding dome on top, and down the back of his neck. Deep-set, grey-green eyes that saved his face from being plain were rimmed faintly with red. He stared for ages. Vee squirmed. Finally, he smacked a palm on the desk in a 'let's get down to it' manner.

'Saskia can't stand you. You're not madly in love with her either. She says you're messing about with the online team, making it hard for her to do her job. Why can't you learn to stay out of her way? You've been here over a year. You should have the hang of it by now.' He glanced at the piece of paper in his hand. 'Meddling.' He looked up. 'Why do you do that?'

Vee sighed. He was quoting from one of the reference letters in her file, and she would bet her right arm this one was from none other than her old boss, Portia Kruger. 'I'm not meddling. Not exactly. It's just . . . Saskia's the office manager but she barely manages. She's fulla *wahala*, everything got to be palaver with her. She's more concerned with running people than she is about quality output. Who cares if I help the web guys? They're understaffed.'

'They're doing fine, all things considered.'

'They're not. What things considered?'

'Backchat and authority issues.' He tapped a line on the piece of paper, nodding emphatically at her sceptical expression. 'Seriously, that's really on here. Kruger's thorough.'

'Can I get a copy of that?'

'What do you think?' He leaned back again. 'What's your deal with Anton?'

Vee threw up her hands. 'You mean Saskia's toilet paper. He's more comfortable with Afrikaans, why can't he be on the Afrikaans editorial?'

'He should get comfortable with communicating well in both languages. Chlöe Bishop does.'

'Chlöe is half Afrikaans. And she studied languages at UCT. Anton can catch up if y'all give him chance to breathe.'

'Propensity to preach and pick up strays,' Nico intoned, making an invisible tick against the paper. Vee muttered a curse and sat back. If he was all systems go for a verbal flogging, she wasn't going to help him at it.

'Oudtshoorn.'

'Hehn?'

'Oudtshoorn. You know where that is?'

Vee flicked through her mental archive. 'Mossel Bay?'

'Further. Out in the south-western Cape, Klein Karoo country. The Grotto Lodge is a two-star establishment out there, and they're gunning for their third this year. They put on their best face during last year's World Cup and still didn't get it. They're not letting it go this year, and that means they need all the stellar reviews they can get.'

He slid a thin manila file, open to a brightly coloured pamphlet, over to her. 'Looks nice enough. Apparently it was a hot-spot during the soccer, though God knows why anyone would want to be some-where as beautiful as the Garden Route when it was pissing down at kick-off last June. Anyway, bloody tourists never seem to give a damn about realities like the weather.' Sighing, he rubbed his eyes hard enough to wrinkle his forehead. 'It's gone up in the revolving door ratings with the number of tourists and ministers wives that have been passing through. If they need more positive spin, it can't hurt. They get publicity, we get advertising.'

Vee gave the leaflet a polite perusal throughout his speech. Adorning the front was a hulking, rustic building of indeterminate architectural style squatting amongst some dusty red boulders. 'Quaint' was the first word that leapt off the blurb inside. She closed it. The look she shot was an admixture of 'I'm not following you' and 'I think I am, but you can't be serious'.

Van Wyk looked weary. 'Look, I'm sure you're aware of Lynne being on maternity leave. Again. She's all we've got on travel and tourism right now. The usual piece on accommodation hotspots can't marinate till she gets back. It needs wrapping up.'

'And who say I know about travel writing? I'hn know nuttin about it. I can't even whip up a dozen synonyms for "picturesque".'

He cracked a whisper of a smile. 'It's a tad more involved than that.'

'Exactly. And I'hn know anything about what those involvements are.' She opened the folder, didn't know why she had, and snapped it shut again. 'Nobody else want this?'

'There are people who do.' He paused. 'No one I'd want or trust to give it to. There are those who could but can't, because we barely have any free hands. That leaves you. And Tinkerbelle.'

The ones you neither trust nor want to hand it over to.

He coughed. 'Sorry, that came out wrong. I'm certain you can handle this.'

'So . . .' Vee took indignant pause. '*This* you're willing to let me do. But you won't put me on the crime desk full-time. When that's the job I was promised.' Khaya Simelane and Andrew Barrow, long-running autocrats of their page, were still holding firm on blocking newcomers. 'I've done courses and learnt so much about web media and editing, which I use all the time working with the online team. But no, I still can't *join* the online team, that's got only *three people* despite that it's more popular than the print edition. Darren appreciates the extra help, but I can't even put my two cents into the webpage without issues. Because of Saskia Schoeman.' *Who you're sleeping with, on top of your liquor problem. Hey, maybe you got drinking problems because you messin' round with her, wouldn't be surprised. But we only here to talk about my shortcomings.* Vee bit the insides of her lips closed.

'It's complicated. And I fully appreciate how empty that sounds. You were candid and emphatic in your interview about not being shunted through various departments willy-nilly as you'd been at *Urban*. For the most part I've kept my word, but—'

'I know. This is an emergency. Always is, always will be.'

Van Wyk replied with a long, granitic look. Vee tipped a curt nod, took the folder and got to her feet.

'Hang on.' He folded his arms and eyed the ceiling, toying with an idea. 'I've been meaning to, and I guess now's as good a mood as any to ask. Did you take it?'

Vee furrowed her brows.

'Year before last, the case you had . . . with the thing . . . and the crazy family . . .' He twirled a finger in the air, indicating she jump in with the elusive words. 'The missing Paulsen girl,' he snapped his

fingers finally. 'The pay-off. That the client offered you for your . . .
diligent services. Did you take it?'

'*Excuse me?*'

'Johnson, come on.' He puffed in dramatic exasperation. 'Listen,
you've got something. First of all, you don't play games, which,' he
clasped his hands in gratitude, 'goes a long way to making my life
easier. Top reason I can't stand working with women. Besides the
dramatics and all the time off they need to pop munchkins, of which
I'm bloody *gatvol*.' He sat up straighter. 'What I'm getting at is, I need
to know my people. Now you *know* there've been whispers about this.
And I know that *you* know that *I've* heard, and if I've heard, then I've
wondered. So . . .' he presented open palms. 'You'd hardly be the first
or last journalist to take an incentive if they felt it was deserved.'

Stock-still, Vee felt a nimbus of heat plume between her eyes. 'You
jokin' me, right?'

Van Wyk shook his head.

'You got to be jokin' me,' she insisted, surprised at the dangerous
rasp in her voice. She turned, swayed through the door and almost
slammed it behind her.

Vee fumed at her desk for a quarter of an hour, eyes lost in the sunshiny
world through the window as a pulse thumped in her neck. Finally,
loosing a string of expletives under her breath, she grabbed laptop,
handbag and keys.

'I beg your pardon?! Where do you think you're going?'

Vee gruffly shouldered past Saskia and continued towards the exit
without a backward glance.

'Hey! Where're you off to?'

She whirled on Chlöe.

Chlöe took a step back, eyes widening. 'For heaven's sake, what
happened now?'

Without a word Vee turned down to the underground parking,
leaving Chlöe staring after her with a 'what the hell?' look on her face.

The Pink Oysters

Shafinaaz Hassim

The athaan pierces the cool morning air. Birds scatter over the rooftops of Mayfair's dishevelled houses, remnants of a colonial past. From my window, I can see a police van – officials trying to disperse the crowd gathering around an old Mercedes Benz, its boot gaping open. I've seen this car in the neighbourhood, often stopping to visit at the house across the road. A dodgy, oily-haired fellow emerges now and then, turns to look around before he goes into the house and hurries back to his car when he leaves. There's no sign of him today, just this abandoned car, and many curious people. I amble across the street to find out what has happened. The police have managed to part the crowd; I slither through the path created in time to see the police photographer flash his camera over a bloodied corpse squeezed into the open boot. The body of the odd, oily-haired man is unmistakeable. His eyes are open, looking fitfully ahead, even in death.

Another athaan echoes, this time from the mosque two blocks away competing for believers' attention, nagging me to get back to my reason for waking early. I return to my modest rented room. The dead man's face follows me through my day. By late evening, a knock on the door makes me reach for a torch and the front door keys. Power outages have become common in the winter. There are too many homes suckling off the city's power grids like ever-hungry babies. I open the door to reveal Mahmood Hassan, a local Somali trader, and my bearer of news and business opportunities. I usher him in, allowing moonlight to poke holes in the dark.

'I brought some tea,' Mahmood holds up a flask.

'Thanks, man,' I say, reaching for two mugs from the dish rack. Mahmood is fidgeting with the zipper on his jacket. He seems nervous.

'So, you see what happened in this street this morning?' he says. I merely nod. I still don't know what to make of it.

'It's a problem for us,' he says, intent on turning this into a discussion. I don't take the bait. I don't really want to know. 'Irfan, do you realise what happened?' he probes.

'I saw it. I saw that guy's body in the boot, it was horrible. Maybe he was screwing some guy's wife while the man was away at work and he got caught,' I spill words and shrug. 'Hectic story, but who cares?'

'Ai, Irfan,' Mahmood snickers. I've annoyed him. 'It's bigger than you think. Come, let's go see old Fidel, he's waiting for me. And I'll tell you the story when we get there.'

'I haven't seen Fidel in months,' I say. I'm not complaining. He's not my favourite person.

'I didn't come see you to make nice chit chat,' Mahmood's tone changes. 'Fidel has a big job for us.'

A groan escapes my lips. Mahmood shakes his head at me and walks out the door, starting up the engine on his motorbike while I grab a jacket and lock up. The smell of death lingers. The face of the dead pervert accompanies us through the streets to Main Road. The bike comes to a stop outside a barber shop, and I jump off. Mahmood cuts the engine and climbs the pavement and then he walks the bike through a narrow side alley. He rests it against a decaying wall stuck with bits of a poster from some Bollywood flick. The voluptuous Kareena's bare midriff and heaving bosom try to replace the dead man's face in my mind. A loud guffaw breaks the effort; Fidel's voice echoes from the canteen a few steps away. Something tells me I'm not going to like this. I drag my feet and follow Mahmood towards the scattered tables. Fidel is seated at one of them with a suited guest, his men sitting at the tables playing card games, turning around now and then to inspect new arrivals. Fidel sees Mahmood and motions to his guest to step aside.

'Mahmood . . . *kay fahaal ya* Mahmood,' he greets. 'Take a seat, take a seat.' His mockery is evident.

'Who is this boy?' an irritated Fidel asks Mahmood, nodding his head in my direction.

'My man, Irfan,' Mahmood offers. 'He'll do our job.'

The ruckus at the table beside us ceases.

'Ah, this is good news,' Fidel passes a toothy smile over me.

I still don't have a clue what this is about.

'That guy fucked it up. And now he's a bag of *kak* in the boot of his car. *My* car. He didn't even pay for it,' he says. 'You sure he can do this?'

'Tomorrow night. Consider it done,' Mahmood says. His eyes haven't left my face. He gets up and pushes me towards the door. I don't see Fidel's face again. 'We need this job. You don't ask questions. I done many things for you. And only you can do this, you look like your Indian brothers. Paki what-what,' he mutters.

'I'm not Indian or Pakistani,' I say, annoyed. 'So at least tell me what this is all about?'

We're walking the bike to Fordsburg. I'm struggling to keep up with him. The smell of tandoori chicken, paan masala and ganja filters in spirals through the crisp air.

'Don't give me excuses, you know what I'm saying,' he reprimands. 'He just wants us to finish the job that stupid Faisal was supposed to do, before he got killed . . . Deliver a parcel. Return with the money. Simple. And you'll fit into the crowd with your clean Paki face. No one will suspect a thing.' We stop at the corner of Mint Road and Central.

'What parcel? How much money?' I dare to ask. I'm wasting my time. He doesn't usually give me details. Cars are whizzing by but I manage to catch his words, somehow.

'Diamonds. Fifty million rand.'

Mahmood briefs me on what I need to do when we get back to my place. Our cut will be huge, enough to keep us happy for a few months.

The next morning, he has a brand new suit delivered to me. Salman brings it over.

'Mahmood says you're going for a job interview,' he says, his idiot grin plastered on his face.

'Eh, yeah,' I say, retrieving the suit and slamming the door in his face.

By evening I'm sliding across town in the back of a private cab to attend the wedding of some Indian industrialist's daughter at the Sandton Convention Centre. I'd had a shave and slicked my hair back the way they do in those mafia movies. I've always wanted to do that. But then I change my mind at the last minute. I don't want to attract too much attention. My clean 'office boy' look will have to do.

It doesn't help that as I make my way up the elevators to the main hall, women who look like shimmering mermaids glance in my direction. The weight in my left jacket pocket echoes my heartbeats. I slip into the reception area trying to figure out how to find my guy. Signals. Something. A short bald man in a white suit approaches me. He has far too many rings on his hands, clutching a glass of something sparkling.

'Areh, Kamal, your mother would be so proud, look how you've grown, son,' he slobbers over me, hugging me and patting me on the back.

'Eh, Uncle, I'm sorry. You must be mistaken . . .' I mumble.

'No, no! I'm quite sure Sarita would have been so proud. Super proud, my boy!' he raises his voice, and then lowers it. 'It breaks my heart, you know. She was so young, so lovely, so very, very young,' he laments, shaking his head, looking tormented.

No. I don't know. I glance around nervously.

He continues to pat and prod, shuffling me towards a table laden with cakes.

A muffled screech of ecstasy from a pink-shrouded shrimp of a woman and my gushing friend is off, leaving me standing beside tables of cake and mithais, biscuits, baklava and fondant. A waiter appears with a tray of samoosa and pakora.

'Do you have oyster, instead?' I test.

'Eh, no sir,' he stutters. 'Only pakora.' But he doesn't offer his plate as he says this, eyes shifty, he disappears out of sight towards what must be the kitchens or serving area.

Almost immediately, another waiter appears.

'If it's oysters that you prefer, they are served on the balcony, sir.' He motions for me to follow him. Password accepted. This is my cue.

Once I've stepped out on to the terrace, he vanishes behind me.

Strong hands grab my upper arms, lifting me slightly off the ground and into the shadows.

I'm patted for weapons and shoved back on my feet.

Something doesn't feel right. I pat my pockets to confirm. They're gone! The bag of diamonds is gone.

'Looking for this, young man?' the man in the white suit steps into view, holding my bag of goods.

I'm confused. And potentially fucked.

'Thanks for the delivery,' he says. He throws a set of keys at me. My early days of playing cricket in the streets of Kabul come in handy; I'm holding the keys to a Toyota.

'Car is in the back. Payment in the boot. Enjoy your dinner before you go. Just don't leave it out there too long, as you know, Johannesburg isn't too safe as a safe.' He chuckles now. 'Get it? Safe for a safe!'

The two guys behind me also burst into laughter.

I'm not getting the lame joke. I make a retreat to where the car is parked.

I don't know where else to go, so I drive to Rafi's place in town. I use my old key to draw open the roller shutters and pull the car in. Rafi is asleep upstairs. I return to the car and click open the boot. A sea of tightly packed wads of R200 notes greets me.

I've never seen so much money in my life.

I guess this must be what fifty million rand in pink notes looks like. The Pink Oysters, as Mahmood said.

When I awake for early morning prayers from my makeshift bed of cardboard and sheets on the floor, Rafi is standing over me nodding his head. 'Where have you been? Did you get a job?' he asks, every bit a reminder to me of my mother, his youngest sister. I'd come to South Africa on his request. Things would be better here, he'd said. He didn't say that a University of Kabul degree in Philosophy would mean nothing, except as a tool to console myself.

'Yes, Baba. I have a job. You know. I told you. I work with Mahmood, the Somali guy.'

'And this car?' he asks.

'Just a delivery for a client,' I say.

He creases eyebrows but says nothing. He turns and walks away.

I dial Mahmood's number from my mobile.

'Ha, who's this?' The line is bad but I can tell that it isn't Mahmood.

'Salman?' I enquire.

'Yes, Irfan bhai,' he confirms. And then he goes silent.

'Where's Mahmood? Why do you answer his phone, useless idiot, give him the phone!'

There's silence. Why does he have Mahmood's phone?

'Mahmood is dead,' he finally says.

'Huh? What shit are you talking?' I manage to blurt, my head buzzing.

'I found him dead in his room last night. I don't know what happened, bhai,' he says slowly.

The line goes dead.

My heart races. Mahmood, dead? Who killed him? Fidel? Or the same guys who killed the oily-haired guy? I could be next. I have Fidel's money. And I don't know what to do with it.

Rafi's linen and towels are stored in a cupboard in the garage. I retrieve a large quilt and pull it over the car. I've locked it. The set of keys feel like a rock in my pants pockets.

I take a walk into the city to clear my mind.

When I return at noon, Rafi is surrounded by customers. Afghan Fruit Shop. His pride and joy for the past fifteen years in this land of opportunity. I used to work here when I first arrived. He gave me R200 a week. The shop earned him about R14,000 a month after expenses. An honest living, he said.

I slip into the garage where I'd attempted to hide the car and slide to the floor next to it.

I'm not sure when it is that I fall asleep but I awake to the sound of Rafi talking to someone at the top of his voice.

The Pink Oysters are attracting flies.

'I don't know where the boy is,' he says. 'If he did the job, he must be at home now.'

'If he hasn't done the job, he better be dead!' the man screams back. I recognise Fidel's voice. But how did he know where to find me?

I peek through the gap in the wooden door between the garage and the front of Rafi's kiosk.

'That Mahmood tried to double-cross me. Just like Faisal, I had him finished off. You better tell that boy of yours, Salman will come after him too,' Fidel warns, kicking the fruit table at his side. Tomatoes, green beans and potatoes scatter on to the pavement. Anger flashes across his face; he returns to his car and drives off.

Rafi remains still. I watch him as he slowly turns around to look for a towel, pulls up a plastic chair and sits down to wipe and cover his face. His mobile rings, he ignores it. It rings again.

'Yes. Yes, I had a visitor. This is getting out of hand,' he says to the caller.

Rafi is disappointed.

What have I done?

I have a car with fifty million in the boot. And I don't know what to do with it. I don't know how to guarantee that they won't just come back and kill me and Rafi once they have their money.

I wait on the floor of the garage until the city quietens down. Then I go back to my rented room in Mayfair. The walk is treacherous, I realise. Any of Fidel's men could be lurking about. But I can't use a car full of hard cash.

When I get to my place, the lock on the door is broken; the street light throws beams through the opening. My dilapidated couch is slashed, spilling fluff where the fabric has been split. Dishes have been broken, my possessions strewn all over the place. I always carry my passport and papers with me. But the money I keep in a small plastic bag under the kitchen sink is gone. Even if Fidel's men have been here, I know that it's been a free-for-all ever since, now that the door has been broken open.

I open the little cupboard under the bathroom sink and find a small roll of money where I'd last left it, wrapped in a toilet paper roll. My last R2000. Some relief: I'm not totally done for. I return to the small front room. The silhouette of a short man in the doorway is unmistakeable. Salman. He flashes a grin at me.

'I've been looking for you, Irfan bhai,' he says.

'How are you, Salman?' I reply with caution.

'So sad about Mahmood, bhai,' he says.

'It's sad,' I say. 'Do you know why they killed him?' I pick my words carefully. 'What was his mistake?'

Salman is silent. He doesn't have a response.

Salman laughs. He can't stop himself now. I stop picking things off the floor and stand up to look at him.

'So you really don't know,' he says.

Another silhouette appears behind him. He barely glances back.

'Irfan bhai, come. The Trader is waiting for us.'

I don't have a choice in the matter. He steps back as two men enter the room and usher me to a car parked outside. I'm made to sit between them on the back seat as we make our way through the darkened streets of Mayfair. Salman sits in front, muttering into his phone. We stop outside a rundown building on the edge of Fordsburg. I am dragged out and we make our way inside, taking a lift to the third floor.

Two raps on the door of 308 and we step inside across the creaking floorboards to face Fidel. The Trader.

'So you found him,' Fidel says. 'Where's my money?' he asks. He lifts himself off the chair he's been sitting in and walks towards me. 'Did you do the delivery, eh?' he slaps me before I can answer. I'm knocked off my feet. His men lift me up.

'So, you and Mahmood think you're clever? You want to take the money and go?'

I have no idea what he's talking about. I knew Mahmood. He would have been happy with the cut from the deal. And Mahmood was no idiot.

'Mahmood didn't want the money,' I say. I'm his only defence. I have to say something.

Fidel laughs. A long menacing bellow emerges from his ugly face. The stench in this room makes me sick.

'I want my money,' Fidel says. 'You take me to it, or I kill that old man. His time is almost up anyway, and we like doing favours for friends, eh Salman?' he says. A big smirk stretches his mouth.

'The car is in town. My uncle doesn't know,' I say. 'I've parked it away at the back of his place. Fidel, you can have your money, I did what I was told. But please don't hurt Rafi. He's a good man.'

'Just give me my money,' he says, shoving me back to the car. Salman drives.

Within minutes we're parked outside the fruit shop. The streets will remain deserted until the early crack of dawn when the mishmash of foreign Muslim traders wake for prayers. I turn the key in the garage door and we make our way inside. The quilt has been moved aside, and the glint of the Toyota's surface is evident. Fidel takes the key from me and opens the boot.

'Nothing!' he gasps. 'You lying bastard!'

I reach his side to stare into the empty boot of the car. The Pink Oysters are gone.

'It was all there,' I whisper. The tip of a blade fills me with dread; I hold my breath. Salman has a knife to my back.

'Liar!' Fidel shouts, his fist jabs my face sending me to the floor.

I hear a creak from the side door that leads to the shop. The last thing I need is Rafi coming in. They'll kill him. I shouldn't have brought them here. They're going to kill us anyway.

The door swings open. An unfamiliar man walks through the entrance, followed by someone who looks like a younger version of Mahmood. The resemblance is striking.

'Fidel, my old friend,' the older man says.

'Bilal Hassan,' Fidel replies, his voice barely audible.

I had no idea that Mahmood had brothers. These look like they might be. But my brain is fried. I could be hallucinating.

And then two more men enter the space. They move to check each of us for weapons. Even Salman is easily relieved of his. He makes no attempt to resist.

And finally, Uncle Rafi enters the garage. He doesn't look at me.

'Fidel,' he says. 'You've finally delivered.'

Fidel looks confused. 'The Pink Oysters were for the Gora,' he says. 'If they don't get their money, they'll kill all of us.'

'The money is in the right hands,' Rafi says.

What does Rafi have to do with this?

'It will help our people. My people and your people,' Bilal Hassan explains. 'If the Gora get it, they will buy more guns and send them across to their soldiers.'

'It was a deal. Mahmood messed it all up,' Fidel begins.

'Ah, you didn't understand,' Rafi says. 'The diamonds were brought from Angola to help the migrant community. Survival is difficult in this country. But you didn't understand. You were greedy, Fidel.'

'But now, you and this Salman; you must pay for Mahmood Hassan's death,' Bilal says. The Gora will take care of you. That is your fate.'

Hassan's men are ushering Fidel and company out of the garage now, and back to their car. I can't make out what the Trader is muttering all this time. I'm in a daze.

Finally, Rafi turns to look at me. 'You did well. And we lost a good man. But it is time for you to leave this country. Your work here is done. You will move on with Said Hassan, Mahmood's youngest brother. We have work for you in the North.'

He looks at Bilal, the oldest of the Hassan brothers. Bilal nods in agreement. The decision is final.

The crackle of athaan can be heard in the distance signalling a new day.

Echoes of Mirth

Abubakar Adam Ibrahim

I used to like my brother's girlfriend, until she desecrated our house with laughter not long after Mammy died. Being just fifteen at the time, I thought it inconceivable that there would ever be any hilarity in the house until Princess came and startled grief with her laughter.

It happened two weeks after Father had put up Mammy's portrait in the dining area, right above her chair that no one had had the audacity to move. The picture had been taken years before, before her eyes had become listless like stale pap and she had withered like a maize stalk in harmattan and her hair had fallen out. Before they had cut off her breast.

Mammy had always insisted that we have dinner together like every family ought to. She simply would not have this ritual violated. Not even Father's caprices or Audu's pungent smell of frustration would intimidate her into giving up dinner time. She would not allow arguments or squabbles at the table and even Father could only fume at most. We would forget about the epileptic power supply, the stifling corruption, the scorching sun, the shortage of rain or its excess, the bad day at school, at work, the ever climbing inflation rates, our combined frustration whose sheer force alone could have blown down the house, and for that sacred hour, dwell in the benign illusion that everything was fine.

We maintained the ritual in her honour even though Audu had indicated he no longer wanted to be part of it. He had missed dinner one night and Father had insisted we wait for him. Asabe, tired of fiddling with her cutlery, fell asleep at the table and Ladidi was yawning like a hungry hippo every other minute. Father and I sat facing each other, trying to avoid each other's eyes, until Audu came back at almost 10 p.m. He was shocked to see us still sitting at the table, eyeing the untouched food.

'Now that you are here, we can eat,' Father proclaimed.

'I'm sorry you waited but I'm not hungry,' Audu said. The muscles on his temple flexed lightly, rapidly, as he ground his teeth, something he always did when he was agitated.

Father looked at Mammy's portrait for a long time and sighed. 'Your mother would not have been pleased with you,' he said gravely and looked down at the spindly green beans on his plate.

That settled the matter. Audu never missed dinner after that. He went to his unhappy work where he taught an unhappy subject to students who, I was almost certain, were equally unhappy. I had never been to his school and he had never invited me. I did not think I would like it because of the smell of frustration that hung about him like a vulture over a carcass. He would come back home and go to the room to read before dinner. After dinner, he would go out – to see his girlfriend, Princess, I suspected.

Power-pole thin and tall, Princess was perhaps even taller than Audu but I could not really tell. Her dark skin, spangled with sweat beads, always glistened and her eager breasts jutted out almost obscenely. It must have been her likes that those first marauding white men saw and decided to call us *blacks*. Her astonishing red lipstick made her teeth look unnaturally white and her smile false. She was always kind to us but I did not want her coming often because that meant I had to keep out of the room I shared with my brother as long as she was around. He had been planning to move out before Mammy died and I had been looking forward to having the room all to myself. But whenever she visited, I would suddenly want to get my football boots or my exercise book or one such trifling thing or the other. Audu would frown each time I knocked on the door.

That day when she came, I found the need to fetch my school bag for my assignment. Twice I went to the door and turned back. The third time, I raised my hand to knock when I heard her profane the house with her laughter over a joke Audu had made. I stood by the door listening. When I left, I went to the flame tree that Mammy and I used to sit under and sulked until Audu came and asked what I was doing there.

'Nothing,' I said and walked away from him, resenting him for even making a joke in the house Mammy had died in. The issue of Princess's laughter never came up again.

Audu did not say much to anyone but his grouchy presence was enough to quell any fermenting unrest in the house. Even little Asabe dreaded him. Sometimes, she would raise some juvenile racket because Ladidi would not let her play with Mammy's trinkets. No amount of pacification would appease her, not even long after she had forgotten why she started crying in the first instance. But once Audu's shadow darkened the threshold, she would slink away and sulk instead.

Ladidi took full charge of the kitchen. She made decisions with aplomb since she no longer had to ask Mammy what we would have for dinner or breakfast; or what she should buy at the open market that was flooded with mud during the rains. She took care of Asabe and did not grumble about washing her sister's clothes, or getting her ready for school on time. And she did not spend as much time at her friend Salia's place.

I got up every morning and went to the tap nearby to fetch water – that was on the rare occasions that the tap ran – otherwise, we had to make do with water from the well that seemed to have been flavoured with iron chippings. I fetched pails upon pails and hauled them to the storage drum. Sometimes, when she felt like it, Asabe lent a hand; that often impaired more than enhanced my efficiency.

Father was often distracted. He would go to work and return early to sit on the veranda staring into the distance as if he expected Mammy to walk out of the setting sun and ask him why he was moping about, massaging his shoulder and telling him everything would be fine, as she always did.

Sometimes I woke up at night and saw him through the cracked windowpane sitting in the dark under the flame tree, a drab blanket draped over his shoulders.

There was a haunting emptiness that had occupied the house since Mammy died. It was like a huge shadow that spewed out of the doors and windows on to the premises, like stealthy, monstrous fingers reaching out to grab you before you could change your mind about coming back home, sometimes reaching as far as the foot of the flame tree. The curtains of gloom that draped the windows since Mammy fell ill seemed to have been dyed with deeper shades of disconsolation. My spirit sank each time I returned from school and came within view of that house. I felt it was bound to remain forever unhappy. We were the trapped remains of the drowned, floating in salty dreariness with no hope of redemption. And so, we would sit at the table and have dinner and no one would utter a word except maybe to thank Ladidi for her cooking, a rote offering previously made to Mammy at the end of each meal. The first time we did that Ladidi wept.

But one night, Father broke the silence and said, 'Audu, when will you be moving out?'

Audu looked up, startled by the question. He stalled by taking a sip of water and took an eternity to set down his glass. Then he cleared his throat. 'In about two weeks,' he said.

Father continued eating, dolloping tuwo dipped in the vegetable soup garnished with smoked fish. We thought that was the end of the conversation. Then, like Audu, Father had a sip from his glass and cleared his throat.

'Your brother is thirty years old now,' he began, addressing no one in particular. Like one of those eccentric poets, he could have been reading a poem to the grasses on the fields. 'He is old enough to be on his own, start a family, have a decent job . . . but he doesn't have that because this country is so warped.' He banged his fist on the table, as if it had anything to do with the country being warped, as if it was part of the problem. He looked at our faces like one waiting to be challenged.

'Audu ought to be on his own, God knows, because I was not living with my parents when I was his age. And so, if Audu decides to leave this house today, I will not blame him. However, Audu should think about this family also, because leaving so soon after your mother's death would not seem to me like the right thing to do because your little ones would want you to be around and guide them . . . I would want you to be around and guide them so that they would not feel

abandoned, first by their mother, God rest her soul, and then by you.'
He was looking into Audu's eyes now.

Ladidi coughed once. The sound filled the silence like a single
gunshot in the night.

'This family must not break apart,' Father continued, this time
eyeing me. 'I will do everything in my power to keep this family intact
and so Audu, if you want to leave, feel free and may God be with you
but I would also want you to think about what I said.'

Father dipped his fingers in the soup again and continued eating.
We were all quiet, looking at Audu, who was looking down at the
half-empty plate before him.

'I understand, Father. I will stay a little longer,' he said at last.

Father nodded proudly. He reached out and squeezed Audu's hand
and continued eating enthusiastically like one assured of victory in the
war to keep his family intact. I did not want to sully his enthusiasm but
I knew he was wrong, that he would lose. I had dreamt about it.

In the gloom-filled ambience there was a consolation of sorts. Salia,
that glittering heroine of my fantasies, would come with a rainbow-
coloured whirlwind in her wake. She would bring smiles and the
fragrant smell of happiness. She became a regular visitor to the house,
mostly in the evenings when she and Ladidi would retreat to the
kitchen and gossip while my sister made dinner.

I would stop by the kitchen entrance, listening to her and imagine
that if light had a sound, it would be Salia's voice. I watched her every
gesture, each gaining some amorous dimension and floating in my
lovelorn mind. Sometimes she would turn and see me, starry-eyed,
looking at her. She would smile and say, 'Hi.' My throat would fill
with bubbles and I would only manage to nod.

'Want anything?' Ladidi would ask.

I would shake my head, my eyes on Salia's slim neck, her bare
shoulders, her graceful hips well positioned on the stool, her sensu-
ous ankle around which was clasped a glittering silver anklet. I would
swallow with difficulty and leave. Sometimes, I went to the bathroom thereafter.

Then, one night, Salia decided to sleep over. Apparently, Ladidi had confessed to her that she was frightened of the dark, increasingly so since Mammy's death. Salia came over with her night things and had dinner with us. She was shy because of Father. And even though not much was said, I think that was the best dinner I had had in a long time. I looked up from my plate periodically to see her. Then everyone else in the room seemed to disappear and I imagined we were alone. She would smile at me. I would smile back. We would have dinner as two lovers.

'Salt, please,' Audu's voice crashed into my daydream. I must have frozen. They were all looking at me – Salia too. She smiled and continued eating. I smiled back, embarrassed.

'Hey, salt,' Audu demanded again. There was a hint of mockery in his voice. I passed him the salt and ate, not daring to look up, mindful so as not to repulse her with any of my loose table manners.

She came to the house regularly after that, sometimes spending the night. I did not know exactly how her father approved her visits. He was neither the gentlest of men nor the kindest of fathers. A towering mobile police sergeant with a fondness for drinking, he had a face always begging for a shave and his crooked nose must have been broken in some drunken brawl. His eyes were bloodshot and his lips darkened by tobacco. He would come home, charging on his motorcycle, his rifle slung over his shoulder and drive straight at those who sat under the bushes of Queen of the Night on his facade. Because of the platform and the sweet smell of the bushes at night, lovers made the place a haven. Often, I had fancied myself and Salia under those bushes, whispering sweet, poetic words to each other. Her father would come and chase those unfortunate lovers from his bushes, hurling curses and stones after them. Sometimes however, he would go about his business, not in the least concerned about their amorous presence. Even on such days, it was difficult not to envisage him as the venal officer he was.

Since his first wife fled from him, when Salia and her brother Bala, my friend, had been very young, he had had one other wife whom he had beaten to a pulp once. From the hospital, she had gone back to her parents', effectively dissolving the marriage. He gave up on marriage and had had a string of girlfriends, some of whom had stayed months in the house and packed out just as unceremoniously as they had been brought in.

Often, I have wondered how something as sublime as Salia could have come out of something as crude as he, or how my personification of love could have been the progeny of as loveless a marriage as her parents had had. But Salia seemed to have handled her troubled childhood with grace as she had everything else. She had been forced to mature early, be wise and prudent and learn to look the other way when her father was at his worst, which, unfortunately, was often.

I happened to be passing by the bathroom one morning when I saw a beige chemise hung out to dry through the half-open door. I had the notion that it would be hers, it must be hers. I pushed the door and went in. It was soft and alluring – silky, just as I imagined her skin would be. It smelt of her; the warm smell of cocoa butter. I crumpled it and tucked it under my shirt and scurried away.

I spread the garment on my bed and imagined her in it, imagined it to be her. I caressed it affectionately as I would her tender skin. I lay on the bed, next to the chemise, dreaming I was lying down next to her, feeling her warm breath on my face, her smooth skin against mine. I imagined kissing her lips, caressing her breasts. It was so real to my mind that I gasped involuntarily and a sublime sensation rippled through my body. I rolled and rolled on the chemise until I was exhausted and fell asleep, dreaming of my dream girl.

'Hey, what the hell are you doing?' Audu thundered. I started and discovered I was encumbered by Salia's beige chemise. I was embarrassed.

'What the hell were you doing?' Audu asked again, sniffing me, looking about him.

'Nothing,' I said unconvincingly.

'What do you mean nothing? What the hell is going on here?'

'I said nothing.' I struggled into a sitting position fearing he would soon alert the whole house.

'Whose stuff is that?' he fingered the chemise, trying to draw it away from me. I held on to it.

'Let go,' I gasped. He was stronger and was gaining. I could see the shadow of menace creeping into his scowling face and I knew he would soon resort to underhand methods.

'Let me have it!'

'Please, let go,' I pleaded.

'What on earth were you doing with it?' He was still tugging.

'I said nothing!'

'You want to be a transvestite, right, *dan daudu,* eh? You pathetic puppy!'

'No!'

'Then what in heaven's name are you doing with ladies' stuff?' He grabbed my hand and started twisting my wrist.

'No!' I screamed. 'It fell. I picked it off the ground.'

'Shameless boy, I will . . .'

'What is going on here?' Ladidi's voice rang with alarm from the door. I looked over Audu's shoulder at her face, trying to make sense of our dubious entanglement. Audu turned, using his bulk to shield her view so she could not see me trying desperately to wriggle out of her friend's underwear.

'What's happening?' she asked, suspicion creeping into her voice. She started coming towards the bed.

'Ah . . . nothing, just rough-housing,' Audu stammered. He stood in front of her. She tried to look over his shoulders but he was taller.

I got out, crumpled the chemise and tucked it between the bed and the wall and jumped off the bed.

'There's something going on and I would like to know,' she demanded.

Audu held her by the shoulders, pushing her gently backwards.

'Nothing is going on,' he said. Looking over his shoulder and seeing that I had concealed the incriminating evidence, he smiled wickedly and let her go. 'What do you think is going on?'

She looked from me to him. He was smiling and I was sweating. She pushed him aside and came towards me and I feared she would find the underwear.

'Ladidi.' Salia's golden voice floated into the room and filled it with a subtle light. Instead of joy, on that occasion it filled me with dread. She was standing by the door, looking into the room.

Ladidi turned to her.

'Hi, Audu,' Salia said.

'Hello,' he said. He was obviously enjoying my dilemma and would have done anything to make it last. 'Why don't you come in?'

While she weighed the invitation, I prayed she would decline.

'I was just looking for Ladidi,' she said.

Ladidi eyed Audu and me with menace before going past Audu and leaving with Salia.

Audu was snickering as he closed the door and turned to me. He looked at my face and broke into a wild laughter that would have startled the night spirits. I never thought I would hear him laugh like that. He fell to his knees, his body jerking, his laughter ringing in my ears. I was, above all, relieved that in his own mischievous way, he had bailed me out. I felt exhausted by my trauma and slumped on the bed. He picked himself from the floor and came and sat next to me, laughing all the time.

'So, you like her, eh, don't you?'

I said nothing.

'But she is older than you, you know, do you think it would work?' he asked seriously.

I turned my back to him.

'Hey, come on, I am on your side, you know. I could talk to her for you.'

'No, thank you.'

'This is a free offer, you know. Just take it and I will work things out for you.'

'No.'

He laughed. 'Well then, if you want to be rolling in ladies' underwear all your life, fine, but don't say I didn't offer to teach you like any decent big brother would do.'

'I won't,' I said, frowning.

He pulled me to him and started tickling me. I did not realise I was laughing at first, perhaps because the sound of my laughter sounded strange even to me. But Audu tickled so hard I was trying to get away, screaming for him to stop and laughing up to the ceiling without inhibition.

When he stopped and we were lying side by side, trying to catch our breath, it occurred to me that I too, and Audu as well, like Princess, had desecrated the memory of Mammy. We had laughed in the house in which she died. And I felt as if I had betrayed her.

But Audu lifted himself on his elbow and said, 'Wow! It's been ages since you laughed.'

And he was tickling me again and I was laughing and laughing and laughing.

The Old Man and the Pub

Stanley Onjezani Kenani

Monsieur Bentchartt's offices are on Rue de Chantepoulet, on the same side of the street as the Payot Bookshop, which is to the right when coming from the Cornavin train station. If you were the well-fed type intending to burn some fat, you could walk all the way to the seventh floor via a steep, dimly lit staircase. But I chose the easier option, via a lift, as I had no intention of arriving here panting.

In the tiny lift, I stood face-to-face with a petite strawberry blonde whose height matched mine. As is often the case in these parts, you don't greet or so much as nod, much less smile or arch and collapse your eyebrows or look into the eyes of a stranger, so I minded my business as she minded hers, my eyes pinned on the digital panel that indicated floor numbers as we ascended. You can imagine, then, how awkward it was to find that both of us got out on the seventh floor and came to the same office where, I discovered, she was Monsieur Bentchartt's secretary returning from lunch.

At once her demeanour changed. She said *bonjour* and showed me a seat as she told me her name – Alina – and I likewise told her mine, Kadam'manja, which she asked me to write down as I had no business card. She attempted to pronounce it loudly, but managed to reach only as far as 'da', and gave up. I put it down to my poor handwriting. Alina started flipping through the pages of her diary, eventually stopping at one where her finger jabbed thoughtfully for a moment. 'From the Irish pub?' she said.

'Yes, I am the owner of the Irish pub,' said I, hoping I did not sound boastful.

'Monsieur Bentchartt will see you soon,' she said, with an attempt at a smile.

This is how I now find myself ensconced in a chair in this office, facing the small, dark-haired bespectacled man who goes by the name of Bentchartt, and who, a week ago, surprised me by sending me a letter summoning me in a matter concerning his client, Mr Brandenberger. Unfortunately for me, today is not an easy day to see this man, who is now leafing through an enormous file, and who, so far, has not said a word to me beyond a greeting. I am supposed to be at the pub, quelling a protest, which may very well flare up into some sort of third world war. All my five bartenders are threatening to resign and, from the glares I got last night when we last discussed the matter, especially from the guy from Burkina Faso and also the one from Guatemala, some are likely to resort to violence. I haven't paid them last month's wages, and we are now well into the middle of another month.

When I came up with the idea of opening an Irish pub ten years ago, after losing my job at Hope for Humanity, there were all the indications that I had made an excellent decision. My bank did not hesitate to support me with capital – a quarter of a million francs – with which I rented the premises on Rue de Lausanne, opposite the old Catholic church of Notre Dame. Although it was a one-man business, I went ahead and called it the Three Little Boys Irish Pub, believing, as it were, that the name gave it an Irish air, and that customers would have no reason to think that the owner of the pub was neither Irish nor that he had never been to Ireland. This, I told myself, was not deception. It was business. I assume you don't need to first visit China to offer Chinese cuisine in your restaurant, or to visit Italy for you to obtain a licence to sell pizza. And I presume any outfit that sells pizza or pasta reserves the right to call itself an Italian restaurant, or whatever nationality the owner wants the restaurant to be identified with, because, as anyone may agree, over his business an individual is sovereign.

The tiny community of Malawians to which I belong was obviously disappointed, but I did not mind. Naming my business the Malawian Bar would signify that I was angling for a slice of the market that comprised African expatriates as customers, and there was already a joint on Rue de Monthoux – the Nairobi Bar – enjoying the lion's share of that clientele. Mamadou Niang, a fellow I once made the acquaintance of, opened a Senegalese Bar on Rue de Berne a few blocks from the Nairobi Bar, and Mamadou's was way better than the Nairobi, as it was more spacious and had two washrooms, but he was unable to attract many clients from the African community, and he found himself compelled to close shop a few months after opening. So, in my case, I had a choice to call it the Malawian Bar, and struggle to build the business – seeing that nobody I met on the streets of the city seemed to be aware of Malawi as a country – or to make a decision that made more business sense.

I did some things to make the place resemble some of the Irish pubs I had been to. I put shamrocks on the walls, fixed television screens in every corner to show football games, piped in the music of Chris de Burgh and other Irish musicians, sold Guinness on tap, and made sure that the atmosphere in the bar was conducive mostly for conversation, with alcohol only as a lubricant. From time to time I tried my best to ensure that some of my bartenders were Irish students looking for opportunities to make an extra buck.

For a while I believed I had hit the jackpot. Not only did I have the whole of Ireland under the roof of my bar, but also clients from mainland Europe flooded in, such that it became necessary to make minor improvements, in the form of interspersing Irish music with classical hits. We were probably among the best Irish pubs in Switzerland. Until a year ago, that is, when real Irish fellows opened a pub right next door. Now I consider myself lucky on those nights when as many as seven customers turn up, and on many nights nowadays the clientele is entirely Malawian. I am even considering renaming the pub the Malawi Bar. I guess I have no choice. I figure I could wrestle business from the Nairobi Bar. I will bring Anna-Maria Ramirez, the girl from Santo Domingo who serves at the Nairobi Bar, to my pub. I will make her an offer she cannot refuse, as they say. I will stop playing Mozart and Mahler, and fill the room with Fela Kuti and Allan Namoko. I anticipate that with such a remake I will stand a chance of attracting more than seven customers. In this awfully expensive city of Geneva, a bar cannot run on the custom of seven people. All my savings have gone towards the rentals and the replenishment of stock and the taxes. I am no longer as lucky with the banks as I was ten years ago. Now things are getting out of hand, as the boys have lost their patience.

In the middle of the brewing riot I was forced to come here. I am curious why this lawyer wants to see me.

'Monsieur,' he is now speaking. 'I act on behalf of the estate of our client, Mr Brandenberger.'

'So you said in your letter,' I say.

'Your name is rather unusual. Where do you come from?'

'What is a usual name to you?'

'I mean no offence. It's simply unusual because I am failing to pronounce it. Which country do you come from?'

'Malawi.'

'Mali,' he smiles. 'I had a friend once who came from Mali—'

'I said Ma-la-wi.'

'*Je me suis trompé*. Where's that?'

'Have you heard of Mozambique?'

'Yes, I have. There was a war.'

'Two wars, actually, before and after independence. We share a border.'

'I see. And what do you do in Switzerland?'

'I own a pub.'

'A pub?'

'Yes. The Three Little Boys Irish Pub on Rue de Lausanne.'

'Why Irish?'

'Why not Irish?'

'I'm just curious.'

'That's a business secret.' He does not laugh.

'So,' says the man, getting down to his business. 'How did you know Mr Brandenberger? How close were you?'

'Why?' I say. 'What has happened to him?'

'Maybe you should first answer my question. Did you know him?'

'I know him, of course.'

'Would you mind telling me on what grounds?'

'But, sir, what do you want to know? What has happened to Mr Brandenberger?'

'First answer my question please, Monsieur. The information you will share is very important for me.'

'Is it to do with the police?'

'The police? Not at all, Monsieur.'

'Ah, Mr Brandenberger . . .'

Tall, lean and feline, Mr Brandenberger was an old man who came to the pub every Friday night, always at seven on the dot, and always in a pair of blue jeans and a white shirt, his white hair combed backwards, his chin clean-shaven, with a pair of large spectacles resting on his nose. There is a corner – the one whose window faces the Notre Dame church – where frequent patrons of the pub avoided sitting on Friday nights, and new customers were discouraged from occupying. It was this corner Mr Brandenberger would walk to at the appointed hour and sit without a word, drinking carafe after carafe of Cabernet Sauvignon Syrah at an alarming but steady rate. He was always alone. He would sit there the whole night, except when he made occasional trips to the washroom, at which point one of us would make sure that his drink was secure until he returned to the table. I never saw him wave or smile at a familiar face. I never saw him tap his foot to the music that filled the air until two in the morning when the bar closed down. As soon as the clock struck two he would take out money from his wallet, and, whatever the number of carafes he had drunk, he would count the cash accurately. He would then add five francs on top as a tip, the meanest tip of the week, all of which he left on the table, put a carafe on top of it, as though he feared some wind might blow it away, after which he walked out of the bar without a word.

For nine years he did that. New bartenders were discouraged from attempting to engage the man in conversation. It was clear his preference was to be left alone. I personally made sure that every Friday night Mr Brandenberger's wine was adequately stocked. If there was none in the nearby Denner shops, suppliers in neighbouring France would be called. The most reliable of them was in Ferney-Voltaire.

About nine months ago, Mr Brandenberger stopped coming. It was a Friday and his corner was reserved but he did not arrive. Other customers asked, 'Where is the old man today?' But nobody knew the answer. He failed to come the following week, and the week after that, and the month after that, to this day. I concluded that he, too, had followed the others to the real Irish pub.

'Is that all?' Monsieur Bentchartt interrupts.

There is more. There were some nights, though such were few and far between, when he would try to outdo himself. On average he drank six carafes a night, which makes three bottles of wine. But on those rare nights he would attempt to take eight or more carafes, after which he would throw up in his corner.

We took care not to reprimand him. He was an old man, about the same age as my father back home. We would at once call for a taxi. I would personally take him to his apartment on Avenue Pictet-de-Rochemont across the lake, where he lived on the eleventh floor. This was how I got to know his name, more than a year after he had started drinking at our bar. I noted on his door that the name panel read 'V. Brandenberger'. I never found out what the V stood for. On some of those nights, he was in no position to pay for what he had consumed, but we never brought the bill to his attention the next time he showed up. We wrote it off. For the trips to his apartment, we met the taxi bills from the bar's takings.

There was one night when, on arrival at his apartment, he seemed to have recovered a reasonable slice of his sobriety. He insisted that I should come in. He asked me my name and where I came from. To my surprise, not only did he know my country, but he also knew the name of its founding president. 'Hastings Kamuzu Banda,' he said. 'A charming fellow, wasn't he? Always going about carrying a white horse-tail for a flywhisk. Why did he do that?' In a city where nobody knows whether your country exists at all, finding someone who knows it well is like chancing upon a man from home. I was in a hurry to return to the bar as it was after the ungodly hour of 2 a.m., but I accepted a shot of whiskey, as he himself reached for tonic water. His apartment was spacious, but its furniture was cheap. There was an old piano in the corner, a painting of a woman on the wall, and lots of books in German, French and English.

'How did you come to know about my country?' I asked.

'Well, when youth and blood were warmer, I used to travel a lot,' he said. 'Somebody spoke of the rare beauty of your lake. I decided to visit Malawi with Tatiana, my wife, God bless her soul. We went to other parts of Africa, to the beautiful national park in Kenya, Masai Mara, and to the Lalibela Temple in Ethiopia. We also travelled to other continents in the thirty-nine years we were together, but it was Africa whose diversity never ceased to astonish us. In all the seventeen years that Tatiana has been dead I have never been outside the canton of Geneva. I see no reason for travelling anywhere alone.' His voice was becoming sad.

I had to leave. The boys would be getting impatient, as they could not leave without handing over the night's takings to me. And on Friday nights, after closing the bar, they descended on Déjà-vu and other nightclubs where girlfriends were waiting to dance with them until sunrise.

One may be deceived into thinking that when he next showed up at our pub, Mr Brandenberger would greet me like a long-lost cousin. But no, he went straight to his usual corner and ordered carafe after carafe, until he paid his bill, added the five francs on top, and left.

In fact we never had another conversation. When I met him on the tram, he looked at me as though he had never seen me in his life before. I once dropped off at the same stop with him on Rue de la Terrassière. He was carrying many things in paper bags, groceries it seemed he had bought from Migros. As he was struggling, I approached to offer to help him carry them to his apartment, a block away, but he refused as though I was a suspicious-looking stranger. He did not seem to recognise me at all. 'Pas de souci,' he said, 'pas de souci.' He left without adding, 'C'est gentil.' I went away having resolved not to offer to help him again, except on those nights of madness in our pub.

It was probably a year after the groceries incident that he stopped coming to our bar. At first, we thought the pub next door had stolen him from us, like they had most of our customers. But we ventured on spying missions to the bar on many Friday nights, and never saw Mr Brandenberger there.

'Why are you asking me all this, anyway?' I say to Monsieur Bentchartt.

'Well,' says the man, 'Mr Brandenberger died nine months ago.'

'Oh, God!'

He takes from his file a copy of the *20 Minutes* newspaper. 'Man bequeaths ninety-five per cent of fortune to charity,' reads the title above a black-and-white photograph of Mr Brandenberger, in all likelihood taken when he was younger than the last time I saw him.

'And he has bequeathed the remaining five per cent, which is three million francs, to your bar,' says the lawyer. 'He says you were, in the later years of his life, the only family he knew.'

I have tears in my eyes, unable to comprehend the kindness of the old man. How could someone be so generous to another whom he hardly knew? I rise from the chair. I want to laugh and dance. I want to hug the lawyer across the table. The bar will not close. 'The bar will not close!' I say, and the lawyer looks at me, puzzled.

I need to buy myself a car and an apartment. I need a holiday, maybe to the Lalibela Temple Mr Brandenberger spoke of. Anna-Maria Ramirez from Santo Domingo, you would be a fool to reject my offer. Come to my pub. Let the Nairobi Bar fold, who cares?

I shake hands with the lawyer who is asking me to send him my bank account details. His voice sounds as if he is speaking underwater. I cannot hear him as clearly as before.

I forget to take the lift and descend the stairs, two at a time, falling, rising, running, until I reach Rue de Chantepoulet, like Archimedes gone mad, shouting, 'Eureka, eureka!'

I run past the Payot Bookshop to the traffic lights at Rue de Lausanne, where I do not wait for green. I cross to the curses of infuriated drivers, and their '*Merde!*' slides like water off a duck's back.

I arrive at the pub where the boys are all perched on bar stools, helping themselves to drinks instead of getting the bar ready for customers. The protest is underway. Plunder and let Rome burn, they think. You can see their stony faces. You can see the way they all ignore me. If they had hoped to see me disappointed, it is they who must be disappointed, because I say, 'Give me a Jameson's, Boys! Make it a double. And a carafe of Cabernet Sauvignon Syrah. Let's raise our glasses to Mr Brandenberger!'

Sometime Before Maulidi

Ndinda Kioko

At the oceanfront, a man in an embroidered hat stands with his donkey, watching the ocean hit the banks, threatening the land beyond it. Above him, at a balcony in the *makuti*-thatched guesthouse, a traveller watches the morning arrive.

The traveller's name is not Anah.

She watches the sun peep its eye into the day, slowly rising from below. The residual darkness that had been lingering on top of the water disappears, and the darkness which had collected in the anchored dhows fritters away. The morning is now the colour of the ocean.

The traveller whose name is not Anah is visiting the Lamu archipelago. She arrived this morning from Nairobi, then Malindi and then Lamu town. She is here for *Maulidi,* Lamu's *Milad-un-Nabi.* She is here to switch off her mind, to get rid of the stain of everyday noise, to shake off the dust that has accumulated over the years, to have a new conversation, to eat new foods, to swear in a different language, to litter another part of the world with pieces of herself, to think of nothing except wonder what it feels like to be a cloud, to dip her feet into the talcum-soft sand, to look at the sea and in the reflection, recognise herself.

At least that's what she keeps telling herself.

But the traveller whose name is not Anah knows why she is here. She is here because she has just buried her husband. It is where she first met him, during the previous year's *Maulidi* festival. She is also here because it is the last place the bus stopped.

As she watches the ocean, she remembers sitting in a coffee shop

with her friend Boni two days before. She remembers him congratu-
lating her for a good funeral, as if it were a birthday party. She remembers him telling her that she is still young, that someone else will find
her; and then wanting to tell him that his tea is getting cold, and
suddenly forgetting, and then getting lost in the crowd below – the life
of the street sucking her in. She remembers watching the street as she
is watching the ocean now – the street, ominous as the ocean; the
ocean, not as seedy as the street.

At the foot of the throng that winds through the city alleys after
5 p.m., she remembers beggars and hawkers laying down their wares,
each one of them fighting for a chance to cash in on Nairobi's rush
hour. She remembers the city council van, parked at a hidden pavement, the *askaris* hawk-eyed, ready to pounce, a woman clutching her
handbag, tight under her armpit, a man bumping into another as they
cross the street, and then before an insult is hauled, the realization that
they know each other from somewhere, an open window, a jump, a
scream, 'My phone!'

She remembers hordes on the street coming and going, crossing and
almost crossing, and waiting for a *matatu* to cross first, and then crossing
and skittering for the only bus.

'*Gari ya mwisho! Gari ya mwisho!*' the touts chorusing, beating their
hands hard on the body of the bus, calling commuters' attention to the
last bus of the night. Each bus is the last bus.

As she watches the dhows bob in the ocean, she thinks about the
people she saw on the street that day. She wonders where they were all
going, where they were coming from, and if they were cared for in the
places and spaces they belonged to.

As with everyone else she has met and is yet to meet, she wonders
if they watched the news the day her husband was murdered on the
street, and what they said if they did. She wonders if they clutched
their husbands and their children close, and if they know loss by its
first name. Then promptly, it hits her how arrogant it is for her to
wonder about such things. She reminds herself that it is in the
loyalty pledge. One pledges their loyalty, their readiness and duty
to endure loss.

'*Suspected gangster killed, two guns and explosives recovered.*'

She remembers his fear of guns almost at the same time she remembers the curliness of his hair and how much she hated his overuse of the outmoded Hair Glo.

The traveller whose name is not Anah remembers thinking about all the mothers she had seen on television, clutching old photographs, speaking of sons who never made it home. She wonders how it must have been for them – sitting, waiting, hoping that each knock on the door was from their son's fist.

Then she remembers the overwhelming urge to be in a moving bus – the hankering to enjoy solitude in motion, and then suddenly asking her friend to take her to the bus station.

'Isn't it too early to go home? You should wait out the traffic.'

She remembers how this reminded her of her grandmother:

'*You have come home with darkness.*'

'*You should go to church sometime, get a pastor to bury you when you die.*'

At the bus, she remembers the man with the receipt book.

'Where to?'

'Where is it going?'

'Lamu.'

'That's where I'm going.'

And then her friend pulling her out of the bus, telling her that it is not so good for a girl to do these things by herself. She remembers texting him after eight hours on the bus, in the potent pride of a lone traveller, apologising for her aloneness.

'I'm learning the world again, alone.'

She is here now, learning how to watch the ocean, alone.

Her attention shifts back to the man in the embroidered hat and his donkey. She watches him watch the fishermen dock their boats and the parade of dhows bobbing in the water. A new crowd of weary visitors, mostly white, alights from the boat that has just docked after the short hop between Manda and Lamu. She watches the awe in their faces at the first sight of the old town – perhaps shocked by the closeness of the town to the ocean, or annoyed by the lack of space.

She remembers Issa's love for the island.

'They don't know our cruel, harried world. Their world has been softened by the ocean and the gentleness of the wind. We should move here'. She remembers him laughing lightly.

'You'd finally get a chance to finish your book.' She remembers forgetting to ask him what he'd be doing.

She pretends he is here. There is a way her heart feels – like the residual warmth on a seat when someone who has been there for a while stands up from it, or the warmth left in your hand after a long, firm handshake, the sudden feeling of contentment, loss and indigestion.

The traveller whose name is not Anah tries to remember why she loved Lamu in the first place. She knows it wasn't for the same reasons Issa loved it, but she cannot recall exactly why at first. But then she remembers being struck by how the fishermen named their boats – *Kipendacho Moyo,* the one the heart loves. *Lamu si Kenya*, Lamu is not Kenya. *Nipe Nikupe*, give me, I'll give you. *Wape Vidonge Vyao*, give them their medicine. She also remembers loving how in the afternoon, the smell of *biryani* and old spices wafted its way from people's kitchens through the thickly coral stone walls into the tiny streets that squeezed their way through the old buildings.

She loved the silence in Lamu.

She hated how everyone knew everyone new. She hated the idea of not being in a moving bus for days, not losing herself into the busy streets in the city. She hated the sight of the arrogant ocean, how it took up all the space, squeezing the people into a tiny strip of land.

Now, the traveller whose name is not Anah is here, learning to love the things he loved that she didn't.

For a brief moment, she wonders what day of the week it is, not sure if it is Thursday or Monday. She might have forgotten, but she remembers one thing; that today is her father's birthday. He chose it one day many years ago when she asked him about his birthday and, unable to remember, he decided it was the expiry date on the insecticide tin he was holding.

She wonders if she should call him, and what she would say if she were to call him. She wants to tell him that she loves him, but between her and her father, such incoherence is known, not uttered. These words are strangers to her father's lips. She wouldn't even recognise them if he uttered them.

But she knows her father loves her. He tells her all the time when it is raining or when he is planting.

'It's raining.'

'We are planting.'

There is a way he says these words – as if the rain carries a message in it from him to her, and each time it falls, she should be listening.

She stops thinking about her father and goes downstairs for breakfast. She sits at a table that allows her the view of the ocean. The waiters watch her watch the ocean. When she eventually goes to the counter to ask about the holdup, the man in blue uniform apologises.

'Most girls who come here do not buy. They smoke cigarettes and wait.'

He brings her *masala chai*, and she holds out her small cup, no paying attention to him. She continues to watch the ocean, responding in a slight gasp each time the waves slap the land with force. She finds it threatening; how the water hits the seawall with force, rising to form an ephemeral wall. She wonders about the language of the ocean; the language between the ocean and the land and the language between the ocean and those it has swallowed. What things do they say to each other when no one is listening?

'You learn to love the ocean,' the man in the blue uniform says. She smiles and sips her *masala chai*.

When she is done drinking, she takes a walk through the maze of narrow, shady streets squeezing their way between the coral stone walls. It is almost high noon, but some of the alleys are dark, too dark to see. The further she goes, the darker and more deserted it becomes. As she makes her way through the alleys whose walls threaten to hug each other, she remembers what the guide said about the slab above some of the narrow streets; it connects the two families once their children get married.

In one of the shadowy corners, she finds a man in his *kanzu*, rubbing his donkey's back. It is the same man she watched in the morning, sitting at the *daka* porch outside one of the intricately carved wooden front doors. She extends her hand in greeting and he ignores it nonchalantly.

'Are you a journalist?'

'No.'

'I was hoping you were.'

Before he continues, the muezzin calls the town to prayer. The shadowy alleys that were empty a few minutes before are now filled with men in full length *kanzus* and embroidered caps, hurrying past her. The man who was rubbing the donkey jumps on its back and hits it lightly on its stomach and riding away, without another word to her.

Later that evening, while having a drink at the floating bar, she meets the man in the embroidered hat again. He stares at her, and in his eyes, they meet, as if for the first time.

'Why are you sitting alone.' It doesn't sound like a question.

She joins him and his friends, and amidst trivial conversations and tremulous laughter that ripples the water at their feet, they ask her who she is here with. She wants to tell them that she is not alone. That she is here with Issa.

She makes an excuse for her solitude, again, explaining that her husband was working. He couldn't get time off.

At some point, when the bar is full and everyone is drunk except her, the man in the embroidered hat invites her for a dance. Even though she is shy at first, she puts down her drink and joins him. Together, they are lost in the slow *Taarab* dance.

Later that same evening, the man in the hat invites her outside for a smoke. She follows him. He leans on the rails separating the floating bar from the water and they listen to the ocean slapping against the tanks that hold the bar above the water. There is something even more threatening about the calmness of the ocean in the dark. In the near distance, she can see Lamu town, numerous dots of light emanating from the high windows.

He hands her a cigarette. She accepts it.

'You don't look like a smoker.'

'I don't smoke,' she says, holding it up for him to light.

Then she holds the lit cigarette between her fingers, watching the stick burn into ash, and then eventually the ash giving up, falling into the ocean. She asks him to light another one, and they sit in silence, both of them inhaling.

The traveller does not smoke. She however loves the smell of nicotine and the dark that grows on the hands of smokers from many years of cigarette burns. As she watches the ash drop into the sea, she thinks about her father, and wonders again if she should call him. She pictures him sitting somewhere in the dark outside his house, smoking one cigarette after another. She can hear his cough.

When they are done smoking, the man in the hat asks his friend for the keys. His friend looks at her and smiles. He then calls the man in the embroidered hat aside, whispers something to him, and then gives him a key. The traveller whose name is not Anah follows the man in the embroidered hat to a speedboat.

In no time, they are back in Lamu town. He leads her to a hotel with a carved teakwood front door. She follows him up the stairs to the rooftop, where she can see almost all of Lamu town sleeping below her. The man tries to kiss her, but her lips are cold, too cold to kiss. He then removes a handful of leaves from his pockets. He smiles at her. She smiles back. He places a pinch of the leaves on a piece of paper and rolls them into a stick. Then he lights it and puffs. He hands her the roll and she smokes it, without a question. From the rooftop, they watch the old town orbit around the building. The more they smoke, the faster the town revolves. They laugh at nothing in particular and at such things as the wind.

He comes to stand next to her, and when he touches her, it is as if thousands of hands have touched her face. She wants to ask him if he knows Issa. He pushes her to the wall and kisses her, without removing his hat and he begins to walk back to the building. She follows him down the stairs, and when they get to the room, she demands that they take a shower first.

'You first,' he says.

She goes first.

When he is done, without wiping the beads of shower water off his skin, he pulls her to him and kisses her gracelessly, and then he asks her to close her eyes.

'I have something to show you.'

After two seconds, he asks her to open her eyes. His embroidered hat is off. He is bald, with just small bushes of curly white hair at the back of his head. Without his hat, he looks thirty years older.

'Please don't leave.'

There is a way he fucks: in chunks, like he is about to give up, and then going back to the beginning and starting again, like a generator that is running out of fuel.

'You have beautiful eyes.'

She kisses him angrily and shuts him up.

She wants to ask how old his daughter is, but instead, she thinks about how changing the position of your reading table or reducing the distance between your bed and your window can suddenly change your life completely.

He seems to have forgotten that she is there with him, and as she watches him in the dim light she feels like she is watching a man masturbate inside her. She drifts off again and begins to think about the man she once dated – and how her dreams were as big as the space between the four walls he paid rent for.

When he is done, he collapses next to her. A few minutes later, he lights a cigarette and offers her one. Then he kisses her. There is a way his kiss tastes; one can tell that it is the last one.

'You never told me your name.'

'It used to be Anah.'

'Why is it not Anah now?'

She is tempted to tell him about the man who gave her that name, but by the time she decides, he is already asleep. She rests on the bed for a bit. As she watches the ceiling, a strange feeling of incompleteness engulfs her. She feels like she is part of a circle that is broken and she doesn't know what to do with herself outside this circle. She dresses and leaves.

The man in whose boat she rides to Shela Beach later that morning has long curly locks, all dyed brown. He does not remember her from before. She asks him if he enjoys what he does, just like Issa asked him when they were riding in his boat a year ago.

They talk about Nairobi, and he refers to it as if it is another country. He tells her that in his thirty-two years, he has never taken the bus. She has heard this story before.

'I have no need for the bus. I don't want to know what's beyond the bus.'

'They hate us there,' he says, after a long silence. As he says this, he cuts through the water with his speedboat, angrily.

She knows what he means. She wants to contribute to this conversation somewhat, to tell him about the pool of blood that day on the street. Before she speaks, he points at another island across the lagoon where mansions and luxurious guest houses stand, their oppressive and clean white almost swallowing the blue in the ocean.

'Two years ago, those used to be our wells.'

He cuts through the water angrier this time.

'A woman was killed there, and then the others started to leave. No one lives there now.'

He asks her what she would do if a man walked into her house and started bringing down the walls. She does not answer.

Later, she walks on a thin pavement at the edge of the ocean, walking back to where schoolgirls seem to be coming from, where everyone else seems to be coming from.

She spots more writings on walls, more writings on docked boats and others that bob in the ocean. *MRC* (Mombasa Republican Council), *Lamu sio Kenya. Pwani sio Kenya.* Lamu is not Kenya. A flag here, and a sketch of a currency there.

She comes back to a restaurant and looks for somewhere to sit. She asks the waitress if she can get a table for one. They offer her a table for two. The binaries of the world refuse to leave her alone.

In the evening, the sun sinks and the lights come up. In the darkness, the shacks in Lamu town and the private guest houses on Manda beach become equal, reduced to light bulbs, each one of them a mote in the oppressive darkness, squeezed into size by the pompous ocean.

Beyond the shack under which she listens to the ocean and watches a Swahili pre-wedding celebration on the street, the water is a few inches away from her, but quiet in the dark. The man wearing the embroidered hat from the night before is leading the dance procession of men. He is the groom's father.

She thinks about the previous year's *Maulidi* festival.

She wants another cigarette.

She should call her father.

from the novel

All Our Names

Dinaw Mengestu

Looking out at the capital from our secluded corner reminded me of a story my father had told me about a city that disappeared each night once the last inhabitant fell asleep. He was good at telling stories – not great, like my uncles and grandfathers, who revelled in the theatrics. Compared to them, a story was a solemn occasion delivered in a calm, measured voice that nonetheless left a lasting impression on anyone who was listening. He told me that story about the city that disappeared at night shortly after I developed a sudden, irrational fear of the dark. I must have been ten or eleven at the time, old enough to have known better than to be afraid of something so common and simple as the end of the day, and well past the age of bedtime stories, but for the first few nights of my terror, my father indulged me. He told me one night about the countries thousands of miles to the north of us where months went by without the sun setting – hoping I would find comfort in knowing that the world didn't end simply because the lights went out in our village.

According to my father, the city in the story was once a real place. 'I'm not inventing this for you,' he said. 'Everything I tell you is true.' I believed him in that semi-conscious way that children have of dismissing reality in the hope of finding something better. 'For hundreds of years,' my father said, 'that city existed as long as one person dreamed of it each night. In the beginning, everyone kept some part of the city alive in their dreams – people dreamed of their garden, the flowers they had planted that they hoped would bloom in the spring, or the onions that were still not ripe enough to eat. They dreamed of their neighbour's house, which in most cases they believed was nicer than their own, or the streets they walked to work on every day, or, if they didn't have a job, then of the café where they spent hours drinking tea. It didn't matter what they dreamed of as long as they kept one image alive just for themselves, and in many cases they would pass that image on to their children, who would inherit their house, or attend the same school, or work in the same office. After many years, though, people grew tired of having to dream the same image night after night. They complained. They bickered and fought among themselves about whether they shouldn't abandon the city altogether. They held meetings; each time, more people refused to carry the burden of keeping the city alive in their dreams. "Let someone else dream of my street, my house, the park, the intersection where traffic is terrible because all the roads lead one way," they said, and for a time, there were enough people willing to take on the extra responsibility. There was always someone who said, "OK, I will take that dream and make it my own." There were heroic men and women who went to sleep each night when the sun set so they could have enough time to dream of entire neighbourhoods, even those that they had rarely if ever set foot in, because no one else would do so. Eventually, though, even those men and women grew tired of having to carry all the extra parts of the city on their backs while their friends and neighbours walked around, carefree. They also wanted their dreams, and one by one they claimed their independence. They said, "I am tired. Before I die, I want to see something new when I sleep." Then the day came when no one wanted to dream of the city any more. On that day, a young man whom few people knew and no one trusted went to all the radio stations and shouted from the centre of the city that he alone would take on the burden of keeping their world alive each night. "Don't worry," he said. "I'll dream of everything for you. I know every corner of this city by heart. Close your eyes at night and know that you are free.'"

From then on, everyone in the city believed they were free to dream about foreign lands, countries they had read about or that had never existed, the lovers they hadn't met yet, the better husbands or wives they wished they had, the bigger houses they wanted to live in

someday. The people gave that young man their lives without knowing it. They had given him all the power he wanted, and even though
they didn't know it, they had made him their king.

Weeks, months, and then years went by. People dreamed of living
on the moon and the sun. They dreamed of castles built on clouds,
of children who never cried, and while they dreamed each night,
their king erased a part of the city. A park disappeared in the middle
of the night. A hill that had the best view over the city vanished.
Streets and then homes were erased before dawn. Soon the people
who complained about the changes went missing. One morning,
everyone woke to find all the radio stations and libraries gone. A
secret meeting was held that afternoon, and it was agreed that the city
should go back to the way it had been before. But by then no one
could remember what the city had looked like – buildings had been
moved, street names were changed, the man who ran the grocery
store on the busy intersection had vanished. There was another problem as well. When asked to describe what the city looked like now,
no one could say for certain if Avenue Marcel and Independence
Boulevard still intersected, if the French café owned by a Mr Scipion
had closed or merely moved to a different corner. It was years since
anyone had looked at the city closely – at first because they were free
to forget it, and later because they were embarrassed and then too
afraid to see what they had let it become.

Those who tried to dream of the city again could see only their
house or their street as it looked years ago, but that wasn't dreaming, it
was only remembering, and in a world where seeing was power,
nostalgia meant nothing.

I thought of telling Isaac that story, but I didn't know how to explain
it to him without sounding foolish. The president cut the lights at
night, he might have said. So what? He did it because it made it harder
to attack. And though that was the obvious reason, I would have
wanted to argue that there was also something far worse happening.
The city disappeared at night, and, yes, he wanted to protect his power,
and what better way to do so than to make an entire population feel
that just like that, with the flip of a switch, they and the world they

knew, from the beds they slept on to the dirt roads in front of their houses, could vanish.

When the doors to the house opened, Joseph was standing on the other side, his tie undone, as if he had just finished a long night at a wedding, drinking and making speeches. He looked at once exhausted and relieved; whatever doubts I had about being welcome vanished as soon as I saw him again and he waved us in with a generous smile and dramatic sweep of the hand. Had I paid closer attention, I might have noticed that, as before, I hardly registered, and that all of his attention was devoted solely towards Isaac.

'You boys must be tired,' he said. 'I apologise for making you wait outside like that. I hope we didn't offend you. My colleagues are a bit nervous and aren't used to speaking in front of others.'

He was the only man I had ever met who spoke like that. It wasn't the accent but the words themselves that were striking, at once formal and yet seemingly more gentle, as if he were trying not just to communicate but to elevate whomever he was speaking to on to the same privileged plane on which he existed.

'We didn't mind,' Isaac said. 'We would have been happy to stay outside longer.'

It had been decided that Isaac and I would share my room on the top floor, and Joseph, the three other men, and the two soldiers with them would take over the rooms on the first and second floors.

'We are going to need all the space we have,' Joseph said. 'This is just the beginning.'

As he talked, two of the house guards quietly entered, carrying a mattress that must have belonged to one of them. Joseph stopped them just as they were climbing the stairs. He had them turn the mattress over so he could see both sides, and then said something in Kiswahili that made both of them smile and Isaac turn away in embarrassment.

That was the second time Isaac and I shared a room – the first had been back in the slums, after Isaac was kicked out of his house. Neither of us had slept well that night, fearful about what would happen next. I felt a similar fear that second night, though it was hard to know what lay behind it. We were safe in that house, at least for the moment, but there was something else at risk. Isaac seemed to know that, too. He didn't say a word to me after we entered the room, just undressed in the dark and went straight to his mattress, which had been placed opposite mine, next to the door. It fell to him to say that everything would be OK, even if we were both certain that it wasn't. As tired as I was, I couldn't sleep while he was visibly disturbed. I turned my back to him so he couldn't see that, though I was lying perfectly motionless, I had both eyes wide open.

Either my performance was better than I thought or, after an hour of silently waiting, Isaac no longer cared. Sometime around 3 a.m., Isaac rose from his bed. I didn't turn around to see him, but I could hear him pull back the sheet and put his pants on. He opened the door just enough to slip out; not until I was certain that he was gone did I turn over.

Whatever I had been afraid of left with Isaac. With him gone, I was asleep in a few minutes. I suppose I knew that night where he had gone, and I suppose I also knew that he was trusting me not just to keep that knowledge to myself, but to ignore it altogether. There was no secret to guard, nothing to deny, because, according to the deal we had silently struck, nothing had happened.

When I woke the next morning, Isaac was back in his bed. His pants and shirt were strewn on the floor just as he had left them when he arrived. He was, to my surprise, deeply asleep. I had never felt protective of him before. I had seen him injured, beaten, and knocked unconscious, and all I had ever felt was pity or sadness and maybe a bit of envy for his reckless courage. He had never needed me to come to his defence, and to be honest, I wouldn't have known how to. Had I woken him up and told him that when it came to me he was safe, he had nothing to worry about, he would have kicked me out of that house, and we would never have spoken again. I wanted him to know that, though, and so I did the only thing I could think of: I picked his clothes up from the floor. I folded his pants and shirt, just as my mother had done for my father and for me — a seemingly insignificant gesture that was still one of the things I missed most about living so far away from home. It had something to do with knowing that even in your sleep you were watched over, and that each morning, no matter what mistakes you might have made, you had the right to begin again. I laid Isaac's clothes next to his bed, which was how my mother had always done it; before leaving, I swept my hands over his shirt and pants to shake off the dirt and smooth out the wrinkles as best I could.

Number 9

Nadifa Mohamed

I have to take care on this floor. My narrow, high-heeled boots strug-gle to find purchase on the smooth white marble, flecked here and there with brown fossilised shells, relics of prehistory within the steel, glass and concrete of Hammersmith Broadway. I pause for a moment by the Tube entrance and gaze at the flower stall heaving with buckets of roses, tulips, irises, sunflowers, and baby's breath and wonder if he will bring a bouquet with him. I stand like a pebble in the cascade of commuters and take a deep breath. I won't get the Piccadilly line, I decide, the vertiginous escalators, the bad-tempered rush through the corridors and the awkward intimacy of a strange man's heart beating against my ribs in the humid carriage are the last things I need right now. I take the battered iPhone from my coat pocket and double-check exactly what he said in his last text:

loking forward c u by statu at 7

He is the fourth from the site and the tallest so far, 6'3" according to his otherwise bare profile. What he lacked in words he made up for in photos, he had uploaded eighteen from his travels but wore large mirrored sunglasses that concealed half his face in most of them. In the handful from Dubai you could see the remains of a woman who had been closely cropped from the images; a heavily henna-painted hand draped over his shoulder, the hem of an ornate abaya and gold sandals beside him and in one close-up the reflection in his lenses of a pretty girl with deep dimples in her cheeks and a red, lacquered smile. Even from that dim image I knew I wasn't as attractive as her. I'm not the kind of woman who makes men's eyes light up or who turns their heads in the street but neither do they seem disappointed when they meet me. The hijab has actually seemed to make them more intrigued in the few months I've been wearing it. The religious guys in ankle-skimming gowns and white prayer caps surreptitiously check me out now rather than scowling and muttering under their breaths, the white guys are the worst though, staring into my eyes as if I'm a snake that might be charmed.

I take the lift to the bus station and check my reflection in the glass doors. I look smart, presentable in a raspberry wool coat and black trousers. My threaded eyebrows are so perfectly arched they open up my otherwise small face. The black scarf around my hair is folded intricately around my jaw and held in place by a constellation of diamanté brooches. My stomach performs a small flip as the lift reaches the floor. I am early enough to take the bus and at this time the routes into central London are quiet; I can put my bag beside me, stretch out my legs and listen to my music in peace. I flip the music player to the next song and hear snatches of Arabic, Somali, Hindi before I finally settle on bass-heavy R'n'B. Walking lazily to the bus stop I speed up when I see a number 9 to Aldwych pull into the kerb. I press the Oyster card against the reader and see that the balance is low again, the money from my temp job at the hospital haemorrhages into these machines; I'm getting sick of struggling in this city alone, coming home to nothing but bills on the doormat. The route begins in the bus station and the Polish driver is still wiping crumbs from his thick blond moustache after his short break. I yank open the narrow, horizontal window to clear the smell of smoked kielbasa from the air and take my favourite position on the right-hand seats above the wheels. I sit a little higher than everyone else and the double-glazed panel serves as a picture frame to the snatches of city we catch from traffic light to traffic light. I know this route intimately, years of un- or under-employment kept me chained to London's buses, my internal clock in tune with the timetables and particularities of certain routes and even certain drivers. I know the impatient, the rude, the gener-ous, the late, the lecherous, all by sight. I also know this ring road

beside the station and the tall, modern office building outside of which
a young woman was raped recently, and the Iranian supermarkets and
restaurants garlanded with strings of light bulbs. The Kensington
Olympia is hosting a wedding show and I turn my head at the couples
exiting with plastic bags full of the crap that weddings seem to involve
these days. Would tonight be the start of that journey for me? I needed
to become like one of those women on the street, they were neither
perfect nor very individual, but had moulded their relationships into
something real and tangible that others could see. I would make him
believe that I was the right one for him; he could close the laptop and
step away because I would be all that he was looking for. He had
written that he would consider women up to the age of thirty-four,
my real age, but I had told him I was twenty-nine. I had fibbed that I
work in public health but in all honesty I sit on reception at an outpa-
tient ward. I also said that I had travelled to Doha and Thailand and
Brazil but haven't left London since a visit to my grandparents a
decade ago. All of these details are insubstantial; they say nothing of
whether I will be devoted, faithful, fertile, the qualities that these men
are looking for deep down.

The bus lane along High Street Kensington is clogged with
double-deckers and I browse the clothes shops as we chug along, the
heater under my feet burning the soles of my boots. A gaggle of Italian
schoolchildren in matching pink T-shirts clamber aboard at the stop
opposite the underground station while their beleaguered teacher
negotiates the fare at length with the driver. Just as the doors beep
ready to close, a bearded drunk staggers on. He presses the orange
cover of a freedom pass hanging around his neck to the reader and then
raises his hands to announce his presence.

The traffic clears and we fly past Kensington Gardens and the Albert
Memorial, the dead prince shining golden on his plinth, what woman
wouldn't want her man struck in metal? Eternally loyal, silent and
hard. I had chosen the Eros statue in Piccadilly as a meeting point to
force some romance into what so often feels like a job interview. The
little iron cherub with his bow and arrow also gave some charm to a
part of the city that teemed with fast food packaging, prostitutes' calling cards and lost tourists. Frigid trees in their winter nakedness stand

against the jewel-toned monument, it's impossible to imagine them lush, green and dense again but in a couple of months they will be clad in leaves and blossoms. The road widens to four lanes and doormen pose in red polyester frock coats outside heritage hotels with chintz curtains in their windows. I notice a nasty smell in my nostrils and turn away from the window; the drunk has moved seats again and is sitting beneath me. His thick, black, wavy hair is enviable but it's also oily and peppered with large grey flakes of dandruff. The smell is hard to pull apart but there is sweat involved and urine and perhaps even vomit. He feels my gaze on him and turns his head sharply back until it hits the rail hard. Our eyes meet and he gives me a hazel-eyed, bloodshot stare. He must have once been a good-looking man, poetic in a way, with strong eyebrows, long eyelashes and a full mouth.

'Suck. My. Dick,' he mouths slowly in an Irish accent, then giggles to himself.

I roll my eyes dismissively and return to watching out of the window. We have passed the new development of hundred million pound flats, and armoured Bentleys and Range Rovers wait, their hazard lights flashing, for their Russian and Chinese owners to return. A bat-mobile-like Lamborghini overtakes the bus with an aggressive roar of its throttle and then has to stop abruptly at a red light. I look inside its leather interior as the bus crawls up beside it; two young Arab men lounge inside in distressed jeans and garish T-shirts, they have the stiff gelled hair and trimmed goatees of low-rent male strippers but they exude wealth from the gold on their wrists and their necks to the stack of parking tickets stuffed carelessly under the windscreen wiper. They speed off with Arabic pop wailing behind them. We reach Harrods and I check my phone. Twenty to seven. Another ten minutes and we should reach Piccadilly.

The sky is indigo now and a squall of rain falls lightly on to my cheek from the open window, I slam it shut. The exterior lights studding the facade of Harrods are lit and the skeleton of the building glows orange. I hate the place; its expense, disorder and incongruous Las Vegasness. The Italian students disembark giddily, boys and girls brazenly pawing each other on the pavement, all tongues, hands and sexual entitlement. At that age I was terrified even to be seen walking beside a boy, the shame alone would have killed me; my desires were lived out only in my mind.

The bus feels airy again even though the smell remains. The drunk's legs splay out in front of him, his battered trainers tied clumsily around his toes with string, he smiles and hums to himself. A wealthy-looking family waits in the gangway for him to make room for their pushchair. The father is middle-aged, tall, sandy haired, wearing salmon pink trousers and a mustard tweed jacket, he must be cold but his face is flushed red. He tries to manoeuvre the buggy into the small gap while his blonde baby sleeps with her hands over her knees. His wife behind him is a narrow, brittle thing with chestnut hair and teeth that look like they have been whitened with Tipp-Ex. A shy boy in the clothes of a wartime evacuee, grey short trousers and a wool jacket with red piping, hides his face behind a new iPhone.

'Do you mind moving?' the mother says sharply to the drunk. Her lips move awkwardly as she speaks and I notice that they look swollen and stiff. Silicone.

He doesn't move but reaches for the baby's hands with both of his grimy ones, 'Allo gorgeous . . .'

The father jerks the pushchair back. 'What do you think you're doing? Leave her alone. You shouldn't be sitting here anyway, can't you see the sign?' he points a finger to the blue and white notice on the side, reserving this area for pushchairs and wheelchairs.

'I'm disabled, yer posh cunt.'

'I told you we should have got a cab,' the wife looks like she is about to implode with anger.

Their son looks with widened eyes to his father then mother and then back again. His thumb is still twitching as he absentmindedly plays a game on the phone.

His father tightens his grip on the pushchair, the skin around his signet ring draining to yellow, 'I'm not going to tell you again, clear off before I tell the driver to move you himself.'

'That playing-fields of Eton shite ain't gonna work on me, pal.'

'I'm not your pal.'

'Why don't you take yer anorexic wife and little ponce of a son and feck off yerselves.' He gestures dismissively to the exit and lounges even deeper into the seat.

I sigh, a fight seems to happen on every tenth ride I take, over petty nonsense like this mostly.

The mother rushes back to the driver and makes an appeal, her son staying close behind her.

People tut, kiss their teeth, curse at the unexpected delay. I check the time again. Eleven minutes until seven. I shouldn't worry, Somalis are always late and even if I'm later than him that will be a good thing. I'll look nonchalant, cool. Not desperate.

The driver turns off the engine and the bus sinks lower to the ground as does everyone's mood.

'Why don't you jump into yer Merc or Aston Martin? Didn't your *queeeen* Thatcher say only lowlifes get the bus? Fallen on hard times, have we old chap?' He puts on a fancy accent and then continues. 'One's been to Harrods and now one's heading to Fortnum and Mason's for one's turnips.'

I laugh despite my own irritation.

The parents huff and puff but they are impotent against him. I get the impression that the man is used to being listened to and obeyed in the same way the consultants at the hospital are; he just looks shell-shocked now, his hand constantly pushing his hair back from his face. His wife on the other hand has an edge to her; she has rolled her sleeves up and keeps trying to push around her husband to confront the drunk.

'We pay our taxes; we give money to charities that help ingrates like you! The least you can do is give room to a working family, you wastrel!' She thrusts her left hand in his face. A large diamond sends flares of light around her. She is more attractive suddenly; she looks alive and real.

'Cha! Jus' let the people sit down, bumbaclot,' a teenage boy with an Afro comb plunged into his hair shouts, poorly imitating a Jamaican accent. 'Why you have to go on? Keeping the whole damn bus waitin'.'

We murmur agreement.

'So youse pay yer fucking taxes, do yer? Bully for you! It's not like yer kith and kin didn't fucking rape Ireland over and over again, is it?

Oh no! You made all of your money from tea and scones and licking Prince Charles' arse.'

'I'm Irish, you dimwit! An O'Sullivan if that makes an ounce of difference,' her brogue comes out now, 'and it's people like you who made me want to leave in the first place.' The veins in her throat are pulled tight and her yelling makes her daughter startle awake. The child begins to cry and her father picks her up and rocks her against his chest.

'Well, you landed on your feet then, duckface.'

The wife slaps him briskly across the mouth and before she can do it again, the driver leaps out from the cab. 'All of you stop, police are coming, *you* and *you* have to wait here,' he says pointing to the mother and the drunk, 'the rest of you can get off.' His foreign intonation sits lightly over his words; he was probably something big in Poland but earns twice that salary driving buses in London.

The boy with the Afro comb in his hair presses the emergency release button above the exit doors and they wheeze open. He sticks his middle finger up at the drunk and shouts another bumbaclot. We follow him off, we're opposite Green Park Station and the traffic is blocked all the way up to the Circus. I decide to run rather than wait for another bus. Soon my shoes begin to slide against the damp concrete, I make slow progress against the crowds and lift my head only occasionally to measure the distance left. I can feel my make-up running from the sweat and damp air, I will look a mess by the time I reach him but I persist, led on by nerves and excitement. I cross the street and run past the Ritz, where I once saw one of my childhood movie crushes standing outside smoking a cigarette, up past Fortnum and Mason which has an ornate display of spring hampers in its windows before stopping to catch my breath. I need to walk so I don't look so frantic when I reach Eros. I pant past the Japan Centre and Waterstones and then take out my compact. I look awful; mascara under my eyes, my nose running, my lips puffy and dry. I wipe Vaseline over them, quickly tidy my eye make-up and then blow my nose. I look across the road but the crowd is too large to spot him. The last bit of natural light is about to disappear from the sky but the large advertising screens cast a digital glare over everything. I take a deep breath

and walk as elegantly as I can on my pinched feet across to Eros. I look
first for men, then black men and then Somali men but I don't see him.
I check the time. Quarter past seven. I swivel my head from side to
side, worried that I won't recognise him from his pictures, for some
reason my eyes begin to well up and I wonder how long I will have to
wait. I can't imagine not waiting, I have waited two weeks already for
this to happen, I don't even have food to go home to because I expected
to eat out with him. I don't care how desperate it makes me look, I'll
wait an hour if I have to. The rain starts to fall again, harder this time
and I move away from my position right under the bow and arrow.
Huddling in a corner with couples snuggling against the cold, I tell
myself that this is the last time this will happen, that I won't be the only
woman who doesn't have a man's arm around her after tonight, nor
the only one getting soaked while they hold their men's jackets over
their heads. I look up at the little iron brat and wonder why he never
sees me. My phone vibrates in my pocket and I plunge my hand in to
grab the call but it stops. I hold the phone close to my face and see a
black message box on the screen, my heart is pounding and I have to
read a few times before I understand what it says.

Sum ting came up, not gonna make it. raincheck?

from the forthcoming novel

Rusty Bell

Nthikeng Mohlele

Rusty Bell was a capable debater. I never knew when she would turn the tables, corner me with overwhelming facts. Once a week, mostly at the stroke of midnight, Rusty knocked at my door. We spoke, laughed, argued and reflected on things under the sun: poverty in the world, how sugar daddies preyed on willing campus sluts, sexual exhibitionism in America and, now, South African music videos. Our sudden friendship blossomed into walks around campus, to the fury and detriment of her multitude of hopeful suitors. I cannot say I did not enjoy basking in that glory, of being chosen.

Those midnight visits took a toll on my sleeping patterns, but the inconvenience of losing sleep was nothing compared to the bliss of seeing her throw her head back in unguarded laughter. It was during those visits that we stumbled on affectionate silences, that we resisted a magnetic desire to kiss. But it never seemed possible. So we kissed on the cheeks, like gangsters, conscious of the itch that got redder by the day. She, months later, developed audacious wishes: that I check her breasts for cancer lumps, for an opinion on a tattoo in provocative places (inner upper thigh, she wore an acceptable mini skirt; immodest silk under-wear), a night in my bed whenever she was at the mercy of period pains.

As much as we knew we were playing with live grenades, the pend-ing moment for looming wild unprintables, we also knew surrender to desire would ruin our friendship. It always felt out of place, incestuous even, every time we almost caved into desire. Besides being tempted by Rusty's elaborate sensuality, I resolved to live with my raging nocturnal terrors, my self-inflicted depravations.

But how, amid such rampant fornication, to new found and abundant campus freedoms, away from glaring prison walls of mothers, fathers and religion, was it possible that we upheld brittle chastity? It seemed like the seventies all over again, only without the rock and roll, without such promiscuity being synonymous with Aids and ruin.

It was, quite alarmingly, within the walls of David Webster Hall that I observed the foundations of adult life: lessons in deception, accidental pregnancies and abortions, flexible romantic thrills without the terrors of marriage.

It was at university that our characters seemed to form: minor triumphs, terrors reserved for our unknown future lives, dormant seeds of frustrations yet to come. I observed campus thrills and cruelties, the hunting Rusty Bells come rain or shine, bedding lovesick ugly girls and later accusing them of being ambitious stalkers. I submitted a paper on this, *The History of Life*, for which I dethroned Columbus with an unheard of ninety-five per cent.

I, to fortify my defences against the inevitable, the gangster kisses that would ultimately evolve into other things, introduced Rusty Bell to Columbus at a *Schindler's List* screening at the School of Drama. That was the day Columbus, laughing as always, disclosed his hepatitis diagnosis. It was only weeks later, with Rusty Bell now firmly the matriarch of the triumvirate, that we knew Columbus would require surgery, an organ donor.

Columbus said, 'Death comes in a million guises.' As it turned out, he was not, as Rusty Bell and I had expected, killed by tragedies of the liver.

I met Christopher Wentzel – handsome, with curly brown hair and watery, blue-ocean eyes – in a History of Art class. It was inevitable that we would be friends, that it would be a perfect friendship, ruined by laughter, by minor perversities of the mind. I, out of fondness and fooling around, pet named him Columbus. We debated: Dali's molten and deformed watches. Modigliani's *Reclining Nude*. That sly Mona Lisa smile. Kentridge. Gloria Mabasa. It was remarkable how Columbus could sit through an entire semester without a whisper; but suddenly shock everyone with a penetrating comment. All of art, Columbus once said, with the exception of a few unrelated artworks, in some way celebrates the beauty of the human body – particularly the nude woman. Artists, he argued, are obsessed with capturing longing and desire and in their fantasies capture naked beings in wood, stone and iron. On canvas. Art, according to Mr Wentzel, was the sum total of human depravation. I had never seen Professor Mbembe so elated, so agreeable, so exalted. So agreeable that he declared the course the History of Human Depravations. Columbus was quick to add, not without Professor Mbembe smiling from ear to ear, that it was 'The History of Measured Human Depravations and Excesses and All the Splendour In Between.'

Rusty and I visited Columbus at Eugene's apartment on Louis Botha Avenue, Orange Grove. He was horsing around as usual, said he was tired of lectures on dead artists of 'meagre' talents. He laughed until he collapsed, clutching his chest. I thought Columbus was clowning around, pulling faces, until paramedics, half an hour later, solemnly declared the unthinkable.

Medically, said the paramedic, it is rare but possible to die from laughter. Cardiac arrest. It is possible that Columbus had, unbeknown to him, problems with his heart.

His death certificate, according to Pete, a giant of a man with a twitchy mouth, said Columbus succumbed to natural causes. Laughter seemed too morbid an excuse for such a solemn incident. A story waited our friends of the future: we had a friend we called Columbus. He was killed by laughter.

Columbus had, in life, had his funeral wishes written down, detailed instructions deposited in a safe box of Spencer & Young Inc., the Wentzel family attorneys on Twelfth Street, Melville. I had the honour of assisting Pete in the interpretation of some of the peculiarities: in other words, advising him which of Columbus's instructions could be ignored, without it being grossly offensive to the deceased. 'C. Wentzel Funeral Commandments' was a detailed list, typed on a typewriter, with perfect punctuation.

The perfectionist in him ensured that not only were his

Commandments legible, he also took the trouble of attaching a separate page with explanatory notes: how to interpret, understand and administer the Commandments. The separate page included explicit task allocations to specific people and a list of substitute persons in the event that delegated people were unavailable. It was, therefore, not an accident that: Professor Mbembe gave a moving eulogy, Zubeida Patel from the History of Art class read out the notes on the wreaths, while I was left alone to mourn. Columbus ensured this was crystal clear: 'My dear friend should be left alone to mourn.' This is exactly what I did by the graveside. I, between my repressed sobs, greatly admired Columbus' foresight, that not even death clouded his meticulous planning, so thoughtful that it took into account even the dreary and depressing dramas of death and burials. It was a peculiar occasion. Columbus had, two years before his death, reflected on the exact details of his funeral: the polished mahogany casket, the tulips in clay pots at the foot of the grave, the twelve white pigeons that were to be released at exactly fifteen minutes before midnight, as well as the custard and the pineapple jelly that was to be served by the graveside, failing which mourners were to be served strawberries and cream.

Columbus insisted, in capital letters, that funeral hymns were completely off limits, that the only scripture permitted was the Song of Solomon. It was a sensual funeral, full of memorable charms that chiselled the grief off our collective bosoms. The week of the funeral was brimming with memories of him – stories of love and kindness: how he bought heaters for old age homes, spent hours at Christ the King Care Centre, his bottomless patience with lazy freshmen who attended his History of Art tutorials, his generosity with his limited finances.

It was proper that our hearts bled, sank with the purplish brown casket, to the meditative grooves of Bon Jovi, playing 'Something to Believe In'. I remember all two hours as a painful blur of mourners in their pyjamas, each clutching a lit candle, resulting in a half sombre event that from a distance resembled a mute rock concert. This was consistent with Columbus' Commandment 8, which clearly stated: 'Bury me in the evening, under glittering stars from above and a sea of lit candles from among yourselves.' Commandment 7 was Columbus at his best: 'For those who understandably feel the urge to weep, please do so with some level of composure.' The lunatic in him then concluded, still under Commandment 7, 'Like all things under the sun, composure is relative. So: bawl your lungs out if so moved by the trag-edy of my passing (till we meet again), but please, don't forget the strawberries in your howling; they are there for your sensual delight.'

Professor Mbembe read the Commandments out loud. We giggled. Laughed. Sobbed. Ate strawberries. Licked cream off our quivering mouths. It was a delightful, memorable evening, devoid of the grief that makes funerals sombre, weepy things. Columbus had, with ten brief requests, ensured the posthumous presence of his peculiar mind – how we in our pyjamas fobbed moths which somehow understood the gravity of our collective mourning, descended on the candles with moderate and guarded interest, a cautious display of insect empathy.

Commandment 4 explicitly declined use of anything remotely resembling a motorised hearse, instructing that the casket be pulled by a single white horse. That horse, with its metal shoes on the tarmac, with its twitchy tail and wet nose, street lights along Jorissen Street bouncing off the polished casket, the clay pots with their tulips, the strawberries and bowls of cream, the unlit candles, the coy pigeons in their temporary cages, constellations of stars above seen from under and through cemetery tree branches, the modest cortège (family and close friends) in pyjamas walked into the Braamfontein Cemetery wherein the silence was molten by AC/DC riffs, where I saw Zubeida Patel's beautiful collarbones lit by her candle, her dimples encouraging inappropriate thoughts, taught me that funerals did not have to be depressing, but that with the right measure of madness, funerals had the potential to be light-hearted and enjoyable things.

Only Columbus could manage such a twisted view of existence, only he could, even in death, pour on to life bucketfuls of pranks. That is why I loved him: for his madness. One last detail about the funeral: when the pigeons were freed, fluttering in the evening light, I in my mind's eye saw my friend at the Heavenly Gates Undertakers, lying cold on a stretcher: calm, rigid, in a soulless, handsome, refrigerated kind of way. It was only when Alfred, a bow-legged aged mortician, replaced the white sheet that covered Columbus that the post-mortem scars bared their ugliness. My friend: butchered and sewn, like an old shoe. It was then that I caught sight of something unlike Columbus: a golden brown nest of curly, rich textured pubic hair. Cheeky, this discovery, for Columbus had in life been an exemplary custodian of male grooming – which I erroneously concluded would include mani-cured carnal gardens. That unfortunate oversight aside, Columbus was a charmer of the finest breed, a rare specimen. Intense. Sobering. Of peculiar thoughts.

★   ★   ★

I have never in my life imagined I would be committed to psychiatric help. I was wrong. I ended up seeing a Dr West, for eight months at first, and countless others that followed. Though besotted with Rusty's beautiful navel – her ferocious intellect, all her sleep-talking about red tractors and aeroplane crashes in sunflower fields, my visits to his office meant I had my eye and heart elsewhere. Audrey.

I confused dates and times for my twelfth consultation. Dr West had indicated he would be travelling (visit to a love child?), during the week of 8 March. It was only when Audrey answered the doorbell that she reminded me of this detail. She invited me in, requested that I pardon the mess caused by her rearranging Dr West's filing system. She wore a black mini dress, a brilliantly tailored gem of a garment with trimmings and openings in the right places: polka-dot collar, a discreet slit over the right thigh, a giant red button that secured the dress over her remarkable neck. A deep red cardigan took care of the upper torso and her red-soled stilettos lay neatly next to one of the couches.

She walked barefoot, thoughtfully, from one filing cabinet to the next. Gorgeous legs. A devastating rear profile. Those pouty lips, begging to be kissed. She mouthed alphabets, mentally arranging surnames of patients. She was, strangely, pleased to see me – all her blushing, all the coy yet deliberate glances. Her toenails could do with a fresh coat of nail polish – a revival of the purplish shade in various stages of peeling off. She offered me a seat, Dr West's chair, the throne from which he deciphered human tragedies, from which he patiently asked questions with discreet judgments, from which he had to think ahead, predict how to deal with unexpected meltdowns. It was from that chair that Dr West blended into the background, seemed insignif-icant, the master of weighing emotional pauses.

His choice of interior decor had ensured witnesses to his theatre of sobs and hisses: pictures of Bill Clinton surrounded by a group of singing children in Uganda, Gabriel García Márquez receiving the Nobel Prize, a jubilant Idi Amin in full Scottish regalia, Mandela sewing a garment on Robben Island, a shot of John Kennedy, Jr. saluting JFK's horse-drawn coffin, that Kevin Carter image of a vulture stalking a starving child. It dawned on me that each picture, no doubt carefully selected, said something (I was not quite sure what) about existence. And what perplexing juxtapositions!

Audrey opened and sealed boxes, discarded out-of-date psychology journals, continued mouthing alphabets: C. Cromwell, D. Dikobe, Z. Maharaj, P. Woodhouse. I, in an effort to seem at ease, helped myself to dried mangoes, on which Audrey nibbled between her filing. 'I better get going,' I said. She looked up, a typed report with red pen underlining in her hand, said, 'I won't die if you stay.'

'Meaning?'

'Stay.'

'Well, isn't it inappropriate, with all these secrets scattered around the consultation room?'

'Says who?'

'Well, doctor-patient confidentiality?'

'Here. John Cromwell: filthy as a practicing paedophile ever gets. Preyed on two-year-olds.'

'Audrey!'

'Audrey what? Some of these psychos are either languishing in jail or dead.'

'What will Dr West think?'

'Nothing. Do you really think he walks around agonising about deviants who fuck watermelons, pathological liars who defraud orphanages, alcoholics who butchered their wives? Is that what you think: that Kevin lives his life cringing and wincing at every blot contained in these files?' She picked up the files, pulled out Dr West's meticulous notes: 'Let's see. What have we here? Amanda Dube, a prostitute who found and lost and found Jesus, Elizabeth Reed drowned her twin daughters to spite a philandering boyfriend, and Colonel Maritz, a Vlakplaas kingpin, specialised in making Africans disappear. These files, all five hundred of them, contain the most hideous, most depraved and ruthless tales you can ever imagine. Do you think Kevin kisses his children goodbye at the school gates thinking of all the rot in these patient files? Most of these horrors are perfectly normal and capable people simply being full of it. Granted there are some, a small percentage, that genuinely need help and affirmation, but the rest are fuckheads abusing their good medical insurance – drowning in self-pity and guilt.'

She smiled, transferred pre-arranged blue and yellow files into filing cabinets, all the while double-checking the alphabetical sequence. Those calves of hers. Those small, efficient hands. The small wristwatch she says was a gift from an ex-boyfriend, 'a perfectly capable, marriage-averse software programmer with a zero-attention span. Besides his computer codes, really shocking lack of concentration. Sleep-with-shoes-on kind of delinquency. Genius? Oh, yes. Looks? Double tick. Style? Spadefuls. Money? Bank vaults. Father is a controlling shareholder of East Platinum, so the Smiths defrost their refrigerators on to bank notes. Bedroom antics? That is private. And, let's see: Dependability? Zero. Bucketfuls for culinary skills. Bruce cooks sinfully tasty meals. And here I am, rearranging confessions from fucking Cromwell (God, he is a dick!) and other delusional, depraved creatures of his ilk.'

One hour, and the files were neatly in their respective filing cabinets – leaving Audrey to polish furniture and empty the trash basket's negligible contents: a twisted paper clip, shredded papers, a perfume box. I knew without asking that Audrey had read my file, though she downplayed her prying eyes by volunteering stories about Cromwell's. I also knew there was something very special about Audrey – something feminine, carefree, something profound – complex even – in how she switched from one topic to the next with breathtaking agility, how she could discuss paedophiles and boyfriends and Dr West in one passionate conversation, a conversation that lingered long after she had moved on with her tasks. She was interesting, hiding her true self, a self far removed from the obedient and efficient PA serving bottled water and dried fruits to psychopaths.

Dr West had, unbeknown to either Audrey or me, never left for

Spain. This was the reason I felt safe to will pleasure into being. My hand travelled halfway up Audrey's thigh, almost all the way, inches short of her humid horizons, transmitted oppressive sensations, while my eyes crept through the giant red button of her dress, where a pair of turgid breasts guarded her muted sighs. I lifted her on to Dr West's desk, stood between her slightly parted legs, fed on her lip-glossed pouty lips – lips that tasted like strawberries, only with citrus undertones. It seemed the longest seven minutes I ever imagined possible, during which Audrey saw, over my shoulder, Dr West staring in absolute horror. We composed ourselves, acknowledged it had to end, that all seven minutes had to be forgotten. But we also (on the telephone) agreed that life would have been explosive had we entered the eighth minute, and every other minute thereafter. How could I explain this to Dr West: strawberry lips with citrus undertones? I would be accused of remorselessness. Loathed. Condemned. I would be crucified for a seven-minute affair, for twelve seconds of weakness; for three seconds of letting my hand wander under Audrey's dress. I thought of Audrey Adams, whom I had, technically speaking, not bedded. How would Dr West weigh the conclusiveness of my intentions – if I would have indeed let my hand travel the remaining sprint to her forbidden spheres? I tossed and turned that evening, stared at the ceiling, plotted and raged and despaired; at how Dr West seemed to enjoy punishment by silence – how he simply walked away.

Cinema Demons

Linda Musita

It was one of those days when a man has done all he can to make sure he goes back home with food. Derrick had tried everything, even offering to do a woman's laundry for just 200 bob. But she refused. She said she did not trust a man to clean poop out of her baby's napkins, scrape vaginal crust off her panties and rub skid marks from her husband's briefs. It was unnatural and how dare he ask?

He had a wife, two girls and a boy to take care of. He wasn't really sure why he'd ever married Beatrice. Those things that happen when you live in certain places and certain things are expected of you. Derrick was an educated man. He had gone to primary and secondary school, gotten into a university as a regular student. Being a regular student meant his parents would not have to struggle to pay his tuition fees. Neither would they have to fork out the ridiculous fees that parallel students pay, as if to compensate the university for their failure to get the right grade to be considered for a loan. The government would definitely grant Derrick a HELB loan that he would start paying back with interest as soon as he got a job.

The Joint Admissions Board assigned him to study for a Bachelor of Science in Recreation and Leisure Management. Beggars are not choosers so he entertained himself for four years and graduated with first class honours.

Derrick looked for work everywhere. People laughed at his papers. They thought he was a very good joke. Ha! Ha! Ha! Recreation and Leisure Management? What the fuck is that, boy? Yes, Derrick, why didn't you change the course? What sort of qualifications are these? Such a waste.

His father told him that a degree is just a degree and he could get a job as a bank teller if he applied himself. He had to remember he had a loan and yadda yadda yadda. Words that only served disillusion and bitterness. Forget employment, he told his father. I will become a life coach. A few seminars and I will deposit a lump sum at the HELB office, just wait and see. He tried to sell his 'I know exactly what you should do with your life after work' muck to corporates and house-wives but they all had things to do and hardly any time to spare until December when they would holiday overseas. He wrote a book, *Ten Ways to Become Leisurely*, applying all he had learned at school. He was sure it was going to be a bestseller. It ended up a green leaflet covered by polythene at a few newsstands.

No money. Loan looming. Needs arising. Tired and confused. Derrick looked for hope elsewhere. He found it in Beatrice. She lived in the next plot and was permanently awed by his one-bedroomed iron sheet house that had electricity, would you believe it? Hers was one timber room that did not have cement but mud on the floor, no electricity and she was always being attacked by every odd kind of insect. But Derrick's house? Wow. Things were in separate rooms. You had to go through a doorway to find a bed. And another doorway to find the stove, pans and plates. Plus all that netting, lace and crotchet around the sitting room wall to cover the rusted iron. How did he afford that? Wow. Beatrice, you have found a man among men.

Thanks to his 200-bob-a-month house in Kawangware, Derrick got a girlfriend. She was not of his class; he had a degree and all. But loca-tion, location, location. That is why she was perfect. His ideal woman probably lived in an extension in Bururburu but he smelled of kero-sene and pit latrine all the time. For that reason, Beatrice would do.

And she did get fat and pregnant successfully, three times. Fourteen years later, he was the oldest tenant, paying 3,000 bob for the same old tin. Going out every day to look for money.

The Bachelor of Recreation and Leisure Management had built houses, sold scrap paper and metal, cleaned toilets, washed cars, cut trees, delivered letters, sold onions, lost some coins in a Ponzi scheme, cooked and sold mandazi, pickpocketed, cut hair, made soap and cobbled shoes to make sure his progeny ate. Just food. No one was going to go to school, even though Daddi had told them that it was a fantastic place to be. And what was the point anyway if a tin was as far as school took you?

But food they just had to have. Derrick knew it. Except for this one day. He was tired and it was too early to go back home. He sat on a City Council bench opposite the Junction Mall, under a city clock, near that great corner and watched the rich go crazy with the paper in their purses and wallets.

To be honest with himself, he was afraid of money. It had caused him so much pain without even allowing him to touch it properly. Money was that woman. The one who hates you so much yet you have done nothing except desire her. The sight of you makes her puke. Derrick made money sick. Money could not believe he wanted anything to do with her and his love grew into fear that if one day he conquered her, he would mistreat and abuse her. He was not really sure he wanted much to do with her. The money game was exactly like playing Double Dutch with barbed wire.

'Praise the Lord, my brother,' a man sat next to him.

He was wearing a white shirt, white trousers and white shoes. The shoes and the cuffs of his trousers had some red dust on them. A sign that he had walked some distance before he got to Derrick. The man was holding pamphlets and a Bible. He was yellow. Not a white man, not Chinese and not Indian. A yellow curiosity that looked foreign and believable.

'Amen,' Derrick said.

'My name is Pastor Agostinho and we speak Portuguese where I come from.' He looked at Derrick like he wanted him to guess something.

'Good for you.'

'Ha! Do you know which countries speak Portuguese, my brother?'

'Not really.'

'Ah, my brother. The Lord is the source of all knowledge.' The man laughed as if he had said the most delightful thing in the world.

Derrick was amused by the yellow cartoon.

'I come from Brazil and the Lord has sent me to you. What is your name?'

'Derrick.'

'Dederick. That is the name. You, my friend, were born to be a ruler. Your name is blessed.'

'Derrick. Not Dederick.'

'No, my brother. Your name should have been Dederick. Derrick is removed from Dederick and whoever gave you that name took your blessings from you, Dederick.'

'My parents.'

'Yes, they cursed you.'

'I am tempted to believe you.'

'Tell me Dederick . . .'

'Derrick. Derrick.'

'Tell me Dederick, what do you do for a living?'

'I do my family for a living.'

'No, I meant do you have a job. Do you earn money?'

'I do not have a job. I try to earn money.'

'You do not have a job because you were cursed and Jesus sent me to help you.'

'How big of him, considering he never had a job.'

'Jesus is Lord. He died for you and has told me that you need the floodgates of heaven to open for you to prosper. I came all the way from Brazil where I had a good life. I abandoned my relatives and followed Jesus here just to help you.'

'Why?'

'Because you need deliverance.'

'Which church is this anyway?'

'The Church of the People of Damascus.'

'From Brazil?'

'No. From the story of Saul who was persecuting the people of God and then saw the light on his way to Damascus. What would have happened if he was not on his way to Damascus? What, Dederick?'

'The Lord would have found him on another route?'

'No. No. No. This is what I mean. This is your road and the Lord sent me here to save you. I will pray for you and things will change for you, my brother. Let us pray. Father Jesus, you said the kingdom belongs to such as Dederick. You said your house is open to them. The ones the devil is trying to steal. The ones hell has already taken like

Dederick. Lord you said they are yours and I, your servant, am here fighting for Dederick's soul. He should not suffer at the claws of demons. Save him! Purify Father Jesus! Send your fire Father Jesus! Purify! Burn the evil. Kill the devil, Father Jesus. Pour your blood on Dederick. Pour your holy blood. Red blood purify your child Dederick. Your sacrifice was not in vain. Make Dederick the ruler he is meant to be. Make him walk on streets of gold and fly with wings to the glory of your kingdom! Oh Father Jesus! Burn the Lucifer! Sanctify! Sanctify! Hallelujah! Hallelujah! We believe! I believe! And you Beelzebub, master of darkness, I command you in the name of the light of the world, leave Dederick's body. Manifest yourself! Manifest! Leave! Go to hell! In Jesus' name! Amen and amen.'

'Amen,' Derrick said.

'How do you feel now?'

Derrick looked Agostinho in the eye. He had never heard such a prayer.

'Dederick, there are six demons in your eyes. They are looking at me with authority over your body and soul. The demon of poverty. The demon of covetousness. The demon of leprosy. The demon of foul smells. The demon of polluting farts. The demon of stagnant faeces. They have refused to come out. You need to come to church this Sunday. The big bishop is coming from Brazil. He has come with power from the Holy Land.'

'Brazil?'

'He will go to Israel before landing in Kenya.'

Agostinho gave Derrick a pamphlet:

Do you have family problems? Are you sick? Do you need a job? Are your children stupid? Do you feel cursed? Do you have bad dreams? Do you need a promotion? Are you an alcoholic/depressed/stressed? Do you want to go to heaven?

Come to the Church of the People of Damascus on Sunday 7 July for the Prayers of the Seven Tabernacles and be delivered.

A powerfully anointed bishop, who just came from a pilgrimage to Mount Moses (aka Sinai), will fight the devil with you.

Come brothers and sisters. Bring your burdens to Bishop Abraao.

It read like those signs Derrick saw in places where people who went to Junction Mall lived. The rich areas had different types of houses, tastes and kinks but they had one thing in common: numerous wooden signs, all nailed to trees. For Dr Ali from Tanzania, Dr Nuhu from Zanzibar and Dr Shabaan from Pemba. The signs said the doctors could clean woe out of lives, enlarge a penis, stitch a vagina telepathically, get a toy boy back, track stolen cars, wear an invisible cloak and tamper with ballot boxes, and like Agostinho they got rid of evil spirits.

'Agostinho, do rich people go to your church?'

'No, the kingdom belongs to the poor.'

'Why are the rich left out?'

'They worship the devil.'

Agostinho left and after four days of hunger-no damn work-quarrelling-undermining-bickering it was Sunday morning.

Derrick needed a break. He still had Agostinho's pamphlet and curiosity made him walk out of his house and trudge on till four hours later he found a cinema hall in town with a huge banner, THE CHURCH OF THE PEOPLE OF DAMASCUS written on it in glorious Technicolor.

He walked through the big doors and found ushers milling around, directing people. Agostinho was there too.

'Dederick, praise the Lord. Come here!'

Derrick went.

'Nice to see you here mighty ruler. At the end of the service you will be a better man. A free man. A very blessed man. Do you believe? Say you believe. Come on!'

'We will have to wait and see, Agostinho. That is all I can say for now.'

'Have faith. I am glad I convinced you to come. Go in, Dederick. The Lord is waiting. And please do not be a doubting Thomas,' and once again Agostinho laughed as if he had said the most delightful words in the world.

'Isn't that a good thing?'

'No! Why would you say that?'

'Because then the Lord would actually come back to life and let me touch his wounds to prove that he really lives. And I will also ask him to spare a few minutes to tell me why he sat back and let life hand me a bad deal. If he does not have a good answer he will have to ask for my forgiveness.'

'I see demons are working inside you, Dederick. But Father Jesus is stronger. Go in my brother. Go in.'

'OK.'

Derrick went into the cinema church. The seats were almost full. He sat next to a young woman who was humming to a nice choir song coming from the wall-mounted speakers.

There was a very good smell about the place that Derrick liked immediately. There was a scent of fresh flowers but there were none in the building. Curious. The music and the scent made him feel at ease though. He looked around to come to complete terms with his surroundings.

At the front was a stage with a pulpit and arches covered with purple and pink curtains. A large blue velvet cross with a silver Jesus hanging on it stood against the white wall.

Ushers came from behind the curtained arches carrying throne-like seats − high-backed and painted white − which they later wiped with equally white pieces of cloth that were now and then dipped in bowls of what looked like Elianto.

As soon as they left the stage, Agostinho and five other pastors came from behind the arches. They each had a wireless microphone. All but Agostinho had potbellies.

'Hallelujah,' they said.

'Hallelujah. Hallelujah. Let us all welcome Bishop Abraao with a mighty clap. A thunderclap, people of God. Open the floodgates. Rain blessings on the man of God. Hallelujah.'

A man Derrick assumed to be the bishop raised his hands, smiled and waved at the people.

'Stand up, close your eyes and feel the spirit. Raise your hands, lift your burdens, open your hearts and tell Jesus you are tired of carrying the cross,' Abraao said.

Derrick closed his eyes. He tried to open his heart. This was a very straight-to-the-point church service. No song, dance and sermon. Just get to the main purpose of congregating: complaining to Jesus.

Some people started talking to themselves in prayer. The woman next to him turned her hum into a low chant. He tried to make out what the others were saying but the din now accompanied by a keyboard made it sound like Tom Mboya Street at 5.30 p.m. How did Jesus comprehend all this? It sounded like Babel.

Then, someone screamed and the cinema was quiet. All eyes opened to see where the evil sound came from. It came from the back. There was a woman jumping and screaming. She removed her blouse and threw it aside as if it had safari ants.

'Close your eyes,' Abraao said. 'The demons know that the eyes are the windows to the soul. You came here to collect blessings not evil spirits.'

Everyone but Derrick closed their eyes.

Abraao told the ushers to bring the woman to the 'altar'. As they did that there were more screams and grunts, as if in defence of the woman.

'Aha, Lucifer's servants and their herd of pigs have felt the presence of the Lord. Bring them all here.'

Derrick watched the ushers battle the demons all the way to the altar and wondered why they were doing it with their eyes open. The demons had a perfect getaway right in front of them and the owners of the windows seemed oblivious of the danger Abraao had warned them about.

There were close to fifty evils spirits crawling on the stage. Demons making faces, hugging each other, calling Agostinho, Abraao, the other pastors and the ushers idiots, nincompoops, losers, philistines, weak, mere mortals, irreparable pots, powerless and stupid. The demons called on Lucifer to save them. They wrestled the ushers and threw punches at them.

Abraao took one demon by the neck and began interrogating.

'Who are you, who sent you and what are you doing in this man's body?'

Boisterous, the demon said: 'I am Zapara the Third. I lead a legion of 10,000. I am a good commander with a few accolades to my name. I am the shit, to be honest with you. No lie. And I have been sent by his wife's ex-husband, Bishop Abraao.'

'What are you doing in this man's body?'

'What are you doing in this man's body?' Zapara mimicked.

Abraao tightened his grip on Zapara's neck.

Zapara coughed and Derrick's eyes grew bigger.

'OK, Abraao, go easy on the neck. It is not mine but it kinda hurts. If you play nice I will give you all the details. Deal?'

Derrick expected Abraao to decline Zapara's offer.

'All right. Speak!' The bishop held the legion leader by the collar.

'I sex him every day and night so that he does not desire his wife. That is my assignment and tell you what? I think he likes it as much as I do.'

'God save us! Holy Father have mercy on us. What is your mission Zapara?'

'To make sure that slut goes back to her real husband. He has paid a good price for her.'

'What price?'

'If I tell you, all the work I have done will be useless.'

'You, won't tell me?'

'No Abraao. Neither will you force me. I know things about you. Demons talk and word is . . .'

'Church, raise your hands towards this man. We are going to kill Zapara!' Abraao said at the top of his voice.

Everyone in the church started screaming and Derrick was so frustrated because he could not make out what Zapara was saying. He really wanted to hear the dirt on the bishop.

The ushers were told to abandon the little demons that were kick-boxing them and form a 'circle of fire around me and Zapara'. And like clockwork everyone started screaming, 'Fire, Fire, Fire, Fire.'

Zapara stopped talking. He convulsed, writhed and fell on the floor limp.

Abraao knelt next to the limp body.

'Wake up, child of God. You are now free. Resurrect. We have defeated the devil. Rise and see the light.'

The man opened his eyes and sat up. Abraao leaned forwards and blew air into the man's eyes seven times.

Every time he blew he said: 'Receive.'

The people followed his lead at the third 'Receive.'

The Zapara-free man stood and jumped up and down with what looked like joy.

Derrick could not help but think that Zapara had pulled a number on all of them and was somewhere in there, dissociated from one of his possible multiple personalities.

Everyone started clapping and muttering praises to the Lord. Their eyes were now open.

Abraao told them to close their eyes again. Derrick's refused to shut.

And he saw demons, talk, fight and mock. They puked yellow stuff all over the white thrones. One by one the spirits were subdued and the people they had possessed gave little speeches about how they had suffered under the demons but now that they were free, they would do anything and everything for Father Jesus and Bishop Abraao.

'This is quite the show,' Derrick told no one.

Abraao, Agostinho, the pastors and ushers were sweating through their shirts and blouses. They looked so tired with their eyes wide open. Their souls had been placed at risk as much as Derrick's.

The bishop began sobbing. So did everyone else except the usual suspect.

Mass hysteria, is what one of his lectures had called this fete. The professor told them that it could be very useful to shrewd men who wanted to entertain themselves or an audience.

Derrick felt lucky to be the esteemed audience at the cinema. But he had mouths to feed and long roads to walk. It was time to go. There was nothing for him to give or take at the Church of the People of Damascus. Agostinho would not set him free. Derrick now knew that his two hands and his sweat would deliver him sooner, later or even never. Abraao and Agostinho were using their hands and sweat in there. It worked well for them. They knew precisely what they were doing with their grand performance.

Tomorrow was coming and Derrick knew what worked for him. The road. So he walked.

an extract from the forthcoming novel

Ebamba, Kinshasa-Makambo

Richard Ali A Mutu

A cool breeze. The sky begins to cloud over. The sun wends its way to set behind the majestic Congo. Hovering above the riverbed, the great red sun glitters and glistens like blood. The river is still as glass, the cool wind unfurls. Night draws in and day slips gently away. The skies are filled with birds fluttering swiftly back to their nests. Still the leaves rustle and add to the cool of the evening. It is just possible to make out the tuneful and melodious sound of a wind that heralds rain.

Today is Saturday, the day when Kinshasa shimmers, shakes and struts its stuff. *Kinshasa-makambo* – Kinshasa the troublemaker – Kin the mysterious, Kin-du-Knoy awash with the golden beers Primus, Skol and Turbo. Kinshasa the party animal. This much is true: to live and die without ever seeing, without experiencing Kinshasa is tantamount to never having lived on God's good earth. See Kinshasa, if only for one night, if only to watch the majestic Congo snaking through the city before you die!

It is coming on for 6.12 p.m. and the bars of Kinshasa are filling up from Nyangwe to Kimbondo, from Tshibangu, Super, Beau-marché and Muguyla-guyla all the way to the last stop on the line which is, as it always has been, the mighty Avenue Oshwé in the district of Matonge. Here, the pleasure, the exhilaration and the excitement is redoubled. Here goat meat and chicken are grilled out in the open air to be snatched up and wolfed down like hot cakes. Beer flows like water. But what matters most is the dancing! Because Kinshasa is also the king of song, the Queen of *ndombolo*!

The evening wears on. Already it is 9.05 p.m. and the *bana nyonka*

– the little serpents – begin to slither from their lairs. Their eyes meet yours which instantly well up with tears, they are unutterably beautiful. They glister like gold. Some wear miniskirts, others skin-tight dresses, some are wrapped in a simple *pagne,* others are sporting outfits that defy description. They are vipers seeking some man to devour or some man to devour them. See them lined up along the Avenue du Stade, on the Rue Inzia, in Yolo Nord, along the Boulevard du 30 Juin. Nameless women, *filles de joie, banaya-mpunda,* our runaway sisters, our bongolo-sisters. They come in every colour: black, chocolate brown, white, mixed-race, albino. They come in every size: small, slender, neither-small-nor-slender, not to mention the dwarves, the deaf-mutes, the blind and the crippled.

At the Muguyla-guyla bar, Ebamba and his friends are dancing to the diabolical rhythms of Ya'Jossart Nyoka-Longo. Throbbing to the irresistible beat of songs like *Mokongo-ya-Koba*, of *Vimba*, of *Mama-Siska*. The demon drink arrives on cue with intoxication not far behind. Under the influence of alcohol, Ebamba begins to lose control. He very nearly touches the breasts of his best friend's girlfriend; his best friend brings him down to earth with a slap across the face. Precisely the right reaction since it means Ebamba stops himself in time.

Ebamba, too, had a date, but Eyenga, his fiancée, has gone home early because she wasn't feeling well. Ebamba had walked her as far as her neighbourhood then raced back to the bar because the party is due to go on into the early hours. It's a birthday party for his childhood friend, his very best friend, his *masta-ya-kati*!

They party on and the atmosphere just gets hotter.

It has not rained, but the lowering threat of rain has brought with it a balmy night. The cool breeze whipping across the dance floor means they can keep on dancing without too much sweating.

At some point, there are a few raindrops, but no one complains, on the contrary, it whips the dancers at Muguyla-guyla into greater frenzy.

1.05 a.m.
Knock-knock-knock!
Knock-knock-knock!
Ebamba pounds on the gate to the compound, having come home

to find it locked. He keeps knocking in the hope that someone will come and open up. Without his mobile phone, he has no way of contacting anyone inside. The aforementioned phone he lost a little while ago at the party – while he was feverishly boogying and boozing, the owner of the bar filched his phone.

No one comes to open the gate. Ebamba is getting impatient. Weak and exhausted, he cannot possibly climb the high wall. The booze has beaten him. Sleep is weighing on his shoulders. He slumps in the gateway of the compound.

1.30 a.m.

Ebamba can just make out the faint footsteps of someone coming. The gate opens. Ebamba struggles to his feet and heads towards the entrance. Maguy has come to open the gate. She is barely dressed, wrapped in only a *pagne* that covers her chest and her hips.

They look at each other. Maguy greets him. Ebamba responds. He reeks of alcohol. Maguy steps aside to let him pass.

The compound is silent. Everyone is asleep, even the dog someone forgot to let off the leash so it could guard the compound. They make no noise and no one wakes.

Ebamba staggers to his tiny studio, fishes out his keys, opens the door and stumbles inside.

Maguy, meanwhile, closes the gate then runs back into the big house.

1.40 a.m.

Soft, cool, tender hands caress Ebamba's cock and slowly he begins to get hard. These same hands move on, unbuttoning his clothes, stroking his hairy chest. Ebamba feels himself floating.

The hands do not stop. Fast asleep, his cock by now rock-hard, Ebamba is in heaven. He feels a coolness, a gentle, thrilling wetness against his chest. An irresistible caress. He is his cock, his hair stands on end, his skin tingles with goosebumps.

The pleasure reaches its apex and, still half asleep, Ebamba dimly realises that this is not a dream. He forces himself to wake up. He sees a woman and jolts upright. 'Hey!'

The woman starts back, releases her prey and recoils a little. Now wide awake, the dumbfounded Ebamba shouts:

'How long, Maguy?! How long have you been doing these things, huh?'

'What are you scared of?' Maguy says softly, seductively, clearly in control.

'What are you scared of, honey?' she says again. 'Did I hurt you? You left the door of the studio open so I decided to come in and make you feel good.'

'Make me feel good?'

'Shhhh, keep quiet. Don't say anything.'

She does not give up. She knows how to seduce a man in his condition. She begins to unwrap her *pagne*.

Standing in front of Ebamba, she is suddenly transformed into Eve, in the Garden, in the moment before original sin: pale-skinned, voluptuous, her young, beautiful breasts pointing to the heavens as she considers her prey.

She comes to him. Body against body. Already, the young man has fallen into her trap. He begins to stammer. Electricity trills through his body. He tries to open his mouth but cannot utter a word. Maguy peels off his shirt and kisses him full on the lips.

She eases down his trousers and pulls them off. Ebamba stands, naked as Adam. They tumble onto the bed. The mattress creaks and coughs. In an instant he is stone cold sober. Ebamba is streaming with sweat. Their bodies tangle and writhe like earthworms.

He has never felt like this. Maguy has intoxicated him. His eyes grow red. His body quivers and his heart pounds. He surrenders to Maguy completely, allowing her to do with him as she pleases. Maguy unsheathes the bullets and arrows of a true 'Mongo', 'a worthy Mungala'.

He has never experienced anything like this in his life.

'Can you bring me a grenadine?'

'Oh, don't say that, my friend! Are you really telling me you've given up beer?'

'Like I told you, Tshiamwa, I will never drink beer again.'

'Don't give me that, we know each other too well – it's just a drunk man's pledge.'

The waitress stands rooted to the spot, saying nothing, doing nothing. She simply stares at them until Tshiamwa gives the order.

'For me, a nice cool Primus, *maman*!'

The girl scribbles this on a slip of paper before disappearing from sight.

'So tell me, my good friend, how did this happen? How can you have come to this?'

'Ah, Tshiamwa, it is a long story, brother.'

Ebamba bows his head.

They sit facing each other with only the café table between them.

The place is a little empty at this hour. It is just after noon. Outside the sun sears and shines, making the most of the cool shade of the tall madamier tree in the gardens of 'Sous le Madamier, chez-le-Pasteur' in Bandal-Bisengo.

After a few seconds, Ebamba shakes his head, looks up at the heavens, then stares at his friend and carries on.

'*Masta*, my friend, I want to tell you my story but I don't know where to begin . . .'

'But the reason we met up here was so that you could tell me. Would you rather not talk about it?'

'No, my friend, that's not what I said . . . we will talk about it. I just wanted to say that this is not easy for me.'

'Ebamba!'

Ebamba looks up.

The waitress has come back with a tray carrying the bottles and the glasses. She sets them on the table. The drinks are ice cold.

'Thanks.'

The waitress simply nods and walks away again.

Tshiamwa picks up the bottle of beer and fills his glass. They drink a toast to friendship. Ebamba sets down his glass, licks his lips and takes a deep breath. Tshiamwa drains half of his glass, refills it and drinks again until he has quenched his thirst.

'You remember the daughter of my landlady, *Maman* Mongala?'

'Oh, I remember her! Maguy?'

'That's right. Well, this is about her.'

'What did she do? Is she the problem?'

'She is indeed, my friend, this girl and her mother have trapped me and I can see no way out.'

Tshiamwa finds himself confused by his friend's sudden assertion and asks him to hold up a moment.

'So what is this problem? What is this trap the girl and her mother set for you?'

Ebamba looks at Tshiamwa for a moment then says, 'Maguy is pregnant, Tshims!'

'So . . . ?'

'So, apparently I'm the father.'

'What? How did that happen! Don't say such things, my friend.' Tshiamwa is shocked. He cannot believe his ears. 'How on earth did it come to this?'

'This is why I asked you here today, my friend, so you can give me some advice.'

'But how on earth did it happen? How could you have got her pregnant? What about Eyenga? Have you forgotten your fiancée? You can hardly tell me Maguy raped you?'

'No, my friend, of course not. Though thinking about it, about the way it started out, you could say that she forced me.'

'Don't be ridiculous.'

Tshiamwa makes it clear that he does not believe what his friend is trying to make him believe. He gives Ebamba a scornful sneer and says:

'Tell me the truth. What possessed you to do such a thing?'

'You remember the night of the Matuka's party in Muguyla-guyla?'

'His birthday you mean? Of course I remember. You went home drunk. '

'Exactly, that was the night I went home in a state of inebriation . . .'

Ebamba tells Tshiamwa the whole story down to the smallest detail. Tshiamwa listens to the tale attentively, though there are moments when he cannot help but make his astonishment obvious.

'And now, how far along is she?'

'Only a month.'

Tshims shakes his head again, scratches his chin, strokes his beard. He cannot believe what he is hearing

'So what are you going to do now? Tell her to get an abortion?'

'*Niet!* What kind of advice is that, huh? I could never tell a girl to have an abortion.'

'But let's be realistic, my friend, what else can you do now? In case you've forgotten, let me remind you that you have a fiancée and you're supposed to marry her very soon!'

'That's the problem, and may I remind you that this is why I asked you to meet me so that we could talk it over. But there will be no more talk of abortion. I refuse to consider it.'

Tshiamwa drains another glass. He exhales nosily and slams his glass down on the table. Picking up the bottle of Primus, he studies the contents and pours the remaining beer into his glass, holding it at an angle as foam spills over the sides and puddles on the table again. Then he picks up the glass, stares at it fervently, nodding as if to say 'What a life!', and drains it before slamming the glass down on the table. Boom.

'What now?' Ebamba asks sarcastically. 'Don't tell me you're drunk on a few glasses of beer!'

Tshiamwa snorts. He rubs his face with his hands as though to wake himself or to lower the level of alcohol in his bloodstream. He sighs again, biting his lower lip. He rolls up his shirtsleeve and glances at his wristwatch.

Tshiamwa looks into Ebamba's eyes.

'You know how much I love and value you as a friend, not only because I personally followed your brilliant career from primary school to university. You are intelligent guy and I always told myself that one day you would be an important figure in this country.'

'*Nanu tokufi te!*' Ebamba interrupts. 'We're not dead yet . . .'

'Oh, yes,' says Tshims. 'As you say, where there's life, we're still allowed to hope.'

'Amen!' says Ebamba with a little laugh.

'So, as I was saying,' Tshims continues, 'it's because I admire you so much that what's happened upsets me – I can't help but wonder how you're going to cope. You have no father and no mother. And you have no job! What does Maguy's mother have to say? Does she know about the situation?'

'No, we haven't told her about it yet. Though I don't know, it's possible that her daughter has talked to her and the two of them have decided to keep me in the dark.'

'Do you love this Maguy girl or what?'

'Oh, my friend, Maguy is not so bad. She is not vulgar; it's just that I have made my choice: it's Eyenga I plan to marry. With my uncle's help, the preparations for our wedding are already well advanced.'

'How many times were you together, apart from the famous night of Matuka's birthday party?'

'More than a dozen times! You said yourself the girl is a real Bangala bomb!'

Tshims smiles. Looking at Ebamba, he scratches his head and nods, then says: 'But what about you, my friend, what about the little deal I told you about? You've done nothing, have you?'

'I've already talked to you about that little deal . . .'

'Yes, but you still refuse to do anything about it, am I right?'

'I've already told you, Tshims, I will never – and I mean never – agree to such a deal. I would rather die. Men with men? Not with me, is that clear?'

Ebamba has raised his voice. Every time his friend mentions this 'deal', he finds himself seething with rage.

Tshims tries to calm him and tells him to lower his voice because the bar by now is starting to fill up.

'Why are you shouting? Honestly, I've never understood why you stubbornly refuse even to consider it! You're missing out on a great opportunity. You're a charming, intelligent man so it's only normal that other guys would be interested in you, like I've been attracted to you for ages . . .'

'What are you talking about, man?' Ebamba looks as though he has just woken from a nightmare, his eyes grow wide, his mouth falls open. He scowls and leans so that he can hear what Tshims is saying.

'Are you listening to me, my friend?'

'I'm listening . . .'

'I've wanted to talk to you about this for a long time but I was afraid of how you would react. I just want you to know that there's nothing wrong with homosexuality! It's exactly like doing it with a woman. And it's got nothing to do with witchcraft or magic like people say, because I'm sitting here with you and I'm no sorcerer, no magician.'

Ebamba's bulging eyes grow wider still. 'Shut up!' he growls. He cannot bear to listen to what his friend is saying. The other customers turn to stare. Ebamba notices and tries to pull himself together. Tshims says nothing. The few seconds of silence feel like an eternity. Eventually, the other customers go back to their own conversations.

Translated by Frank Wynne

from the forthcoming novel *Durban December*

Sifiso Mzobe

By the Tracks

The downpour is over in ten minutes, just the heat remains. A single agitated crease on Jabu's sweaty forehead deepens as he brutally changes down and kills the diesel engine at the pedestrian gate of D 11773.

Because this part of D section has been affluent since the inception of Umlazi Township in 1965, D 11773 is a double-storey delight of dark, chocolate-brown brick only slightly bleached by time. A mansion among mansions – tended gardens and manicured lawns. This part of the township has been loved by the well-to-do – graduates and business people – since way back.

Climbing out of the car, Jabu adjusts his T-shirt to cover the state-issue Z88 pistol that sits heavy and snug on the hip of his cargo pants. He is still in flip flops – the urgency in Commander Sithole's instructions, the muggy heat of the night and the hangover colluded to make him dismiss changing into sneakers. Torch in hand, he slips a slim camera into his pocket and grabs a pair of the latex gloves that Zinhle nicked from the clinic.

The pedestrian gate is unlocked. A group is congregated in the brightly lit front yard of the house.

These originals, the first ones to live in Umlazi, are grandparents in their seventies and eighties now. All of them are in pyjamas, robes and slippers. The fabric of nightwear is cotton of the finest ilk, silk is true silk. Age has blurred sight, so most wear spectacles. Before they hush down as Jabu nears, he hears the last of their final whispers: 'An hour after we called, they arrive? This is not professional!'

Jabu gets on with the business at hand. 'Can I talk to the owner of the house?'

The lights of D 11773 reflect on their glasses as he searches their faces for a response. They don't reply. Instead, they usher him into the centre of the circle where a scruffy man is sitting on the lawn. As Jabu gets closer he wonders how these people stood the stink for an hour.

The ratty man reeks of a blocked toilet; his hair turned into dread-locks by an aversion to taking baths. His eyes are shackled by shock. Tears pour out and roll down, cascading over older salted tracks. His trembling, filthy hand points Jabu to the general direction of what has him shook.

'It smells of death. I am sure it is death. I've never smelled it so bad. He is dead! He is dead!' he mumbles through a clenched jaw.

'What are you talking about?' Jabu enquires.

The dirty man loses it. He falls on his side, tumbles and breaks the circle of elders around him by rolling like a log on the lawn.

'How long has he been like this?' Jabu asks the septuagenarian next to him.

'Close to an hour. He was rambling, so we decided to call you. But this, the rolling, he started now . . .' says the bespectacled, straight-shoot-ing grandfather, tucking his hands into the silky robe that is tied too tight over his ample midriff.

'Has anyone seen what he is talking about?'

'It is dark – no one can see. But we had to call you because he keeps saying the same thing, pointing to the tracks.'

'Does anyone know where he lives? Have you seen him around here before?'

'He lives by the stream. He's a hermit. Something is really wrong with him. Maybe he is confessing to a crime – human blood weighs heavy on the soul, you know. It talks, detective.'

The homeless man is clearly terrified by what he has seen. Jabu has caught many criminals and he knows that murderers don't just appear in front of you on a silver platter. They don't stick around and alert the world to their crimes. Something is amiss.

In a momentary pause that lasts just seconds, the homeless man stops rolling. Jabu searches for the hobo's eyes but their pupils don't lock.

The vagabond gawks beyond him, too far into the humid night sky. The look is blank and his body shivers in the Umlazi night. Soon he is in the foetal position, his numbed stare cast into the grass.

'So, what are you going to do?' asks the elder.

'I'll check what is out there. Probably nothing, but to ease your concerns I'll have a look.'

'Umlazi was once a wonderful place to raise children. This area, especially, was once peaceful. Now we have break-ins and muggings. Last year we asked for vans to patrol our streets, now that would be a solution to nip these problems in the bud, but your boss is a hard man to work with. Sithole is big on promises but doesn't do much. I have been in touch with Provincial SAPS. Their communications officer is a former student of mine. Now there is a brilliant mind. Excellent ambidextrous brain. She could have just as easily excelled in academia, to tell you the truth. She told me they will address my concerns. You see, my son, institutions must function for us, the people. But . . .'

'Let me get on with what I'm here to do,' Jabu says, cutting short the developing monologue. 'Nobody leave the yard. I still have to talk to all of you for my report,' he adds, heading to the back yard.

The Umlazi originals leave the vagabond shaking on the lawn and follow Jabu to the edge of the tracks.

You'd think it would have cooled down after the storm, but it is the sweltering opposite. The humidity in the air, the fragrance of a fruiting mango tree, and the smell of freshly cut grass mingle with the stale taste of the whisky from a few hours ago. Jabu wipes sweat from his brow as he steps on to the track ballast, crushed stone crunches as he climbs up to the track.

There is an eerie hush, a near absolute silence in which Jabu hears the quieting cries of the vagabond.

Jabu torches his way forward, instantly making out a shape in the darkness, a shadow on the friction-polished tracks. It is right at the curve where the tracks go under a bridge. The back yard lights of the mansions don't reach this far but the lump is darker than the night. He treads on, away from the group of elders until he hears only his steps and sometimes the crunch of crushed stones when he misses a concrete sleeper.

A breeze comes to him, hinting that the night is cooling down. Jabu inhales the cool air, but with it he gulps down a sharp smell that burns his nose, windpipe and lungs. The attack is so sudden, so disorienting, that he unknowingly pulls in another breath and croaks into a phlegmy cough. It hits him hard – physically it looks as if he has taken a heavy punch that has winded him. He kneels and spits. A collective sigh from the crowd of elders cuts through the silence. Jabu takes off his T-shirt, folds it, wraps it over his nose and ties it tight at the back of his head. His eyes itch and water, his torch falls. He picks himself and the torch up and waves the light back at the originals, showing them he is up and moving on.

The lump is large. If it is indeed a human body, it is a big fellow. The odour that fills his throat steams off the lump, which he now sees is covered by a green plastic sheet. Three steps from it he looks back at the crowd.

When he peels back the green plastic, the cool breeze blows away the sharp smell for a few seconds. Jabu has seen his share of gore but it still shocks him that there are two bodies under the green sheet, one on top of the other. The top body has a single gunshot wound, a clean shot – just a hole exactly the size of a bullet in his left temple. Jabu's torch reveals a young man, twenty or so years old. Pulling on the latex gloves, Jabu feels that heaviness that slumps his shoulders every time he comes across a fatality.

The young man died in expensive clothes – a YSL big buckle belt, T-shirt and jeans, ankle-high Lacoste sneakers and a Diesel chrono-graph. Jabu lifts the designer T-shirt and checks for injuries on the young man's torso. There aren't any. And he bled only slightly from the gunshot wound – the red line does not even reach his jaw. His pockets are empty.

Jabu drops the torch and rolls the first body to the side. Picking up his light, he starts at the feet of the second body. This young man died in even better clothes. Sneakers are Iceberg. He is bound by rope at the ankles, knees and waist. Jeans are True Religion. His hands are tied behind his back. Torchlight exposes stumps where his fingers should be, they have been severed at the first joint. His belt is genuine Louis Vuitton. His T-shirt is soaked in so much blood that it is impossible to make out its original colour. Jabu moves his torch up from the torso to examine the face, estimate age, but the second body has no head.

A gust of the vapour coming from the windpipe of the decapitated body puts a halt to Jabu's shocked inspection. The sharp smell cuts through the layers of the T-shirt over his nose, it burns his throat and eyes. He bolts away from the bodies, but the breath he holds is full of the foulness of death. He needs fresh air and he runs to it. Halfway between the crowd of originals and the bodies he can hold on no more. He removes the T-shirt and gulps in.

It is the second lungful of fresh air that does him. That second gulp brings the smells of the weekend flying back to him. Stinking goat sellers, the smell of the slaughter, the persistent reek of goat hide, the stink of slippery innards, torn tendons and dismembered joints, wood smoke, whisky, Card's cologne, frying onions, weed, the wetness of earth, the plate of food he warmed and ate before he came to the crime scene, a fruiting mango tree, latex gloves, the bitter, lung-singeing smell of death.

He kneels, sick, and his stomach empties violently. Exactly three times he bellows like a bull on its last breath after it has been fatally wounded. Thrice his internal organs attempt to jump out from under his skin and overtake it so that all that is inside is out, the out in.

'He's dying in front of us! Call for help! My son, what is wrong?'

And a few screams from the grandmothers in the group of Umlazi originals. Cries of the vagabond rise again. Jabu hears a sound that rings from inside his ears, a shrill continuous buzz that blocks out all other sounds. He stands up, lighter than a feather. The ground sways side to side then round. The track gives out from under him. Next thing he knows he weighs nothing, and then the track crashes into his face.

Jabu mistakes the hiss in his ears for the breezy winds of heaven. His eyes open just as the oxygen tank shoots out an especially dense white mist that escapes through the sides of the mask. He is sure the white fumes are the famed fluffy clouds of heaven, but the whiteness clears quickly to reveal a starry sky.

He hears the baritone of Commander Sithole in the distance and feels a tightness gripping his left arm. Yet another hit of white from the oxygen mask clouds his view. When it clears he sees the source of the tightness – the inflatable cuff of a blood pressure monitor strangles his upper arm.

Jabu quickly realises that he is lying on a stretcher. He tries to sit but fails and turns his head to the side instead. He sees old people, the originals of D section. The regaining of his bearings ends with the last thing he saw before the track rushed into his face and it was lights out, he sees it again in his mind – the bodies, the absent head. He deliberately inhales hard on the aerosol for an oxygen high to banish the gore he witnessed from his mind.

Jabu is out for no more than a minute. The oxygen buzz wears off and he wakes to see the railway track in the distance. It is now better lit, not pitch dark like when he foraged, found the mess and blacked out. His partner, the old hand Shezi, is in and out of view, holding a flashing camera. Commander Sithole is also in and out of view. He looks around and finds the source of the sudden brightness – the new light from the station. There is yellow police tape around the horrors, right where the track disappears into the tunnel; it barely flaps in the windless night. Commander Sithole and Detective Shezi have secured the scene.

Jabu turns back to the originals and tries to raise his head. The elders nudge each other. A few grandmothers smile encouragingly at his valiant attempt. He strains and tastes his own blood as his tongue runs over a burst lip.

Jabu tries to sit up. He fails four times, only succeeding when the helping hand of Commander Sithole pulls him up. The inflated cuff on Jabu's arm is about to burst. He adjusts to the sitting position, closing his eyes to the sudden dizziness that overwhelms him.

Sithole is next to him. He looks at the scene – Sithole does – and at the elders, then back to Jabu. 'The force of the fall cut your lip. You were bleeding profusely when we arrived. Totally out. Your face half-buried in crushed stone,' he says.

'Have you ever seen anything like it?' Jabu says through the oxygen mask. The mask seems to reflect what he says back into his head. His words ring inside his cranium and he is within a whisker of gagging.

'Once. When I had just started on the force. It happened on the N2 near Mtunzini – a bus full to capacity rolled and caught fire. We arrived before the fire engines and there was nothing we could do. We watched for fifteen minutes while the people trapped inside burned alive. We watched, waited for the fire engines, helpless, and heard, one by one, their screams fall silent. But that was an accident. This is murder.'

Jabu recalls the crudeness of the smell that burned his nose, throat, eyes. It is tattooed in his memory. Luckily the oxygen tank thwarts his recollection with another hit of white mist. A government mortuary van reverses into the yard, stopping as close as possible to the edge of the track. They are quick in their recovery. Jabu watches, seated on the stretcher, only half believing what is happening in front of him. He is there but not really there, watching himself from above, not as high as, say, a news helicopter but maybe two metres over the unravelling scene. From this view the undertakers return with only one body bag.

'Where is the other body? There were two bodies . . .' Jabu says from behind the oxygen mask. His words echo back into his head. He hates how he sounds – weak and shaken.

'We took him to hospital. He was still alive. We found a faint pulse,' says Sithole.

'What? The boy with a bullet in his brain is alive? How come?'

'It baffled everyone. His pulse was faint, though. I doubt he will make it through the night.'

'Commander, I don't believe you.'

'Believe it.'

The paramedic is back from a smoke break. He takes Jabu's blood pressure and deems it time to remove the oxygen mask.

'You will be fine. Your blood pressure is stable,' he tells Jabu, taking off the inflatable cuff. 'Try to stand up.'

Jabu sits for a while then he stands and takes a step, then another.

'Is it true he is alive?' he asks the paramedic.

'I was also shocked when I checked him and found a pulse. He is in surgery at Prince Albert Luthuli as we speak.'

A call crackles on the young paramedic's two-way radio. He collects the stretcher and equipment and takes it all to the ambulance. There is another emergency and he is quickly gone.

'This is yours, you and Shezi,' says Station Commander Sithole.

'You go home, get some rest. I'll help collect the evidence, seeing as you are in no condition to work, but when morning comes this case is yours.'

'Are you sure he is alive? The boy with a bullet in his head?'

Jabu looks at the ground, trying to get it to steady. When he looks up again he finds that Sithole is on his way back to the heart of the crime scene.

In the van Jabu attempts to get himself together, a cigarette burning in his trembling hand. His recollections are repetitive, each one ending with the absent head. The shrill whistle of his phone shakes him back to reality, but his trembling hands drop it and he has to fiddle between the pedals until he eventually finds it. The message is from Zinhle.

'Where are you?'

'Coming home,' he replies.

from the forthcoming novel

My New Home

Glaydah Namukasa

Today Jjaja did not smack my ankles. She did not call me devil's pet. She did not even spit at me! She simply handed me the plastic jug and a one thousand shilling note and asked me to wait about for the milkman. Mukulu has been away for two days now. I want him to return soon so that I can tell him about Jjaja. Mukulu loves me. He calls me his grandson.

The morning air is freezing. A few moments ago, the sun glanced at me. I saw its face peeping through the branches of the *kifenensi* in the middle of our small compound. It blinked and gave off warm, fluorescent light that gracefully danced through the leaves. Then the sun closed its eyes and disappeared, leaving the gloomy grey clouds to gaze at me. I do not look back. My life is no longer that shade of grey.

For the three years I have lived with her, Jjaja's hatred for me has been steadfast. Her hatred was born the minute she opened the door of her mud-and-wattle house to let me and Aunty Lito inside. When Aunty Lito introduced herself as Mama's former friend and explained that I was the child of Jjaja's only son, the late Damulira, Jjaja told Aunty Lito not to talk ill of her dead son, and then she hurried to the bedroom and returned with a bowl of water. She darted around the house, dipping a small bundle of *bisenke* grass into the bowl and spraying spurts of water in the corners and on the walls. She said she was safeguarding her house with holy water because I wasn't her grandchild but a curse.

I was seven years old then. Now I am ten and I know that she sees me as a pest. She tells me that I am different from the other children because I don't have a mother or a father. Or any known relative. That I am a destitute orphan rambling through life like a plastic bag flapping about in the wind.

But yesterday the routine of my days changed. Jjaja did not pull me out of bed at cockcrow so I could make the fire for smoking her left-over tilapia and Nile perch. Instead she served me millet porridge with milk and sugar! She let me smear my whole body with Movit Herbal Jelly for the first time. Last night she served me a piece of fish ball. First I delicately peeled off the crust. Then I slithered the pieces of fat in my mouth, enjoying the salty cream.

I am sitting on the small veranda of our house with my knees drawn up to my chest. The milk jug is safe beside me, the money secured in my right hand. I cannot understand the meaning of Jjaja's goodness. This new pattern is scary. But I love the fish balls. The milk and sugar, and Movit Herbal Jelly. The milkman is taking too long to come. I grab the jug and hop my way to the kiosk that separates our house from the bucket latrine shed. This is where the milkman parks his bicycle.

A band of boys charge from J.J's film shack across the trench. J.J racing after them. He has a bamboo rod that he keeps swiping and hitting in the air. He gives up. Last week these boys were rounded up by police for going to film shacks during school time. Their punishment was five strokes of the cane each but they didn't learn the lesson. One of them, the one with a head shaped like a Sejembe mango, waves a hand in my direction. 'THAT BOY DRINKS ALCOHOL.' They all stop and turn to stare at me.

'No. He doesn't!' another one shouts. I know this one. Juma. He lives with his mother at Kadopado where Jjaja sends me on Tuesdays, Thursdays and Saturdays to buy fried fish balls. He is short and has a big stomach that protrudes through his shirt, like mine. I don't like Juma. He never shares fish balls with me.

But now he is defending me.

'He goes to bars with his grandfather,' Sejembe-head.

They think I drink alcohol but I don't. At the bars, Mukulu buys me *mubisi*, a sweet juice made from ripe bananas. At Tongo's bar, Mukulu buys me Fanta soda, my favourite.

'I tell you he doesn't drink. He only goes because he has to hold his grandfather's walking stick.' Juma.

'Lujuuju!' Sejembe-head.

Juma lunges forwards and grabs Sejembe-head's throat.

I put the milk jug down and watch Juma go. Warm blood streams through my veins and wakes up my entire body. The chill disappears. I am filled with warm laughter and it is a good feeling. So different from the cold fear that always pinched my heart when Jjaja looked at me before.

Juma is Jackie Chan. Springing forwards snake-style to bite Sejembe-head. My happiness is unstoppable. It's like the sunlight seeping into every crevice in our locked-up house in the mornings. I chant, 'Juuuma, Juuuma, Juuuma.' The other boys join in.

Juma! I will forage the neighbourhoods for marbles and *janto*. Together we will dig small holes in the ground and play *duulu*. We will live our playtimes in delight; laugh, play, roll in the dust, run about. I will share my thoughts with him; tell him that when I grow up, I will work hard, get money and buy fried fish balls daily.

Oh, no! Jjaja is bending the corner of the kiosk! The boys disperse. I missed the milkman.

'He hasn't come yet, Jjaja.' I am on my knees now and a piece of gravel has dug into my skin but I swallow the pain.

'That's OK. We will go to the shops and buy fresh dairy milk instead.' As she passes by me to enter the house, she hands me a black *kaveera* containing clothes. I receive new clothes instead of a clout on my head! This is more frightening.

Joshua Mondo dressed in a blue T-shirt with the picture of my favourite footballer, Didier Drogba at the front. A smiling Didier Drogba. Joshua Mondo clad in a pair of jeans! That's me. A few moments ago Jjaja scrubbed me up with a rag she cut from the worn-out burlap sack we no longer use to keep coffee. Soaked me up in a foam she made with Dettol soap. Scraped my head hairless with a piece of broken glass – a quick, rough experience that left too much broken skin – and smeared my body with Movit Herbal Jelly. Then she dressed me up in the smiling Drogba and the jeans.

It's already dark. I love it that I am dressed in new clothes but I hate it that I cannot go out to show off my smiling Drogba. I don't even know why I am dressed up at this time. I am sitting on the fibre mat in Mukulu's bedroom where Jjaja told me to sit and wait. Mukulu is drunk asleep. He returned after sunset with a half-litre empty sachet of *kasese* peeping from his coat pocket. Before I could tell him how my day had rolled on fresh diary milk, fried Nile perch, rice, new clothes, and Jjaja Mukyala's baffling goodness, he slumped across his bed, feet hanging over the side. I am waiting for Mukulu to wake up.

A knock? A persistent, impatient knock on the front door. Rapid blows obviously made by a fist not the knuckle of the forefinger. I jump off the mat and sneak to the bedroom door and position my face against the slit in the lower hinge.

Two people enter the house; a man and a woman, both wearing *kitenge* fabric. The man has a matching cap that makes his head look like a box. He sits down on Mukulu's stool, facing away from me. The woman takes the mat that Jjaja spreads next to the heap of my rolled-up bedding. She is facing me. The scarf on her head is wrapped so that there are two stiff ends hanging beyond her ears. The ends appear like horns. A buffalo head on human shoulders.

'You came at the perfect time. The old man is out of our way.' Jjaja is down on her knees, her fingers moving. She is plucking at her skirt as if she is picking *sere* spikes from the fabric.

The man rises, picks up the left side of the *kitenge* to reach into his trouser pockets. He extracts something which he holds towards Jjaja. She instantly jumps up to receive whatever is being handed to her. She doesn't plant her palms down for support as she rises. Whatever she has received has given her the strength to rise unaided.

She is smiling. I see her clearly. As she buries that something in her brassiere, she faces the kerosene lamp. I have seen this smile before. Last Monday I sneaked up on her in that *matovu* shrubbery behind our house. She was counting a wad of shillings which she later secured in her bra. She had that smile: a rapid movement of the lips twitching, nose flaring. A rabbit happily chewing *kanyebwa* weed.

The man bends towards the light; he pushes his arm forwards and looks at his watch. Then he turns back to stare at Jjaja. I scuttle back to where she left me because this time Jjaja is shambling into Mukulu's bedroom. I sit down and rest my head at the back of their bed and feign sleep.

'Joshua, dear.'

She bends over and pats me, repeating my name. I rise slowly. I am trying to listen to the sound of my name as it crawls on her tongue. A violent chill rushes through me, digging through my skin, flesh and bones. I am afraid. Jjaja's tenderness is eating me up. I can't see, can't think, can't walk normally. I shuffle behind her, clutching on to her hand. I am a goat being propelled to the slaughterhouse.

The woman smiles at me. A big, happy smile like the one Jjaja gave me this morning. Her smile widens to expose the whole set of her teeth. The man only glances at me. When I turn to look at him he looks away and focuses on my rolled-up grass mattress in the corner of the room. I am scared of him. Scared of the oversized, full-length green *kitenge* and the matching headgear. I am scared of his big belly that cannot be hidden by this large attire. He looks like the men I have seen in Nigerian movies. Mukulu says such men hide wickedness behind big stomachs and full-length outfits. If Mukulu could wake up now, he would tell me to keep away from these strangers.

'*Mutabani wange!*'

The woman speaks, calling me her son. Her words rattle in my ears like falling pieces of scrap metal from a truck. She jumps off the mat and hurries to take my hand. I withdraw it and she instead strokes my head, grazing the open sores in my burning scalp.

Jjaja snatches my hand and forces it into the woman's. 'Joshua, dear, she is your mother. The one who gave birth to you. And he is your father. I finally found your parents.'

I stare at Jjaja in bewilderment. I know that Mama died. Aunty Lito told me. 'Don't call me Mother. Call me Aunty Lito. Your mother died. She used to be my friend. Even Karo was your mother's friend. She took care of you when you were a baby. Before she brought you to me. The parents who gave birth to you are both dead.'

According to the jumbled details of my life, my birth parents are dead. And dead people can only resurrect when Jesus comes back – so

Aunty Lito used to say. But Mukulu told me Jesus will never come back, so dead people will never be resurrected.

'My parents died, Jjaja. Aunty Lito told me. Even Mukulu told me so.'

She smiles. Not the rabbit smile. This time her teeth are barred. She is grinning. 'If I say that these are your parents, it means they are.'

'Mukulu told me I am his grandson. I want to stay here.'

'Shut up now and listen to me. You are going away with your parents. Now!'

'Going' dashes towards me like a rock let free from a catapult, shattering my ears. This is a nightmare. I am settled into Mukulu's home. Mukulu's love gives me strength to endure Jjaja's cruelty. This is home. I can't go away from Mukulu. I glance in the direction of the room where Mukulu is snoring. I need him to walk through the bedroom door and explain all this. He is the only one who can save me from these lies. But I know it would take pouring a basin of hot water on him to make him wake up.

Jjaja talks on. I listen with my ears closed, see with sightless eyes. I am choked up by my own helplessness. The woman has her hand clutched around mine. Jjaja is giving me away. I hate her. I hate the new clothes she gave me. I hate smiling Drogba!

Suddenly the man rises off the stool, steps towards us and within moments he has me lying across his chest in a manner one carries a newborn baby. I wriggle and scream. He cups my mouth.

'Behave, you devil!' Jjaja pinches my ear.

By the half smiling, half glaring look on her face, I know that I have lost my life once again. I have lost four lives in my ten years of existence. I am leaving. Again.

The person who opens the door is tall and skinny. His shoulders are hunched as if weighed down by his long arms. He is dressed in a sleeveless white T-shirt with a shredded hem, and a pair of loose pink-flowered shorts from which two long legs descend to the ground and end in two gigantic ostrich feet.

Ostrich feet waves to the man and woman, who immediately dash back to the car and drive off. I stand in sheer confusion, terrified of whatever will happen to me in this strange place. Ostrich feet shows me the way through a winding trench of a white corridor. I count my steps, one by one, steadying myself, spreading my arms to keep balance. The white walk is scary. The smooth white tiles are thorns under my calloused soles. The white ceiling is Jjaja's water drum sitting on my head. The white walls are the open jaws of a python.

The corridor ends in a semicircle of six closed doors all painted black. Six doors arrayed hand in hand. I step aside to let him pass. He looks at me head to toe, and smiles before reaching into his pocket for a bunch of keys. He easily spots the key that opens one of the two doors in the middle of the semicircle. Another wave signalling me to enter. The room is dark. I raise my face to look at him, hoping he will see the terror in my eyes.

Our eyes lock. He opens his so wide that the whites of his eyes threaten to swallow me up. For a moment I pray that Mukulu will appear from along the corridor and ask me to take his walking stick and wait for him outside. I see myself outside, hurrying into the friendly darkness of Kikuubo slums, smelling the stagnant sewage that always welcomed me home to Mukulu's house.

A rough tug on my shoulder wakes me from my daydream. The room lightens as soon as I step inside. A small room housing a spiral staircase that leads to an ascending fierce darkness. An overwhelming urge to turn back and disappear jumps to me. I want to shove backwards, knock over Ostrich feet and disappear down the white corridor. But I can't. The white corridor has turned black. And Ostrich feet is right behind me. The lock clanks. The spiral opens into another white corridor. It seems like the lights in this house depend on human presence; coming to life soon as we enter a room, and dying as soon as we leave.

Another semicircle of closed doors. More lights coming to life. A beautiful white bed squatting lonely in the middle of a large room. This time Ostrich feet enters before me, and in a few strides he is sitting on the beautiful bed. I did not see him shut the door, did not hear the lock clank but I feel the locked door behind me. Just as I am beginning to think Ostrich feet is mute, he speaks.

'Take off your shirt.

'Put it down.

'The jeans . . .

'I mean take them off!

'Put them down.

'Turn around!'

I stand in naked shame, my eyes glued to the white tiles beneath my feet.

He jumps off the bed and wades past me to the door. 'Dress up.' He slams the door behind him.

The morning is as white as the sheets I slept in, as white as the pyjamas Ostrich feet gave me last night. I don't know if I slept at all. All I know is that Ostrich feet dragged me by the collar and buried me inside the white sheets I was afraid to sleep in. He warned me I would wake up dead if I left the bed before he came back. Then tears started gushing down my cheeks. The tears are still flowing. Under my cheek is a damp patch of drying tears: a large blot of shit on the white sheets!

Ostrich feet scares me but he is not as scary as my strange surroundings. Not as scary as the prospect of never seeing Mukulu again. This cannot be my new home. I don't see myself, Joshua Mondo here. I belong to Mukulu's mud-and-wattle house. I belong with the trenches, stagnant waters, rubbish heaps, broken bottles, rotting dogs. I belong in Kikuubo. I belong with Mukulu's drunken love and Jjaja's sober hatred.

Key turning. Lock clanking. Ostrich feet.

'Good booooy.' He hurries to pull out the sheets he tucked in last night. Then he reaches for my hand to pull me out of bed. His hands are so soft they feel like a ripe avocado.

'I can see you didn't get out of bed. Big bro is always right, you know. Do as he says and you will always be a good booooy. Now come on, Kato is waiting for you.'

The white walk down corridors, staircases, and through black doors leads us to a boy whom I at once guess is Kato. He is seated alone at a round table making sketches on the glossy black surface with his fore-finger, and shielding whatever he is sketching with the palm of his left hand. He pauses, gazes at me. His face looks angry. Lips bunched. Nose flaring. But I can't see the same anger in his eyes.

Ostrich feet waves me over to the pulled-out chair facing Kato. I can't take my eyes off Kato. I am trying to know him. Trying to find out if he, too, was brought into this house by the man in the Nigerian attire and the woman with a wild headscarf. Was he deceived that they were his parents? Did he leave behind people like Mukulu who love him?

Ostrich feet bends over the table and says something to Kato.

'No! I don't want to go there again. Help me big bro.'

'Stop it.'

'I can't go there again.'

'I said stop it!' Ostrich feet bangs the table. The bang hits directly into my bladder. I jump off the chair and press my legs together to contain the rebellious urine but it spills. Through the white pair of shorts, down my legs, to the rubber sandals Ostrich feet gave me this morning.

'And you? Going anywhere?' Ostrich feet glares at me.

I slump back on the chair.

Kato has resumed sketching, forefinger grazing the table like it would perforate through the wood. The left hand shielding his sketch is trembling. He keeps glancing at me as if it is my fear that he is sketching.

I'm Going to Make Changes to the Kitchen

Ondjaki

how terribly absurd
it is to be alive
  Luis Eduardo Aute, *Sin tu Latido*

I've picked my ashtray up again.

My little ashtray, made by hand and with feeling.

Feelings are like ashes – suggestions of past attachments and pleasures.

The kitchen is empty. Silent. My ashtray survived all the kitchen earthquakes. Tiny little ashtray, made from sweat and pieces of me. In the small hours. Far from the kitchen.

Near to me, I have an unlit cigarette, an old lighter cased in dark wood, a lit incense stick, a window onto the unlit world, two or three lit stars, brown sandals, a faint smell of rice, a fresh teardrop and my ashtray. My ashtray.

The unlit cigarette greets my dry, desiring lips. I smoke a sort of future. A sense of peace takes hold of my hands and breasts. I savour the prospect of the pleasure that will soon be ignited.

The ritual is underway. The smoking will come later. The burning in the eyes, the itching of the hands.

'You shouldn't smoke so much.'

Father smokes more than I do. And he hasn't the habit of lingering over yet-to-be-lit cigarettes. I discovered the ritual by chance. In a protracted search for a lighter. Rituals come to us to show us how to survive our other routines.

I won't enter the kitchen with the unlit cigarette. I try not to mix private rituals and marital environments. Or, to put it more openly: perhaps everything in the kitchen has become invadingly private.

'Above all else, you must love your husband.'

The lighter is the same one as always. That's why I call it old.

It hides from me on Sundays. Doesn't want to be found. But I know of plenty of matches in this house. It occurs to me that matches can ignite kitchens as well as cigarettes.

But I resist.

'Everything has to be at peace in the house, so that you can love your daughter.'

If one day my daughter turns out to be a smoker, I'll have to give her a simple lighter. I'll have to remember to say to her: with this lighter, if you have the heart and your fingers have the will, you can ignite a kitchen. She'll laugh. Assume her mother is being playful. You shouldn't play with fire, Mother. Well no, dear. But there are kitchens and there are kitchens. Here's hoping you never need to know about fire.

The lighter is the same one as always because it hides from me but wants to be found. The kitchen never hides.

When I light the incense, the lighter licks at the smell of cinnamon, lavender, opium. A lit incense stick is not much like a star, but I think of stars whenever I light incense. These associations of ideas have never been explained to me. Since being married, I've lost any sense of what the word kitchen means to other people.

'You have a home to care for. Everything else is of little relevance.'

Father likes words. He likes the word relevance.

The smoke from the lit incense tells me stories. Recollections of people from different cultures, people I've never been acquainted with. Paths. Myths. Pains suffered by women other than me.

'Perhaps it's time you thought less about yourself.'

The smoke of the lit incense lets me know if there's any wind in the heat of the night. The dense lonely night.

★ ★ ★

I keep the house lights switched off so as to watch the red breathing of the incense. And there is wind. A mild, windy-breeze.

'Keep the house tidy. The home clean.'

Outside my window is the switched-off world. Because I believed in it when it was switched off. I'll have to unbuild it first, then rebuild it anew. In celebration, if possible. In rediscovery. In bloom.

The world appears switched off to a woman who looks at the world from her window and feels switched off from it. The woman has an unlit cigarette in her dry mouth. The woman has a quarrel with her kitchen. Or perhaps with more than just that.

I call my window 'window to the switched-off world', obviously, because I wanted a different window or a different world. A world with a different kitchen.

When I light an incense stick, I think of stars. When I visit lit stars, by looking at them, I think of the desert.

'In short, you will try to be a dedicated wife.'

Because the desert could be the mirror the stars use to revive their shine. The prints left by camels' feet are not tracks, they're not boundaries: they're mysteries. Poems we can't see or digest. It's impossible to see so close up.

One day, my daughter's eyes will surely shine with passion. Love will harbour in a new quay. Without saying a word, like a mature woman, she'll surely present the shine for me to comment upon. Here's hoping I have the clear-sightedness and courage to warn her: tell your partner not to get too close, or he might lose sight of you. 'Oh, Mother!' my daughter will say. And she'll understand.

My sandals are always close to my body. Grounded, airy and malleable. Unlike men.

'You must be patient with your husband. Patience and dedication.'

The sandals take me from the kitchen to the living room, and from the living room to the bedroom. They protect me from the coldness of the floor; they don't protect me from the coldness of the kitchen. They make me walk almost silently. If I leave them in the bedroom, it's because I require absolute silence. I haven't left them in the bedroom today, and so I talk.

I wanted a salty smell to come in through a gap in my window. Not necessarily the sea. Perhaps a forest, perhaps a mountain. Spaces of freedom and positive emptiness. Places the sandals have yet to show me.

I have my sandals close to me. As comfort, as a second skin.

From the kitchen comes the innocent, Indian smell of rice. Gentle basmati afternoons. The poetry of my hands in contrast to the drama of my nights.

'You have to find a way to understand him. To understand and accept.'

Garlic in the rice and on my nails. I don't wash them properly. To leave traces. A bay leaf. A little salt. I remain still while it gently bubbles. I leave the kitchen and await the smell of readiness in another room. The basmati of my past, without the collateral damage caused by certain flights. A tranquil time when I was the wife of a tranquil man. A man who laughed and cried. I'd started to cook rice at night, as is done in other homes.

Sometimes this strange stillness comes to me, even when I'm unaccompanied. I can tell by the smell that whatever's cooking has reached its optimum point. I'm hesitant. Lately I'm hesitant whenever I have to enter the kitchen.

Still. I try to get myself moving.

More than everything else, what's taken me by surprise is a teardrop. They don't usually come so early.

Worried, I realise disorder has entered my tears. I usually sense the approach of feelings that bring their onset. Light tremors. Particular thoughts. Queries and poems.

I call it the unexpected teardrop, and its coming could be worrying. A certain existential tiredness. The end of prolonged pressure. This teardrop, today's teardrop – I think – is different. It announces, if anything, a new season. I'm crying because the tough times will soon be over. I'm crying because the past is too recent, as are the words. I'm crying because I'm rediscovering myself.

'Is it really so hard for you to understand that this country is at war?'

Is it really so hard for you to understand, Father, that I never wanted war in my home?

I've picked my ashtray up again.

I light the cigarette. I extinguish the flame beneath the rice. I like the rice to cook through in the leftover steam. Let it soften; allow the taste of garlic to intensify.

I made this ashtray with my own two hands and all the feelings I had back then. I made it for you. You still shared cigarettes and moments with me. You flew different planes from those that drop bombs on people. Our relationship was far from war, from the screaming, the bombs. Our kitchen, the wood that you polished, rested undisturbed every night. The small hours were ours. Far from the kitchen.

'Perhaps your seeking God might be a solution.'

Father hadn't yet started with his ridiculous advice. Our daughter could greet you before bedtime.

I didn't want to know the number of your plane. I found out because they told me unexpectedly, and no one can constantly guard against being given the key to their suffering. I don't know how long it will take us to forget – will we forget? – the number of times you, the way you, the brutality with which you ripped out the cupboards in the kitchen. I found out what your plane was called today. The bombs. I found out everything. Though really I knew all along. Knew from your eyes, from your hands ripping the love from our home, tenderness disappearing out the window. At the beginning of our life together, I said let's escape this war. It's too late, you said. I was pregnant; you were busy with your flights.

My voice. My silence.

My heart, frightened and wrecked.

The kitchen is empty.

I switch off the stove and ask myself again how my ashtray survived all the kitchen earthquakes.

There is great disquiet in our house. There's our daughter who needs raising.

I smoke the cigarette.

I want to change out of my skin.

I look at the ashes in my ashtray, like feelings that lack density. I'm left holding onto nothing. Like soldiers after violent combat, that's to say, like their losses. What they lose of themselves.

I just wanted to tell you: I'm going to make changes to the kitchen.

Translated by Jethro Soutar

Rag Doll

Okwiri Oduor

In the thick yellow air, the wind hums in the bramble, pushing engorged berries against the twigs, so that thorns prick them and the jam inside starts to trickle out.

Tu Tu and Mama wear matching lace dresses with bows sewn on to the back. They each try on a wide-brimmed hat that they found fluttering in the dust devil outside their window, and when it falls over their faces and covers their eyes, Mama pulls at the latch and tosses the hat back to the dust devil.

With her hands on her hips, Mama says to the dust devil, 'Next time, bring us something we can use, you hear?'

Tu Tu imagines it – the dust devil will knock on the dusty pane and say to Mama, 'Here are some things you can use, Solea,' and there, on the window ledge, shall be poinsettias and sugar icicles and browning pages from autograph books, pages that read, 'Just wake 'em up in the usual way, Spencer – we'll leave "Flight of the Bumble Bee" for some other time.'

Mama takes out jute bags from the pantry and they pull strings out of their corners and fasten the strings like ribbons round their tresses, and then they bow at each other and giggle like girls who fry their hair and light scented candles and go to the cinema with silk handkerchiefs pinned to their cardigans.

Hand in hand, they march across the yard, crumbling anthills beneath their bare feet, singing,

Snuff out the sun
And pour porcupine juice

In Tu Tu's keyhole.

They pick only the crimson berries, the ones that pulsate and burst in their fingers, and they tie them inside the scoop of their frocks, and the hot jam runs down their legs and glues together the spaces between their toes.

In the dying light, they race each other across the yard, fireflies crackling in their hair, lighting their path. Tu Tu slips on a moist snail and she clutches at the hem of Mama's frock so that Mama slips too, and the two of them crumple down in a heap, laughing and sputtering until their panties are soaked and their tresses are filled with dead grass and earthworms.

When the dust devil comes back, Tu Tu and Mama run to the window and pull at the latch and push their heads outside. This time, the dust devil has brought them a porcelain jar with a chip broken off its mouth. Mama takes it in her arms and cradles it, singing,

Girls are dandy,

Made out of candy.

She takes Tu Tu's hand and they stand in the musky bathroom and untie the scoops of their frocks, letting all the berries fall into the old tub. They sit inside the tub, porcelain jar nestled between them, and they knead the berries between the heels of their palms until the jam becomes a kind of sticky red treacle.

They hear the milkman whistling out in the yard, and Mama calls out, 'Oe! Kinu, bring the milk here!'

The milkman comes in, gumboots squelching, leaving ace-shaped prints on the wood floor. 'Solea?' he says, peering into the hallway.

'In here.'

Kinu slowly pushes the bathroom door. It creaks, as though resenting his touch. He emerges piecemeal – elbow, shoulder, chin, ear, eyes. His face is crinkled, half anxious and half apologetic, as though he yearns both to come in and to flee.

He places the bottles by the tub, puts on his hat and says, 'Me, let me go now,' as though anyone has stopped him from going.

But he does not go. Tu Tu sees him stand in the hallway and peer through cracks in the door. He watches Mama pour all the milk in the tub, watches them lay steeping inside it. Tu Tu does not know when

Kinu leaves. Her thoughts wander off without her noticing it, and she thinks of blaring fire engines and of pigeons pecking at crumbs on the windowsill and of tiny globs of snot that someone flicked from their nose. Then she remembers Kinu watching them and looks, but he is gone already.

Tu Tu and Mama are at the Oasis of Grace church. On the outside wall of the church is marked:

Bricks for sale,

Each for 2/=

Adjacent to the church is a field where golden star grass rises ten feet in the air, hiding a grave whose epitaph reads, 'They went off together.'

Tu Tu and Mama sit down on the headstone.

'Where did they go off together?' Tu Tu asks Mama.

'Do you really want to know that?' Mama says.

'I do want to know.'

'The church sent some of its members on mission duty to Kindu Bay. They rode in the pastor's Toyota station wagon, twenty men and women, each squeezed so tight that they coalesced, and when the pastor's car rolled, they became a dollop of flesh, indistinguishable, each of their peculiarities – whether they liked their maize boiled or roasted, or whether they chewed mints or sucked them – gone, and so all twenty of them were buried together.'

Tu Tu and Mama bend backwards over the stone, their tresses grazing the dirty terrazzo of the mass grave. Their distended navels pop out and poke through the fabric of their frocks, and their nostrils flare and gnats dart into them.

Abandoning the headstone, they climb a tree, higher and higher, to the very top branches. They sit there, swinging their legs below them, toes wiggling and the coarse wind scratching the soles of their bare feet.

'Look at the stone angels,' Mama says, pointing further out in the field.

Tu Tu sees them, an entire battalion of them, standing tight-lipped, watching them.

Mama climbs down the tree. 'Come, let us look.'

Tu Tu jumps down from the tree, scraping the back of her thighs against the rough bark. The hem of her frock tears. Mama lifts the frock up to Tu Tu's waist. She scrutinises the scratches on her thighs.

'You are bleeding,' she says. 'Does it hurt?'

Tu Tu nods.

Mama spits into her hand and rubs the saliva over the scratches. 'There now, it won't hurt any more.'

They wander to the stone angels, hand in hand, chanting,

Suzie my best friend,
Come out and play with me
I've got a dolly – see
And an apple tree.

The stone angels are scattered over the yard, as far as the eye can see. Some have wings spread out, flapping in the air. Some have swords held menacingly across their chests, ready to slay any brutes that cross their paths.

In a corner of the yard, where a fig tree was felled by the wind, one stone angel lies face down, her open mouth filled with earth. Tu Tu and Mama stare at her.

'Is she still alive?' Tu Tu asks.

Mama pokes the stone angel with a twig. The stone angel does not move. Mama throws the twig away and falls down to her knees. She picks the stone angel up and brushes earth from her eyes and nose. Her arm is broken off and lies on the ground.

'Look,' Mama says, and Tu Tu leans in to see the words inscribed on the stone angel. The words say,

Mbekenya Mwisya,
She started out so well.

Mama hugs the stone angel to her breasts. 'She started out so well because she had been standing upright, but then the wind tipped her over and she broke her arm and now the other angels don't want her any more,' Mama says. 'We have to take her home with us, Tu Tu. She is lonely.'

That night, Tu Tu brings out a bowl of wheat flour and warm water, and Mama makes some wheat glue. They bend over Mbekenya the stone angel and put her arm back together.

'Bring me a needle, Tu Tu,' Mama says, and when Tu Tu does, Mama inscribes one more line on to the stone angel, so that now the words on her say,

Mbekenya Mwisya,
She started out so well . . .
But her story is not yet finished.

The sky is melting and the marsh is roiling, and Tu Tu and Mama take out empty milk cartons and fill them with air and bring those with them for extra supply. They swim all the way down to the bottom of the marsh, where the sludge is hot and bubbling.

Later, they lie down on their backs with their arms folded beneath their heads, and they stare out into the sky and watch dandelions quiver, and when it starts to rain, they stick their tongues out and taste the beautiful, terrifying creatures of the far-off sea.

'Oh, how I miss the seaside,' Mama says.

'What do you miss most about it?'

'My brother Haji,' she says. 'He rose from the green bog of Old Town, among cawing ravens and the dusty deflated umbrella bodies of decaying sea urchins. His stick went kong-kong-kong on the narrow coral-paved streets and on the sagging fish-stuffed bellies of alley cats. He was blind, you see.'

Tu Tu turns on her side, so that she watches Mama's face as she speaks. She stares at the dimple on Mama's chin and at the slight severing of Mama's earlobe from the side of her face, as though she had once enraged a person and they had pulled at her ear too hard, almost tearing it off. Mama's eyes are set deep inside her sockets, and her irises dance maddeningly, even as she fixes Tu Tu with an unwavering stare.

'Your brother,' Tu Tu says, 'where did he go?'

Mama plucks at a blade of grass and nibbles on it. 'Through the town.'

'Did you go with him?'

'All the time. I described to him the things he could not see.'

'Like what?'

'Like the men sitting in their fruit-filled rickshaws or on their cabbage-laden donkeys. The ships on the sea, too. I told Haji that they were large iron snails crawling slowly, leaving a trail of thick, white mucus on the blue water. I told him that no matter how hard one stared at the iron snails, one could never see them move. They only moved when one was not looking. Some had names like *M. V. Britannia* and *Tausi Ndege Wangu.*'

Tu Tu watches a pair of marabou storks forage, their feathers turning green in the steaming marsh.

'When the sun was high up in the sky,' Mama says, 'we sat beneath the tamarind tree, where the housewives of Old Town hurled mouldy biriyani and polyester rags and orange peels and month-old foetuses. Sometimes we found nice things there.'

'Like what?'

'Once we found a child's caramel smile, and we took turns wearing it on our faces. Another time we found a billy goat that could turn into a beautiful woman in the night. Once we found a mganga from Zanzibar who knew how to remove seven-headed jinnis from inside people. Another time we found the music of the muezzin trapped inside a cooking fat tin.'

'Did you sit beneath the tamarind tree even when it rained?'

'Aisha took us in then. She owned the tea shack down the street. She spent her days standing at the door of her shack, staring up at the sky, mulling over whether or not it would rain. Well, when it did, she came out waving a stick at us, cackling that we would catch colds and die. She gave us boiled blue marlin and rock buns and coconut milk to warm us up, and as we ate, she cut Haji's hair and plaited mine and snipped our toenails with a razor.'

'Why did Haji not come to the big city with you?'

Mama sits up, bringing her knees up and hugging them. 'He tried to come with me,' she says. 'We didn't have any money, so the conductor only let us ride in the luggage compartment of the bus. All was well until we got to Voi. The sea must have realised then that Haji was gone. It started heaving, throwing a frightful fit, and all the ships on it and all the beasts inside it crushed in a pile of mangled iron and rotten wood on the seashore. So Haji had to disembark and return quickly-quickly to calm the sea. And every time he ever tried to leave, the sea would not have it.'

It is dark now. Tu Tu and Mama walk home slowly, exhausted from their swimming, drowsily chewing on stalks of grass.

The wooden beams above Tu Tu's head hem and haw, and the walls lean closer. They like to do that, the walls, to play *Broken Telephone*. When someone says a thing, the walls lean in to catch snatches of it. The walls then tell these words to other walls, stretching them and smothering them in turn, so that when you finally hear them, the words have become tiny, pea-shaped whispers that would burst like maize grains if one held a candle to them.

Tu Tu seeks out her mother, finding her in the grotto they once dug out in the backroom. Mama sits by the window, tipping back and forth in a rocking chair.

The rocking chair; they found it broken and discarded near the marsh, and they put it on their backs and brought it home and fixed it. They cut rattan with a penknife and soaked it in glycerine and plaited it, and when the rattan made cuts in their arms, they spread cow lard and saliva on the cuts.

They did that with everything they own – found it and put it on their backs and brought it home and fixed it. Their house, too. It had been thrown away in the dumpster behind the market square, and they put it on their backs and climbed the hill, singing *Ten Green Bottles*, and when the last green bottle fell from the wall, they put the house down and built a home.

Mama's face is to the window, spangled, golden beads dancing on it. Outside, the guava tree shakes, its glossy leaves rasping, the quilt that hangs on its branches flying, dragging in the grass.

'Catch it!' Mama says, her voice shrill.

Tu Tu chases it down like a cockerel. She catches it and it squirms and squirms and she restrains it beneath her arm. She closes the door and kneels by Mama, the quilt spread out before her. She plucks out red-headed caterpillars and yellow beetles and little black jack needles.

A few months back, they made a dozen trips to the seamstress' stall, filling their pockets with rags that the seamstress no longer wanted. When they had gathered enough, they sat down on the kitchen floor and darned and embellished and overcast, and the rags became this quilt which they lie on each night and dream grainy rayon dreams, dream of silver coins spinning and spinning and disappearing beneath dressing bureaus, dream too of butter-smudged fingers scratching at bumps in walls.

'They don't want us here, Tu Tu,' Mama says.

'Who?'

'Them,' she says, pointing out the window at the bramble.

'The berries?'

'No, Tu Tu. The people out there. We make them uncomfortable.'

'How do you know they don't want us here?' Tu Tu says.

The walls fidget about, blabbering indecipherable things. Mama raises her hand to shush them. She says to Tu Tu, 'Come I show you.'

Mama takes Tu Tu to the kitchen. 'This was here when I got home from the posho mill.'

The carcass of a cat is hooked to the wall above the door, wire poking through the back of its neck. Flies swarm about it, buzzing, their backs sparkling. Draped over the back of a nearby chair is the cat's skin, like a scarf that someone forgot.

Tu Tu retches into the washbowl. Outside, Kinu the milkman whistles, bottles clanging in his crate. Tu Tu and Mama watch as he stands his bicycle against a tree, as he takes out their milk and places it on the doorstep.

'Kinu,' Mama says. 'Do you like cats?'

'What?'

'Cats. Do you like them?'

'I do not really care for them.'

'But you would not hurt them, would you?'

'By God, no.' Kinu has his half anxious and half apologetic face again. 'It was the chief and his cronies that did that. Me, I am just a milkman, what could I do to stop them?'

'Well, then?' Mama says, but it is not a question, rather, a command.

Kinu takes his hands out of his pockets. He takes the cat down from the hook, holding it as gently as if it were a newborn infant.

Mama fetches a hoe and they go out to a clearing by the bramble. Mama chooses a spot between two clumps of aloe vera. 'Well, then?'

Kinu places the carcass down, and he begins to dig.

'You have to make the hole deep, else the stray dogs will burrow in and take it out.'

Kinu digs and digs until Mama says, 'There, now.'

He buries the cat.

Mama says, 'If you scrub your hands out in the back, I will make you some tea.'

Tu Tu watches Mama light the kerosene stove and put on a sufuria of water and milk. When it boils, she adds tea leaves and masala and sieves it and pours it into three cups. She hands one to each of them.

Sipping on his tea, Kinu says, 'Why did your mother name you Solea, like the petroleum jelly?'

Tu Tu almost chokes on her tea. She had never considered the fact that Mama might have a mother herself. In her mind, Mama had always just *been*.

'Why do you assume that it is my mother that did?'

'It is not?'

'Well, if it had been, she would have named me something that had spirit. Like Mbekenya Mwisya.' Mama sips on her tea. 'Do you want to see her?'

'Who?'

'The stone angel.'

Kinu nods. Mama takes his tea and places it in the washbowl.

'Well, then?' she says, and it is a command for him to rise up and follow her.

He stands by the side of the bed, stroking the stone angel's face. Mama pats down Tu Tu's tresses. She whispers, 'Would you like it if Kinu became your father?'

Tu Tu tries to imagine the things that Kinu would do if he were her father. He would sip water from a glass and pass it to Mama, and Mama would sip it too and pass it back to him. And the water glass would go back and forth between them, until the water became a piece of string at the bottom of the glass, and the mouth of the glass would have bubbles of spittle from both their lips. Then Kinu would clip the branches of the pear tree and build a new pantry at the back of the house for their berries.

When the sun went down, Mama would tilt the Thermos flask and pour some millet gruel into a mug. Slowly, she would turn so that she was facing Kinu. She would bring the mug to his lips and blow it until the gruel bubbled and raged, and some of it would splatter against the daffodils embroidered on her dress, over her breasts. And Mama would motion to Tu Tu and offer her some gruel too, and Tu Tu would slurp a tiny portion of it and turn it about her tongue, not swallowing it, for the remainder of the night.

Tu Tu watches as Kinu pulls at the bows in the back of Mama's dress. Mama says, 'Wait, I take Tu Tu out first. She should not see this.'

Kinu gives Tu Tu a sidelong glance. 'Jesus, Solea! Tu Tu is just a rag doll. Rag dolls don't *see* things.'

So Mama drops Tu Tu on the bamboo table and shrugs out of her frock. Kinu pulls Mama beneath him, and then he slides deeper and deeper into her, and when he slides back out, he sits at the edge of the bed and pulls his slacks on.

'Will you not tell me your real name, Solea?'

Mama turns in the bed, so that she lies with her back to him. 'My real name is the marks on my body,' she says. 'Call me by the chinks in my chin and the discolourations in my toenails. Call me Trembling Eyes. Call me Torn Ear.'

This is How I Remember It

Ukamaka Olisakwe

I was eighteen and stupid, and I never anticipated we would become friends after that encounter in Conflict Resolution class. You remember? It was Mrs Clara's class and she was reading out her rules for the semester when you walked in. You were thin, busty and perfect. And the way you walked? Like you were slow-dancing. Swaying from side to side. Throwing out one thin leg after the other. Your nose in the air. Lips in a pout. We all watched you. Mrs Clara too. I was smiling when you got to where I sat.

Until you said, '*Shift!*'

I moved a bit and you sat and crossed one leg over the other. You did not look at me. Did not even pretend to look at me. I wanted to touch your shoulder, to tell you that we had met before, but you turned to me with this scrunched up nose, these rude eyes, Jesus, they were like slits on your face. 'You are staring,' you said, 'and that is fucking rude.'

I tried to breathe. Tried to read. But, dear Lord, your words came smashing my ego with machetes. I crawled into myself, moved farther away from you. You crossed and uncrossed your legs. Unfazed. You didn't *see* me. Didn't even notice my hurt.

You called yourself Bisi, when Mrs Clara asked your name. You asked questions when no one else had any. Your hand rose into the air every time, seeking clarification. You had an opinion on every topic. Your eyes blazed with interest as you talked about the trivial conflict situations: if a woman caught her husband in bed with the housemaid, which conflict resolution strategy would Mrs Clara recommend; if a girl stabs her uncle who raped her, which resolution style would the family adopt? Questions that had no place in Mrs Clara's book. Questions Mrs Clara knew that even Mrs Clara didn't have the answers to. You scored the highest in her first assessment. You impressed her, made her putty in your hands. Thunderbolted through her classes. Blurred out every other student. It was just you and Mrs Clara. You ask, she smiles. You opine, she smiles. Others snore. I scowl. At a point I wondered if she was in love with you. By the fourth week, I hissed each time you raised your hand to ask a question and yawned each time Mrs Clara sought your opinion.

We never had the briefest of conversations, never pretended that we were even course-mates, until that afternoon when you poked my shoulder and said, 'You are sleeping,' loud enough for everyone to hear. I began to stutter. Mrs Clara's face contorted in disgust. I began to deny it, but Mrs Clara was already frowning. I stood before her, hopelessly struggled to mouth the words that clung to my throat. A sense of failure enveloped me, one that swooped on me not because I did not know how to articulate my defence, but because I did not know how to articulate it while you stared. Because with you, words took leave and scaled, reducing me to a stuttering buffoon.

That evening, I lay in my bed. I thought of Papa. I thought of you. Then I said my prayers. For you to break your neck. For Amadioha to shave your hair with a blunt razor. *Ka kitikpa lachapu gi anya, anuofia!* But my meditation was broken by hard knocks that came from my door. I got it. Then stopped, stunned. Oh! You stood before me, an impish smile on your face, a tub of ice-cream in your hands.

'Oge,' you called me, 'I apologise for everything.'

You sounded sincere.

Nobody has ever barged into my life, playing proprietary, like they'd been there all their life. I trusted you to be there. To *see* me. I listened to you talk. And I didn't want you to stop. You never stuttered. You know that I think my words first, before rolling them off my tongue. But you, you spoke like your tongue grew words, and you were in a hurry to set them free. I reassessed myself – my dress, my hair, my make-up. I was the timid girl who didn't belong there. Who didn't belong to you. You were the only girl I'd seen in a long time who didn't spend forever before a mirror. Who didn't cake her face or coat her eyes, layering herself, until she became a masquerade. Who wasn't obsessed with her beauty. And that absence of narcissism, is beauty in its purest form.

During classes you started using lines like, *'My friend, Oge, once said this . . .'*, *'My friend Oge once said that . . .'*, quoting smart things I never said, amplifying simple things I once said, presenting me like I was someone more intelligent. Mrs Clara began to look at me more kindly.

You wanted to know what my first sex was like. I said I'd had never had sex. You stared at me, your mouth wide open, waiting for something I did not know I was supposed to say. You were utterly, innocently shocked, that a girl my age hadn't had sex. And then you were laughing. I began to laugh too. I laughed because you were clutching your stomach, your tears streaming down your face, your chest heaving from the strain. I laughed because it was the prettiest sight I had even seen.

Bisi, there is a vacuum here. What we had transcends friendship. It has a name.

And I trembled that day you told me your whole story: you dropped out of a girls' boarding school because the girls in your school were notorious for many things but famous for touching themselves in closed spaces. You always caught them slipping their fingers under their panties. Once you walked into your senior prefect's room, found her splayed on her bed, her legs spread apart like a book, and the labour prefect's face buried at the place the legs met. You said it almost made you puke. That you ran but they caught you, held you down, touched your breasts. That they slipped their fingers under your panties. You fought them, but they were stronger. You yelled. No one burst through the door to help. The world was coming to an end. You would be stuck there forever with those two. You scratched. Kicked. But they were stronger. You struggled, then weakened, then began to cry. Your legs grew smarter. They fled. Carrying your numbed mind along, rushing you to Principal's Office, all the while you thought you would fall on your face. At Principal's Office, you walked past the snoring security guard, and pulled the door open. And wished you hadn't. There. Head

Girl stood before the Principal, reeling out names of the girls who jumped the school fence the previous day, the girls who were said to have partied with the boys from the neighbouring school. You were still unable to speak as Principal hurriedly summoned all the girls to assembly. You stood before the girls, before the ones who tortured you, wishing for the ground to open up and swallow you. You could see their smirks when you were asked to kneel. You could hear their laughter when Principal whipped your hands. You survived long enough before your mother pulled you out of that school.

Bisi, your story ruined my *coming out*. You glared at the floor long after you were done talking. But you became Bisi again. 'That is in the past now,' you said, smiled. You pulled off your blouse, because the room had grown hot. You sat before me, in all your glory of breasts and braids and pretty face, fanning yourself with the *News Magazine*, laughing at something you were saying. You sat there. Without shame. Without inhibition. Without an inkling of the riot that went on in my mind. I wanted more, but each time I dared to, your words came back slashing that yearning with a machete.

You were desperate to rid me of my virginity. So you wanted me to meet your writer friends. I was a little apprehensive, but you were smiling in that sincere way. I said 'OK', and the next thing you did, I didn't even expect it. You grabbed my face, plopped a kiss on my cheek. I stared, stunned. You began to laugh. I held your eyes, sought for that confirmation that said you understood my affection for you. That you understood the emotions that racked my ribs and caused the liquid warmness to seep into my underwear each time we were together. But you were laughing in that careless way. And saying, 'You look ridiculous. It's just a kiss!'

You put on the CD, and began to dance *kukere*. My eyes burned with tears. You kept dancing, rolling your waist, shaking your buttocks, your breasts jumping about in rhythm. You made funny faces, twisting like you were pole-dancing, twerking and breaking my heart into tiny, miserable pieces.

That evening, we went to the staff club to meet your friends. You said they were the only students allowed into the club, because Nenye, the leader, was sleeping with the VC.

We got to the old club. Frowned at the large swimming pool. Shook our heads at the chipped tiles. Smiled at bright lights. Scrunched up our noses; the air was heavy with alcohol and music and urine. At one end, a group of lecturers lounged on sofas, sipped from cups of beer, chatted discreetly like they were talking top secrets. Your friends talked gibberish, laughed like Motor Park touts and clinked bottles of beer. It was hard to imagine they were writers. They welcomed you with hugs and taps and pecks and kisses. They observed me like old meat in a butcher's stall. They stared when you introduced me as your best friend, and then they returned to assessing me. The boys undressed me with their eyes, but feigned disinterest when I glared back. The girls looked at my shoes and my dress and my hair, and they struggled to hold their mocking laughs, though they spilled from the sides of their big mouths. I clenched your hand tightly as you introduced them: the sulky one was Nenye; the skinny one was Tope; the fat one with the dreadful hair was Nkem; the one in the god-awful blouse was Mary. You also introduced the boys: the one acting like he was the biggest boy on campus, what with the way he arced his leg on the table, was Kene; the one with the stupid smile and big nose and rabbit ears was Femi; the overdressed one was David; and the one with the mug-me look was Kevin. You sat and pulled up a chair for me. I stared at the faces first, then I sat on one buttock. You ordered a special called 'homework' and two bottles of Smirnoff Ice. I asked for a bottle of Maltina. Then you were talking with them and the conversation took away the previous tense silences. Once, you tried to include me in the conversation, but they all went mute, like NEPA had cut off power. The waitress returned with the orders. Homework turned out to be two chicken heads with their respective feet shoved down each throat and strung with chicken intestine.

'Try it,' you said. 'It is fantastic!'

Your girlfriends kept observing me. But Femi, the guy with the big nose and rabbit ears, smiled and said, 'Order one. You will enjoy it.' He would have looked handsome if you placed a hand over his nose and pulled back his ears.

I ordered homework.

Group discussion skirted from the looming ASUU strike to the stories of Buccaneers warring with Black Axe, and then to the female student who did juju with her vagina and slept with her abusive lecturer; he woke up the following morning screaming himself hoarse and tearing off his clothes.

Nenye said, 'He has been admitted to a psychiatric ward.'

Mary said, 'Suits him best!'

Kene said, 'That's nonsense talk! Perhaps she wanted marriage and he refused!'

Mary said, 'Then, zip up if you can't own up.'

Nkem said, 'That's one penis down. Next on the line please!'

Kene began to speak but Nenye gave him the talk-to-the-palm.

You, you hardly spoke. Something dark climbed into your eyes. I wanted to ask what bothered you, but Femi was saying these things to me: asking about my course of study and where my hostel was. I took one look at his ears and glared at him.

Nenye lit a cigarette. The girls lit theirs too. They smoked and puffed like firewood. I wanted to throw up. The speaker which hung from the wall began to croon Flavour's 'Ada Ada'. The tranquil song melded with the loud chatter from the group.

'I love this song!' Femi said, moving in closer, unfazed. 'You wanna dance?'

I got up and went to the smelly restroom. When I returned, Flavour's 'Shake Ukwu' was blaring from the speaker. You swung your bottle of Smirnoff Ice over your head, twisting your body in tune with the music.

Nenye said, 'You guys are wasting this fine music,' got up and began to dance. Kene joined her. You stopped swinging your bottle and dropped it with a thud on the table. You sat back, your gaze on the dancing couple for a minute, before you pulled out your own cigarette pack and began to fumble with your lighter. Your movement was cold. Your face was set in a grim mask. You finally lit a cigarette and puffed smoke in my face.

'You are surprised, babe?' But you were looking at the dancing couple.

Something was not sitting well with me. It was in the way you watched Kene. The way your eyes shot arrows at Nenye. The way my pee filled up my bladder. You jerked off your seat and began to dance, a slow rhythmic sway of your hips, from side to side, like tree branches during harmattan. Kene pulled away from Nenye and drew you from behind, moving with your slow rhythm, his body perfectly melding with yours. Flavour's *Ashawo* switched on and your dance steps changed. You began a slow dance, your right leg raised and your crotch slapping against Kene's thigh. Later, when the music ended, you became brighter and chattier. I wanted to just get up and leave, but my legs stuck to the floor.

Femi pulled out a paper and began to read a poem, something about love and obsession. When he ended, Kene said, 'I hate it. It didn't give me the fucking *whoosh*!'

Nenye read her own story. Kene scoffed and said, 'Depressing.'

David read a story about students who died during a Boko Haram attack, and Kene said it was agenda writing.

You read a story about a girl becoming aware of her sexuality. It was almost about me. My eyes burned with tears. I held your eyes. And I realised this was love, this thing that always made words screw themselves over and leave me stammering before you. I wanted to say that the story was beautiful. But Kene beat me to it.

'It reads like a personal opinion masquerading as fiction,' he said.

I was offended. You weren't. You smiled in that sincere way that was beginning to piss me off. And then you jotted down notes, making the fucker feel like he was the best thing to have happened to the group. I wanted to shake you until your teeth rattled. Then I wondered if you were in love with Kene.

Later, Kene read his own story. You could tell it was carefully written, studiously edited and languorously rewritten. But you didn't take him on. Didn't even see how he thought he sounded like God. Instead you sat there, the stupid smile tearing through your face and peeling your lips back.

'This story is so antiseptic,' I said. 'I could as well soak my head in a bucket of bleach!'

Kene froze.

David gasped.

Nenye's jaw dropped.

Femi began to cough.

I could feel Nenye's disdain. I could see Kene's hate. And the cold war began. We fought with our eyes, gathered guns and arrows and machetes and shot and slashed and attacked with our stares. All the while the air was swollen with anger and silence and hate. Others stood by and watched as the war raged. I would not budge for them, would not be intimidated by their rudeness.

Femi began to laugh. 'I love this babe!'

I turned to you. But you were watching Kene. He took his time folding his paper into tiny squares, his eyes glued to his task, his shoulders struggling to stay high. Then you looked at me. Then you smiled. I gave you the eye and you got up and said we had to leave. They did not attempt to call you back.

We walked out of the club, our hands clasped together. Outside, in a dark parking lot, you pulled me in a hug. The breeze was cool against my face. I gulped in air, to keep from crying, but my eyes burned still. For the first time, it felt so right, this affection, this thing that obliterated reason, leaving me in that space where hope fluttered, weakly at first, and then determinedly as I inhaled your scent of flowers and soap and cigarettes and alcohol. It blossomed as I kissed your cheek and you didn't cringe. It winged boldly, uncontrolled, as I kissed your neck. The trembling started in my stomach and then I was shaking. And then I was crying. And then you begged me not to cry. This was love. But it beckoned for a new name, so you would understand – because you were supposed to understand – that I wasn't like every other girl. That I was meant for you. But you held my face, wiped my tears, called me, 'My best-friend-sister'.

How do you weigh friendship? At what point should the other party begin to perceive that it has become something much more?

You lay on my bed, dressed just in your underwear, your head propped on the pillow, and you were saying something about the walls breathing fire, all the while your breasts hung atop your bra cups like large oranges on bottle corks. Liquid warmth swirled in my stomach. I was paralysed by it. I could not breathe well. I could barely hear you as you talked about visiting home; about your town, Abeokuta, and its rocks and dusts and little rusted-roofed houses. But I was staring at your breasts, at the bulge that was your nipple, wondering when you would ever get it.

'You will love Abeokuta,' you said.

'I love you,' I said.

You sat up. You held my hands. You said, 'Oh, babe, I love you too. I want this to remain even after we marry our husbands and have our own children.'

It was then the anger clouded my vision. It raged, pulling down all my restraints and silences and hopelessness. You were supposed to be intelligent but how could you be so stupid, so blind? How could you not see something as simple as this?

'I love you like a boy does a girl.'

You dropped my hands.

'You are mad,' you said.

'Maybe . . . I . . . Papa always said there is something not right with me.'

You did not say I sounded stupid. Instead you cracked, your face crumpling and squeezing and morphing. You grew into someone else. Someone scary. You pulled the duvet to your chest. My initial bravado began to seep out of my pores.

'You are homosexual,' you said.

'I am different-sexual,' I whispered.

'What the fuck is . . . When did this begin?'

Your voice, it was cold, cold, cold. I stared at my palms and the words would not come.

This is how I remember it, Bisi. This is how you left me: you pulled on your dress. You slipped on your shoes. You grabbed your bag. You picked up your phone. You walked out of the door, without a second look back. Leaving only the memories. Of things that used to be; of things that never would be. You never came back. Your number is unreachable. And weeks later, ASUU embarked on an indefinite strike action.

Bisi, it has been five months and fourteen days since you left. School will reopen next week and I know I will begin to know what hell feels like. I will see your big eyes again. I will walk alone now. I will hurt every day. But it will get to that point when pain will begin to take hold. And then, I would begin to hold my head high.

I will slip this letter under your book when classes begin. I hope you read it. So you would know just how I remember us.

from the forthcoming novel

The Wayfarers

Chibundu Onuzo

Everyone hates soldiers, even we, Chike Ameobi thought that morning. How will you enter a village and kill a young man because he cannot explain where he slept last night? The first time he had slept with a girl, he had no explanations for his mother the next morning.

They tied the boy to a stick and blindfolded him. The strip of cloth was so worn that when Chike passed it round the boy's forehead, he could still see his terrified eyeballs moving. The villagers gathered to watch this riverside show. A few women were weeping demonstratively, throwing their hands to the air and beating their heads in the dust but for the most part, the audience watched in silence.

The boy was convicted on baseless evidence. One of their men had been killed last night in a patrol ambush. One attacker had been of slight build and wearing a red shirt that showed in the dark, even as he escaped. In the early hours of the morning, their C.O. had driven to the nearby village and demanded that the culprits be brought forward. Rounds had been fired in the air and a few men had been kicked to the ground but no one came forward, as was expected. They were about to leave, when his C.O. saw this young boy going down to the river in a red shirt and torn khaki trousers.

His 'Where were you last night?' had caused a series of stammering answers, two of which conflicted. Sergeant Bayọ, who could barely see in daylight, had identified the boy as the assailant from last night and the military tribunal of one sentenced him to death.

★ ★ ★

The line of twelve soldiers began to step backwards. A young woman, perhaps his sister or girlfriend, broke away from the main group of mourners and rolled towards the boy, stopping just before his feet. She lay there with her face to the sky, keening like a wounded bird. It would have been better to shoot the boy in the head, quickly and quietly. It was such displays that stirred up hatred, folding it into the villagers' souls.

Seven, Chike counted out loud. Whenever a firing squad was assembled, it was the shortest man's legs they used to judge. Wherever he stopped after ten steps, the group readjusted. In battalions with crack shooting teams, it was the tallest used to measure. For a division like this, Yẹmi Ọkẹ, with his stumpy bow-legs, was best.

'Attention!'

They stamped unevenly, their feet syncopating the ground.

'Aim!'

Their guns clicked in a rhythmless staccato.

'Inemo go,' the boy screamed.

'Fire!'

The bullets from eight guns tore his chest open as the girl rolled to safety. One shot managed to find its way to the boy's head, pumping blood out of his ears.

'Cease fire!'

The boy's body slumped forward as their guns came down, as if obeying the same order. The girl was dragged away by some villagers, sliding through the dust, unresisting as a corpse. Still on the ground, but weeping in a more restrained fashion.

Chike and Yẹmi were chosen to cut the body down from the stake and bury it. His C.O. maintained there was nothing unconstitutional about them but still, he refused to submit the open-air trials to the legal expertise of others. The boy's palms were still moist but his trousers were dry.

'You didn't shoot,' Chike said as they lifted the body between them.

'No. You, nko?'

'No.'

Was it rebellion they were fermenting, Chike asked himself when they got back to base. He did not know. Unrest in the ranks was often the effervescence of weevily beans and maggoty rice. Tolerably fed and kitted African soldiers did not grumble because of ideas. Still, on many occasions, he found himself whispering his discontent to Yẹmi, who, even if he did not agree, did not stop the words of his friend, an act convictable in their C.O.'s court.

Their Commanding Officer was an Ijaw man, inconceivable but it was so nonetheless. He had sat on the tribunal that convicted the Ogoni geologist who claimed the oil spills would make his homeland uninhabitable. Rock scientists do not often rouse people but this onyx-black man with his rushed, unpunctuated speech heated the Niger Deltans until they erupted on to the streets in protest.

Tear gas was thrown, property destroyed, shots fired into the crowd and a military court assembled to determine the sequence of events. As the only Niger Deltan, Chike's Commanding Officer was held up as proof that disaffection in the region was exaggerated. Perhaps Opuowei Benatari had fought for the geologist on the other side of the panel doors the tribunal retired behind briefly but when the verdict of guilty was passed, he stood shoulder to shoulder with his comrades.

There was no way back after such a betrayal and so forward Colonel Benatari marched with his morning drill mantra: 'The army is my mother. The army is my father.' Under the military rulers in their dull khaki and now, in civilian rule, Benatari had served in the Delta. His name was an expletive in the region.

They found him in their canteen, sitting with the senior officers. Chike felt pity for these men whose rank entitled them to meals with Benatari. The Colonel swung between jocose familiarity and an exacting attention to military etiquette.

'You two, come here.'

They went to his table and saluted.

'Have you disposed of the rebel?'

'Yes, Sir.'

'Go and get your food then. Beans and dodo today. What do you think of that?'

'Good, Sah,' Yẹmi said.

'And you?'

'Very good, Sir.'

'Remind me of your name.'

'Lieutenant Ameobi, Sir.'

'All this Sir, Sir, when you talk to the junior officers,' Colonel Benatari said, turning to the men who always sat on either side of him. 'At ease. Not you,' he said, when Yẹmi too relaxed into a slouch. 'Are you a graduate?'

'Yes, Colonel.'

'What did you study?'

'Zoology, Colonel.'

'Wonderful,' he said, turning to his supporters. 'Gentlemen we have a zoo keeper for our company of animals.'

The officers who flanked him laughed, slapping their knees. Those outside Colonel Benatari's circle smiled but continued to stare down at their plates.

'Dismissed.'

It was harmattan now and the evenings were cool. Cool enough for some men to wear warm mufti to the mess if Benatari was in a good mood. The clothing at Chike's table reflected the guilty conviction of that morning. One man wore a woollen hat, another had exchanged his camouflage shirt for a blue cardigan and the man opposite him had tied a wrapper over his trousers. Their camp was a makeshift affair. In well-ordered barracks, officers did not eat at the same table with the other ranks but in the Delta correct manners had begun to slide.

He liked to sit with the men and listen to their banter. At first they had been guarded around him, wary of the officer in their midst. The most experienced of them could never rise to the officer rank and the most incompetent of his kind would never sink into the other ranks. It was the way of the army. Some were trained to lead and others to follow. They stretched their fists forward in salute when he and Yẹmi sat down but the conversation did not stop.

'O, boy, you see Tina today? That her bobby.'

There was a new worker in the kitchen. Youngish and pretty enough. Since she started two weeks ago, she had been the subject of every wet dream in the barracks.

'Her nyash.'

The men's common language was a very basic version of pidgin that allowed for little more than sex and food. Benatari hated to see them grouped according to tribe, so on patrol and at meal times, conversations were confined to this Neanderthal fare. But in a smoking huddle by the lavatory, or on the way to the river to fetch water, he would hear softly spoken Igbo and Yoruba and Hausa. He knew enough of each to understand when a brother was sick, or a father had died, or a new governor was judged inept.

It surprised him how often these soldiers discussed politics. At NMS, they had been taught that officers and gentlemen did not get involved in that dirty game of persuasion and manipulation. The ethos had clearly not trickled down. Further proof of the disconnect between the officer class and the men they led.

Some of the other platoon commanders had no patience for the new privates.

'Women and children,' he had heard Lieutenant Ademọla complain when one of his men dropped his rifle during an attack. They had handled guns for so long, they could not fathom fear of them. His first time was when he was twelve; induction week in the Nigerian Military School, Zaria. Ten paces to his left was his bunkmate Ogboi, who had an older brother in the school and knew everything about everything. When Instructor Aminu shouted 'Fire!' Ogboi swung his AK-47 at him and held down its trigger. Too surprised to run, he had dropped his gun and raised his hands to shield his belly.

Strangely, Ogboi was laughing. 'Blanks,' he said, wiping tears from his eyes. 'We don't get bullets till SS1. See your face like Sallah ram.'

Instructor Aminu had caned them both.

'Why me, Sir?' he had asked before he bent to receive five strokes more than Ogboi.

'Because a soldier never drops his weapon unless to surrender and a soldier never asks why.'

He would have followed Ogboi to the Nigerian Defence Academy if not for his mother's obsession with higher education.

'Just in case democracy should come back. I want the military to stay for ever because my son is there but you must still prepare for rain in harmattan.'

★ ★ ★

'The beans sweet today.'

'Dem over boil am. The thing dey poto poto,' Yẹmi said.

'Private, this place no be restaurant,' said Godwin, the Pentecostal who had seen Chike drop a Bible and begun spreading rumours that he was a wizard.

His books had not been allowed into the Delta. '*The Communist Manifesto*,' the officer said, reading off the cracked spine of Marx, an author discovered on a final year elective. 'Lieutenant, we do not want any manifestos on our base. We are soldiers, not politicians.' In vain did he try to explain that the words in the book had lost almost all power to inflame, and only the most academic on the base would even be able to understand them. The slack-jawed man has seized not only Marx but Hegel and Aristotle and John Grisham out of spite.

The only books on base were the Bible and the Quran. The latter was written in an Arabic script that was solely art to him. He started reading the Bible, flicking to a new passage each day. With time, he grew expert at bibliomancy. Knowing that one's fingers sought the middle, he dropped the book on the floor, letting the uneven cement decide which passage he would read. It was this Godwin had seen and branded him a wizard.

'Sah, the Colonel no go like this.'

Benatari was a Catholic, or at least he wore a rosary wound round his wrist, a silver Christ, dangling crucified to his palm.

'And who will tell him?'

The matter had ended there but since then Godwin had become his enemy, so far as a soldier of lower rank could be the enemy of an officer.

'Private,' Godwin said, speaking to Yẹmi but looking at him, 'Just close mouth and eat your beans.'

'Before nko? I go open mouth eat am?'

Yẹmi was the lowest-ranking man in his platoon but he was also one of the sharpest. He needed no defending. Chike got up and left the canteen.

With the exception of Yẹmi, the men of his platoon did not like him. It was not an active dislike. They obeyed his orders and stood at attention while he inspected their kit but they could not warm to him. Officer training had not prepared him for this. He had been taught to lead men who would idolise him and to bring to heel men who would buck at his every order, sneering at his age and inexperience. But there were no lessons for apathy. What to do when eyes slid away from his attempts at contact.

He had tried to broach the matter with his Sergeant but either the man did not understand, or he had no intention of playing nursemaid to his new platoon commander.

'They will soon get to know you,' Sergeant Moloku said, cracking his knuckles. 'It's just our last Lieutenant, before he died suddenly, was so popular with them.'

His friendship with Yẹmi had come about by chance. The man had been a loner before Chike arrived. Perhaps it was his face that drove people away – with eyes that were two slits, shielding his soul from scrutiny. His thin lips were un-African and as alien as his long nose, which ended in a point. Yẹmi was also blunt, rude even, to soldiers and officers alike. With the latter, he was more circumspect but still, he would often find himself on extra patrol for mutterings, cloudy with insubordination. On the surface there was little to like in this man who freely admitted he was a coward.

'I no want die,' he would say, when the other men laughed at him for always finding his way to the back on any attack. Chike had not taken much notice of the lowest ranking member of his platoon until he chanced upon him one day, crying. Not in the attention-seeking way you would have expected from one so buffoonish but short, snivelling tears, wiped before they could fall.

'Nah young girl. E no good,' was all he would say. There were others who felt the same about the woman they had shot for harbouring militants in her hut but the only protest he had heard was from the butt of his platoon.

On leaving the canteen, he did not bother to join the groups holding cigarettes. The members would drift off like fireflies should he wander into their midst. No matter how amiable, Chike was still an officer. He could go to the tent that the officers had commandeered as their mess but increasingly he loathed the company of his peers. They were all complicit in Benatari's crimes.

His quarters were a cramped affair, six bunks piled into a square with only one window, but he was lucky to have a room. Although each officer had a limited number of possessions, in the small space, the room took on an air of a badly kept store. Chike brought out his Bible and his torch.

The news that two sentries had been killed was all over the base the next day. Benatari was as quick in disposing of their corpses as he was with the victims of his trials. No one in the ranks saw the bodies before they were buried. Some said the hands were tied together with a stick shoved between the palms. Others said a note had been left over the face of one, 'In revenge for our fallen hero.' A few said Benatari had had two men shot and dressed in khaki so he could blame the village. An even smaller faction said the story was made up as the Major had said nothing about it all morning.

Benatari soon made light of the last rumour by assembling the men on the parade ground. He was dressed in full regalia, his white gloved hand resting on the hilt of a sword.

'It is with great sadness that I report the loss of the two brave soldiers. We have been gentle with these people because our superiors have told us to promote national unity whenever we can. They don't know what is on ground. The Niger Delta is not a place for ideas. You tell an Ijaw man about nation building, all he wants to know is what's for lunch. These are stomach people and it is time to show them we are muscle people.'

Not for the first time, Chike concluded that Benatari was a man who enjoyed killing. You sensed that, if permitted, he would string the scalps of his enemies on to a belt and do away with the leather and steel contraption that circled his waist. The men would kill readily if they had to but they would not choose it over a morning lie-in or a night with Tina.

'This evening, we attack,' Benatari shouted.

They had attacked a few villages before. Benatari called it 'smoking out the rebels'. A convoy of jeeps would drive through a village, shooting in the air or, if it was a floating village, they would take their patrol boats. They would round up the men, forcing them to kneel in the square or tread creek water. Anyone who tried to run or swim away was judged either a militant or a collaborator and was shot.

Once, he watched an old man struggle to keep his head above the oily slick that threatened to swallow him. He would go under and come up, each time his head taking longer to resurface. Chike had lowered the butt of his rifle into the water and tapped the man on the shoulder. Help, even mute help, is recognisable. The man grasped the bottom of the gun, his grip so strong Chike feared he would pull the weapon from his hands. He did not. He bobbed below less frequently and when Benatari was ready to go, the old man swam slowly back to his hut.

They would attack another village tonight. No work was given that day. No marching in the afternoon. Double lunch rations. A smoggy expectation hung over the base. Tina was not in the canteen today. She was a spy, the men said. A sexy spy. Chike wondered if she was from the village they would attack that night.

Evening swept briefly through the Delta: half an hour of mauve before the sky bruised to black. They could not all go. A station of seven hundred men could not possibly approach a village unheard. A century had been chosen and Chike's platoon fell in the batch.

From their approach, the village seemed asleep. Inside the houses no doubt, there would be people lingering over meals, telling stories and having sex but as their small settlement had never been put on the national grid, they would be doing this in candlelight or darkness.

Tonight's formation was different. Instead of roaring into the village, they drove slowly to its perimeter, Benatari and a group of ten officers continuing on foot. The moon was hidden. When the cloud passed, Chike saw the Colonel and his men walking laboriously under the weight of jerry cans. At every hut they passed, they flung what must have been petrol on its roof. A spark appeared in someone's hand and jumped to a thatched roof.

Was it the heat that drew the villagers from their huts or the smell of smoke?

'Disembark.'

It sounded like Major Waziri, a thin, pallid man whose shout could be heard from one end of camp to the other.

'When the villagers begin to run this way, shoot. The Colonel will also be shooting on the other side.'

'And what if we refuse?'

'Who said that?'

The men by Chike remained silent.

'Anyone who refuses will be shot.'

Men were dashing into houses and rescuing the bric-a-brac of their lives. Women were carrying babies and smacking children who strayed too far from the family group. At the sound of gunfire, the young and the very old were startled into flight. The latter did not get very far but the children had almost reached the jeeps when Waziri said 'Fire!'

For a moment, there was silence. Only Colonel Benatari and his contingent were shooting. This is a mutiny, Chike thought. Unplanned and unconcerted, they had all decided to revolt. Here was the will of the people, with no king needed to divine it. Then the first gun stuttered into life and the others found their voice.

'Let's go now before we take part in this.'

The men of his platoon turned when he spoke, fingers relaxing from triggers. Perhaps if he had led them, really led them instead of only giving orders, they would have followed him. They all had reasons to stay. Private Usman was newly wed, Lance Corporal Okachi had an elderly father and Sergeant Moloku's dependents were too many to be counted. Only Yẹmi remained unencumbered.

'Oya,' he said. 'I don tire for this their army.'

Hope's Hunter

Mohamed Yunus Rafiq

Hope's hunter leaves home for the hunt of a lifetime just as the hornbills have begun to announce the severity of the impending drought.

This is the land: once teeming with galloping and prancing antelope, now a desert of fine dust. This is the land where the chatter of contented voices rang around the warm embrace of the fire from which roasting meat released its aroma into the balmy darkness. But now, shrunken heads are sunk deep on cadaverous chests or against bony lower limbs. The war song that no one dares sing still rings in the villagers' ears.

> *Eeh; eagle soaring in the sky above*
> *Tell my family I'm bound for battle*
> *I'll be back with food*
> *Or return as food*
> *The food I bring I'll share with all*
> *If as food I return*
> *Feed on flesh*
>
> *And become what I am*
> *But care for those I love the most*

Hope's hunter leaves behind him the fire that has tied his family together more securely than the most ingenious knot. He leaves behind too the pleasant smell of the evergreen mtarakwa tree that hugs the walls of his homestead. He leaves behind the tobacco-coloured mountains that caress the low pregnant clouds that never deliver. The cracked earth that no longer shows evidence of roaming antelope. All this urges him forth to find the elixir that will ward off the impending calamity. He leaves behind the eyes of his children staring at his depart- ing and diminishing form, eyes as blank as dead stars.

Resolute, Hope's hunter turns his back on his relatives' scrawny, beck- oning hands; hands so powerless they have let fall the empty gourd of the sap of affection for the retreating pilgrim. But still they beckon, as if defying the wisdom in the children's song that urges:

> *Be not like a chair*
> *With legs*
> *That do not walk*

The traveller moves on, for it is the glory of a man to be on the move always, like the river; unlike the mountain whose majesty is in its stillness.

In his departure, the traveller also leaves behind some painful, yet sorrowful nods of approval; nods reminiscent of the lizard's resignation to the inevitable setting of the sun. The traveller tips down his throat the bitter herb that is the agony of departure as he stands at the mouth of the forest.

A baobab stands formidable here; roots firmly sunk into the earth. The hunter is dwarfed by the great tree, whose branches lift like strong arms into the sky. The hunter feels the presence of the uncountable prayers of the wise that have been offered here. He only wishes he could hear them. His eyes are glued to the robust trunk of the tree and his mind records the shifting script and pictograms presented by armies of ants and other insects enacting before his eyes the daily struggle of their lives.

He sees kingdoms take shape, stand valiantly and fall here on the vast trunk. He sees the flow, swell and ebb of hope as one army advances with a huge prize of the fresh succulent cadaver of a green grasshopper.

In the translucent sap that covers part of the trunk, he sees armies sailing in canoes and beholds them as they crash into the vortexes of rapidly swirling waters and sink into chasms of spider webs spanning some depressions on the branches of the baobab.

And what is that fleeting spear? Oh, it is the lightning-fast tongue of the chameleon as it zaps into its mouth some unsuspecting juicy grub. The hunter is enthralled. No sooner does a question pop up in his mind, than the answer emerges right before his eyes. Why is it that the prey fails to see enemies who tower over it like mountains? That is because the prey lives to gather and store; while the enemy lives to hunt and eat and rest and be fresh for the next meal.

He feels that he can almost sniff the object of his quest now. At least, he reasons, he has found the bow and arrow and he has grasped it firmly. His hope soars into the sky and he half wishes his people could see it the way they see the clouds. He was eager to alleviate their suffering. But he remembers how even clouds in the sky no longer kindle hope in their faces.

He finds a stone conveniently close to the baobab tree on which he sits to reflect. He can still read the scripts and pictograms from where he sits. Hope rises like a serpent rearing its head not only better to survey its foe, but to intimate its menace. It is so strong in him that he journeys through many hot suns and cold moons. He grows so accustomed to the facial expressions of the moon that it is as if she and he hold nocturnal conversations. He is buoyed by the waxing of the rounded moon; left bereft with its waning. As he trudges on, it seems that the only balm for his lips is the song he sings to his ancestors, the one that bubbles from deep within and flows from his lips and wafts into the air around him where it seems to hang like an invisible mantle. The sonic forms and esoteric meanings in the songs of yore pulsate in the surrounding air enshrouding the traveller from snakes bites, deviant whispers and piercing thermal spears.

After many moons he comes upon a fig tree. Here he reflects on whether he has earned the honour required of him in order to help his people. Hasn't he borne the assaults of the elements? Isn't his skin

covered with a thick enough layer of sweat to cement the most irrec-
oncilable enemies? Although he cannot name what he seeks within
himself, he feels the object of his quest is near, and it is bright as a ray
of light dancing on the surface of a river.

He plants the staff that he has been holding firmly on the ground.
As soon as the feeling of discovery dissipates, feelings of despair flood
his heart, he sees himself like a star spun off from its ancestral group-
ing and left alone in the vastness of the sky. He staggers and falls on
the ground, his hands still clenching the staff. His ear on the ground,
vibrations pulsate throughout his body building back up his strength.
After the thermal convulsions end, the hunter feels an emotion so
profound that the dusty kiangazi wind of the dry season slapping his
spare frame does not register in his consciousness. He is able to
resume his journey.

Trees, shrubs, sand, stones, hills and mountains give way to endless
plains. His countenance resembles that of a fisherman who holds a
rod at which a mighty catch mischievously tugs. He does not care
for the savannah grass that waves in the wind like myriad robed
priests bowing and swaying in worship. If he cared it would be only
for the reason that these priests intercede on his behalf. As he has
countless nights before, he lays that night under the sky that places
over him a ceiling decorated with jewels. The frogs and crickets
produce a melodic rhythm that rocks the hunter into a pensive
tune:

> Travelling is seeing, *kusafiri ni kuona*
> Migrating is healing, *kuhijiri ni kupona*
> Depth is in reflection, *kufikiri ni kina*

These are the words that beckon him towards the friend who awaits
us all at the end of the day. The *kusafiri na kuhijiri* lures him to sleep.
The next morning, he continues with his solitary journey.

His hope soars as he comes upon a riverbed, drawn by the promise of
water and food – elemental needs. At last, he is able to drink and eat

and continue his journey. With his back arched like a tightened bow, the hunter combs the shallow banks of the river for buried oysters and aquatic snails. He gorges on their white leathery flesh like an ousted mongoose, their juices escaping down the sides of his mouth and tiny bits of flesh flying in the air, mixing with the water below. His flaring nostrils draw in huge draughts of air and there is a joyful rhythm as his sandaled feet come in contact with the sand. His feet can kiss the sand now and not fear that the sand will cling to them in a spider-like embrace as he had feared before this moment. His soul chants a victory chant: greenness is life, *ubichi ni uishi wa binaamu*, those who fear should not live, *aogopae na asikae*, and more intensely, real death is to cease searching, *kifo ni kuacha kutafuta*.

The dusty wind jerks him out of his reverie. In front of him, the clump of densely populated tree encircles the riverbed. Here are the legendary medicinal trees such as the mbuyu of the leafless branches with twigs pointing up at the sky like long fingers; the elkilotri with its yellow flowers reminiscent of a flock of goats; the mwarobani in its sunny red majesty.

The hunter notices a gap in the middle of this clump of trees. His face is tear-streaked now, and he advances to the opening in the middle of the trees as if drawn by some magic. On the ground, hoof prints of the numerous animals of the forest etch the muddy path. There are so many that it is hard to make out which print belongs to which animal. Feathers from the plumage of various birds wave gently in the calm breeze. It is clear to the hunter that this path was well worn. On the other side of the copse the tunnel opens up into a clearing at the centre of which there is a huge gleaming coil that seems to be swaying gently to the breeze. Or perhaps it seems to be inflating and deflating rhythmically; surely, it is breathing, and, and, wait, this is a huge python. The sight of this massive creature mesmerises the hunter. The python's mouth opens wide and a stream of water gushes forth from it like a mighty waterfall. It is as if the great snake never ceases pouring out its precious substance and what races through the hunter's mind is the thought that if only he could drink from the snake fountain he could regain the wisdom of old.

★ ★ ★

The hunter beholds a colony of bedraggled frogs beside the river. Their skins appearing as tattered travelling cloaks, their eyes sunken from lack of food and water. It is a long journey across the plains to this riverbed. Though miserable in appearance, these frogs sing songs of jubilation and triumph. In unison, they take a sip of the precious water and like the fleeting sight of a leopard, their shabby appearance begins to dissolve and give way to shiny coats and their eyes begin to glow like the brave koroboi. He feels in him the sweetness of the reward of all the travailing that the frogs faced to arrive at this place. The python, as if sensing the stirrings in the man, blinks and in the process sends waves rippling over the sacred water and the waves add zest to the breeze that dances over the calm waters. Like him, the frogs have come to this riverbed to partake in the life-giving waters pouring fourth from the generous python. The hunter thinks out loud, 'What troubles have forced these amphibian cousins to leave their abode and venture this far?' He recounts the adage: 'Don't see a man walking; he carries mountains on his shoulders.' The mountains of drought, broken dreams, splintering families and vanishing forests cleaved the hunter from his people, bringing him here to this secluded riverbed. But does not one traveller aid another when the dry winds of the world blow them in different directions? Humbled, the hunter waits.

He rubs his hand over his eyes better to see the spectacle before him. It feels as if the fatigue is falling from his eyes in sandy sized particles. When he eventually returns his gaze once more to the giant serpent, he catches his breath in horror and staggers to lean against a nearby tree. The python is dead and its white, weather-worn skeleton is suspended on the dry vines that cling to an acacia tree. He cannot explain how the splendour of a few moments before could have disappeared. He feels a betrayal reminiscent of a worshipper who responds to a stirring call only to find that the shrine lacks a priest. In the place of the gleaming water of the river now lie the roots of a huge dusty caldera.

There is not a trace of the green vegetation or the water that sustained it, regardless of how vivid his recollection and how

unchanged the exact spot at which the python had stood. The para-
lysing reality is of the frogs that have metamorphosed. They now
bare sharp malevolent teeth that remind the hunter of a
mad-with-hunger hyena. With bloated bellies, the frogs emit violent
grating sounds, ruefully eyeing the serpent's dry white skeleton.
There is no doubt in the hunter's mind that they are the ones that
devoured the serpent. Now they are satiated while the breeze lashes
at the serpent's skeleton. Gone too are all traces of the precious fluid
that had issued from the mouth of the serpent. Maybe that has also
been consumed by the frogs. And now the frogs are struggling as
they drag their big bellies along the ground. He fights the bile of
rage and nausea that wells up from his gut.

Now the rapacious frogs turn on one another and begin a gory,
blood-churning spectacle of tearing and ripping at each other. The
sun, as if to turn its back on a world gone awry, begins rapidly descending to its nocturnal abode. It leaves behind a savannah reluctant to bid
it farewell.

The hunter turns his gaze up at the grey streaked clouds that seem
to assume the shape of arrows. Every day the clouds and the land seem
to put up a fight against the departure of the sun, an occurrence they
cannot stop and every morning they welcome the sun even before
men and women begin to stir. The constant positive and negative
interplay seems, to the hunter's mind, to be a primal pattern. He
wonders though, where is the mid-point between the positive and
negative. Maybe it is not necessary since the cycle always repeats itself.

He finds his steps homeward bound. But he stops and fights this
stirring urge within him to return; he looks to the python's skeleton
for some moments. Then he starts walking towards it, passing the frogs
immersed in their ritual blood bath. Seeing him pass, heading towards
where the snake's skeleton hangs, the frogs bare their sharp fangs and
violently swing their clawed limbs at the hunter's feet. Unrelenting,
the hunter dodges the attacks, pushes them aside with his feet and
heads to the acacia tree where the python's skeleton hangs. He loads its
body on to his shoulders. The python's skeleton wraps around the
hunter's torso like a beaded mantle. The sound of the frogs gnashing at
each other is now no more significant than the breeze playing through

the trees around him and caressing his face. The frogs register the calm on the hunter's face as they try to catch the last rays of the sun at the door of their rocky hideouts.

He walks away shouldering the smooth bones of the python, and says out loud, 'We are going home.'

from the novel

Ghana Must Go

Taiye Selasi

Fola wakes breathless that Sunday at sunrise, hot, dreaming of drowning, a roaring like waves. Dark. Curtains drawn, humid, the wet bed an ocean: half sleeping still, eyes closed, she sits up, cries out. But her 'Kweku!' is silent, two bubbles in water that now, her lips parted, run in down her throat, where they find, being water, more water within her, her belly, below that, her thighs, dripping wet – the once-white satin nightdress soaked, wet from the inside, and outside, a second skin, now brown with sweat – and, becoming a tide, turn, return up the middle, thighs, belly, heart, higher, then burst through her chest.

The sob is so loud that it rouses her fully. She opens her eyes and the water pours out. She is sobbing uncontrollably when the tide subsides abruptly, leaving no trace whatsoever of the dream as it does (much as waves erase sand-script, washing in without warning, wiping the writings of children and of lovers away). Only fear remains vaguely, come unhooked from its storyline, left on damp sand like a thin sparkling foam. And the roaring: sharp racket in dull humid darkness, the A/C as noisy as one that still works.

Sparkling fear-foam, and roaring.

She sits up, disoriented, unable to see for the drawn mustard drapes so just sitting there, baffled, unclear what's just happened, or why she was crying, or why she's just stopped. With the usual questions: what time is it? where is she? *In Ghana*, something answers, the bulbul outside, so-called 'pepper birds' bemusedly joining the racket in ode to oblivion to things that don't work. So not night-time, then: pepper birds, the morning in Ghana, the place that she's moved to, or fled to.

Again.

Without fanfare or forethought, as flocks move, or soldiers, on instinct, without luggage, setting off at first light: found the letter on a Monday, in the morning, in Boston, sorting mail at the counter (coffee, WBUR, 'a member station supported by listeners like you'), bills for school fees, utilities. One dropped to the floor. Rather, floated to: pastel blue, flimsy, a feather, slipping silently from the catalogues of Monday's thick mail. A proper letter. And lay there. In the white light of winter, that cheap airmail paper no one uses any more.

She opened it. Read it. Twice. Set it on the countertop. Left for the flower shop, leaving it there. Came home in the dark to the emptiness, retrieved it. Read again that Sena Wosornu, surrogate father, was dead.

Was dead and had left her, 'Miss' Folasadé Savage, a three-bedroom house in West Airport, Accra. Stood, stunned, in her coat in the kitchen and silence, soft silver-black darkness, tiles iced by the moon.

Monday evening. Left Friday. JFK to Kotoka. Nonstop. Without fanfare.

Just packed up and left.

Now she squints at the darkness and makes out the bedroom, unfa-miliar entirely after only six weeks. Unfamiliar shapes, shadows, and the space here beside her, unfamiliar entirely after sixteen years, still.

She touches her nightdress, alarmed at the wetness. She peels the drenched satin away from her skin. She touches her stomach as she does when this happens, when fear hovers shyly, not showing its face yet, when something is wrong but she doesn't know what or with which of the offspring that sprang from this spot. And the stomach answers always (the 'womb' maybe, more, but the word sounds absurd to her, *womb*, always has. A *womb*. Something cavernous, mysterious, a basement. A word with a shadow, a draft. Rhymes with *tomb*). She touches her stomach in the four different places, the quadrants of her torso between waist and chest: first the upper right (Olu) beneath her right breast, then the lower right (Taiwo) where she has the small scar, then the lower left (Kehinde) adjacent to Taiwo, then the upper left (Sadie), the baby, her heart. Stopping briefly at each to observe the sensation, the movement or stillness beneath the one palm. Sensing: Olu – all quiet. The sadness as usual, as soft and persistent as the sound of a fan. Taiwo – the tension. Light tugging sensation. But no sense of danger, no cause for alarm. Kehinde – the absence, the echoing silence made bearable by the certainty that *if,* she would know (as she knew when it happened, as she knew the very instant, cutting pastel-blue hydrangea at the counter in the shop, suddenly feeling a sort of seizure, lower left, crying, 'Kehinde!' with the knife slipping sideways and slicing her hand. Dripping blood on the counter, on the stems and the blossoms, on the phone as she dialled, already knowing which it was; getting voicemail, 'This is Keh—' call waiting, clicking over, frantic sobbing, 'Mom, it's Taiwo. Something happened.' 'I know.' She knew as did Taiwo the very instant that it happened, as the blade made its way through the skin, the first wrist. So that now, a year later – more, nearly two years later – having neither seen nor heard from him, she knows. That she'd know). Last, Sadie – fluttering, butterflies, a new thing this restlessness, this looking for something, not finding it.

Fine.

Sadness, tension, absence, angst – but *fine,* as she birthed them, alive if not well, in the world, fish in water, in the condition she delivered them (breathing and struggling) and this is enough. Perhaps not for others, Fola thinks, other mothers who pray for great fortune and fame for their young, epic romance and joy (better mothers quite likely; small, bright-smiling, hard-driving, minivan-mothers), but for her who would kill, maim, and die for each child but who knows that the willingness to die has its limits.

That death is indifferent.

Not *she* (though she seems) but her age-old opponent, her enemy, *theirs,* the common enemy of all mothers – death, harm to the child – which will defeat her, she knows.

But not today.

The fear recedes. The roaring persists. The rough snuffling slosh of the broken machine. The heat grows assertive, as if feeing ignored.

The bedsheet and nightgown go suddenly cold.

She gets out of bed, knocking her knee as she does, quietly cursing the house, its deficient A/C. The night watchman Mr Ghartey was meant to have fixed it, or meant to have had his electrician-cousin come fix it, or meant to have called the white man who installed it to come fix it – the plan remains largely unclear. 'He is coming' is the answer whenever she asks. 'I beg, he is coming.' For weeks now, hot air. But the relationship is young, between her and her staff, and she knows to go slow, to tread lightly. She is a woman, first; unmarried, worse; a Nigerian, worst; and fair-skinned. As suspicious persons go in Ghana, she might as well be a known terrorist. The staff, whom she inherited along with the house and its 1970s orange-wool-upholstered wooden furniture, sort of tiptoe around her, poorly masking their shock. That she moved here alone. To sell *flowers*.

Worse: that she arrived on that Saturday, from the airport, in the morning, in the white linen outfit and open-toe shoes and, alighting the cab, said, 'How *are* you?' incomprehensibly, with British *a* and American *r*. Worst: that no man alighted the taxi thereafter.

That she shook their hands, seeking their eyes.

That, leaving her suitcases (three? were there more? was this all? a whole life in America?) by the cab, she proceeded directly to the wall to put her face in the crawlers. 'Bougainv*iiii*llea!' Still incomprehensible.

That she greets them in the morning with this same odd 'How *are* you?' and thanks them as bizarrely for doing their jobs. '*Thank* you' to the houseboy when he washes her clothing. '*Thank* you' to the cook when he sets out her meals. '*Thank* you' to the gatekeeper when he opens the gate and again as he closes it.

That she smokes.

That she wears shorts.

That she wanders around the garden in these shorts and a sun hat with cigarettes and clippers, snipping this, snipping that, hauling her catch into the kitchen, where she stands at the counter, not pounding yam, not shelling beans, but arranging *flowers*. It amuses her, always has, this disregard of Africans for flowers, the indifference of the abundantly blessed (or psychologically battered – the chronic self-loather who can't accept, even with evidence, that anything native to him, occurring in abundance, in excess, without effort, has value).

They watch as research scientists observe a new species, a hybrid, herbivorous, likely harmless, maybe not. Masked, feeding her, washing for her, examining her clothing when they think she's not looking, whispering, watching her eat. She hasn't yet told them that she once lived in Ghana, that she understands all they say in hushed Twi about her flowers, flowered nightdresses, distressing eating habits like pulling out and eating the weeds (lemongrass). She learned this from her father, who spoke the major Nigerian languages plus French, Swahili, Arabic, and snatches of Twi. 'Always learn the local language. Never let on to the locals,' he'd say, a cigar at the end of its life on his lips, giving birth to a laugh – upper left.

There it is.

The movement she was feeling for.

Left upper quadrant, in the vicinity of Sadie but closer to the heart, not a tugging or a tightening or a throbbing of dread but an echo, an emptiness, an emptying out. A familiar sensation. Not the one she was feeling for, fearful of (auguring harm done the child) but remembered, unmistakable, from four decades prior, a memory she forgot she still has.

She sits back down absently, abandoning her mission, whatever it was, a word with Mr Ghartey perhaps, or a smack to the side of the wall-mounted machine, or a fresh set of bed sheets, a post-nightmare drink.

And thinks: *odd,* to be returned to the death of her father, which she thinks of so rarely, as one recounts dreams, out of focus, diluted, not the event but the emotion, a sadness that's faded, dried, curled, lost its colour. The *event* she can see clear as day even now: Lagos, July 1966, the short chain of events. First: the waking up gasping, cold, thirteen years old, all her posters of the Beatles stuck with tacks to the walls, sitting alarmed in the dark with that space in her chest, unfamiliar with the feeling (the same odd emptiness as now). Second: making her way from her room down the hall, to her father's room, forgetting that he'd travelled to the North, gone to see about his in-laws, her 'grandparents', the Nwaneris, whom she'd never actually met and never would. No one said it. Never him, her kind, broad-shouldered, woolly-haired father, who wept for the loss of his bride every night, kneeling down by his bed beneath the portrait above it, Somayina Nwaneri, fair, gold-eyed. A ghost. Twenty-seven.

Fairy ghostmother.

Had bled out in labour.

A stranger to Fola, no more than a face, so unusually pale that she looked in her portrait as if she'd been born without blood, cut from ice. Still so pretty. Stuff of legend. Local celebrity in Kaduna, Igbo father as famous for his post in the North as for plucking one rose from the grounds of the mission and marrying her, a Scotswoman, auburn-haired Maud. And the rest of it: shame, stillborn son, successive miscarriages, the shaking of heads and the wagging of tongues, *see, the Scotswoman can't bear the Igbo man's child,* then the one white-skinned daughter, the magic mulatto. Little princess of Kaduna. Colonial Administrator's daughter. Won a bursary to study nursing in London after the war, promptly met and immediately married Kayo Savage, Fola's father, lawyer, late of the Royal Air Force. Felled in childbirth, etc. No one said it. No one mentioned that they never came to see her, Rt. Hon. John and Maud Nwaneri, never called nor sent a gift, but she could guess it: that they blamed her for their only daughter's early death, as she would come to hate them for his.

But not yet.

First: waking at midnight with space in her chest. Second: slipping down the hallway to her father's bedroom, vacant. Third: ascending to his empty bed, still warm with scent (rum, soap, Russian Leather) and covering her face with his thick kente blanket, then lying, unmoving, eyes open, heart racing. Still as a corpse, swathed in cotton and sweating, with the A/C not on, with her father not there, gone to Kaduna that morning, having heard from some friends that the Igbos in the North were in trouble again.

'*Again?*' she'd sighed, sulking, loudly slurping her breakfast (*gari,* sugar water, ice), already knowing he was going by his having prepared this. 'A bush girl's breakfast' as he called it, mocking. Powdered yam in ice water, her favourite. If this grandfather of hers was as rich as they said, with his Cyclone CJ and his split-level ranch, then why must her father go 'check on him' always, she'd asked, crunching ice, but she knew. He had to go, always, to appease them, to redeem himself, to beg again forgiveness for the death of Somayina (which was, technically speaking, not *his* fault but hers, infant Fola's, the doctor's at least, or the womb's).

'They're always in trouble, these Igbos. *Na wow o.*'

'Your mother was an Igbo.'

'Half.'

'That's quite enough.' But when she looked he was laughing, coming to kiss her head, leaving. 'I'll be back before Sunday. I love you.'

'Mo n mo.'

There was no equivalent expression for *I love you* in Yoruba. 'If you love someone, you show them,' her father liked to say. But said it nevertheless in English, to which she'd answer in Yoruba, 'I know.'

Mo n mo.

Out the door.

Just like that.

Stood, set down his coffee cup, kissed her on the forehead once, hand each on her Afro puffs, walked out the door. Gone. Woolly hair and woollen suit and broad and buoyant shoulders bobbing, bobbing, bobbing out of view. The swinging door swung open, shut.

Fourth: fourteen hours later in his bed beneath the blanket, sliding down beneath the kente into darkness, absence, scent and heat, a still and silent ocean. And remaining. In the quiet. Lying ramrod straight, not moving, knowing.

That something had been removed.

That a thing that had been in the world had just left it, as surely and simply as people leave rooms or the dust of dead dandelion lifts into wind, silent, leaving behind it this empty space, openness. Incredible, unbearable, interminable openness appearing now around her, above her, beyond her, a gaping, inside her, a hole, or a mouth: unfamiliar, wet, hollow and hungry. Unappeasable.

The details came later – such as details ever come, such as one can know the details of a death besides one's own, how it went, how long or calming, cold or terrifying, lonely – but the thing happened there in the bedroom. The loss. Later, if ever alone, she'll consider it, the uncanny similarity between that and this moment: alone in the dark in the sweltering heat in a room not her own in a bed far too big. Mirror endings. The last of a life as she'd known it, at midnight in Lagos, never suspecting what had happened (it simply wouldn't have occurred to her, that evil existed, that death was indifferent), yet *knowing* somehow.

This was the event for her, the loss in the concrete, the hours in which she crossed between knowing and knowledge and onwards to 'loss' in the abstract, to sadness. Six, seven hours of openness slowly hardening into loneliness.

The details came later – how a truckload of soldiers, Hausas, high on cheap heroin and hatred, had killed them, setting fire to the mansion, piling rocks at the exits – but the details never hardened into pictures in her head. So she never really believed it, not really, couldn't *see* it, never settled on a sight that would have made the thing stick, put some meat on the words (roaring fire, burning wood), put a face on the corpses. The words remained bones. They were no one, the 'soldiers'.

They were shadow-things, not human beings. The 'Nwaneris' were what they'd always been: a portrait on the wall, a name. A pallid cast of characters. Not even characters, but categories: civilian, soldier, Hausa, Yoruba, Igbo, villain, victim. Too vague to be true.

And not him.

It was him. He was there without question (though they never could confirm it, his bones turned to ashes, in REM, dreaming, his 'Fola!' two bubbles), as rampant anti-Igbo pogroms kicked off the war. But she simply couldn't see him, not her father as she knew him, as she'd seen him from the table, bobbing, bobbing out of view. It was someone else they'd killed that night, these 'soldiers' whom she couldn't see, this 'victim' whom they didn't know, anonymous as are all victims.

The indifference of it.

This was the problem and would be ever after, the block on which she sometimes feels her whole being stumbled: that he (and so she) became so unspecific. In an instant. That the details didn't matter in the end. Her life until that moment had seemed so original, a richly spun tale with a bright cast of characters – she: motherless princess of vertical palace, their four-storey apartment on Victoria Island; they: passionate, glamorous friends of her father's, staff; he: widowed king of the castle. Had he died a death germane to their life as she'd known it – in a car crash, for example, in his beloved Deux Chevaux, or from liver cancer, lung, to the end puffing CAOs, swilling rum – she could have abided the loss. Would have mourned. Would have found herself an orphan in a four-storey apartment, having lost both her parents at thirteen years old, but would have been, thus bereaved, a thing she recognised (tragic) instead of what she became: a part of history (generic).

She sensed the change immediately, in the tone people took when they learned that her father had been murdered by soldiers; in the way that they'd nod as if, yes, *all makes sense, the beginning of the Nigerian civil war, but of course*. Never mind that the Hausas were targeting Igbos, and her father was a Yoruba, and her grandmother Scottish, and the house staff Fulani, some Indian even. Ten dead, one an Igbo, minor details, no matter. She felt it in America when she got to Pennsylvania (having been taken first to Ghana by the kindly Sena Wosornu), that her classmates and professors, white or black, it didn't matter, somehow believed that it was natural, however tragic, what had happened.

That she'd stopped being Folasadé Somayina Savage and had become instead the native of a generic war-torn nation. Without specifics.

Without the smell of rum or posters of the Beatles or a kente blanket tossed across a king-size bed or portraits. Just some war-torn nation, hopeless and inhuman and as humid as a war-torn nation anywhere, all war-torn nations everywhere. 'I'm sorry,' they'd say, nodding yes in agreement, as one says *I'm sorry* when the elderly die, 'that's too bad' (but not *that* bad, more 'how these things go' in this world), in their eyes not a hint of surprise. Surely, broad-shouldered, woolly-haired fathers of natives of hot war-torn countries got killed all the time?

How had this happened?

It wasn't Lagos she longed for, the splendour, the sensational, the sense of being wealthy – but the sense of self surrendered to the senselessness of history, the narrowness and naïvety of her former individuality.

After that, she simply ceased to bother with the details, with the notion that existence took its form from its specifics. Whether this house or that one, this passport or that, whether Baltimore or Lagos or Boston or Accra, whether expensive clothes or hand-me-downs or florist or lawyer or life or death – didn't much matter in the end. If one could die identityless, estranged from all context, then one could live estranged from all context as well.

This is what she's thinking as she sits here, wet, empty, a newly wrecked ship on a beach in the night: that the details are different but the space is unchanging, unending, the absence as present, absolute. He is gone now, her father, has been gone for so long that his goneness has replaced his existence in full. It didn't happen over time but in an instant, in his bedroom: he was removed, and she remained, and that was that.

That is that.

The Sack

Namwali Serpell

There's a sack.
  A sack?
A sack.
Hmm. A sack. Big?
Yes. Grey. Like old *kwacha*. Marks on the outside. No. Shadows. That's how I know it is moving.
Something is moving inside it?
The whole sack is moving. Down a dirt road with a ditch on the side, with grass and yellow flowers. There are trees above.
Is it dark?
Yes, but light is coming. It is morning. There are some small birds talking, moving. The sack is dragging on the ground. There is a man pulling it behind him.
Who is this man?
I can't see his face. He is tallish. His shirt has stains on the back. No socks. Businessman shoes. His hands are wet.
Does he see you?
I don't know. I'm tired now. Close the curtains.
Yes, *bwana.*

J. left the bedroom and went to the kitchen. The wooden door was open but the metal security gate was closed. The sky looked bruised. The insects would be coming soon. They had already begun their electric clicking in the garden. He thought of the man in the bedroom, hating him in that tender way he had cultivated over the years.

J. washed the plates from lunch. He swept. A chicken outside made a popping sound. J. sucked his teeth and went to see what was wrong.

The *isabi* boy was standing outside the security gate. The boy held the bucket handle with both hands, the insides of his elbows splayed taut. His legs were streaked white and grey.

How do you expect me to know you are here if you are quiet? J. asked as he opened the gate. The boy shrugged, a smile dancing upwards and then receding into the settled indifference of his face. J. told the boy to take off his *patapatas* and reached for the bucket. Groaning with its weight, J. heaved the unwieldy thing into the sink. He could just make out the shape of the bream, flush against the inside of the bucket, its fin protruding. J. felt the water shift as the fish turned uneasily.

A big one today, eh? J. turned and smiled.

The boy still stood by the door, his hands clasped in front of him. His legs were reflected in the parquet floor, making him seem taller.

Do you want something to eat?

The boy assented with a diagonal nod.

You should eat the fish you catch. It is the only way to survive, J. said.

I told him about the first dream but I did not tell him about the second. In the second dream, I am inside the sack. The cloth of it is pressing right down on my eyes. I turn one way, then the other. All I can see is grey cloth. There is no pain but I can feel the ground against my bones. I am curled up. I hear the sound of the sack, sweeping like a slow broom. I have been paying him long enough – paying down his debt – that he should treat me like a real *bwana*. He does his duties, yes. But he lacks deference. His politics would not admit this, but I have known this man since we were children. I know what the colour of my skin means to someone of our generation. His eyes have changed. I think he is going to kill me. I think that is what these dreams are telling me. Naila. I cannot remember your hands.

They lifted the bream out of the bucket together, the boy's hands holding the tail, J.'s hands gripping the head. The fish swung in and out of the curve of its own body, its gills pumping with mechanical panic. They flipped it on to the wooden board. Its side was a jerking plane of silver, drops of water magnifying its precise scaling. The chicken outside made a serrated sound.

Iwe, hold it down!

The boy placed his hands on either end of the body. J. slid a knife beneath the locking, unlocking gills. Blood eased over their hands. The fish bucked once, twice. Stopped.

I needed your help, J. smiled.

He deboned and gutted the fish. The boy wiped the chopping board, hypnotised by his own hand tracking thin loops of purple and yellow entrails across it. J. fried the fish in cooking oil with salt and onions and tomatoes. He served a piece of it to the boy, setting the plate on the floor. He set a portion of the fish aside for himself and took a plate with the rest of it to the man in the bedroom.

The room was dark but for an orange patch on the wall from the street lamp.

Who is here?

The *isabi* boy. J. put the plate on the side table and turned on the lamp.

The man began to cough, the phlegm in his chest rattling as he heaved and hacked. J. helped him sit up and rubbed his back until the fit ceased. When it was done, the man was tired.

Why is the fish boy still here? Did you not pay him?

I gave him supper.

As if I have food to spare, the man grunted. He took the plate on to his lap and began eating.

In the first dream, the sack is full and it is being dragged. In the second dream, I am inside it. What will the third dream reveal? You laugh. You say that dreams move forwards, not back. That I am imagining things. But that is why you chose me, Naila. Or at least that is what I fancied then. Now I am not so sure. Some days, I think you loved me for my hands. Other days, I think you threw stones to decide.

The plate on the kitchen floor was empty. The boy was gone. A tongue cleaned that plate, J. thought as he went to the doorway. The security gate was scaly with insects now, some so heavy their bodies chimed against the hollow metal bars. J. opened it and descended the short set of steps outside. He squatted to open the thatched door of the coop. He could hear the creaking, purring sound of the birds. Light from the house slivered the dark. J. inched along, his hipbone clicking as he went from one chicken to the next. They pivoted their heads and puffed their feathers. The last chicken sat upright on its nest but it wasn't moving. J. heard a shudder and scanned the wall. The boy. Crouching in the corner, light-mottled.

J. turned back to the chicken and inched closer, reaching for it. The feathers were strung with light brittle spines. The bird fell limp in his hand. Then he saw them, hordes of them, spilling down the chicken's body, rolling around its neck, massing from its beak. J. started back. The chicken caved in as a flood of ants washed over it. J. stood, hitting his head on the thatched roof. The chickens were yelping and flapping, feathers rising from the ground. The ants snipped at his skin. As he hunched his way out of the coop, a chicken beat its way past his ribs and loped across the yard, head at full piston. Methodically, J. brushed his body off. Then he reached back and pulled the shaking child from the shadows.

My chest is full of cracked glass. That is how it feels when I cough. But the glass never shatters – there is not even that relief of complete pain. I am sick, Naila. Working for me has only made him stronger. Why does he bother? I thought at first that it was the money. But now I think he has been waiting. I wonder at the dwindling of our cares. We began with the widest compass, a society of the people, we said. But somehow we narrowed until it was just us three. Jacob, Joseph, Naila. You replaced yourself with the baby you birthed. So there were still three. But then your family took our son away. And now there are only two. Every day this sickness bites into my body and soon there will be only one. In the dream that just woke me, I am on the ground. It is night. The man kneels at my side. The face is melted but his hair-line has washed back with a froth of white hair and he has those same strong arms. His hands are wet. He is tugging the mouth of the sack up over my thighs. This must be when he puts my body into it. We are in the garden. I woke to the smell of smoke.

J. burned the coop. The four chickens left – one had disappeared in the night, snatched by a lucky dog – huddled in a makeshift corral. The fire smelled good; the dead chicken was practically fresh-cooked. From the kitchen doorway, J. watched the last of the smoke coiling up to join the clouds above. The sun took its time. His saliva was bitter and when he spat in the sink, he saw that it was grey. The boy was sleeping on a blanket on the kitchen floor. J. leaned against the counter, watching the boy's chest catch and release. His skinny legs were clean now, greased with Vaseline. J. had hosed the ants off him and anointed the rash of bites. J. made a cup of tea – Five Roses, milk, no sugar – and balanced it on a tray.

The bedroom was ripe with the metallic smell of dried blood. A copper dawn lit the window: *Kwacha! Ngwee . . .*

The man looked up when J. entered the room. What was that fire?

I burned the chicken coop.

Why?

J. put the tray on the side table and began to leave the room.

Do not walk away from me. The man spat.

J. wiped the spit from the floor with his sleeve. White ants, he said.

Bloody superstitions. The man sucked his teeth. Is that bloody fish boy still here? I don't like people coming here. They find out who I am and ask for money.

He doesn't know who you are. He's too young. This boy has no family, J. said. We could use the help.

The man lifted his cup, his hand trembling. He sipped the hot tea and winced with pleasure.

The boy goes. I can't afford such things.

The light had gone from copper to white gold, the day spending itself freely. J. squatted on the stoop outside, shelling groundnuts to cook a dish of pumpkin leaves. Students in pale blue uniforms flirted in the dirt road. J. watched them with fond pity as he pressed the knuckle of his thumb to the belly of a shell. He hadn't tasted *chibwabwa ne'ntwilo* in twenty years. Naila's favourite. When he returned to the kitchen, he could hear voices in the living room. J. looked through the gap between the door and the frame. The man was leaning against the far wall, his pyjamas low on his hips. J.'s eyes narrowed: the man hadn't left his bed in weeks. He was shouting at the boy, who stood with his back to J.

Isa kuno, the man said sternly. Come here! Are you deaf?

The boy moved hesitantly over to him and the man's hand fell trembling on to the bony shoulder. He used the boy as a crutch, levering himself to the sofa. His breathing rasped, shaving bits of silence off the air. In the dull light of the living room, the boy's skin was the colour of a tarnished coin.

There, the man pointed at a picture frame face down on the floor near the sofa. What is that?

J. opened the door. Leave him, he said.

The boy rushed to J.'s side.

He broke it, the man snarled, picking up the framed photograph.

He doesn't know, J. said, looking down at the boy leaning against his leg.

I don't want him here, the man panted.

I owe it to him, J. said.

The man gaped, a laugh catching in his throat. The only debt you owe is to me, old man.

J. pushed the boy ahead of him into the kitchen.

I did not think I would walk again. These dreams give me strength. Not enough. I only got halfway to the kitchen, to the knives in the drawer. They wait like a flat bouquet: their thick wooden stems, their large silver petals. I will gather them up in my tired hands and I will hold them out to you. Naila. Look at you. There is a crack over your face because that bastard boy dropped the picture. But you are lovely in your green *salwar kameez*. Why do you look down? I never noticed before. Your eyelids are like smooth stones in this picture. I am a fool beside you. We reek of arrogance, all of us, J. with his Nehru shirt. How far he has fallen, sweeping and cooking for me like I'm a *musungu*. This picture must have been taken before the Kalingalinga rally, the one that led to the riot. Do you remember? We were so hopeful. So very young.

J. stood above the sleeping man. He watched him for a moment then slapped his hand against the wall to wake him. A gecko in the corner shimmied upwards, its eyes a black colon punched in its face. The man's head fell forwards and he began coughing himself awake. When the phlegm had settled, he blinked.

Supper, J. said, placing a hand under the man's armpit to help him up. The man swept his weight against J. like a curtain falling from its rails. J. guided him back towards the bedroom but the man raised his hand.

No. I'll eat in there, he nodded his head at the kitchen door. J. shrugged and they proceeded slowly in the other direction. J. kicked the door to the kitchen open and as the *isabi* boy watched warily, he lowered the man into a chair by a small table.

Fish again? the man smiled at the boy.

J. placed a plate of food before the man and a bowl for the boy on the floor. The man stared at his plate. The fish was in pieces, its skin a crimped silver, its eye a button. When J. went to sit on the stoop, the man complained: Join me, he said.

My dream in the living room was short. A man is holding an ankle in each hand on either side of his hips. He drags the body towards the empty sack. It leaves a dark irregular trail on the ground. J. was standing over me when I woke up. You would say that these visions are an old man's nonsense. That no man dreams backwards. Can you see us sitting across from each other now? He eats in silence. The boy on the floor hums a rally song. J. must have taught him that. They are trying to confuse me. I know this boy is not my son but I have to concentrate to keep it in mind. I insisted on this last supper. I am resigned to it. You laugh: you know I am resigned to nothing. You escaped my wilfulness only by dying. I will see this out. We will wrestle like Jacob and the angel.

I do not want the eye, the man said. J. reached for the plate.

Am I child that you must cut my food?

J. stood and wiped his hand on his trousers. He walked around the boy on the floor who was already burrowing into his *nsima*, humming a song in loops, and opened a drawer and took out a short knife with a wooden handle.

Yes, that one, the sharp one, the man said.

J. sat back down, watching the man insert the point of the knife into the cavity in the fish's head and cut the eye out carefully, tipping it on to the edge of the plate. He put the knife on the table and began to eat in that slow noisy way of his.

So, the man said, picking at his teeth with his fingernail. J. was at the sink, rinsing pots. What will we do about that broken picture?

I can get it fixed. We are still comrades, that glass cutter and me, J. said.

Comrades? *Nts.*

J. leaned against the counter, his arms, damp from dishwater, folded across his chest. What word would you prefer? Friend?

What do you know about that word? The man sucked his teeth again. The boy looked up at them, his cheeks dotted with white bits of *nsima.*

Yes, *bwana.* I know nothing of friendship, J. said.

The man looked at him. Rage beat across the air between them. Eating across from each other at a table again had kindled something.

I did not take her from you. J. released the words one at a time.

I've been having dreams, the man whispered.

No. I will not listen to your dreams. I have had dreams, *friend.* J. spat. He paced the room with the easy vigour of an animal, flaunting his vitality. His words cut through the smell of fish and illness, through the boy's whimpering hum.

I dream of her cunt, J. said. The English word was steely in his mouth. I pull a baby from her cunt. The baby's stomach is round and full and I can see through the skin, I see another baby inside it, five fingers pressed strong against the inside. I look at her face, sweating from labour, and I say, How is this possible? She laughs. Then I know that this is what happens when you use a woman with a used cunt.

The man looked away first. J. strode to the sink and spat in it. The boy was gone, his bowl upside down like an eye on the floor. J. stooped to pick it up and looked back at his boss. The man's eyes were closed, his hands under the table.

We should not talk about that woman.
    She is gone.
    She has been gone a long time.
    And the boy?
    The boy is gone too.
    The man turned on to his side, gingerly hitching up his knees. J. looked down at him. J. had long ago decided to hate that woman: a feeling which had clarity and could accommodate the appetite he had once felt for her body. But he knew that the man still loved her, that he scratched invisible messages to her in the sheets. J. was sorry for his old friend. But to say sorry would be preface to leaving and he would not leave until it was done. The sick man hiccupped in his sleep like a drunk or a child. J. switched off the lamp and left the room.

When the door clicked shut, the man's eyes opened. He reached under his pillow and the blade snipped him. The tiny pain in his thumb pulsed inside the throng of pain in his body, a whining in the midst of a howling. The man sucked the blood from his thumb and carefully nestled his hand back under the pillow to grasp the knife handle. He could not slow the reversed momentum of these dreams, but he would not succumb like a dog. He kept his eyes open as long as he could.
    A man shuffles through the dark, carrying a body over his shoulder. The legs dangle down the man's front and bounce as he moves unsteadily down a corridor. He faces forwards but steps backwards. He turns and fumbles with a door knob. The bedroom door opens with a sucking sound. He bends slowly and lays the body on the bed. It tumbles down piecemeal, buttocks, then torso, then arms. The man stands and looks at it for a long time. All of a sudden, he pitches over the body. He seems grappled to it. A moan lifts and trips and falls into a scream cut short.
    Which comes first? The knife handle abrading his palm? Or the wide agony in his chest? The man's eyes open, he gasps. J.'s face floats above as if he had exhaled him: flat as day, dark as night. His fist is

pressed hard to his own chest, his palm around the knife's handle. J.'s fingers are wrapped around his, their hands a bolus of flesh and bone, wood and blade. Together, they wrench the knife free of its home. Blood washes over him, its temperature perfect.

The boy stood in the doorway of the kitchen, looking out. It was night. His *bwana* was at the bottom of the garden, busy with a black lump and a grey sack. The boy's mind was empty but for a handful of notions – love, hunger, fear – darting like birds within, crashing into curved walls in a soundless, pitiless fury.

from the forthcoming novel

Harlot

Lola Shoneyin

By the time I was twenty-six, I knew how people could use their mouths to darken the skin of a banana coming into ripeness. I also grew to know the *asiri* of womanhood. Believe me, there are things that those who call women 'harlots' do not understand. You can wear the sole away if you march in a shoe for too long. And when you hammer a nail into a hole in a wall, the mud around it will begin to crumble. But, there is nothing like that thing between a woman's thighs. It is like a well-treated mortar and no amount of pounding can damage it. It is not like the penis that will raise its head and falter. It does not slacken or waste away with use.

I tell you, it has neither measure nor clock. It is like a spring in the hills. It is the place to find delight or bury your sorrows. It can give life to those who want life and bring death to those who seek it. It is a woman's strength, her fount of power.

The women who know the treasure that is clamped under their wrappers use it well. Those who do not will turn their mouths to those who do when sacks of sadness hang from their throats and their tongues hide gourds full of curses. I have come to understand that this is how it is for women. What they don't have, no one else can enjoy.

I was born in 1940, sixty-three years ago, in Ilara-Remo. My father, Awoyemi Folarera, was a goldsmith and my mother, Iwalola, sold anything that grew, ran or died on our farm. We were not poor and we were not rich. We ate guinea fowl only at Christmas and Easter but we had leather shoes for church. Left to my mother, I would have become a tailor but my father said I should go to school and learn to read like my three brothers. It is because of my father that I can speak the small English that I speak today.

In 1949 while he was hunting in the deep forest, Baba's trap caught an antelope. After the hunters cleaned it and smoked it, they gave my father the honour of dividing it. He carried up the cutlass to cut the head of the antelope but the blade came down on his pointing finger, slicing it at the second knuckle. The hunters had to carry Baba home. They said the blood that left Baba's body that day could fill a calabash. When the medicine man arrived to wake Baba with a bull's horn, he said the veins of death had crept into Baba's eyes.

Those who once called my father spider-hands stopped coming to his workshop. He could no longer make beautiful butterfly pendants in brushed gold. He could no longer make anything. What was a man to do with only four fingers? So, to make him feel like a man again, in 1951, my father took a second wife.

When the new wife arrived, my mother cried for many days. But our people say it is only a selfish woman who wants to enjoy her husband alone. The new wife moved into a room in the three-bed-room house that my father had used his savings to build. Baba did not ask my own mother to move there with him so she started behaving as if Baba had poured *sombo* all over her body.

Mama twisted my ears and called me a wayward child whenever she caught me coming out of the new wife's room, licking palm oil from all the five fingers of my right hand. She said the woman would soon poison me. I did not listen to Mama. I liked the woman's soup. I would eat it even if I would die. Mama hated me for my disobedience. She told people I did not remember whose breast I had suckled. Her friends would use their eyes to cut my feet from under my legs but I always went back to the new wife's room. Even then, as a child, I did what my heart wanted. I had a hand in my own destiny.

Today, the Police Commissioner with the big stomach asked me to become his third wife. I told him I did not want to marry. He forgot that I was not one of his corporals. The slap he gave me left the mark of three fingers on my cheek. The next day, he came back crying. I asked him to remove all his clothes. When I finished with him, he slept like a rotting fruit, swelling from pleasure. I rubbed his penis with hot peppers. That day, he saw his ancestors and never came to my door-mouth again.

The good Reverend Joshua said the world would end in 2016 but when my sweetness sank into the back of his head, he cried and asked Jesus to forgive him. The first time he did this, I was ashamed and afraid. I told him I did not want to make him sin. Reverend told me to bend over and continue God's work. God's work! I laughed that day. The things men say when pleasure takes them make me laugh.

I cannot remember them all. Many men have known the inside of my room and my inner chambers. I have taken pleasure from them when I needed it. I don't know how women build their nests around one man.

Many wives should be grateful to me because I drove their husbands back to them. After I used the men like rainwater and threw them out, they would crawl back to their wives. In their stupidity, they would then put their mouths together and call me a harlot.

Some women believed the lies; they believed the stories of how I used my powerful thighs to capture their husbands. They would come to my shop to look at me with bad eyes. Some women admired me secretly and told me so; others envied the way men desired me. They tried to befriend me so I would reveal my secret.

But the truth is I had no secret. I did not want my childlessness to reduce me to clay. That I did not have a husband was not a reason for me to forget the ticking between my thighs. The gods gave me a soft core and I was determined to use it. For this, they called me a harlot. They used my name to frighten their young daughters. And when their sons brought home unsuitable girlfriends, they would say the girl had a face like mine.

I will never be ashamed of my life because I have lived the way only a few women can. I have lived like a man. I have lived like seven men. If that makes me a harlot then I wear the name with pride.

★   ★   ★

Age is a woman's enemy. Five years before, no woman in Lagos was complete unless she had a piece of jewellery that was bought from me hanging around her neck or hooked around her wrist. But by 1973, many women were selling gold. And diamonds were everywhere. It seemed like my time had passed. Women with bigger breasts and blacker lips were snatching and devouring husbands as if the men were just fingers of roasted plantain lying by a fireplace. These reckless women opened their thighs for money and let men trample on them. If they had asked me, I would have told them that when a woman is too generous, men will suck her last breath. These women became slaves to men. I was not like them.

When a road was so bad that it was difficult for cars to pass, I would pay engineers to repair it. If children were sick and their parents could not afford a good doctor, I would call in favours from people in my past life and ensure that they were seen by specialists. It is good to know many people. I bought many sewing machines in those days. You know how Ebute Metta is full of old tailors today? Go and ask who bought many of them their first sewing machines. If you have money and you do not use it to do good, it is no better than ashes.

I thought often about my money and what would happen to it when I was returned to the soil. I could not have children and it worried me that the weeds around my grave would be uprooted by strangers, if at all. At these times, I would think of my village and the days of my childhood. I would think of the forest, and the fruits I used to pluck with my friends. I wondered if my friends had children. My money gave me a hundred wells but I desired the sound of a running river.

Later, in 1979, a man came to my shop. When he saw me, he prostrated himself and asked to see Madam Rolake Folarera. He did not recognise me but I knew who he was right away. I thought of the story about the brothers who sold Joseph into slavery but returned to bow down before him.

The man scrubbing the floor with his nose was Adenuyi, my eldest brother. I remembered the day he came to call me from the churchyard when Iya Ibeji died. There were many years between us, too many for us to be friends, too many for us to have much to talk about.

As a child, he never offended me but sometimes silence is a sin. All the time my mother was making my life a pot of tears, he did not raise his voice to comfort me.

When I told him who I was, he did not seem surprised. He slowly got on his feet. His eyes were full of shame. He was bald. His clothes were worn and faded. He smelled as if he had been tending cassava all day, under the heat of the sun. There were patches of dry skin on his arms, as if the shea butter had been rationed.

'Our father is dead and we have no money to buy a coffin,' were the first words that fell from his lips. I should have known that he needed something from me. All the years that had gone by, not a dog, not a goat from my village had come to find me. Misery can make strangers of strands of hair on the same head. I told him that they should throw our father into the earth as he was.

'So you are kind enough to buy my daughter a sewing machine. You are generous enough to repair the road that my son lives on but you do not care about your own father and whether he is buried in shame?'

'What daughter? What do I know about you?'

He told me that one of the women I'd bought a sewing machine for, just months before, was his daughter whom he had warned not to reveal her identity.

'So you thought I would not help her if I knew?'

'Yes. For the same reason you are rejecting your father. I know that anger has kept you from us. The tales of your life reach us in Ilara. We wanted to visit you but shame would not let us. Baba wanted to touch you with his eyes but death was already claiming them. Every time we thought a day would be his last, he would climb into the next one. Mama has nursed him all this time. All the money we have, we have used to support him. What we have borrowed, we will never be able to pay back. We live like beggars. Finally, last week Friday, Baba woke up with clear eyes and asked why strangers dressed in white were carrying his clothes out of his room. We knew they were death's messengers. As if he had dreamed the last thirty years, he asked when you were coming home from school. He said we should save you some red *omini* bananas because you liked them so much. He slept that

afternoon and did not wake up.' Adenuyi took off his cap and prostrated again. He begged me to forgive him.

I could not lie. I could not say I was still angry with my mother or
my family because I had just forgotten them. My destiny was different
from theirs. Living my life like an orphan was better for me. I leaned
forward and lifted him up. He was my senior brother and I did not
want to humiliate him. I asked about the village. I did not ask about
Mama. I was afraid to.

I bought my father a coffin made from the finest bronze. I gathered
the most expensive lace in my shop, the one I reserve for the wives of
kings. I took my best gold to put round his neck. I bought him a
leather wallet and filled it with money. I bought him two pairs of shoes
– one for him to wear and a spare pair for the rocky roads that lead to
heaven. I bought him a fan for the heat and a walking stick to ease each
step. I wanted the ancestors to stop and stare when Papa walked
through the gates of heaven.

For the funeral celebrations, I bought ten bags of rice, three cows,
six goats and eighty chickens. Three buses followed me and my brother
as we drove to Ilara in my new Volvo.

I was surprised to see how little the village had changed. There were
electricity poles but no evidence of electricity. The main road that used
to look so wide now resembled a foot-beaten pathway. The houses
were tiny, many of them made of mud, a few with little concrete
extensions. There were children running about. Young boys pushed
an old tyre rim around with sticks, girls played hopping games and
threw up sand with their feet.

Adenuyi wanted to be seen. He beckoned to them with the wave of
a hand. He wanted the villagers to know that we had arrived. They left
whatever they were doing and followed the car.

Mama was standing outside holding the hand of a young man for
support. The boy was moving from leg to leg as if he wanted to urinate.
I saw him and my stomach felt like there was a bead moving inside it.
It was Olujimi, Mama Ibeji's son. He was a man. I did not take my
eyes from him as I got out of the car.

I surveyed everything that I had left behind. I felt tears come to my
eyes. The woman who had made me suffer so much as a child was

running towards me but her legs could no longer carry her. I ran to catch her so she would not fall. She embraced me. I embraced her. She called me by my praise names, names I had forgotten I owned. She pulled away to look at me. She began to dance. Her head tie fell from her head. No teeth, no hair, no breasts, no husband. Yet here she was. Crying with joy.

Olujimi waited for me to finish with Mama. I called him by his name. He looked like his mother. I embraced him and my tears rolled down his back. He told me not to cry. He took my hand and led me into the house to see Baba.

My father lay on a low wooden bed. He was thin and shorter than I remembered. Death had darkened him. I checked his hand and saw that his left hand was still as it was.

I stared at him for a few minutes and imagined that if I widened my ears enough, I would hear his voice. I thought how small, how helpless he looked, how death was more merciful than life. Light and life together, gone from the egg of his eyes. Why, Baba? I asked. Why didn't you wait for me? His spirit could not have gone far. He could hear me. I asked him why he did not come to meet me. I asked what I had done to make him abandon me. I told him that it had been too long but I was happy to see him whole again. I reminded him to dazzle his ancestors with his butterflies. Spider-hands. I touched his hand and swore that no one in our home would hear of poverty or pain again.

I celebrated my father's funeral in a way Ilara will never forget. Every masquerade came out to pay homage. Every reverend in the diocese came to the church service. The party that followed the burial was a carnival. I invited my friends and they came from Ibadan, from Port Harcourt, Ilorin, Kaduna and Lagos. Old friends, new friends and forgotten friends. They all came to set my father's feet on his journey.

I have lived a full life, a life with tales worth telling, tales that women will hear and remember. I have known love. I have felt passion. I have seen poverty. I have had riches. People have passed through my life. Some have come with bad heads but my *eleda* has made us strangers.

Some have come with goodness and they have stayed to dine with me. Some have found their purpose and some have lost themselves. Some whom I had forgotten, I have found again. Who can judge whether a life was worth living except the person who has lived it.

from the forthcoming novel *¡Azúcar!*

Nii Ayikwei Parkes

Arroz Azucarado

Aguana

In 1959, the year Fumaz, our great, green, island country, freed itself from the tyranny of churches and colonial impositionists, no one would have believed you if you said that our president would become a victim of his own decree that the person – for he was nothing if not a man who believed in equality for all, and we all know women grow beards too – with the longest beard would be the ruler of the land. But to see him now, bent double with the weight of a waterfall beard that he hired more and more people to help him clean, you couldn't help but feel that he, Guerrero Candia Rosario Austral – Guerrero Rosario for short – had enslaved himself. Guerrero was a peopleist who had aligned himself with the Union of Soviet Socialist Republicans, much to the annoyance of the United States of the Americas, who felt their half-decade colonial subjects should at least show some loyalty to those who first exploited their land and labour. I pause here to point out that for the people of Fumaz, the Fumazero, there was great entertainment found in arguing about the aforementioned states (USSRs and USAs) as they sounded the same when abbreviated – something along the lines of USERs.

In any case, I only mention Guerrero Rosario because his actions had a direct impact on the genesis of the history I am to recount. His choice of fraternal nation led to the USAs enacting an embargo on Fumaz imports in 1962, which meant that there was plenty of sugar with no buyer. For a few days after the announcement reached our island, it was not uncommon to see young Fumazero farm folk, covered in sweat and sugar, dancing in protest along the same country roads they had jubilated on with drum, song and dance following Guerrero Rosario's ascent to power. Pursued by flies, and assaulted by ants when they stood still, they created an almighty buzz. Still, the fuss was soon calmed when the USSRs stepped in to buy the surplus sugar – to annoy their eternal rivals in trade, arms and exploitation. It is when the idea first took root in the head of Diego Soñada Santos, already in his distinguished years, of watering his rice paddies with sugar solution so that his rice would be sweeter than any of his competitors' harvest.

Isla de la Inocencia

His name was not Yunior; it was Oswald Kole Osabutey Jnr. When the Spanish tutor first asked for his name, he had said it clearly, but Profesor Hernandez had forgotten, and the next time he wanted to call Oswald to conjugate a verb, instead of pointing and asking him what his name was, as he did with some of the other students – mainly boys from Angola, Southern Sudan, Cape Verde and a sprinkling of girls – Profesor Hernandez snapped his fingers and blurted out, 'Yunior.'

Overwhelmed by the newness of everything; the fertile green of the vegetation he could clearly see from his seat by the open window, the weight of concentration it took to follow what he was being taught, he responded, 'Si.' He was never called Oswald after that.

Playing football in the open yard between the teaching and boarding buildings on his compound, shouts of *Yunior* rang out whenever he had to pass the ball; or dribbled past two, three, four opposing players; or scored one of the spectacular goals he would become known for, his team mates piling on top of him in celebration, cementing the name in myth and reality.

Yunior's Escuela Secundaria was one in a cluster of five lettered A to E. In spite of their separate identities, they were enclosed by a perimeter of barbed wire, anchored at intervals to pillars of solid concrete. When Yunior first arrived, he felt as though he had been sent to a prison. The carefully trimmed bushes lining the enclosure, for all their order and occasional flourish of rogue papaya or mango trees bursting oranges, yellows and reds like lanterns in the uniform green, did not conceal the barbed wire. It looked like the military barracks he had passed by in trotros near Cantonments in Accra. It wasn't what his mother had described; a safe, secluded environment where your child will learn Spanish and all the required secondary level subjects before progressing to sponsored higher education of a world class standard.

Yunior had jumped at the chance. He didn't like the secondary school he had started in Accra; Christian Methodist Secondary School had a uniform that consisted of brown shorts and a deep purple shirt, which he detested. At twelve, he had been the youngest in his first year of secondary school and was teased and picked on continually. Some of his classmates were starting secondary school at fifteen and sixteen – they had had hard lives selling groundnuts, coconuts, air fresheners, puppies, newspapers and sweets as hawkers on Accra's roads to pay their meagre contributions towards their education, already world weary before they started to learn about the world from books. Yunior's mother, Naa Okailey, had protected him from that. A food trader herself, she worked at the central market close to their home in Adabraka, and earned more money than his father, a minimally skilled government clerk. She had invested faithfully in Yunior's education, but with two younger kids, she was relieved when her husband came home with the application form for the Fumazero scholarship. Her relief wasn't because she didn't think they could afford to continue to scrape enough together for Yunior's education. Working under an increasingly hot sun in the market, she had seen the ground turn harder, bereft of rain; heard the prices of food, shouted across zigzagging walkways, shoot higher; smelled the despair in the air as, even she, for all the friends she had who sold bread, had to send Yunior to queue for bread.

Ghana had fallen under the spell of dry Sahel winds and the ensuing drought was beginning to bite hard. Fewer people were buying the cooking oil Naa Okailey sold in smaller, repackaged units at the market; some of her friends who sold vegetables had stopped coming to the market altogether as they could not reliably make up the daily fee they paid for their stalls. The spaces they vacated, previously as sought after as gold dust, were now covered in common dust. For rice, one had to go to one of the Food Distribution Corporation outlets around the city with a chit. When local corn ran out and some aid finally came from the West, there were queues for yellow corn, a thing so alien that it drove old ladies half-mad – corn was supposed to be white. All things were rationed. The lines of chit-bearing families grew longer and more dust-beaten as the year progressed.

And then the Agege-Ghanaians – omo Ghana – started to arrive with their sad tales, new dances, and memories of Chief Commander Ebenezer Obey's wedding song, King Sunny Adé's velvety voice – Fuji music. Thousands and thousands of them. Deported from Nigeria for no reason that anyone could agree on, they arrived mainly by road, clutching patterned bags to their chests, in trucks hired by the Ghana government. They were mainly teachers and mechanics, a few musicians who were not part of Nigerian-led bands, dancers, nurses, traders – even doctors. They claimed to have lost everything, they said Ifako had been razed to the ground by bulldozers: their houses, their TVs, their VW Beetles, were gone. In time, the bags they clutched in 1983 would come to be known as Agege Sacks or Ghana Must Go bags. With their arrival, the food shortage turned acute. Hunger had arrived and it was staying for a while. It is for this reason that Naa Okailey was prepared to let her son go to Fumaz.

On Isla de la Inocencia there was food – three times a day – and Yunior was grateful for that, regardless of what he thought of the barbed wire perimeter. He had been living on one full meal a day in Accra – without meat and often without even bones. He also preferred the uniform on Isla – burgundy shorts and a white shirt – a mirror of the buildings, which were painted burgundy on the lower halves of their walls. In time he would answer more readily to Spanish than Ga or Twi; he would learn to play street baseball as the local youths did, wielding a bat with affected nonchalance; he would come to appreciate peopleist philosophy and spend his weekends helping younger children with their homework. With every passing year his body fell more easily into the rhythm of samba, his fingers sought and moulded themselves to the tension of guitar strings and he blended with the countryside; its fertility, its undulating earth, its cycles, the muted music of its flora flourishing and fading, its temper when hurricanes flashed nearby. Losing the city's pulse inside of him, he became a boy of the countryside – muchacho del campo – his fellow students at Escuela Secundaria Basica en el Campo B – ESBEC B – became his comrades.

Although they dispersed like wind-blown silk cotton seeds after their secondary education, they kept in touch by hearsay and letters. Those who, like Yunior, had learned to play an instrument occasionally ran into each other at university music events, or at concerts in Aguana where their idols from Fumaz or neighbouring islands, such as Alberto Sanchez (who had been born not far from ESBEC B) and Elena Burke, were playing with big bands in which all the players were – to their ears – perfect. Soon their letters were referring to shortages of canned goods from USSRs, which formed the basis of most diets in Fumaz, and it became steadily clear to Yunior that they were heading for a food shortage like the one he had escaped in Ghana. But this shortage was different; in Ghana, deprived of water for months, the soil could not support new growth so the solutions for their food shortages had to come from outside, or from adaptations. In Accra, they had begun to eat the bɔkɔbɔkɔ leaves that grew wild – along walls, in the cracks that lined open gutters, atop the wide walls of the rich, down back streets where gangsters congregated to split their loot, and at the edges of wells that mocked searchers with reflections from their almost-empty depths – instead of kontomire, which had all but disappeared with the cocoyams that formed its roots. Here, the soil was fertile, there was rain and there was manpower, but for years they had only farmed en masse for export, never planting to feed themselves.

With his realisation of what was coming, by the time *half-time* arrived in 1991, Yunior, by now at the Universidad Agraria de Los Cien Vientos del Oeste, in Bana, Western Provinces, was already keeping a plot of varied food crops. He had made arrangements with a nearby sugar-producing family, the Gonzalezs, to cultivate a section of their plantation based on organic agricultural production methods, as the price for sugar began to drop. Once the real shortages set in, in mid-1991, he was able to help the Gonzalez family and the neighbouring farms to switch their output from cash crops to local consumption based crops. It was not a straightforward process; most of the farmers were used to the convenience of using tractors, combine harvesters and mechanised irrigation and struggled to adapt to manual methods. However, the decline of the USSRs' economy and its subsequent division into new nations meant that the petroleum that Fumaz used to get in exchange for its sugar was no longer forthcoming. The farmers had no choice but to adapt. Stories of how their grandfathers used to farm became the order of the day as they trekked to and from wells and standpipes. To sell produce outside of Bana, the eleven horses in the town were called into action – they were haltered, saddled, bridled and attached to carts. Their crownpieces were pulled into place behind their ears, their breast collars checked, they were patted on the head, and put to work. But several of the farms, their soil decimated by years of planting cane and sustaining volumes by using fertilisers, took years to produce a good harvest.

It was the Gonzalez men who told him the perennial joke about his name.

'Do you know what Yunior is?' asked Julio, the father.

'Yeah, it's my name.'

'No,' Julio laughed, 'it's the name of a one-night stand. You know why?'

Yunior shook his head.

'There are so many Yuniors, and they are very hard to trace – unless you know the full name. So, when a girl is asked out and her date says he's called Yunior, we assume he just wants a good time – there's no plan beyond one night, for how would she trace him?'

This is how, on Yunior's first visit to Aguana to play in a live band, he was able to tell the joke to the drummer, one of only two native Fumazero in the quintet, whose brother shared Yunior's name. Warming up absent-mindedly, his hardened fingertips skimming guitar strings, he overheard the man lamenting how his brother, resentful of the way Guerrero Rosario's policies had curtailed their wealthy family's influence, had decided to migrate to the USAs.

Yunior cut in with the joke and added, 'At least over there his name may be less of a code for a one-night stand and more of an identity.' He extended his hand. 'I'm also Yunior, by the way. By accident, but that's my name now.'

'Marcos,' the drummer replied. 'Manjate told me a lot about you, Yunior. You sing as well, yes? Like a Fumazero?'

'I am Fumazero.'

Bana

Marcos was the reason Yunior started taking food from his farm to Aguana at the height of *half-time*. It was never planned; it just happened once and grew into something that could no longer be ignored.

The quintet Yunior played in with Marcos, Los Puntos Estelares, were offered a fortnightly slot at one of the leading salsa clubs, Verde, a place where, regardless of local conditions, foreigners still visited and spent good money on alcohol, cigars and the promise of love. Knowing the difficulty of getting good food in Aguana once supply from USSRs dried up, Yunior travelled to the two-night engagements of Los Puntos Estelares with some basic supplies – three carrots, a head of cabbage, a handful of frijoles Negros that swelled to three times their original size when soaked overnight, and two red onions. The first time he travelled east, mindful that Marcos had a young daughter, he harvested an identical mix of vegetables for him, making a mental note to add some frijoles from the sack he kept on his kitchen table. Then, surveying his half-acre plot, its boundary marked by a thigh-high chicken run that held six clucking red- and brown-feathered hens, Yunior shrugged and uprooted carrots and onions for his other band mates. Peopleist philosophy was now almost instinctive. In a break during rehearsals, he handed to drummer, trumpeter, pianist and bass player, roughly-cut sugar sacks sewn into quaint, small bags with visible spirals of twine.

Marcos, having opened his makeshift bag, stared at its contents almost without recognition, then he jumped up to fold Yunior in a bear hug. 'I haven't seen cabbage for so long, brother. So long.'

The rest of the band converged on Yunior, mumbling their appreciation and light-heartedly describing the wonderful meals they were going to cook, until they heard Marcos's bass drum ringing with the beat of their first song. They still had to rehearse.

Yunior took his position at the front of the quintet and prepared to sing their signature song, *Vivimos Juntos*. He lifted his guitar strap over his head. As he lowered it on to his left shoulder, he noticed his shirt was wet with Marcos's tears. Yunior hadn't realised how bad *half-time* was until that evening; everyone was being stoic, managing their struggles in silence.

It was soon after he started adding eggs to the rations he packed for his band mates that he was approached by the owner of Verde about supplying produce to his brother's grocery store on a side street close by.

'I don't produce much,' said Yunior. 'Only a half-acre, and I only come here twice a month.'

'It's OK. Even a little will be helpful to the locals.'

Gente had already lost the right to be called a grocery store. Its shelves swept bare by the lack of imports from USSRs and the direct-to-hotel trade of fresh produce, it only held a supply of locally-produced cigars in a cabinet to the right of the till. The shelves, painted in alternate greens and yellows, that appeared to have been borrowed from the same palette that created the Fumazero flag, looked like wings abandoned by small planes that had lost the desire to fly. Flor and Tomas, the owners, had kept it open by taking in laundry from the same hotels that had severed their lines of vegetable supply from the farmers. In fact, it was a launderette disguised as a place where one could go and find the means to end hunger, and it remained a launderette after Yunior arrived with his first delivery.

'You won't display the vegetables?'

'No,' explained Flor, 'we cannot sell like this. It is not official. We will tell the people at home and they will come.'

Boxes of onions, potatoes, carrots, cabbages, lettuce and tomatoes were packed in a back room, and before Yunior left, he was relieved to see a bare-chested boy walk in with a note for Flor, hand over a clutch of pesos, and leave with a bag of potatoes, onions and a head of cabbage.

Yunior charged Flor and Tomas no more for the vegetables than he made at government-backed produce markets in the Western Provinces. They only had to cover the extra cost of his transporting the hundred-kilo assortment of vegetables by horse and the converted military trucks that ferried hordes of people along the same route that Western Province traders and mercenaries of old, such as Diego Soñada Santos, used to build their empires of influence. When he arrived from Bana for performances with Los Puntos Estelares, Yunior always spent his spare hours lost in theses on crop rotation, subsidence and the long-term effects of fertiliser use; papers on efficient farm-layout, wild medicinal herbs that were threatened by large-scale agriculture and low-cost irrigation. He was still a student; he had no time to visit produce markets in Aguana, so he wasn't aware that vegetables, when available, fetched far higher prices there. When the locals, who still saw him delivering crates and sacks to Gente stopped waving at him, calling out *hermano*, he didn't notice. The growing, striped flamboyance of Tomas's shirts and the sparkle of Flor's new shoes when they visited Verde to dance, didn't catch his eyes. Yunior loved seeing them happy, embraced them with customary exuberance, shared in the laughter that lit their eyes like diamonds.

Flor often held his face and kissed him on the lips, ruffling his growing Afro. 'Twenty-two. So hard-working, so good-looking. It's a pity we don't have a daughter for you.' Tomas punched his arm and they all laughed. He didn't know that Flor and Tomas had stopped selling vegetables to all but their closest friends, that they were taking deliveries from him and reselling the produce to the hotels that glowed like enemy posts in Aguana nights – hotels that paid ten times the price he charged them.

Leaving the club one evening, a dark woman with loose black curls that tumbled to the shoulder of the clinging red dress she wore, grasped his arm and followed him outside.

'Hi, I'm Loretta.'

He was stunned, both by her radiance and her forwardness. 'Yunior.'

'Do you have something with that woman?' She jerked her head towards the door of Verde, still holding on to his left arm, her low heels keeping beat with his strides.

'Flor? No.' He flashed an amused smile. 'Were you jealous?'

'You are her business partner?'

Yunior frowned at the turn the conversation had taken. 'No. I sell vegetables to her store sometimes. She is a friend.'

Loretta stepped up to walk ahead of him and mumbled, 'Come with me.'

Yunior's frown eased into a grimace of realisation. His first encounter with the secret police.

Following Loretta into a Spanish-style villa turned dull by night, Yunior was ushered into what must have once been a lavatory where a young man in tan trousers, a green T-shirt and a flat cap, informed him that they had been observing the counter-revolutionary activities of Flor and Tomas for five months. They had started in May 1991, nine months earlier, when Yunior first delivered vegetables to Gente, but stopped after a month having spoken to locals who said that they were able to get affordable produce from Flor and Tomas. In September, an old lady complained that vegetables were no longer available, although they still saw Yunior arriving with boxes twice a month.

'We went to Bana and saw the good work you are doing there with the farmers. The Universidad say you are a brilliant student too.'

Yunior nodded, finally leaning back in the low chair he had been given.

'We just had to be sure that you weren't involved in the black market trade with the hotels like Flor and Tomas.'

Yunior was to say nothing of his arrest as Loretta would be observing the Gente operation for another month to identify all the counter-revolutionaries. The Agriculture Minister was interested in his organic farming work in Bana and the smaller project he had started recently on a visit to Isla de la Inocencia.

It was on his way back home, the Agriculture Minister's long arm reaching across him to point, that he first saw the Soñada Santos rice estate in Asadon.

'The owner is a good supporter of the Rosario revolution. The family gave half of their land to the local peasants after our liberation in 1959,' said the minister, pushing his sunglasses further up his nose.

'It doesn't look very productive.'

'True. I think their yield has been falling for years, but it doesn't matter. The rice from here is worth its weight in gold – it's the sweet-est rice in Fumaz.'

Excerpt from Work in Progress

Novuyo Rosa Tshuma

For Abednego, the sweats began the day he dreamt of Black Jesus and Farmer Thornton's wife. The two always followed one another, a seductive sickness which had the effect of curing his erectile dysfunction, an infirmity that started the year he went to Lupane to see the Commission of Enquiry people, near the mass grave where Thandi and his mama lay.

Black Jesus began to afflict him after the Solomon incident. Solomon and his lofty idealism, which he had imported along with the Syrian woman he arrived with from Cuba in '91. He had returned a haunted man, Solomon, lanky, with a Fidel Castro T-shirt, a beret worn to the side, and gaunt eyes which seemed to beckon a dismal future. He was sick, sick, sick in the head as much as in the body; hadn't Abednego tried to tell the family that all that talk about land and revolution and Guantánamo City were the ramblings of a man who had lost his bearings? Well – he scratched his balls – no, he hadn't, but he should have, because he had suspected it from the very beginning.

Solomon decided, as he lay dying on the mat in Aunt Po's hut, to impose an impossible request: 'Bury me where my ancestors lie.'

He knew two things, Solomon:

one: to deny the request of a dying man was suicide

and

two: his was an impractical request.

Everybody knew that the land in question was located in Farmer Thornton's sprawling fields. Aunt Po, swamped by grief, sagged beneath her son's request. And so it was left up to Abednego – he puffed – as were most important decisions in the family, to coax out one last shaft of reason; he grabbed his cousin's hand.

'Please, mzala, anything else.'

'When my body lies in the ground, I want to be able to greet my ancestors on the other side.'

'Anything else mzala. Please.'

'I want to wake up in the spirit world of my clan across the Dongamuzi Mountain.'

'Cousin, don't say that, ngiyacela, please.'

'It's the grief of having to drive past the stolen land of my people which has killed me.'

'Cousin, it is Aids which has killed you . . .'

Aunt Po let out an indignant shriek.

'When they stole the land they stole our souls. Don't let me wander in the spirit world without my soul.'

'Cousin . . .'

'Bury me in the land of my ancestors. Do you hear me? I will come back and haunt you if you don't.'

Solomon chose this moment to draw his last breath; the pact was sealed.

The crime was committed in the dead of night. It was Abednego who led the excursion. Aunt Po insisted on a patch of land right in the middle of Farmer Thornton's pumpkins. It was the farm workers who heard the *conk-conk* of the hoes against rock, and, loyal little mutts that they were, the little shits*, they alerted the farmer. And so, beneath the glower of the farmer's flashlights, his rabid mongrels, his loaded shotgun and the local constabulary – who, fearful of spirits which when unfulfilled wandered the earth in search of vengeance, refused to help the farmer – Solomon Ndimande was buried. The family and what few friends had decided to brave the spectacle congratulated themselves on a job well done and went on their way.

And that was that.

★ The most disenfranchised of the affranchised slave-class.

Until.

Three years later, when, under the assistance of a court order from Judge Muponde – a drunk, a womaniser and a civil servant of the overzealous, irritating kind – Farmer Thornton and his band of latifundia thugs congregated to dig up Solomon. Aunt Po threw herself on to the grave and rolled and rolled, rolled and rolled, tearing at her tangle of frizzy hair. Abednego stood with his hands hanging awkwardly at his sides. It was Farmer Thornton's son, a finely etched shadow of the father, who telephoned the police, and it was Black Jesus, who happened to be visiting the area, who arrived with a gang of terrified constabulary in tow. Before he knew it, Abednego was doubled over, retching; how could it be that after eleven whole years, the man was still disarming in all his magnificent ugliness? He had never been sure if the man had a frightful face simply because it was ghastly or because he was Black Jesus. For years, he had obsessed over photographs of the man on television and in newspapers, safe in the illusion that his rage was a weapon biding its time. Before him, this rage whimpered and died. Oh, not only was it unforgettable, that face, the colour of the rich black clay that could be found along the Gwayi River floodplain in Tsholotsho, near Lupane, but each twitch of those lips – the shape of a flat-bellied heart – and each contraction of those cheeks – protruding from either side of the columella in the distinguished silhouettes of smoking pipes – gave those loathsome eyes a savage sophistication that was at once dreadful and beguiling.

Abednego turned away, still gagging, clamping and unclamping his hands.

Black Jesus seemed to relish the task of dragging Aunt Po off Solomon's grave; he slapped her *one two three*, successive claps on each cheek, and flung her at Abednego's feet, where she began to tear at her pastel dress, the only remembrance Solomon had brought her from Cuba. Cousin Solomon was dug up and flung at his mother's feet, spraying her dress with maggots.

'Nincompoops. Good-for-nothing peasants. Distracting the important work of the farmers with your silly superstitions. You want to be shitting everywhere, heh? *Sniff sniff my ancestors are here my ancestors are here* – you are worse than dogs,' Black Jesus spat. Spittle dribbled down the sides of his lips.

After he left, Abednego wept. The greatest indignity of all was how the man, whose impact Abednego had never been able to forget, hadn't even recognised him.

That was when the nightmares started; first, of Farmer Thornton's wife, who Abednego hadn't thought of in a long time, and then of Black Jesus, who he could not stop thinking about. The nightmares stopped only after he made the trip to see the Commission of Enquiry people in Lupane in '96. Two years of night-sweats, sleeplessness and a sensation of drowning which left him haggard. Two years and then he had managed to retrieve his sanity, thanks to the Commission of Enquiry people, who had, ironically, brought on a different, flaccid kind of anguish.

Afterwards, as he made the trip back to Bulawayo, Abednego hadn't been able to get rid of the smell of singed flesh, and the feeling that he was back in the Liberation War.

Because it had wafted in the smog like braaied carabeef, the stench of the charred soldiers. He had cradled in his arms men he had played with as boys, slipping on outcroppings of Precambrian rock, struggling with firearms they didn't quite know how to use. Lost inside themselves, deep in the Matobo Hills.

Slushy rain and slippery hearts.

Skinny Zacchaeus, his brother, in an oversize helmet and glasses that looked like a handyman's goggles, wailing like a woman at a funeral:

'We are going to die, *going to die,* oh fuck, are we going to die, Abed?'

'Will you *shoosh,* are you trying to get us killed?'

'Best we surrender and negotiate, yes? You know I was the first president of the debating team at school, I can lobby on our behalf—'

'Just shutt*up*, please!'

'Why didn't we just take Muzorewa's deal, why didn't we just deal with this like civilised human beings, heh? I don't blame them for thinking us savages. What is this, heh? This *gorilla* warfare deliberate play on the similar sound of "guerrilla" and "gorilla", and the idea of blacks being "savages" warfare. Like we're still wearing animal skins in the bhundu? Heh? We'd better give ourselves up. Me, I can't die here, I've a degree from Oxford, destined for great things, I'm not a violent man, me. I—'

'I *swear* if you don't shut that trap I'm going to put a bullet in that dwala head of yours!'

He had receded, skinny Zacchaeus, into a shuffling, rather loud type of silence. Sniffling while Abednego held the men as they died, gagging in an atmosphere polluted by sickly fumes of bauxite. He had been a soldier in the ZIPRA military, had fought in the liberation war from '76.*

He had smelled death then, every waking moment, had smelled *of* death. It had hung in the air, taunting, hiding in landmines beneath the underbrush. Popping out of the ground like phantoms out of Pandora's pithos, springing a cruel 'Surprise!' The first time it happened, he was crawling in the bush in enemy territory, about to invade the camp at Fort Hare. He clung to his Kalashnikov, his mind trying to sieve through the haphazard training that had been brow-beaten into the Zimbabwean recruits at Camp Pyonyang:

What is it that we always strive at?

Dialectics – the art of arriving at the truth through the logical deduction of logical arguments.

And what is it that capitalism aims to do?

Provide an antithesis – to rule through the logical deduction of illogical arguments.

What is it that we fight against?

The forcing of the peasant off his land, his only real power, into slavery so he may sell his labour.

---

* It had been a glowing moment for the peasantry: tongues frothy with nationalist rhetoric, mud feet marching to the promise of a Maoan revolution, rural hearts pitter-pattering to the vision of dozens of little Dazhai villages culled from the white agricultural scape. A nation of workers chugging along in solidarity to reach Marx's great ideal of the triumph of labour over capitalist exploitation. These men and women who, having nothing already, and therefore with nothing to lose, clung to the utopic postulations of their intellectual leaders.

How drunk with ambition!

For the people by the people.

But first, they'd had to die.

His father, forced off the patch of land he had adopted and worked quite successfully at the Thornton Farm, into the Tribal Trust Lands where not even the thorn tree dared flourish, so that he found himself – a father and husband, strong and proud with the gait of an ox, and whom men from the surrounding homesteads came to consult – slaving away in the Tsholotsho mines. He would never forget what the old man told him, pried from unravelling strands of senility, the last thing of substance Abednego ever heard from his father: 'It was as though, Zacchaeus my son, my manhood had been chopped off.' And he had wept. Abednego had wept too, for himself.

What is it that we are aiming to do?

Communism is a hammer which we use to crush the enemy!

Mao fluttering on the wall above, wearing a seraphic grin.

What is our ultimate goal?

The people, and the people alone, are the motive force in the making of world history!

Was that fluttering Mao winking?

The Chinese soldiers had spat as they walked past, refused to share the same plates as the Zimbabwean recruits. Welcome to slit-eye Rhodesia, Abednego had thought with a wry smile.

When, in '77, the landmines at Fort Hare exploded, Abednego did not assume the foetal position and cover his head, as did his comrades. Instead, he stumbled through the smoke, yelling for his brother Zacchaeus. He found him scrunched up beneath the flimsy limbs of a mkhemeswane brush, bruised but unharmed.

Zacchaeus had been one of the blacks to slip through Britain's sanctions following Ian Smith's Unilateral Declaration of Independence, and had been awarded a scholarship to study in England. He'd left with the avowed intention of acquiring a law degree, had instead returned with a wispy BA in English Literature – from Oxford, he always made sure to emphasise – and a new way of speaking in roundabout sentences that were too foggy for a career in politics. Zacchaeus, who, in '79, almost became a traitor, having allowed his reverence for all things British to cloud his judgement of a six-course English meal hosted by Bishop Abel Muzorewa; 'Smith's tea-boy,' Abednego quipped, his comrades demolished by laughter. Out of the corner of his eye, a glimpse of Zacchaeus, who was too much like a shadow nowadays, fading deeper into himself.

Zacchaeus playing spittle-spattle on the fine soil of his father's homestead: arch back, neck distended like an ostrich's and in one lazy lunge, aim a nice, frothy globule of spit at the base of the pawpaw tree. His brother metamorphosing into a distant being Abednego could no longer recognise.

'You have become a, a thing which . . .' Abednego began.

'A thing which what, brother?'

'Which is not real, brother. A thing which lives in *books*.'

'But, brother, you don't understand. A society's greatest asset is its poet, for only he is capable of submerging himself thoroughly in its irony, thereby holding up the mirror of many truths—'

'We don't need more ideas here, brother. We need more fighters.'

'Among all fighters, is there a fighter?'

'I don't understand what England did to you. Who recruited you? Was it the Thatcherics, heh? This is war, and you won't side with the capitalist cockroaches!'

And so Zacchaeus, head hung, had grabbed a pair of Abednego's boots and marched to the guerrilla camp at Mbulilingwane.

'Look after him,' Abednego's father begged him.

'What about me, Father?' Abednego said, though he knew he shouldn't have bothered, really.

'The missionaries were right; he's Jacob, and you, my son, have become Esau. Protect him now, for in the end, it's he who shall protect you.'

Abednego smarted. 'I'm your eldest son! That wimpy little nincompoop can't even hold a gun properly, who is he going to protect? All he does is read his books and write that nonsense nobody understands. *I* am the fighter. And yet . . . forgotten, unappreciated . . . un*loved* . . .'

They made it through the war. 18 April 1980 was a Friday giddy with swaying crowds and freedom curdled like sweetened amasi and flowers mingling their heady scents in the heat. As Prince Charles lowered the Union Flag, Abednego* raised a fist, yelled, '*let a hundred flowers bloom!*'

---

* Face pasted into a careful smile; oh, but the hatred, the *hatred*!

In his fist, a little red book.*

The Rufaro Stadium was so packed that the crowd burst through the gates and out on to the parking lot. When Bob Marley and the Wailers climbed the stage and began wailing 'Zimbabwe', the stadium went mad with applause. Guitars tickling air, air reverberating, seducing drunken crowd. Fireworks bombing night, cheerful flag aflutter, prancing in light, a pause for applause, a blow kiss, like soft air on cheek, prance again. Oh! The sweetness of it! Like a tub of Dairy Moon strawberry ice-cream . . .

On hearing Bob Marley, the crowds outside, high on the opium of independence, began to press against the gates, trying to get in. Those inside, propelled by this force, moved towards the stage. The police, overcome by fear, sprang into action, their bodies falling into animated violence like a second skin; they began thwacking the people with their batons, and the people wailed, so that their independence brimmed over into the night, and made a horrible sound. The police flung cans of tear gas into the crowd; at first, uncomprehending, the people cupped their hands, welcoming yet another gift of their independence – were there free Coca-Cola cans? – and then, when this independence stung their eyes and threatened to make them blind, they began to cry.

The VIPs, penned in their elevated stand, were caught by the cameras in what was later proclaimed as joyous weeping, overwhelming emotions at this momentous day, this emancipation of the black-and-brown peoples of the House of Stone . . . but, in fact, the

---

* History, of course, would not remember the names of the masses. Too many to name, really. What was a skull, what was a chopped limb, what was a gutted heart, what was a muddy-face with a name too long to pronounce, who cared who'd remember? Indispensable to the struggle indeed but . . . So who, on this auspicious day, this symbolic emancipation of the black-and-brown peoples of the House of Stone, would History focus her lens on? Of course! Of course! The intellectuals, those charlatans who could not be counted on to speak for anybody, not even themselves! Those prittle-prattlers with the talent for abstraction who History, even if only very briefly, loved to revere. There they sat, in pomp on an elevation penned from the People: Lord Christopher Soames, Prince Charles, Prime Minister Indira Gandhi, President Shehu Shagari, President Kenneth Kaunda, President Seretse Khama, Prime Minister Malcolm Fraser and not forgetting his Excellency and his entourage, the then Prime Minister Comrade Robert Gabriel Mugabe. Titles and honorifics and honorifics and titles, those tactful distractions from the specificities of nationalist ambitions.

overzealous policemen, in a state of frenzy, had flung tear gas whichever way, including at the cordoned-off stand, much to the Very Important People's pompous chagrin.

A hush finally descended on the crowd when Zacchaeus lumbered on to the stage, after Bob Marley. He adjusted his glasses, cleared his throat:

'Oh, but what is a flower?
That decay of sunken spirits?
Soft-petalled.
Flame-Lily sandals at my feet.'

He bowed solemnly as his voice boomed:

'Out of all lovers, is there a lover?'

Straightened up, hushed:

'A heart's private desire,
Smouldering in hatred cauldron
Oh, but listen!'

He cocked his ear.

'Oh, what is that?'

Capped his head with his hand, squinted into the distance.

'It's the cockerel – cock-a-doodle-doo!
On the blistering horizon.'

'That's my brother!' Abednego yelled above the buoyancy as Zacchaeus clambered down the stage. 'Hey, hey, that poet is my brother! He even performed in front of Lord Carrington and Prime Minister Mugabe at the Lancaster House Conference! Yes, *I know him very personally, he's my brother*!'

It was the last time he remembered them so happy together, intoxicated by the future, falling into each other's arms like true brothers of the revolution. For once, their father's bias forgotten.

They were among the first to jump and shout as Tuku ran on to the stage, his dancing queens in close pursuit, chunks of thigh wonderfully displayed beneath skimpy Traditional Attire. Abednego clutched Thandi's hand as his eyes ran over those wiggling buttocks. He smacked his lips. She pouted. He laughed, tilted her chin and gave her a good long kiss.

'Your kiss is so delicious, better even than my Mama's Chakalaka Sunday Special. What a beautiful feeling it is, to be able to kiss as much as we like, wherever and whenever.'

Her pout bloomed into laughter. The light carried particles which danced around her yellow skin like misty translucence.

He stepped back and put his hands on his slim hips, throwing his Michael Jackson 'fro this way and that as he raised an imaginary whip in the air and said, in precise English tones:

'Two licks for insulting my eyes with your black nonsense, sah. You blacks, don't even know how to kiss! You look like two baboons trying to bite the lips off each other. Now, bend over!'

Thandi was doubled over before he was through with his act. 'That's not how they used to do it, man, thank goodness you never considered a career on the screen!'

He laughed, pinched her cheek. Her skin reminded him of pawpaw. Full lips the texture of the fleshy inside. Complete with dark spots around her nose, like the seeds. She was his own pretty, ripe pawpaw.

They were caught in the throes of song and dance, melting amongst the other revellers, when he whispered in her ear, 'If it's OK with you, I'd like you to be my wife.'

She looked up into his face with a mischievous twinkle in her eye, but when she saw that he was serious, she frowned. 'I wish you'd be a little more romantic about it, you know.'

He got down on one knee and took her hand, made a mock gesture of searching for a ring in his pockets. 'Oh, my goodness! Where is that ring? Now where did I put that ring? Will she ever accept me without that ring . . .'

Those within earshot began to clap and cheer.

'Say yes!'

'Make him a happy man tonight!'

'Let the cows come home!'

Thandi laughed, attempted to pull him to his feet.

'That's the most melodious laugh I've ever heard. To wake up to that laugh every morning would make me the happiest man.'

'Oright oright, now get up! People are staring.'

'Let them stare. Dipping into your beauty feels like tasting freedom for the first time.'

She giggled.

Freedom, like a whiff of fresh air.*

Bauxite, like a waft of bad breath that refuses to go away.

So happy. To think that he had thought . . . it would be for ever . . . and then Black Jesus happened . . .

* How stupid, of course, to have thought that something as chronic as war, holding in its grip the hard currency fear of a people, could be over just like that, in the naming of a day.

from the novel in progress *Mood Indigo*

Chika Unigwe

Soham's Mulatto

Life's fare is sorrow cooked or baked
Served up with trials great and small
All these misfortunes fate has shaped
Sure in its quest your joy to stall
Joanna Bromley

London, August, 1856

Joanna wakes up every day stunned to discover that she is still alive. She spends the first moments awake imagining that if she keeps her eyes shut long enough, she might slip light-footed out of this world into the next, the hem of her nightdress swishing as she leaves, her thin, frail body – so frail she cannot abide a corset – klikklikiking all the way to eternity. Death does not frighten her. But there are reasons why she does not want to go just yet. Her husband, Henry Bromley, is one of them. She does not live with Henry in this catacomb with small, dark rooms and the hallway that is no bigger than a tunnel but which she does not mind. At the foot of her bed, Fido is still asleep. This is the best part of the day, she thinks. This period between being fully awake and sleeping when her mind is blank and her brain is slow and her bones forget that they ought to be aching. Before breakfast and the clearing of it, when she has to leave her bed (and confront her aching joints) so that the maid can begin her sweeping day. Joanna has to ask as she does every day if the bed has been thoroughly brushed, all the edges and corners of the sacking-bottom where dust can settle inspected. She is particular about this because she fears that odious plague of London homes: bed bugs, and she knows, regrettably from past experience, what can happen when a maid does not pay attention to the work but rushes over it because she is not supervised. Joanna had had to bring in a carpenter who took the bed apart and washed the frame with chloride of lime and water for several days.

At the beginning, with this new maid, Joanna had supervised the cleaning, making sure that the bed was entirely uncovered, the bedding hung over the two chairs in her room, with an old sheet thrown upon it, and then the bed, the curtains and the valance brushed; the bedposts and stock well rubbed until there was not a particle of dirt to be spied. The pillows must be removed and placed on the sofa, she told the maid, and the window opened, no matter the weather, so that the beddings receive some fresh air. Now, she trusts the maid to do the job on her own but she still asks nevertheless, 'Done a good job, Sarah?' 'Yes, Ma'am.' This asking, even when the response is obvious and never changes, is a habit from when she taught Sunday school.

A good teacher always asks even when she's sure of the response. Henry's words. Joanna was a good teacher.

Experience, they say, is a good teacher. If experience is a teacher, she thinks, then she, Joanna Bromley, formerly Joanna Vassa, mostly known as Jo-Jo to people with whom she is on a first-name basis (of which that number has now shrunk to a great degree) has been a good and dedicated pupil. But what is the use of experience if whatever lessons she has learned have come too late for her? If she could live her life in reverse, then all that learning would be useful. She would know to avoid Henry for one. She does not want to think of him. She has always tried not to be a slave to the past but these days, against her will, that has changed. This is how she knows that for her the end is near. The past is a flame burning her up from the inside, charring her innards. It is ash on her tongue. The past is not this woman who refuses to wear a dozen flounced petticoats to support her skirt so that her dress falls loosely around her emaciated frame. She imagines that she can count her ribs when she is fully undressed. The sight of her body shames her. No, not shames. It disgusts her and she often wishes she had the will to dress up, corset and flounced petticoats and all, so that at least while dressed, she could trick herself into believing that she does not look that bad. The mind is an easy thing to train. Who said that? She cannot recall. It might have been her father.

Her father was a Negro, dead before she was three. Her maternal grandmother – an Englishwoman from Surrey – who raised her, always told her that she was yet to meet an Englishman so intelligent that her father, though African, could not match. 'Gustavus was dark as coal. He was certainly one of the darkest Negroes I ever saw. Naturally, I was against the marriage at first. I could not imagine having a Negro son but your mother so wore me down with her pleas that I could not help but give in. Also, Gustavus was a good Christian. Were he not Negro, he would have made a good Englishman. He had a gentleman's soul and intelligence. He trained his mind to be English for like he said, "The mind is an easy thing to train."' So it was her father after all from whom the quote came.

And she has trained her mind to forget Graham. Why is he back now? And why is he eager to see her?

Soham, 1816

In a handsome cottage on Churchgate Street in Soham, Cambridgeshire, Joanna sat in front of a mirror brushing her hair. She was in something of an ill temper. She grumbled under her breath as she dragged the brush through the thick, dark hair. Once. Twice. Thrice. She paused to draw breath. Then began again. Once. Twice. Thrice. Pause. She grimaced in pain, exposing a healthy set of astonishingly white teeth. She repeated the ritual, working the brush quickly through her hair. She stopped, then held the hair back and stared at her face as though seeing herself for the very first time, as if it were a stranger staring back at her.

Hers was an uncommonly beautiful face: high cheekbones. Huge round, black dots in pools of white, like a startled animal's. Her skin did not possess the alabaster tone – with its ghostly translucence – so richly favoured by society, but that of rich, warm honey. When the desire to be like everyone else overwhelmed her, Joanna reminded herself that that translucent pallor would not have suited her anyway for her features were better suited to a darker hue. Full lips. A rounded chin. And a nose which, while aquiline, was not thin. That was consolation enough at times. She let go of her hair and the mass of curls, dark as a winter's night, fell in gentle ringlets around her face. She pulled and tugged, pushing the hair away from her face as if it were a live, annoying thing, perhaps a cantankerous animal needing to be subdued by a tremendous amount of force. It is obvious that this hair was the cause of much distress to her and that her battle with it was nothing new. There was practised determination in the way she handled her brush. She bared her teeth at the mirror and for an instant looked like a strange, wild, beast. The sight made her laugh.

She grabbed a fistful of hair and grumbled under her breath. If her grandmother could hear her language now, she thought, the poor woman would have a fit. But her grandmother had never had to struggle with hair such as hers. Her grandmother was not 'Soham's mulatto'. Tolerated but never quite fitting in because no matter how often she bathed her skin in the concoction of strawberries and milk touted by everyone as the way to keep it soft and white, her skin would never lose its tint. She was lucky, her grandmother said, not to have inherited more of her father's colour.

Her aunt Charlotte, her deceased mother's younger sister, used to tease her about her hair, good-naturedly of course for this aunt was very fond of her niece. 'What will you do with all these knots?' she would ask while touching the accursed hair, stroking it as if it were a much-loved house pet. But not even Aunt Charlotte who loved her without reserve and understood more than most, could ever have known what it was like to be her.

She missed Aunt Charlotte. All of her childhood memories were served up with the image of this aunt, said to look like her own dead mother, bustling around the house like a wind on her way to somewhere, raising her skirt higher than was polite, complaining that life was unfair and that Soham was dead and she must get away from it before it consumed her.

That was a long time ago now. And the young woman could not be entirely sure that her memory was a faithful recollection of this aunt or

if she borrowed this memory from hearing her grandmother complain
about this daughter who 'went to the devil a long time ago with her
multitude of complaints!' Memories are uncertain things, after all, and
even Charlotte's face was becoming increasingly hard for Joanna to
recollect. This pained her. This forgetting of the face of one of whom
she had once been very fond, trailing her like a shadow around the
house, imagining that she was her mother come back from the dead.
The face of this woman who told her, even though she might have
been considered too young to understand, 'Read. Read especially the
books they don't want you to read.' Like many of the instructions her
aunt threw randomly at her while teasing her about her hair, she was
only now, as an adult, beginning to make sense of them. She was only
now starting to understand why her aunt was the way she was. What
other options did she have?

    She did not want to think of it, but Aunt Charlotte might be dead.
No one ever returned from Australia so it did not matter whether she
was alive or not, she would never see her again. It had been many years
since Charlotte had left Soham and moved to London, 'For the diver-
sion,' she said. 'The only exciting thing that ever happens here is
ploughday! And all the men here I would not wish even on Henrietta
Bell!' The said Miss Bell being her very worst enemy. When Charlotte
was caught stealing trinkets from a shop on Oxford Street the magis-
trate banished her, manacled and shamed, to Australia to serve out her
sentence. 'She is frail and will never survive Australia even if she
managed to survive the voyage,' the grandmother had said. It was only
then that the old woman sounded almost regretful. 'She could have
done well for herself. She was always splendidly attired. And yet she
would not take any of the advantages life gave her. She was the devil's!
She's brought it all on herself,' her grandmother said whenever Aunt
Charlotte's unfortunate circumstances were mentioned. 'She was the
devil's. She was a wicked, wicked child. Always was. Why she could
not turn out like your mother, I cannot say. I tried my best, to heavens
I did, but why the devil gets hold of one and refuses to let go sometimes is beyond human comprehension. Every Christian must bear
their cross quietly. She is my cross and I am bearing it as best I can. The
good Lord, who consoled Job even after he had lost everything, will

console me too. You will marry and give me many grandchildren, will you not my darling Jo-Jo? Help me forget the cruelty of your aunt.'

Sometimes Joanna wanted to shout at the older woman and tell her, 'She was convicted for shoplifting! There are others who have committed worse crimes. Whoring and counterfeiting coins!' Even if she dared to say so, she was well aware that it would not change the old woman's mind. She knew that in her grandmother's eyes there was no difference between her aunt's misdemeanour and other, more heinous crimes.

'She's dead to me,' her grandmother said once. 'She's as bad as that John Rolfe for she has killed me also in cold blood. She has made me the mother of a convict. She has tarnished her family's name. How is she better then than a murderer?' John Rolfe, hanged on the Ely gallows three years previously for killing his poaching partner and friend, was at once the most despicable character ever heard of in recent time and the subject of fascinating anecdotes retold at dinner tables across the country. Many people had gone to witness his hanging – as many as five thousand, if stories were to be believed – and up until this day, the impression his body made encased in a gibbet cage and suspended from a twenty-four-foot-high gibbet erected upon Padnal Fen for all to see was still fresh in people's minds. It was said that he had a sneer on his face, so lacking in remorse was he of his crime, so unmindful of the fact that he was destined to burn in hell, even though some people who were there testified that they heard the fires of hell crackle at the very moment that he died and felt a surge of hot air envelop them in a terrible embrace.

Joanna shuddered to think of John Rolfe on a day such as this, and dragged herself back to the present moment. She arranged the curls about her face, and reached for a bonnet. She could have a maid do this for her but she would rather do it herself. She would not say she was embarrassed at how arduous a task it was to brush hair the texture of hers, but she did not wish to make a spectacle of herself in front of a maid, crying out in pain. Maybe she should ignore fashion and chop it off. Oh what liberty then! She imagined the freedom of short hair, shorn like a sheep's. She could almost hear Aunt Charlotte goading her on, telling her, 'Your life is yours!' But she knew that she would never do it, never have the courage to go so against polite society in so brazen a manner. But this was not her only rebellious thought. She had many more, planted by her aunt, but she dared not let them in now for once she did, they wormed their way into every part of her body and filled her with a heaviness that she could not bear. Today of all days, she must be happy. She must block out that voice.

She tied her bonnet, pulled a shawl across her shoulders and smoothed her gown. It was a yellow dress, devoid of any decoration, very much like a mourning dress save for the colour. The fabric was slightly faded, as if it had seen its fair share of the washing tub. Nevertheless, it was easy to see that the material out of which the dress had been made was of superior quality. It had a low neck, a rather low waist and was designed to be worn with a corset. It was obvious for its old-fashionedness that the style belonged to another century, certainly not in vogue in 1816. But Joanna, young and fashionable at other times, wore the dress with some pride. She had a sentimental attachment to this dress which had once belonged to her mother. Besides, she knew it would make her grandmother happy to see her in it, especially today. She ran a hand over the dress, slipped her feet into a pair of beautiful leather boots, a present from her grandmother for her birthday, and wriggled her toes for circulation. Then she let out a deep sigh. On a day like this, it was impossible for her not to feel inconsolably sad. Her sorrow today was not brought about by a vigorous young mind, open to what she saw as the injustice of the world in which she lived, but was precipitated instead by personal loss. It was of a deeper, insular quality, making her lethargic. She would have liked to have family around. That is not to say that she did not appreciate the company of her grandmother – the woman who spoiled her with love since she was an orphaned toddler, but she would have liked to have her parents, her sister, her Aunt Charlotte. She felt the weariness setting into her bones so that she felt not just twenty-one years of age, but five times that.

Joanna scanned her face again in the mirror, a habit that was becoming more frequent the older she got. She was amazed to see that she did not yet look as old as she felt inside. She had inherited her mother's nose and her high, fashionable forehead too, according to her grandmother. From her father she inherited some colour and tenacity. Her grandmother called her tenacity stubbornness, telling her off often for it, admonishing her that strong headedness was not an attractive trait in a woman, certainly not a woman such as herself. 'Your father needed it to succeed. You are a woman, a young woman. It's got no place in your life. See how far it got your aunt!' She never contradicted her grandmother. But she often thought the opposite.

'It is because I am a woman, that I need to be tenacious,' she said to herself. Apart from the strong headedness, she also inherited her hair from her father. And today she was turning twenty-one and would inherit a lot more. Close to a thousand pounds! Her father, Gustavus Vassa Esq., also known as Olaudah Equiano, had made for himself not only a name but some small fortune too. She picked up her parasol. Uncle Audley would be waiting.

Migrant Labour

Zukiswa Wanner

'I am sorry my broer. I know that you were to get a salary review every six months when you signed the contract with us. Now,' pause, 'your work has been exceptional but the organisation is not in a position to give you a raise right now, our budget just does not allow it,' the Secretary General of AfriAID, James Congwayo said, giving me the same response I had received from his predecessor, Livingstone Stanley.

I was AfriAID Regional Manager for the SADC region. The only person in the organisation since Mzi had left who had on my Rolodex several powerful SADC ministers, influential MPs, knew on first-name basis the leaders of the regional national organisations we worked with and yet again I was being told that I could not get a raise.

I wanted to curse but couldn't. This was not working for me.

I had done everything right that those go-getter male magazines said one needed to do before asking for a raise. I set up a meeting for a salary review highlighting the major things I wanted way in advance. I made sure the email requesting a meeting (and the meeting) were both on a Friday (when bosses are said to be more relaxed and therefore feeling more generous) and yet here I was, being told that the organisation had no money to give me a raise.

Me, Tinaye Musonza. With my vast knowledge of regional relations.

And yet the Secretary General's monthly salary was large enough to fund a few wars in the region.

I had had enough. Perhaps I could transfer my work permit and go and find work elsewhere? There were many organisations willing to pay someone with my expertise a better salary. A friend had told me of a job that he could hook me up with in the corporate sector right up my alley. Director of Diversity or something. Had to do with political correctness in the corporate world. More title than work but I could use the relaxed hours as well as the large salary with incentives.

'Perhaps you would allow me to transfer my work permit and look for a job elsewhere?' I asked tentatively.

Congwayo looked at me intently, his blue eyes seemingly staring straight into my soul. Yes, I said blue eyes. His own gaze was harsh enough but add the blue eyes in the dark complexion and when he gazed upon you, you could not help but feel as though you had erred greatly. For some strange reason ever since he married an Afrikaner woman a few months back, he had started wearing blue contact lenses. He had also started ranting against the system and how the whites exploited 'our people' which was rather rich coming from him if one knew his history.

Congwayo, you see, was one of those South Africans with a wonderful ability for reinvention. A former Special Branch man, according to the Human Resources Manager and my colleague Maki, when the winds of change were beginning to blow towards South Africa – way after Harold Macmillan's speech but before Mandela became president – Congwayo aligned himself well. He started feeding bits of information about his colleagues in the Special Branch to the UDF, making himself appear as though he had a Saul-like conversion. The leadership of the UDF accepted him as an informer for the other side but there were those who still looked at Congwayo with suspicion. It's said that until now, there are certain neighbourhoods he can't walk in Soweto without encountering threats of grievous bodily harm for responsibility for the deaths and disappearances of many locals.

He talked a good game, did Congwayo, but I was proving a wee-bit too clever, so when I suggested I transfer my work permit elsewhere his pupils dilated before he said in a voice full of disappointment, 'After all the resources we put forwards so you could come here, you want us to transfer your work permit so you can work elsewhere?'

He paused meaningfully before continuing, 'Are you aware, young man, just how many young people in this very country are looking for jobs? Do you have any idea how many of your fellow Zimbabweans with degrees are sleeping at the Central Methodist Church because they have no work permits?'

Why did South Africans always do this when someone complained of unfair labour conditions in their country? I really couldn't give a hoot at that moment how many of my compatriots were sleeping at the Methodist church or wherever. After all, this was a meeting about *my* salary raise. I would have told him this but I couldn't afford to be disrespectful when I was the one who wanted a favour from him.

I shook my head, 'No, Comrade James.'

He insisted on being called comrade. I think it made him feel like a benevolent leader. Or made him feel like he was making up for his shady past (his work CV conveniently forgot to mention about his Special Branch days but waxed lyrical about his contribution in the UDF).

'*No, Comrade James?*' he paused as though talking to a three year old. 'Right. Plenty. The way I hear it, half of your country, qualified or not, is in this country because your damned leader thought he could run the country without white capital. '

Congwayo sometimes overstepped his mark. He forgot that he was supposed to be politically correct – working in the NGO field as he did. Did he also forget that South Africa was an African country?

'I am disappointed in you,' he said, shaking his head again. 'I really believed you were out to make a difference.'

I answered, seeing the blackmail before he had finished, 'Of course, sir. But if I am going to make a difference, I need to do so on a full stomach. It would be hypocritical of me to tell everyone to stand up and speak out against poverty when I am not speaking out against my personal poverty.'

Congwayo's eyes twinkled. He seemed to enjoy my turn of phrase but then he continued as though I had not said anything at all. Or maybe I hadn't? Maybe that was what I *wanted* to say? What I would have said? Then why did he smile? 'So here it is, Mr Musonza. If you want to leave you can go ahead but you can't transfer our work permit elsewhere. Those who are offering you a job will have to get you a work permit as well as pay us for the rest of your contract. Now. Are you staying or are you going?'

'I am staying, comrade,' I replied in a whisper.

'Sorry, I didn't hear you,' Congwayo stated, seeming to relish my discomfort.

'I said I am staying, sir.' I said a little louder, emphasising the 'sir'. Comrade my foot.

He patted me on the shoulder with a smile that did not quite reach his blue eyes. 'You are a good man, Musonza. A good man. Maybe after the next six months our donors will see that we have men of your calibre and give us more funding so that our finances will be better and I'll bring the possibility of your raise to the board. If that is all . . .' he said dismissively.

I stood up wishing that I was financially well-cushioned enough to tell him to take his job and shove it. But I had become a slave to this job. If it were just me, I would have survived but my father's salary – which had seen me through one of the best private schools in Harare – now seemed just sufficient to get him to work and back. The family depended on me to send money for my sister's tuition (which for some unknown reason was paid in US dollars and constantly had to be topped up every term) and to pay for other essentials like the telephone and DSTV (Yes, I just called that essential. Anyone who has had to sit through an hour of ZTV will tell you why). If my younger brother Rusununguko – or Russ as he called himself – had been getting an income it would have helped but he had decided he wanted to help at the farm, which really meant selling what he could whenever he could get away with it and driving around picking up girls in the city although he had a wife with two children staying at the farm.

Then there were my own expenses. Sure, I wasn't starving. I was renting a two-bedroomed house in Melville. I could afford to take myself to a restaurant for dinner every once in a while but add my parents' expenses and mine and I often found there was, as the saying goes, always so much month at the end of the money.

My contract was for four years. Three years and the extra trial first year. Just a year less than it would have taken me to qualify for residency. I had been in this country for three years. From the way Congwayo looked at me after I asked for a raise, it was highly unlikely that I was going to get the contract renewed after it lapsed. I was in a quandary.

I started thinking of this country that I loved that didn't want to love me back. I remember how excited I had been when I left Oxford. How I nurtured a dream of coming back to Africa and joining hands with other like-minded Africans to save the continent. But since I arrived I had realised something.

In South Africa, an African country, I was just what I had been in England. An immigrant. To the white South Africans who sat on the board of AfriAID, I was probably filling the quota of the black head count. To black South Africans I was one of them *kwerekweres* because I allegedly took one of their brothers' jobs. I would think (without ever vocalising), 'Aren't I a brother too?'

Other immigrants had the benefit of escaping in their work or having a salary that they could sufficiently utilise to give themselves little vacations and weekend treats of a glass of single malt. But not me. I no longer had job satisfaction – neither from the love for my job nor from the pay (or was that peanuts?) I earned.

I wanted to quit but I couldn't. If I quit, I'd no longer have a valid work permit. People in the developmental field were a dime and dozen in the UK, so there was no way I was going back there.

The only other place I could go to was Zimbabwe and I could not, would not, go back there. Only a fool would repatriate while the rest of the country was escaping. There had to be a way that I could stay in my beloved Jozi but with a job that gave credit to my academic training without reducing me to a yes-man, to an annoying sell-out of a black man.

Then I had what I thought was a brainwave. I scrolled down my cell phone and dialled her number.

'Grace speaking, hello?' she answered.

'Well hello to you too. What, you don't call your old colleagues to see how they are doing?' I asked.

'Oh, my God, Tinaye, is that you?' she screamed and I had to hold the phone a little distant from my ear.

Grace had been a receptionist at AfriAID. She got disillusioned when she was asked to help with the bookkeeping and realised she was the lowest-paid employee but could never convince the powers that be that she needed a raise. Grace was going to be my ticket out of AfriAID while I continued staying in Joburg.

In this business, I deal with statistics all the time.

According to Stats SA, South African women work twenty-six per cent longer hours than their men. I was willing to work hard. I was not bad looking either with my brilliant mind and good looks. That made me a catch. If I could get a job that allowed me to stay, I could work my way to marrying a South African woman, get my residency, and eventual citizenship.

I had decided Grace would be that woman.

I see you are judging me for being mercenary. How easy it is for you. You are probably South African, or have never faced my dilemma. I never planned to hurt anyone. All I wanted was a fair chance to earn an honest living but had the misfortune of not being born in.

My friend and former colleague Mzilikazi had left to work in Cape Town because he had that flexibility. I couldn't do the same.

Grace was an easy choice for me.

When she was still at AfriAID, I always had the feeling that Grace was interested in me. Whenever she came to me to sign documents, she would linger a little too long chatting and lean into me. I had not entertained her then but there was no reason why I couldn't entertain her now. There was no conflict of interest and she was a beautiful woman. I only hoped there was no boyfriend lurking in the background. As I said before, Grace was a beautiful woman.

'Yes, it's me. How are you?'

'I am lovely thanks,' she answered.

'I am just calling to see whether you have any plans this Friday?' I asked.

I heard Grace drawing a breath and then sighing.

I knew I had her.

Even if she had plans, she would probably cancel them.

Her response was coy. 'It depends on what you have in mind,' she said.

'What I had in mind was dinner, perhaps some dancing, and some drinks, and then we see where it goes. What do you say?'

'I would love to. Can you come and pick me up from my work-place then?' she enquired.

'Sure thing. Give me the address.'

And that is how Grace and I became an item.

She worked in Rosebank and on that first date when I walked up to Primi Piatti with her, I could sense every man in the room looking up and wishing they were me.

Grace was the embodiment of beauty – African or otherwise. She had luscious lips that were made for kissing, a nose that was just perfect for her face and dimples that seemed to be etched on her face as they stayed in place whether she was smiling or not.

Her greatest features though, were her eyes. Large and expressive, even when what they expressed was not much, which was frequent. They had long lashes that had nothing to do with any of those television-advertised volumising mascaras. A man couldn't look at Grace for any length of time without feeling as though they were drowning in her eyes. I still commended myself for self-control for not having dated her when she was at AfriAID.

She was almost as tall as me with a fair complexion – what South Africans term a yellow bone. She had the long legs of a catwalk model and now as always, she wore them to advantage in a miniskirt and heels.

Forget Beyoncé, this girl had a bum that was curved and firm as though worked on by some architect who'd had all the time in the world.

And that was Grace. Beautiful.

We sat down and ordered.

'So what took you so long to call?' she asked as I drank my double whisky and she sipped on her Smirnoff Spin while we waited for our starters.

Ah ha. So she had been waiting for my call.

'I wanted you to break up with your other boyfriend first,' I answered.

'What other boyfriend?'

Great. She didn't have a boyfriend. Or he was so inconsequential she was willing to lie about his existence. This was working well for me.

We had sex that very first night, just as I knew we would and she spent the weekend at my place.

Soon Primi became our spot and Grace my weekend shift. However, beautiful as Grace was, conversations with her were painful. In conversation she had nothing to add and when she picked up a newspaper, it would be to relay to me some 'fact' that she had read of, such as some woman being raped by a tokoloshe in Limpopo, or something along those lines.

The sex was good. The conversation was expectedly dull. Grace wasn't the brightest light bulb in the tool shed. Whenever she came to 'sleep' at my Melville home, I had perfected the art of feigning sleep after sex. Marriage to her would be a tedious affair but I knew, with a good job, I could always get lost in my work so long as I paid the bills and bought her a twelve pack of Smirnoff Spin on the weekends.

Perhaps it's true that we men are never content.

But that was probably said by some bra-burning, man-hating woman.

I was content with Grace, I swear I was. It's just that I kept getting the feeling that there was something better out there.

But time wasn't on my side. I had decided I would date her for a respectable six months then propose to her. We would get married. I would become a resident, and then get a better job. Then I'd leave her after a reasonable amount of time.

And then it happened.

In the fifth month of my courtship (for that is what I now thought of it) with Grace, I met Slindile.

I should have ignored Sli. I didn't need any complications to my perfect Grace plan, but temptation was strong. And I, I was weak.

Hiding in Plain Sight

Mary Watson

The witch had been riding her back again. She sometimes did in the small hours of the night when everyone else was asleep. Meg felt, though could not see, that there was someone just above her chest, as if dropped from the ceiling. Her arms were pinned down, tied by invisible ropes. She wanted to turn on the lamp but could not move.

'Old hag,' her mother told her. '*Kanashibari*, if you're in Japan.'

In bed at night, Meg was plagued by screeching fiddles from distant houses, by rats scurrying across narrow roads. She was bothered by mice nestling in her boots, slugs burrowing beneath the grass. Light leaked in through the chinks in the curtains and seeped into her dreams. During the day, ravens and crows beat their black wings towards her, or else hovered just off the edge of her vision, biding their time. Her mother insisted it was nonsense; there was no way that she could hear the fiddles and rats. She just needed to be still. Shut your eyes. Shut out the light and fall asleep.

'The ravens and crows aren't interested in you,' her mother said, stuffing a white envelope with an application form for a job at a school. 'Put a pillow over your head.'

Those early months in Ireland were marked by an elusive disquiet. They had arrived at Kiln House with four suitcases, a dog-eared copy of *You* magazine, a Table Mountain key ring in Meg's back pocket, and a small beaded doll with crazy eyes from the airport curio shop.

'But you don't have any keys,' her mother had said, nudging towards the departure gate.

No keys, no house, no home. Meg's father had died because of his kindness to strangers. And because her husband was gone, Catriona had wanted to leave. She seemed to blame her adopted country for the death of her husband. Within a few short months, they had packed up their things, sold their house and arranged new schools for Meg and Damien. They would squat with their Aunt Maire until they were settled in Ireland.

'Is that a present for me?' Maire eyed the doll in Meg's hand as she entered Kiln House. Not really a doll, but an artefact. A souvenir from her life before. Hot sunshine, the lemon tree in the garden, taxis scream-ing through the main road, the colour and noise of a different world were bound up in that doll and in the plastic mountain-shaped key ring.

'No.'

'She's rather like her father, isn't she?' Maire said in a voice that belied her broad smile. Uncle John carried their suitcases in.

Kiln House was pockmarked with grey pebbledash. It had low doors that forced Uncle John to stoop, and a narrow, dark staircase that sucked you up inside its guts. The house was so obscurely located that Meg was sure the mess of low stone walls was designed to misdirect visitors. A higgledy-piggledy house surrounded by higgledy-piggledy stone walls in a teeny tiny village called Arse End, Nowhere.

Kiln House served a dubious function as a bed and breakfast, the kind with smoke-stained net curtains and faded floral tablecloths draped over chipboard tables. Plastic carnations in made-in-China rosebud vases. Inexplicably, they had a decent passing trade, which seemed to be made up of customers who returned over the years. Maire was tighter than a gnat's chuff while Uncle John was inclined to hand out free things to his friends. And it only took a drink or two to become his friend. Meg had seen him handing over a clutch of miniature soaps and shampoos to bewildered children. It was something of a nervous tic, the need to hand over his worldly goods. It was impossible to have a conversation without him trying to give her sweets or money or his handkerchief or whatever he could lay his hands on at the time. Uncle John was one of those men with a shed. The exact purpose of the shed was a mystery, but whatever it was seemed to need a large amount of time. Meg tried looking through the windows, but couldn't see beyond a jumble of mismatched furniture and electrical objects.

Maire, on the other hand, had an impressive collection of Mills & Boon's hidden in the utility room cupboard so Meg decided to make a study of human relationships from these probably flawed texts. At sixteen, her own experience was non-existent. Reading them from behind the covers of books about hobbits, Meg was seen to make an exceptionally slow journey to Mordor that wet May. She had inhaled several of the purple-covered Mills & Boon's and had substantially improved her education. Though she possibly learned all the wrong things from those books. They placed an unnecessary emphasis on tall strangers with imperfect social skills.

Lethargic from her late night reading about gasping virgins and commanding men, Meg took to walking in the afternoons, climbing wobbly looking dry stone walls. And she would find a soft grassy spot, buffering the damp with a fleece. Or, if it was really wet, she would sit at a window and watch.

'It's only weather,' her mother said, misunderstanding.

Catriona underestimated weather. Because there was something frightening about the Irish countryside in the late spring. Things grew too eagerly. It would seem mild and idyllic, new life emerging after a sleeping winter. But after intermittent sunshine and extended damp, the budding trees and flowers flourished, the growth unchecked. Briars tendrilled towards Meg, catching at her clothes and pulling her into a damp slug-ridden undergrowth. The smell of fresh, that reek of new life, assaulted her sinuses. Even when it was dry, the leaves budded on trees at an alarming rate; if she fixed her eyes on them, Meg was sure she could see them actually growing. That May at Kiln House, it seemed that the countryside was quietly hysterical.

The Clearys arrived just before the end of May. Most visitors stayed only a night, stopping on their way between two points. The house was never a destination in itself, only an interruption on the way to somewhere else. This puzzled Meg because the house did not appear to be the mid-point to anywhere. It felt tucked away, hidden and obscure. Years later, she found out that it was no more than five minutes from a busy arterial road – one of those narrow, winding country roads with a speed limit of one hundred kilometres an hour.

Mr and Mrs Cleary came for a week, as they had every year since their honeymoon ten years ago. There was not a spot like it, Mr Cleary announced in his great big voice, his thick accent putting strange shadows on the words. He was not wrong: it was a pretty place with a stream at the bottom of the garden, a wood nearby. There was a puzzle of meadows that opened up into each other, all of them carpeted with buttercups and dandelions. The whitethorn was in full bloom and as Meg looked across the fields, it was like bridal bouquets strewn as far as the eye could see.

Mrs Cleary was a broad, strong woman. They were farmers straight out of a story book. She was nearly six foot and he was taller; they were both muscled and weather worn. Her only vanity was her hair, a pale dirty colour, which she wore down to her waist, stretching out across a white cotton shirt with a pretty lace trim. Afterwards, Meg remembered that trim because it softened Mrs Cleary's blunt features and stubby fingers.

The couple went out walking or cycling together in the mornings and in the afternoons Mr Cleary would either disappear to a neighbouring farm or to the village pub. Mrs Cleary would join Catriona and Maire in the kitchen and garden or, if the weather was fine, go out walking by herself.

Mr Cleary, for all his booming comments about ten wonderful years, seemed to pay a lot of attention to Catriona. Meg reluctantly conceded that her mother was not a bad looking woman. Her mud-brown hair had been disguised as blonde for as long as Meg could remember and it suited her. With large green eyes, freckled skin and a neat mouth she was utterly unlike Meg. While Damien resembled Catriona, Meg was more like their father and strangers frequently didn't realise that Catriona was even related to Meg.

When Catriona walked upstairs with a pile of clean bedding, her hair bobbing in a pony tail, Mr Cleary would swoop down beside her and lift the load. If she was down in the garden weeding those unbridled beds, he would be at her side holding a small spade. Meg did not like it. A large man, he exaggerated her petite blondeness. It made her seem younger, more vulnerable. It reminded Meg of those books in the utility cupboard.

The afternoon walks seemed to suit the ever-serene Mrs Cleary. She always returned with her hair pleasantly whipped about and her rosy cheeks glowing. Unfazed by most things, Mrs Cleary would sit in the kitchen, shelling peas and peeling earth-stained spuds while Catriona and Maire muttered in the corner like a pair of witches.

On the Clearys' last day, Meg was in the mood for a medical romance, a bit of doctor love, so she took one of the blue books from the utility room. Walking through the woods, she came to a meadow on the other side. That meadow lead into another field, and she continued until she was three fields deep. She was about to sling down her canvas bag, when she heard a sound. It was an animal noise, and she rather fancied herself an animal lover.

It came from a field beyond a small path. She heard the noise again, a kind of pained harrumph, as she climbed the gate and lowered herself into a small patch expecting to see a horse or cow. Instead, after turning a corner, Meg faced an incomprehensible display of molten limbs. There were several pale, hairy legs, and she was sure she remembered red socks, or perhaps she added that later. She must have seen the vision from the side, because she remembered a dangling breast held – no, cupped would be the more correct terminology – by one hand as it fed a large nipple into the mouth below. It was as if the two people there had melted into each other.

It was so very different from what she had studied in the purple books. There seemed to be fewer pants and sighs and much more grunting. Surely it was not meant to be painful? The books had said nothing about that and Catriona had always encouraged Meg to avert her eyes during the wet bits in films. Meg stepped closer.

In her aunt's books it always seemed a graceful, transcendent experience that was communicated through ready euphemisms like 'he entered her' and his 'manhood'. What she saw that day, the huge angry red penis and matching socks, the rutting in the fields, was dismayingly different to what Meg had imagined. Mrs Cleary was on top, her breasts swinging, her love handles gripped by the man beneath who used them to push her back and forth. Meg watched the full white bottom bounce, and found it simultaneously terrifying and strangely alluring. It was fleshy, earthy farmer sex. Meg wondered if Mills & Boon had thought about a brown cover range that featured copulating farmers in flower meadows.

There were loud shrieks and then Mrs Cleary fell face forwards. Slumped down, Mrs Cleary slowly turned her head and saw Meg standing there. She leapt up with alacrity, revealing all of her voluptuous curves. Her untrimmed lady garden. Meg had not realised that it could grow so wild. She was transfixed by the magnificence of that bush. It looked out at her like a small furry animal disturbed from its nap. Mrs Cleary stood before Meg, her chest heaving, hair spilling down her shoulders. Only after considering his penis and the socks, did Meg realise that her uncle John stood naked in the field. She knew too well that he was a compulsive giver: a sweetie, a few coins, a little shag in the flower meadow.

Mrs Cleary was breathing heavily. She grabbed her cotton shirt, the one with the lace trim, and covered herself. Uncle John, on the other hand, just stood there. It was interesting to see that moment of deflation; it was another thing that the books had not prepared Meg for. The other side of it all. Distracted by Uncle John's waning manhood, it took her too many seconds to realise that they were very, very angry.

Meg turned and ran. She disappeared through the fields, through the woods and into a meadow on the other side. Finding a spot behind a rock, Meg hid. She stayed there for a long while, her heart beating. She had lost all interest in her book. Instead, she sat and reflected on the details of what she had just witnessed.

Eventually, exhausted, she fell asleep. Several hours must have passed. When Meg awoke, it was to find herself paralysed. She opened her eyes, but the rest of her body refused to move. She could feel the plastic mountain jutting into her bum. She tried to shift position, but her body would not obey. Then she realised that she was held down by Mrs Cleary. One hand pressed down on Meg's chest and the other clamped her mouth. Meg thought she would receive a stern warning about spying on people having extramarital sex. How she should avert her eyes when her elders and betters were cavorting, but Mrs Cleary didn't say anything.

Meg tried to get up but Mrs Cleary pressed harder. She watched Mrs Cleary's face, as calm as when she shelled peas, her hand closed over Meg's mouth. Meg could taste hand lotion, a light flower fragrance, and her own fear. The hand grew heavy and pinched against the thumb to cover her nose. Meg struggled, but she could not break Mrs Cleary's hold. It was a different kind of intimacy to the one she had witnessed earlier. In that moment, Meg absorbed the details of Mrs Cleary's face: the large mole flecking her lip and the nose pinpricked by blackheads. Green eyes like a murky lake.

Meg was sure that this was the end. She thought of her father, of his concentration as he changed that flat tyre, unaware that his time was up. Both hands taking worn rubber down. But there it was again, that flash of earthy sex. The socks on bare naked legs. The lace and cotton blouse awkwardly gathered at Mrs Cleary's chest. The fury on her face. The plastic mountain jabbed deeper into Meg's rump.

When she found herself again, the sky had changed. The field was a play of light and shadows. Shards of pale sunlight peered out from behind indigo clouds. Meg had been dreaming of her father again. She had slept deeply and, now ravenous, she was filled with nervous energy.

At Kiln House, they were having dinner in the kitchen. Uncle John was at his usual place at the head of the table while Mrs Cleary spooned spuds into her mouth. A bottle of wine was open and Mr Cleary topped up Catriona's glass. Her cheeks were flushed and she laughed, low and rusty as if it hadn't been used in too long. Meg felt like an intruder. They hardly seemed to notice her, apart from a vague 'Ah, there you are' as Maire passed a floury explosion of potatoes with ham and veg.

It was the Cleary's last night at Kiln House and spirits were high. Meg lagged a course behind: the others ate their ice-cream and apple tart while she hacked at the pink meat. Maire lavishly spread all vegetables with butter and sugar, happily diluting their nutritional value. Damien appeared, and disappeared, while Meg sat at the table intent on the pile of food on her plate.

'Oh, go on, let her have a bit. Like the French.' And next thing Mr Cleary had poured red wine into a tumbler and placed it before Meg.

'I can tell you a few things about the French,' her mother's voice did not sound like her own. Catriona looked at Meg and finished the sentence in Irish. Her words were swallowed by her glass, and she did not see Mr Cleary shift that bit closer.

'What's this? You on a diet?' Maire cleared the half-eaten plate, making Meg conscious of her rounded arms, the tops of her thighs that spread and touched. She hadn't finished eating. She was still hungry.

They seemed to forget to give her only a small bit of diluted wine. Her glass was topped up once by Mr Cleary and another time by Uncle John, who still didn't look her in the eye. Catriona was telling stories that had them shrieking like banshees. Her eyes gleamed, her skin glistened and her hair was spun gold down her back. Mrs Cleary smiled, but it was an almost polite concession: go on, have your fun.

Maire placed down a bowl of butterscotch ice-cream where Meg's plate had been. She didn't like ice-cream. Hungry, she ate a few mouthfuls and drank it down with wine. She was beginning to feel detached from herself. She looked down at her hands, amazed that they were hers. She checked again, and there they were. Slightly above her legs, fingers sticking out as if on guard. It made Meg feel panicky, as if she were trapped inside her body. Something had loosened and wanted to get out but it was trapped, like a fly buzzing against a window. She couldn't bear the cackling and loud stories, each one trying to outdo the other. The language switched from English to Irish – the Clearys didn't speak it – and back to English again. The wine flowed and Maire disappeared into the utility room to get a bottle she had been saving. Mr Cleary and Catriona seemed awfully close. Meg couldn't stand it any longer.

'I need—' Meg was unsteady on her feet. Mr Cleary half rose. He eyed her like she was a skittish pony, uncertain what damage she might do.

'I think it's a bug,' Meg said. She stood for a moment, all attention on her. Even Mrs Cleary finally fixed those cold piggy eyes on her. Meg's heart thudded and she could feel the beating of black wings.

'I found it!' Maire sang from the next room. Cheers from the table and Meg was forgotten. Uncle John got up and fetched his fiddle from the sideboard. At the door, she turned and looked at the tableau before her: Uncle John tuning his fiddle in the corner. He was just a few metres away from Mrs Cleary. But it was unmistakeable, like a big stain. Even though not touching, their bodies angled towards each other. Their eyes sought each other out, stared, then dropped as if too hot. How had she not noticed before? A willed blindness, the others did not see.

'I saw you,' Meg said quietly and Mrs Cleary looked in her direction. But it seemed Meg was invisible: Mrs Cleary heard the voice but couldn't see Meg. With a stony gaze, she looked just over Meg's shoulder, as if transfixed by a blot on the wall.

The others continued with their wine. Their voices grew louder, echoing the wings beating inside Meg's head. The crows and ravens were coming for her. Uncle John was tuning loudly and the sharp fiddle scratches grated. Meg's words were lost in all that racket. But she wanted Mrs Cleary to know. More than the romp in the field, it was the hand over her mouth and nose. She wanted Mrs Cleary to know that she knew what she was capable of. So Meg raised her voice and squared towards her, saying loudly: 'I know what you are.'

Just then, Uncle John stopped his infernal tuning. Maire stood at the door holding her special bottle. The pressure of those meaty hands, the taste of it on her mouth.

She said it one more time: 'I know what you are.'

Then she left the room, went upstairs and fell upon her bed. As she hit the mattress, she realised that the plastic mountain was no longer in her pocket. After everything, it was the loss of the key ring that made her want to cry. For her mother, who was saddest when she laughed out loud. For her father, who should have been there, who would have found a way to make it funny. For Maire who was so tight and pinched that she had squeezed John all the way out. But Meg didn't cry. She lay upon the bed and waited for the darkness to complete and the old hag to come again.

Notes on the Authors

Chimamanda Ngozi Adichie was born and raised in Nigeria. Her work has been translated into thirty languages and has appeared in various publications including the *Financial Times, Granta,* the *New Yorker* and *Zoetrope.* She is the author of the novels *Purple Hibiscus*, which won the Commonwealth Writers' Prize; *Half of a Yellow Sun*, which won the Orange Prize, was a National Book Critics Circle Award Finalist and a *New York Times* Notable Book; and the story collection *The Thing Around Your Neck.* Her latest novel, *Americanah*, was published in 2013 and has received awards including the National Book Critics Circle Award for Fiction and the *Chicago Tribune* Heartland Prize for Fiction and was named one of the *New York Times* Ten Best Books of the Year. A recipient of a MacArthur Foundation Fellowship, she divides her time between the United States and Nigeria.

Monica Arac de Nyeko is from Uganda. She won the Caine Prize for African writing in 2007 for 'Jambula Tree'. She is working on a novel.

Rotimi Babatunde's fiction and poetry has been published internationally. He is a winner of the Meridian Tragic Love Story Competition organised by the BBC World Service and was awarded the Cyprian Ekwensi Prize for Short Stories by the Abuja Writers' Forum. His story 'Bombay's Republic' was awarded the 2012 Caine Prize for African Writing. His plays have been broadcast on the BBC World Service and produced by theatres including the Young Vic in London, the Halcyon Theatre in Chicago and Sweden's Riksteatern, among others. He lives in Ibadan, Nigeria.

Eileen Almeida Barbosa was born in Senegal to a Cape Verdean mother and a father from Guinea Bissau. She was raised and now lives in Cape Verde. In 2005 she won the inaugural National Pantera Revelation Prize for Short Stories and the Pantera Revelation Prize for Poetry. Her story collection, *Eileenístico,* was published in 2007. A translator and communications specialist, Barbosa blogs at soncent.blogspot.com. She works as an advisor to the Prime Minister and is currently writing her second collection of short stories.

A. Igoni Barrett was born in Port Harcourt, Nigeria. His first story collection, *From Caves of Rotten Teeth*, was published in Nigeria in 2005. His second collection, *Love is Power, or Something Like That*, was picked by NPR as a best book of 2013. He is the winner of the 2005 BBC World Service short story competition, the recipient of a Chinua Achebe Center fellowship, a Norman Mailer Center fellowship, and a Rockefeller Foundation Bellagio Center Residency. His short fiction has been published in journals including *AGNI*, *Guernica* and *Kwani?*. He lives in Lagos.

Jackee Budesta Batanda was born in Uganda. She is a short story writer and independent journalist. The Africa regional winner of the 2003 Commonwealth Short Story Competition, her stories have been performed on the BBC World Service, BBC3 and radio stations throughout the Commonwealth as well as appearing in various international anthologies. She has written for publications including the *New York Times*, the *Boston Globe* and the *Mail & Guardian*. She was the recipient of a 2010 Uganda Young Achievers Award and named by *The Times* (London) in 2012 as one of twenty women shaping the future of Africa. She is currently at work on a novel.

Recaredo Silebo Boturu is a poet, playwright, storyteller and the co-founder and director of Companía Teatral Bocamandja. Born in Bareso, on the island of Bioko in Equatorial Guinea, his writings explore themes of social change and seek to re-establish oral traditions. He is among the most important advocates of theatre in his country and his works are performed in every region of the country, and have earned him considerable recognition. He is the author of two books *Luz en la noche, Poesía y Teatro* (*Light in the Darkness: poems and plays*) (2010) and *Crónicas de memorias anuladas, poesía y teatro* (*Chronicles of obliterated memories: poems and plays*) (2014) published by Editorial Verbum. His writings have been published in a number of anthologies and magazines, including *Caminos y veredas: narrativas de Guinea ecuatorial (UNAM)*, *La Palabra y la Memoria: Guinea 25 anos después* and the *Afro-Hispanic Review*. Translations of his work in English have appeared in *Bengal Lights*, *Molossus*, and *World Literature Today*. He has participated in conferences and spoken at universities in Spain, Columbia and the USA.

Nana Ekua Brew-Hammond is a Ghanaian-American writer living in New York. Her fiction, poetry and essays have appeared in publications including *African Writing*, *Ebony* magazine, the *Village Voice*, NBC's The Grio and in the anthology *Women's Work*. *Publishers Weekly* hailed her novel *Powder Necklace*, published in 2010, as 'a winning debut'. Most recently, she founded the blog People Who Write.

Shadreck Chikoti is a Malawian writer, public speaker and social activist. His awards include the 2013 Peer Gynt Literary Award for his forthcoming futuristic novel, *Azotus, the Kingdom*. His short story 'Child of the Hyena' was published in *To See the Mountain*, the 2011 Caine Prize Anthology. He is vice president of the Malawi Writers Union and Director of Pan African Publishers Ltd and recently founded the Story Club Malawi, a social gathering for artists.

Edwige-Renée Dro worked as a marketing assistant and community journalist in the UK before moving back to Cote d'Ivoire, where she was born. Her stories have been published in *Prima* magazine and africanwriter.com. She is currently completing work on her first novel and is the founder of Abidjan Lit, an African fiction book group.

Tope Folarin was born in the United States to Nigerian parents. He made his fiction debut in *Transition* with 'Miracle' in 2012, for which he was awarded the Caine Prize for African Writing in 2013. His work has also appeared in *Africa Report* and the *Virginia Quarterly Review*. He is a graduate of Morehouse College and Oxford University, where he earned two Master's degrees as a Rhodes Scholar. He is a recipient of fellowships from the Institute for Policy Studies and *Callaloo* and serves on the board of the Hurston/Wright Foundation. He lives in Washington DC and is currently at work on his first novel.

Clifton Gachagua is a Kenyan writer. He is the recipient of the 2013 inaugural Sillerman Prize for African Poetry for his debut collection *The Madman at Kilifi*, which was subsequently published in 2014 by the University of Nebraska Press. In 2013 he was longlisted for the *Kwani?* Manuscript Project for his novel *Zephyrion*. His work has appeared in publications including *Saraba*, *Storymoja* and *Kwani?* and the science fiction anthology *AfroSF*. He is currently an editor at Kawani Trust and Jalada and television scriptwriter and blogs at thedrumsofshostakovich.com.

Stanley Gazemba is a Kenyan journalist and the author of three novels: *The Stone Hills of Maragoli*, *Khama* and *Callused Hands*, and eight children's books. A recipient of the Jomo Kenyatta Prize, his articles and stories have appeared in publications including *'A' is for Ancestors*, the Caine Prize Anthology, the *East African* and the *New York Times*. In 2013 his novel

Ghettoboy was shortlisted for the *Kwani?* Manuscript Project and his new book, *Callused Hands*, has been published by Nsemia Publishers. He works as the East Africa Editor for Music in Africa.

Mehul Gohil is a writer born and living in Nairobi, Kenya. He was the winner of the 2010 *Kwani?* 'The Kenya I Live In' short story prize. His fiction has been published in *Kwani?* and on several online platforms including Short Story Day Africa. His journalism has appeared in publications including the Sahan Journal and chessbase.com. He is a founding member of the literary collective Jalada.

Hawa Jande Golakai was born in Germany to Liberian parents. She was raised in Liberia until the start of civil war in 1990, and has since lived in several other African countries including Ghana, Togo and Zimbabwe. Her debut novel, *The Lazarus Effect*, was shortlisted for the 2011 *Sunday Times* Fiction Prize, the University of Johannesburg Debut Prize and longlisted for the Wole Soyinka Prize. She currently lives and works in Monrovia, Liberia, as a medical immunologist and is completing her second novel, a sequel.

Shafinaaz Hassim is a South African writer and sociologist. She is the author of several books including *Daughters are Diamonds: Honour, Shame & Seclusion – A South African Perspective* and *Memoirs for Kimya* and the novel, *SoPhia*. *SoPhia* has been converted into performance theatre and staged at the State Theatre during August 2014 prior to its national tour. She is the editor of the Belly of Fire anthologies for social change. Her new anthology, *Soul Seeds for Shade & Solitude* has just been launched. A social commentator and contributor to the *Mail & Guardian*, her work has been shortlisted for the K. Sello Duiker Award and the University of Johannesburg Debut Prize for Creative Writing.

Abubakar Adam Ibrahim was born in Jos, Nigeria. His debut short story collection *The Whispering Trees* was published in Nigeria in 2012 and was longlisted in 2014 for the inaugural Etisalat Prize for Literature; the title story was shortlisted for the 2013 Caine Prize for African Writing. In 2007 he was the winner of the BBC African Performance Prize and was named the 2013 Gabriel García Márquez Fellow. He lives in Abuja, Nigeria where he works as an arts editor for a national newspaper.

Stanley Onjezani Kenani was born in Malawi and currently lives in Switzerland. He has twice been shortlisted for the Caine Prize for African

Writing, in 2008 and 2012. He is the author of the story collection *For Honour and Other Stories* and is currently working on his first novel.

Ndinda Kioko is a Kenyan writer and filmmaker whose short fiction has appeared in several literary magazines and anthologies. Her story *Death at the End of the Bougainvillea* is published by Jalada Africa. Other works appear in publications including *Fresh Paint – Literary Vignettes by Kenyan Women*. She is currently working on her debut novel and producing a fifty-two episode television series for M–Net.

Dinaw Mengestu was born in Addis Ababa, Ethiopia. He is the award-winning author of the novels *The Beautiful Things That Heaven Bears*, *How to Read the Air* and, most recently, *All Our Names*, published in 2014. His journalism and fiction appears in publications including *Harper's*, *Granta* and the *New Yorker*. He has been named as one of '5 Under 35' by the National Book Foundation and was amongst '20 Under 40' writers to watch by the *New Yorker*. The recipient of numerous awards including the *Guardian* First Book Award and a 2012 MacArthur Foundation Fellowship, he currently lives in New York City.

Nadifa Mohamed was born in Hargeisa, Somaliland and moved to England with her family in 1986. Her first novel, *Black Mamba Boy*, was longlisted for the Orange Prize, shortlisted for the Guardian First Book Award, John Llewelyn Rhys award, Dylan Thomas Prize, PEN Open Book Award and won the Betty Trask Prize. *The Orchard of Lost Souls* won a Somerset Maugham Prize in 2014. Her work has been published in 16 languages. Her writing has appeared in the *Guardian*, *Granta*, *Virginia Quarterly Review* and the *Independent*. She lives in London and is currently working on her third novel.

Nthikeng Mohlele was born in 1977 and grew up in Limpopo and Tembisa township, South Africa. A graduate of the University of the Witwatersrand, he is the author of the novels *The Scent of Bliss* and *Small Things*. Two new novels, *Rusty Bell* and *Pleasure*, will be published in October 2014 and October 2015 respectively.

Linda Musita is a Kenyan writer, editor and lawyer. She is a literary agent at Lelsleigh Inc in Nairobi, and a subeditor and legal officer at the *Star* newspaper. Her fiction has been published on the Storymoja publishers' blog and the *Daily Nation*. A Storymoja Hay Festival 2012/13 fellow, she is currently working on her first novella.

Richard Ali A Mutu writes in Lingala and is considered one of the Democratic Republic of the Congo's most promising writers. The winner of the 2009 November Mark Twain Prize, he published his first book *Le cauchemardesque de Tabu* in 2011 when he was just twenty-three, and the second, a novel written in Lingala, *Ebamba, Kinshase Makambo* by Mabiki editions. He is the founder of the Young Writers Association of Congo (AJECO). He has also written poetry, essays, monologues and theatre performance pieces.

Sifiso Mzobe was born in Durban, South Africa. His debut novel, *Young Blood*, was published by Kwela Books and went on to be awarded the 2011 Herman Charles Bosman Award, the 2011 *Sunday Times* Fiction Prize, the 2011 South African Literary Award and the 2012 Wole Soyinka Prize for Literature. He currently works as a freelance journalist and is writing his second novel.

Glaydah Namukasa is a Ugandan midwife and writer, and is currently chairperson of the Uganda Women Writers' Association, Femrite. Her short stories are published in anthologies in Uganda, South Africa, the UK, the US and Sweden. She is the author of one novel, *The Deadly Ambition*. Her young adult novella *Voice of a Dream*, was awarded the Macmillan Writers Prize for Africa in 2006. She is the recipient of a Rockefeller Foundation Bellagio Center fellowship and in 2008 was awarded the title of Honorary Fellow by the International Writers Program at the University of Iowa. She is currently completing her first novel.

Ondjaki was born in Luanda, Angola. He is the recipient of numerous prizes, including the 2008 Grande Prémio de Conto Camilo Castelo Branco awarded by the Portuguese Writers' Association and the Prémio Jabuti. His novel *Os Transparentes* was awarded the Saramago Prize in 2013. He has lived in Lisbon and New York and is currently at work on various cinema and film projects and now lives in Rio de Janeiro, Brazil.

Okwiri Oduor was born in Nairobi. She is a 2014 MacDowell Colony fellow. She is currently at work on her debut novel. Her story, '*My Father's Head*', won the Short Story Day Africa *Feast, Famine and Potluck* story contest, and also won the 2014 Caine Prize for African Writing.

Ukamaka Olisakwe was raised in Kano State, Nigeria. Her debut novel, *Eyes of a Goddess*, was published in 2012 by Piraeus Books LLC, Massachusetts. Her stories have appeared in various online journals and blogs including *Saraba, Sentinel Nigeria*, Short Story Day Africa and Naija Stories and her essays have been published in the *Nigerian Telegraph* and *African Hadithi*. Her screenplay, a movie series, has been accepted for production by an award-winning production stable and is set for release on major TV stations throughout Africa in 2015. She works as a customer service representative for a Nigerian Bank and is currently completing her second novel.

Chibundu Onuzo was born in Lagos, Nigeria. The youngest ever author to be signed by Faber and Faber publishers, her debut novel, *The Spider King's Daughter*, was longlisted for the Desmond Elliott Prize, shortlisted for the Dylan Thomas Prize, the Commonwealth Book Prize and won a Betty Trask Award. She writes comment pieces for the *Guardian*, with a special interest in Nigeria. She lives in London and is currently completing a PhD on the West African Student's Union. Her new novel, *The Wayfarer's Daughter*, will be published by Faber and Faber in 2016.

Nii Ayikwei Parkes was born in the UK and raised in Ghana. He is a writer, editor, broadcaster and performance poet. His debut novel, *Tail of the Blue Bird*, was shortlisted for the Commonwealth Prize and translated into Dutch, German, French and Japanese. He is the author of poetry collections including the Michael Marks Award shortlisted pamphlet *ballast: a remix*, and *The Makings of You*. In 2007 he was awarded Ghana's national ACRAG award for poetry and literary advocacy. He is the publisher at flipped eye publishing, one of the most respected small presses in the UK, and curator of the African Writers' Evening reading series.

Mohamed Yunus Rafiq is a Tanzanian writer and independent documentary film maker. Prior to his career in film and creative writing, he worked for five years as Baobab Connection country co-coordinator where he published monthly articles on globalisation and youth issues. He is the co-author of a poetry collection, *Landscapes of the Heart*, a member of the internationally acclaimed hip-hop group X Plastaz Collective based in Tanzania and the co-founder of Aang Serian Peace Village, a youth-led cultural preservation organisation.

Taiye Selasi is a writer and photographer born in London of Ghanaian and Nigerian parentage. Raised in Massachusetts, she now lives in Rome, Italy. Her debut novel, *Ghana Must Go*, was published to international acclaim in over sixteen countries and was selected as one of the ten best books of 2013 by the *Wall Street Journal* and the *Economist*. In 2013 she was named one of *Granta*'s Best of Young British novelists. She is currently writing her second novel.

Namwali Serpell was born in Lusaka, Zambia. She is an associate professor in the English Department at the University of California, Berkeley. She is the author of a book of literary criticism, *Seven Modes of Uncertainty*, published by Harvard University Press. Her fiction has appeared in publications including *Callaloo*, *Tin House* and *The Best American Short Stories 2009*. She was shortlisted for the 2010 Caine Prize for African writing for her first published story, 'Muzungu', and is a Rona Jaffe Foundation Writers' Award recipient.

Lola Shoneyin is the author of three volumes of poetry and two children's books. *The Secret Lives of Baba Segi's Wives*, her debut novel, was longlisted for the Orange Prize and won the PEN Oakland Josephine Miles Literary Award and the Ken Saro-Wiwa Prose Prize. Her work has appeared in publications including the *Iowa Review*, *Chimurenga*, *Poetry International* and *Orbis*. She founded the Book Buzz Foundation in 2012 and is the director of the Aké Arts and Book festival. She lives in Lagos and is currently at work on a collection of poems and her second novel.

Novuyo Rosa Tshuma was born in 1998 in Zimbabwe. Her short fiction has appeared in publications which include *A Life in Full and Other Stories* and *Where to Now, Short Stories from Zimbabwe*. She was awarded the 2009 Yvonne Vera Award for her short story 'You in Paradise' and was shortlisted for the 2012 Zimbabwe Achievers Literature Award for her short story 'Doctor S'. *Shadows*, her debut collection of a novella and short stories, was published by Kwela Books in South Africa in 2013 and was awarded the 2014 Herman Charles Bosman Prize. She was a judge for the 2013 Short Story Day Africa *Feast, Famine and Potluck* contest. Novuyo holds a Bcom in Economics and Finance from the University of Witwaterstrand, and is currently attending the renowned MFA Creative Writing Program at the Iowa Writers' Workshop, where her writing has been recognized with several fellowships.

Chika Unigwe was born in Enugu, Nigeria. She is the author of the novels *On Black Sisters' Street* and *Night Dancer*. A winner of the BBC Short Story Competition and a Commonwealth Short Story Award, she was shortlisted for the Caine Prize for African Writing in 2004. She won the Nigeria Literature Award (for fiction) in 2012 and her work has been published extensively in journals and papers around the world including the *New York Times* and the UK *Guardian*. She currently lives in the United States where she is at work on a new novel.

Zukiswa Wanner is the author of novels *The Madams* (2006), shortlisted for the K. Sello Duiker Prize; *Behind Every Successful Man* (2008); *Men of the South* (2010), Commonwealth Best Book Africa Region; and *London Cape Town Joburg* (2014). Wanner is also the author of non-fiction satire *Maid in SA: 30 Ways to Leave Your Madam* (2013); the children's book (an African retelling of Rapunzel) *Refilew* (2014); and co-author with Alf Kumalo of the Mandela home biography 8115: *A Prisoner's Home* (2010). Wanner is Zambian-born to a South-African father and a Zimbabwean mother, and live in Kenya.

Mary Watson is a South African writer. She published her debut story collection, *Moss*, in 2004 and was the 2006 winner of the Caine Prize for African Writing for her short story 'Jungfrau'. She is the author of the literary thriller *The Cutting Room* and a contributor to several anthologies. Her work has been translated into languages including Arabic, Italian, German and Dutch. She currently lives in Galway, Ireland.

Notes on the Translators

Lucy Greaves translates from Portuguese, Spanish and French. The winner of the 2013 Harvill Secker Young Translators' Prize, she was one of the Free Word Centre's two Translators in Residence during 2014. Her translations of Eliane Brum's *One, Two* and Mamen Sánchez's *Happiness is a Cup of Tea with You* are forthcoming in late 2014 and early 2015 respectively. Her work has been published by *Granta* and Words Without Borders, among others.

Jethro Soutar is a translator of Spanish and Portuguese. He has a particular interest in Ibero-African literature and his translation of the Equatorial Guinean novel *By Night the Mountain Burns*, by Juan Tomás Ávila Laurel, is published by And Other Stories. Soutar recently co-edited and co-translated *The Football Crónicas* for Ragpicker Press.

Frank Wynne has won three major prizes for his translations, including the 2002 IMPAC for *Atomised* by Michel Houellebecq and the *Independent* Foreign Fiction Prize. He is also the translator of Tomás Eloy Martínez's *Purgatory*, Marcelo Figueras's *Kamchatka* and Carlos Acosta's *Pig's Foot*.